Life Goes On 5:
No Turning Back

Frank Tayell

Surviving the Evacuation: No Turning Back
Life Goes On, Book 5

Published by Frank Tayell

ISBN: 9798771260549

The world is full of big people who have big adventures and little people lucky enough to lead little lives. But beware when the little people tire of being dragged into the big people's war.

Post-Apocalyptic Detective Novels
Work. Rest. Repeat.
Strike a Match 1. Serious Crimes 2. Counterfeit Conspiracy
3. Endangered Nation 4. Over By Christmas

Surviving The Evacuation / Here We Stand / Life Goes On
Book 1: London, Book 2: Wasteland
Zombies vs The Living Dead
Book 3: Family, Book 4: Unsafe Haven
Book 5: Reunion, Book 6: Harvest
Book 7: Home
Here We Stand 1: Infected & 2: Divided
Book 8: Anglesey, Book 9: Ireland
Book 10: The Last Candidate, Book 11: Search and Rescue
Book 12: Britain's End, Book 13: Future's Beginning
Book 14: Mort Vivant, Book 15: Where There's Hope
Book 16: Unwanted Visitors, Unwelcome Guests
Life Goes On 1: Outback Outbreak, 2: No More News
Life Goes On 3: While the Lights Are On, 4: If Not Us
Life Goes On 5: No Turning Back
Book 17: There We Stood, Book 18: Rebuilt in a Day

For more information, visit:
http://www.FrankTayell.com
www.facebook.com/FrankTayell
http://twitter.com/FrankTayell

8th April

The Story So Far
The *Diaz Gallegos*, The Caribbean Sea

In the galley of the Chilean icebreaker, the *Wenceslao Diaz Gallegos*, a young Australian by birth and an older Australian by assumed identity sorted through supplies salvaged from the cartel killers on Corn Island.

"Are you any good at cooking?" Zach asked.

"I can manage beans, eggs, and snake," Corrie said, picking up a can of tinned mangoes. She placed it on the counter.

"Snake? Oh, yeah, I forgot you used to live in the bush," Zach said. "That was in Commissioner Qwong's patch, wasn't it?"

"It was a few hundred kilometres from Broken Hill," Corrie said, "but Inspector Qwong, as she was in those days, kept an eye on me while I kept an eye on the dingo fence. On the whole, it wasn't a bad life. Not one I'd have chosen, but one which ended up suiting me."

Zach opened, then immediately closed, the door to the walk-in pantry. "Smells like something died in there."

"Zombie?" Corrie asked.

"It can't be," Zach said.

Corrie grabbed the broom, and pushed the door open. "Clear," she said. "What a waste. All that food, left to rot. It'll need a scrub before we can put anything on the shelves. Let's work out a menu for dinner first. Those large cans of papaya and two cans of mangoes can be dessert, so we just need an entree."

"Can we skip the starter and just have a main course?" Zach asked. "And I don't think four cans will be enough. We've got ten Kiwi sailors plus Captain Renton running the ship. There's Commish Qwong who's actually in charge, Colonel Hawker, Nicko, Clyde, and me. Doc Flo and Doc Leo, you, your brother, and…"

"And my sister-in-law," Corrie said, smiling, as she picked up another can. "I guess things did work out okay in the end for Pete and Olivia. Yeah, add another can of mangoes to dessert. Does *cebollas* mean onions?"

"Dunno. What language is that?"

"Spanish, I reckon," Corrie said. "My languages are rusty. I haven't spoken much except for English and 'roo since I moved Down Under."

"The cartel didn't speak Spanish to you while you were a prisoner?" Zach asked.

"They barely spoke to us at all," Corrie said. "Except for Mikael, and he preferred trying to teach me Russian. Ah, this one contains *tomate*. I can guess what that is. Look for a few more of these. Now, if the labels were in Python, C, or binary, I'd have no problem telling you what they said."

"That's right, you're a programmer, aren't you?" Zach asked. "How come you ended up living out in the bush?"

"I was on the run," Corrie said. "Hiding from the cartel, and from Lisa Kempton."

"I thought Kempton was on our side," Zach said.

"It's complicated," Corrie said. "*She's* complicated. But when I was about your age, I was a hacker. A coder, too, but hacking was a lot of fun. So much fun, I didn't pay enough attention to the people watching out for people like me. I was caught hacking into NORAD, but a guy called Tom Clemens pulled me out of trouble. He was a political fixer, and he got me the job with Lisa Kempton so I could spy on her for him."

"That bloke was working for the cartel?" Zach asked.

"No, he was working *against* them, and he still was when the outbreak happened. He didn't trust Lisa, because, to stop them, she had to get close to her enemy. The cartel had to think she was on their side. Like I said, it's complicated. Anyway, when I learned what was really going on, that there was a cabal of politicians aiming to kick-start a new feudal empire with the help of an international killer-cartel, I bailed."

"You ran away?"

"To keep Pete safe," Corrie said. "As long as the cartel couldn't find me, they wouldn't bother abducting Pete for leverage."

"Why? What did you know?" Zach asked.

"Everything, I guess," Corrie said.

It was a truthful answer, but necessarily vague. A long time ago, a bug had been introduced into the various global positioning satellite systems used by the nuclear powers. Corrie had created the bug, and a patch to fix it. The patch also contained a hidden routine which, once initiated, would retarget any ICBM that pinged the satellite for a location-confirmation, sending the missile to the most isolated spot in the nearest ocean. After which, the satellite would be irretrievably bricked.

When Lisa had pitched the idea, Corrie had seen it as a puzzle. It was only afterwards she'd realised it was terrorism. Lisa herself had clearly seen the folly in the idea as she'd invested vast sums into in-orbit docking, and just prior to the outbreak, she'd built and launched three repair and refuelling satellites. While Corrie had been long out of contact with Lisa by then, it was obvious to her that Lisa's real goal was to erase any trace of that code. But, being Lisa, there was a secondary purpose: to create her own satellite network which would outlast any apocalypse.

"I found the soap," Zach said, opening a cupboard. "And some rags. Oh, it's an apron."

"That'll do," Corrie said. "And that box'll do for the trash."

"We'll need more than one box," Zach said as he re-opened the walk-in pantry. "So when you say you knew *everything*, you mean about the cartel, the zoms, and the nuclear war?"

"Not the zombies, no," Corrie said. "Lisa Kempton had been fighting this group of politicians, and the cartel, for years. The politicians used the cartel as muscle to bribe, blackmail, and murder their way to power. The cartel hoped to win legal immunity and legitimacy. But each time Lisa foiled a scheme, or defeated a politician, their plans became more desperate, more extreme, until they were plotting a nuclear war. Because they were getting desperate, Lisa thought she'd won."

"Guess she was wrong," Zach said. "But I get why you'd run away from all of that. How did she find you? She did, didn't she? Isn't that how your brother ended up down in Oz?"

"A few months ago," Corrie said, "Lisa learned the cartel had an agent in her inner circle. Before Lisa made her final move, she needed to remove that spy. She suspected it was one of her pilots. So she sent both of them, and her plane, to Australia. As a pretext, she sent Pete with them, with a message for me, one of Lisa's old employees. To avoid arousing suspicion, Lisa first bought the carpet company Pete and Olivia worked for. He thought he was going to a training seminar in Hawaii."

"That's how she avoided suspicion, by buying an entire company?" Zach said. "Strewth, to be a billionaire."

"It's how she thinks," Corrie said. "And I guess it's *because* she thinks like that, she grew rich enough to snap up entire companies on a whim."

"Well, your brother was lucky he *didn't* get sent to Hawaii. The islands were swamped."

"Yep, he ended up in Australia," Corrie said. "While the pilots waited in Broken Hill, Pete came to the outback. He had a message from Lisa, that I should call her. And I did. She knew the cartel was about to try something, demonstrate something, and that it would take place in New York."

"You mean the zombies?" Zach asked.

"Maybe," Corrie said. "Lisa didn't have any details about the demonstration, but I can't imagine it was anything else. Not when the first outbreak occurred in Manhattan a few hours later. No, Lisa didn't know it was going to be zombies. I can't believe the cartel did, either, or the politicians. Maybe I'm wrong."

"And like they say, the rest is the end of history," Zach said, sweeping the rotting contents of a shelf into the box. "Yeah, we'll need more boxes. That's how you met the commish?"

"Yep. Me and Pete were conscripted when we got back to Broken Hill. We helped Tess, and we helped Mick Dodson at the airport. But the cartel had sent a few of their people there to kill the pilots. After the outbreak, those killers wanted the plane so they could escape. They attacked the airport. There was an Australian pilot there, a friend of Tess's called Liu Higson. Her daughter was in Vancouver. With the satellites down, there was no contact with anyone, anywhere. Canberra was sending some soldiers to Broken Hill to use that plane to fly to the very north to make contact with the government. When the cartel attacked the runway, and worried the plane would be damaged, Liu took off, with me and Pete, and her son, aboard. Liu took us to Vancouver, where we found some survivors organising an evacuation of the city. While Liu went looking for her daughter, me and Pete went east."

"Looking for Olivia, right?" Zach asked.

"Kinda, yeah. But also trying to find out more about what had happened across North America. I don't think even Pete really expected he'd find Olivia. But we did, though we found Dr Avalon and Dr Smilovitz first, at a small airfield called Pine Dock on Lake Winnipeg. They went west. We went south, across Lake Michigan, through the State of Michigan, and to Indiana and South Bend. And we did find Olivia, and her dog, Rufus, and some kids she'd kept alive."

"What happened to the dog?" Zach asked.

"Lisa has him now," Corrie said. "We raced back through Michigan, and escaped via a boat plane, and ended up in Thunder Bay."

"Good name," Zach said approvingly. "Where's that?"

"On the western shores of Lake Superior, and on the Canadian side of the border. That's where Pete, Olivia, and I, and Rufus, joined General Yoon's army, working for Judge Benton. She was the civilian authority. Those were good times."

"Compared with what happened next, you mean?" Zach asked.

"No, compared to any," Corrie said. "Growing up was tough for both of us, though worse for Pete, I guess, since he's younger. When I escaped, I left him behind. The years since, even when I was safe in the outback, I was always terrified of being discovered, and felt guilty about abandoning Pete. But in Canada, with Pete and Olivia, there were a few brief days of family happiness when we thought the world might be saved. But then came the bombs. We were sure General Yoon and her army were wiped out. Judge Benton hoped to unite the survivors and lead them north. We were sent west to Vancouver, to make contact with the Pacific."

"That's when the cartel caught you?"

"Yep. Though first we found Lisa Kempton."

"Small world," Zach said.

"Except it wasn't," Corrie said. "Years ago, Lisa set up post-apocalyptic stash houses. Some were rendezvous points where her people could be picked up. Others were places with food, weapons, and strong walls from which local survivors of a nuclear war could be organised. This place in Canada was a bit different. It was a radio telescope she was building on the off-chance that this mission of hers was almost over. She wanted to create a different kind of legacy. But we went there hoping to find supplies to help us on our journey west. Instead we found she was being held prisoner by the cartel as they waited on their bosses to arrive."

"The Herrera sisters?"

"Right. The same thing happened to us on Corn Island. I'd say there's a good chance the sisters are dead, and most of their people are scattered, trying to find Lisa, or her people. Olivia bumped into a guy called Herrera back in South Bend. A young guy. An *evil* guy. A stone-cold killer hiding behind a police badge. We talked a lot about him when we were in prison on Corn Island, and whether he was related to Mikael and the sisters. But how could he be? The cartel don't have a monopoly on evil, after all. Anyway, yes, we rescued Lisa, but we went our separate ways. She went east to hunt down more members of the cartel and their pet politicians. We continued west. And she took Rufus. Good thing too. Because when we reached Minnesota, we were captured."

"That's in America, right? Why did you cross the border?"

"Because Lisa owned a crossroads gas station near a runway. It was another of her redoubts, and we needed gas and ammo. But the cartel were waiting. They flew us down to somewhere in West Virginia, and then on to Corn Island."

"How was it?"

"You mean captivity? Rough," Corrie said. "The torture was mostly psychological, but you've seen what they can do?"

"You mean skin people alive, yeah," Zach said. "They left a video in Colombia for us to find, but we found people like that in Canberra, too."

"They made us watch as they killed the locals," Corrie said. "Mostly, they left us alone. Mostly." She shrugged. "But they're dead, we're alive."

"Shame we didn't find the sisters on the island. Only the brother, Mikael."

"He was bad, but not evil," Corrie said. "Is evil an absolute? Is it on a scale? He had a son, who was supposed to become the sisters' heir. Mikael barely talked about him. There were no photographs of him, and he had a lot of photographs, but they were mostly of his boat. But... no, the son can't be the same guy we came across in South Bend and then in Canada. Anyway, it doesn't matter now. The sisters never reached the Canadian telescope where Lisa was being held hostage, or got to Corn Island where we were being held, or Colombia where they kept their supplies. No, they must be dead."

"So that's one half of our mission complete," Zach said. "Or a quarter. I was never good at maths. Doc Flo's been trying to teach me, but I always prefer words."

"You should try coding," Corrie said. "When we're done here, I'll show you some."

"I don't think that'll be much use in the years ahead," Zach said.

"Software makes life easier, and the end of global civilisation just made living a lot harder for everyone. You were conscripted in Canberra?"

"I volunteered," Zach said. "But yeah, I lived in Canberra. It must have been after you flew away from Broken Hill, the commish came to Canberra to report in. Mick Dodson flew her there. Ms Dodson wouldn't let her dad, or Tess, leave. The commish got a promotion. Our team of conscripts was assigned to clear some houses in the suburbs, and she was assigned to lead us. When she realised there was a coup in progress, she didn't know who to trust, so came to us for help."

"You stopped the coup?"

"Yep. I mean Clyde and the others helped," Zach said, with a pronounced lack of modesty. "We got the politicians, Vaughn and Lignatiev, and then we went hunting for the cartel killers. Got them, too. That's when Team Stonefish became the official support squad for the commish."

"Team Stonefish? Did you come up with the name?"

"Have you ever stepped on a stonefish?"

"They're not that common out in the bush," Corrie said.

"They don't look like much, but they're deadly, like us," Zach said. "That's what the cartel learned, and what Sir Malcolm Baker learned."

"Baker? What did he have to do with it?"

"Oh, he was funding the cartel. His son-in-law was supposed to take over after the coup. But we caught him, so he'll go on trial with those cartel prisoners we caught on Corn Island and that Captain Adams has taken back to the Pacific."

"That'll be some trial," Corrie said. "You met Captain Adams in Mozambique?"

"Yeah. Team Stonefish was supposed to be accompanying Anna Dodson on a tour of refugee camps, and the commish was supposed to have a hundred U.S. Army Rangers to go with her to Africa. When we reached Perth, the soldiers were gone, and so was the plane. So Mick flew us to Africa with Tess."

"That was to Mozambique?" she asked.

"Yeah, a place called Inhambane, and… oh, it was so sad."

"Why sad?"

"Because it was almost beautiful. You've travelled, right? I mean, not just America and Australia?"

"Sure," Corrie said. "I went to a lot of places while I was looking for somewhere I wouldn't be noticed."

"I haven't been to many places, except in books," Zach said. "Tofo Beach would have been paradise if it weren't for the zoms. The African Union had been running an evacuation from the African coast. When the ships arrived in Madagascar, they found the infected had beaten them to it. The ships couldn't unload, so they had to turn around. I guess they let some more passengers come aboard, and some of them were infected. Soon, the ships were full of the undead. The crews fled, or died, and the ships began to drift. Some of those passengers, crammed on the decks, had been wearing life jackets. When Captain Adams blew up the death-ships, the zoms with the life jackets floated with the current and came ashore, right onto the paradise beach. Yeah, that was grim."

"Do you know how many died?" Corrie asked.

"Nope. I know only a few thousand survived," Zach said. "Mick organised an airlift to some island runway, but there weren't enough planes, or fuel, or time, for everyone, so thousands set off in a giant convoy, driving to South Africa. We got onto Captain Adams's ship, and sailed there. Only the African Union's advance team arrived. The rest hadn't turned up before we left. I saw Robben Island, though. That was cool."

"Why didn't you wait for the African Union to reach Cape Town?"

"Because a plane flew overhead," Zach said. "It was Mick. He didn't land, but he radioed to us, and us to him, so we knew that a rescue ship was on the way. That was our one chance to sail on further. Originally, Captain Adams wanted to go to some Atlantic island. Ascension, I think it was called. We were a few days away from it when we picked up these weird radio signals. I still don't know what they mean, but then this Russian sub attacked us, but it was sunk by a British sub. We'd stumbled into this weird underwater battle, and because the surviving submarine wouldn't reply on the radio, Captain Adams took us west. She didn't want that submarine following us back to Robben Island. That's how we ended up off the coast of South America. Saw a lot of crocs there. You know they swam away from the zoms?"

"Really?"

"Yeah, I've got some video of it," he said, reflexively checking his pockets. "Oh yeah, Doc Flo's got my phone. We headed north to Colombia, to the mine. Sir Malcolm Baker had given us the address, and destroying it was part of our original mission. When we got there, it was almost deserted. The locals, the miners, they'd rebelled against the cartel. They even uploaded a video to the internet before it broke."

"I think I saw that," Corrie said.

"The cartel gassed them using VX dropped from a plane that took off from Corn Island. There were no survivors. The supplies were still there, in the tunnels below ground, until we blew them all up. Then we went north, because checking up on the Panama Canal was another part of the mission."

"How was it?"

"Captain Adams thinks it can be cleared, but it'll take months," Zach said. "That's where we found the mega-yacht with the journal that mentioned there were survivors in Puerto Morelos, and in Savannah. And it was around then we saw the plane overhead. We followed the plane to Corn Island, and we found you."

"And the cartel. Thanks for saving us."

"Yeah, no worries," Zach said. He picked up a box, now full of rotting debris. "How long will the food we found on Corn Island have to last?"

"I guess that depends if we find more food in Puerto Morelos," Corrie said. "And on how far we go after that."

"You want to go back to Canada, right?"

"I wouldn't say I *wanted* to," Corrie said. "Where we go now, and when we turn around, will be up to the commissioner. I guess we'll see what we find in Puerto Morelos, and take it from there."

"I know Doc Flo wants to go to New York," Zach said. "Originally, she wanted to go to Britain, too, to get some of the vaccine, but I think they decided that was a lie."

"Yeah, there's no way they can have developed a vaccine so soon," Corrie said. "Why does she want to go New York?"

"To gather samples," Zach said. "She's sort of developing a weapon. Except she also thinks there's a video of a zom just dying, right after the outbreak. If they're already dying, then we don't need a weapon. It's not just zoms the weapon would kill, you see? It'd wipe out trees and plants and everything else, too."

"If they are dying, that would be fantastic news to take back to the Pacific," Corrie said. "Whether they are or not, we need to crack on with dinner. Have you seen any saucepans anywhere?"

"Any chance of service?" Sergeant Nicko Oakes called from the other side of the small serving hatch.

"Not until we've found the can opener," Corrie said.

"No worries," Nicko said. "I'll help look for that. Doc Leo wants you up in the science centre to help solve a riddle over the conductivity of lead."

"I was never that good at chemistry," Corrie said.

"I think he means there were too many bullets fired up there, and everything needs to be rewired," Nicko said.

"Ah, no worries," Corrie said. "I'll go fix that, if you can help Zach fix dinner."

"Sure, what are we eating?" Nicko asked.

"Whatever you can cook," Zach said.

2nd April

Prologue - Final Justice
CDC Eastern Command, Raven Rock, Pennsylvania

Lisa Kempton crouched on the hillside, using binoculars to examine the uniformed figure leaning against the fence half a kilometre away.

"What is *your* opinion, Rufus?" she asked, glancing down at her companion. "Alive, or undead?"

Rufus bared his teeth.

"My thoughts exactly," Lisa said, shifting her gaze to the sentry post and the road beyond the gate. The *real* question was what lay beyond that, inside the mountain itself.

"It takes a special kind of mind to think a bunker inside a mountain is a solution to any of the world's problems," she said. "Especially one whose location is so well known. The cost could have funded a space race to Mars, and probably beyond."

Rufus, sensing that there was going to be no swift action, sank onto his haunches.

"Yes, I suppose it is hypocritical of me to level such a charge against the old government when I wasted so much on vanity projects of my own," she said. "I count three figures between the gate and the hangar entrance. They are almost certainly undead. But what of the people inside, Rufus?"

Rufus turned his eyes up to the vultures circling overhead.

Lisa returned to the binoculars, hunting for an answer to the pressing question. She didn't need to look at the dosimeter to know she couldn't linger long. The high mountain winds created a maelstrom of radioactive particles dragged skywards from blast sites further north and south. But the missiles had missed this obvious target.

This was her fourth stop since Maine, and it was her last. Not just the last stop of this particular journey, but of her nearly life-long quest to save the world. Her target was Mary-Ann Beaumont. Fifty-nine years old, mother of two. Christened Mary Andrews Beaumont-Lafayette, she'd trimmed her name and shuffled the hyphen after her first two failed congressional bids, but not before a donor had paid for her to take a holiday in Cancun. A week later, an Ohio representative had died. Beaumont had jumped into the race. Three days before the election, her opponent had died from an apparent accidental overdose. Beaumont had won, and won re-election. She'd given the response to the State of the Union and been spoken of as an obvious presidential candidate until she'd announced she was stepping back from politics. She returned to the law, was nominated for a federal judgeship, and then to the Supreme Court.

Beaumont was one of *them*, one of the cartel's pet politicians. The last of them. And here she was, inside the bunker at Raven Rock. But was she still alive?

"Well, Rufus, what do we do?" Lisa asked. "We can go on, or we can go back, but we can't stay here for much longer. There are zombies outside, and no living sentries. If there are people inside, there won't be many. They might even be trapped. But if the bunker doors are closed, we won't be able to dig them out."

Rufus's ears pricked at the challenge, before he settled back to watching the vultures.

"We've come this far," Lisa said. "We must see it through to the end."

She opened her bag and extracted the modular rifle, carefully assembling it before attaching the scope.

"Watch the road, Rufus," she said, as she took aim.

The gate-zombie was a soldier in camouflage battledress, stained with dried blood on its sleeve and neck. Its face was already withered, emaciated, and desiccated. The left ear hung loose. Scratched eyes bulged from sunken sockets. Broken teeth jutted from exposed gums, and when the mouth opened, she saw the chewed stump of a tongue.

Lisa adjusted for wind, remembering the lessons taught to her by her beloved. Those had been aboard a ship, for, if you learn to shoot accurately *from* a moving platform, you can hit a moving target from any firm footing. That was Tamika's advice, though from a different time when they'd both been naive enough to think one bullet, one assassination, might save the world.

Lisa settled her sights on the zombie's head and fired. Despite the suppressor, the rifle cracked, while the body clanged into the gate before thumping heavily to the ground.

"Did we wake any others?" Lisa asked, resting the rifle on the boulder before picking up the binoculars. "There's one. There's the other. Ah, there *is* a third. Is there a fourth? No. Good."

She dismantled the rifle, putting it back in the bag. With only four bullets left, they weren't to be wasted on the undead.

"Come, Rufus, it is always best to confirm the worst," she said, picking up the bag.

She was already well inside the militarised perimeter of the facility. The outer gates had been closed. The roads beyond had once been guarded, though those guards had long since departed. Whether their exodus was in rebellion against Beaumont taking charge, or because this bunker had proven ineffective against infection, the road leading to the tank-width gates was free of vehicles, though not of bullets. Lisa left her bag at the guard post, noting the brass casings lying among the grit. A small battle had been fought here, but she only counted three corpses.

Beyond the gate, three zombies walked towards her. She unslung her submachine gun. The MP5 came from one of the many stashes she'd set aside during those early years of planning when she'd assumed her post-nuclear role would be as the leader of a resistance group battling the terrorist-governments who'd brought about the end of the world. She'd not bargained for the undead. Nor, it seemed, had her foe.

"Now to get inside," she said, as the last body fell. "Rufus, are we safe?"

Rufus took a step forward, but then stopped. She took that to be a warning of trouble ahead.

While the main gate would require a tank to break through, the locks to the sentry post had been disengaged. Despite the expended cartridges, there were no bodies inside.

Beyond, it was a different story. Yes, there were the bodies of the undead, but also a few pecked bones belonging to the immune. Lying among them were sets of smaller bones: the remains of greedy vultures who, post-feast, had been too sluggish to escape the undead.

Rufus overtook her, so she followed him as he picked a route between the bodies. He was moving slower than usual, still growing accustomed to the Kevlar booties and protective coat she'd salvaged from a police station. That had been five days ago. Or was it four? Four days, yes. They had gone to the police station just after visiting Beaumont's home. The justice hadn't been there, but in the office, on the desk, was a note addressed to her daughter, saying that she had come here, to Raven Rock. Thus, so had Lisa.

The hangar doors had been advertised as strong enough to withstand a direct hit on the mountain itself. Lisa doubted it, but there was no way they would open. There was, however, a pedestrian access point to the south, through another guard station. Like the sentry post, the locks had been disengaged.

"I think this tells us the fate of those inside," Lisa said.

Rufus took a step back, away from the door.

"No, we must go in," Lisa said, checking that the bodycam was still recording. "One last time, I promise, and then we will find a refuge of our own. And somewhere far more sensible than a hole deep below ground."

Beyond the guard post, arrows painted on the blood-stained floor indicated how visitors could gain access to the deeper levels of this tomb. But there was also a window, overlooking a staging-ground hangar where thirty-two Humvees had been brought up, ready for deployment. Parked in four regimented lines, each was painted white, with a red cross on the roof and the sides. That had been a recent amendment to the CDC guidelines, to make any military units assisting the civilian power look less like an occupation force and more like help. Ultimately, it had been a waste of paint, since these vehicles had clearly never been deployed.

Beyond the vehicles were another set of blast doors, smaller than those outside. They were closed, but beyond would be a spiral road leading down to the levels where more vehicles would be kept. Below those would be the store houses, the living quarters, and the control rooms. But from how the undead staggered between the Humvees, she expected she'd find zombies below, too.

At least fifty uniformed undead lingered between the Humvees. About half were heading towards the window and her. The others, so far, remained stationary. Squatting. As if they were conserving energy.

"Come, Rufus," she said, and made her way out of the guard post, and along the corridor, following the blood-stained arrows. She had her answer. Raven Rock had fallen. The soldiers were dead. If any survived below, they would have gone to the armoury, collected weapons, killed their infected friends, and re-engaged the outer locks. Yes, she had her answer. And yet she still walked on.

Rufus growled, darting ahead to stop just ahead of her, teeth bared.

At the end of the corridor, a woman in a white jumpsuit staggered through the open airlock door. Lisa fired. The suppressed shot whispered from the gun, far softer than the heavy thump made by the corpse. From the hangar beyond the wall to her left came a swoosh of cloth, a whisper of flesh brushing metal, a sigh of air being dragged into dead lungs as the dead soldiers moved towards the faint sound.

"Almost done," Lisa said. "Almost. I promise."

Beyond the airlock door was a small antechamber for the elevators and stairs leading below. On the floor were bodies. They wore fatigues rather than uniforms, except for two who wore jeans. It was impossible to be sure, after so long, but she didn't think they'd all been undead. From how they'd fallen, and from where the bullet casings lay, the shooter had stood in the doorway to a guard post. Inside were dark screens and no bodies, but there was one more door at the very rear. While that door had a mechanical keypad, there was also a key, and it was in the lock.

Lisa kicked the door and listened before looking at Rufus, but his attention was on the way they'd come. Lisa turned the key.

There was no one alive inside. No one undead, either. There were four bodies. One military, three civilians, dead inside a small armoury filled with racks of non-lethal riot gear. All had been shot in the head, and probably by the woman who'd shot herself. Murder-suicide? That made no sense. But the older woman was Beaumont, Lisa was certain. The younger woman might have been her granddaughter, or perhaps it was someone else's child. The soldier and the other civilian were unrecognisable.

"They were locked inside," she said. "Locked inside, and then Beaumont shot the girl, the other two, and then herself. Why?"

There was a bucket in the corner, covered in a jacket.

"They were locked inside for some time," Lisa said. "They thought they would die, and so she opted for a quick end. Who locked them in? Did they return?"

Rufus let out a low growl.

"Yes, I concur," Lisa said. "It is time we departed. As promised, we shall make for the Delmarva Peninsula. Tamika might be there with my ship. After which, Miami, and then retirement. But first, we have one minor detour to make."

Part 1
Honeymoon

The Caribbean, Quintana Roo, Florida, and Georgia

8th April

Chapter 1 - Honeymoon Activities
The Caribbean Sea

Pete Guinn leaned on his mop. "They oversold the Caribbean," he said.

"Who did?" Olivia asked, not taking her own eyes from the section of bulkhead she was furiously scrubbing.

"Joan and Dave," he said.

Olivia paused with her brush half raised. "You mean Driver-Dave, and Joan with the squint?"

"Don't you remember, when they came back from their honeymoon and showed us their vay-cay pics? They said the Caribbean was the perfect honeymoon destination."

"I remember the picture of him on the beach," she said. "*So* much hair." She shook her head, and continued scrubbing. "But we can't compare experiences, until we've gone ashore without a gun at our heads, which I guess will be at Puerto Morelos. Does that still count as the Caribbean?"

"It's close to Cancun and Cuba, so it must," Pete said.

"I never thought of Cuba as being in the Caribbean," Olivia said. "It's just too large. They went to Oregon, didn't they?"

"Dave and Joan? Yep," Pete said. "He was going to drive a school bus, and she was… ah, I forget, but it had something to do with her cousin's jewellery store. It sounded shady."

"Maybe they found somewhere safe," she said.

"Maybe," he said.

In contemplative silence, they continued scrubbing.

The corridor, just above the waterline and just below the science centre, was wider than most on the old icebreaker. Two people, walking in opposite directions, could pass with only the slightest back-to-wall shuffle. The cabins here were larger than most, too, though Pete was basing that on reality TV shows rather than any personal experience of sailing. Some cabins had two bunks, some had just one. All had a little closet space, a chair, a screen, and a few creature comforts, but this was a working ship.

Ten years ago, the Canadian icebreaker had been sold to the Chilean government and renamed the *Wenceslao Diaz Gallegos*. It originally had a complement of fifty-five, with half of those being scientists, and five being the pilot and mechanics for the helicopter, which, sadly, was missing from the helipad. Now, it had a crew of ten New Zealand sailors and was captained by Lieutenant Renton. But the expedition was being led by Commissioner Tess Qwong. With her were three Australian soldiers: Colonel Bruce Hawker, Sergeant Nick Oakes, and the retired Major Clyde Brook. Along for the ride was the mononymous Australian teenager, Zach. For scientists, they only had two: Dr Florence Avalon and Dr Leo Smilovitz. Both were Canadians who'd led a U.N. crisis team preventing biological and environmental disasters. Corrie, Pete, and Olivia Guinn rounded off the crew.

The ship's science and research centre was bigger than the bridge, and its two secure labs weren't much smaller. The vessel was ninety metres long, with a helicopter deck and a giant deck crane. Having a displacement of six and a half thousand tons, the ship was content ploughing the waves at fifteen knots, with a range somewhere between twenty and twenty-five thousand kilometres.

As the Panama Canal was impassable, from their current position, a day's sailing north of Corn Island, Australia was beyond range. On the return leg of their journey, they would have to refuel in French Guiana, after which they would probably continue south to the Cape of Good Hope, and then into the Pacific. The final decision on the route, and with how far north they would travel, would lie with Tess, though it might be decided by what they found in Puerto Morelos.

"Nope. Now I've travelled a bit, I don't see the attraction," Pete said.

"Of travel? You've only been to two countries," she said.

"Six," he said.

"How do you count six? Don't say you're including the U.S."

"Okay, we'll call it five," he said. "Australia, Canada, Corn Island, Michigan, and Mexico."

"You can't count Mexico until we actually get there. But I'll give you Michigan." She scrubbed a little harder at the smear of blood splashed across the corridor's wall. "Michigan really did feel like another world and another time. Okay, next vacation, we'll skip the hot weather unless I can have beaches and bars and an air-conditioned hotel room."

"And no zoms," Pete said.

"Obvs. Do you think there are still beaches in Australia?" she asked.

"They can't all have been flooded," Pete said.

"I mean beaches where you can still swim," she said. "Somewhere we can drive our car, park, and wade into the ocean. Somewhere we can look out to sea and not see any land for months."

"Do *you* think they still have private cars in Australia?" he replied.

"Ah, good point."

"Did you hear what the Australians said about the beach in Mozambique?" he asked. "Zoms in lifejackets who'd survived the passenger ships being sunk."

"Oh. So even if we do have a car, we can't go swimming?" she asked.

"Not in the sea. That's another plus-point for lakes."

"You could still have some zoms in life jackets," she said.

"Ah, but there are no sharks in lakes," Pete said.

"Done," Olivia said. She stepped back. "That's as clean as I can make it without paint. Your turn."

He sloshed the mop along the deck, picking up the flecks of paint, dirt, and blood. She scrubbed the walls of the icebreaker and he mopped the floors. Sometimes they swapped. Together, they spent their first day of married life washing away the signs of where the ship's crew had been murdered by the Rosewood Cartel.

"It's nice being useful again," Pete said.

"It's nice just moving around freely again," she said. "No way will I ever make a joke about marriage being a prison."

"We've got to enjoy each moment. That's my lesson from this year," Pete said. "And there are worse chores than mopping."

"You can take a turn scrubbing if you like," she said.

"In a bit," he said. "I'm still debating whether I prefer mopping to sweeping."

"I didn't know it was a contest," she said, as she opened the door to the next cabin.

"I was thinking about what we'll do when we get to Australia. Do we want a sea-job or land-work? There's less sweeping at sea, but less mopping on land."

"We want a land job," she said. "Because there might be zoms at sea or on land, but there's absolutely no such thing as a land-shark. Not even in Australia."

"There are spiders," Pete said. "And a sun so hot, it makes an Indiana summer feel like a Wisconsin winter."

"That I can cope with," Olivia said. "We'll become nocturnal. Sleeping through the day and working at night."

"Or sleeping all day, *and* all night," he said. "I'll go empty the bucket."

Their nightmare wasn't yet over. If anything, being rescued by Tess and her team was a sign he'd woken to find the dream-terror was real, unstoppable, and irreversible. But he no longer faced the dangers alone. The Canadian scientists, the New Zealand sailors, and Australian soldiers were the best in their fields. He might have instigated this continuation of the mission northward, but he was barely more than a passenger. A honeymooning passenger. With his wife. Olivia Guinn *nee* Preston. He grinned. He'd *actually* married her. Him! *Her*! Yep, the nightmare might now be reality, but dreams could still come true.

On deck, the icebreaker's motion created an artificial breeze that masked the tropical sun's heat. At the stern, in the shade of the deck-crane, Commissioner Tess Qwong was slowly practicing tai-chi.

"Hey, Pete," Tess called, pausing mid-movement. She winced.

"Are you okay?" he asked.

"No worries," she said. "I think one of the bullets I took to the vest fractured a rib. I'm just testing my limits. Good to know what they are before we next get into trouble. Do you have a workout routine?"

"Staying alive," he said.

"That takes practice," she said. "Want to join me?"

"We've got to finish cleaning the corridor," he said. "After, though, definitely."

"Hey, Mrs Guinn," he said when he returned to the cabin Olivia was still searching. "Guess what?"

"What's that, Mr Preston?" she replied.

"The organisers of our cruise are running a tai-chi class. Want to go?"

"I'd prefer lounging by the pool with one of those blue drinks with an umbrella," she said. "But we can give it a try."

"Did you find anything interesting in the cabin?"

"No one was killed in here, so that's something," she said. "This cabin belonged to an older guy who was about your size. Tropical gear is in the locker by the bed. Cold weather stuff is in the closet by the door. He left some boots. Two pairs. Your size, I think. Try them on."

Pete collapsed into the cracked leather armchair, releasing a cloud of dust.

"My musty old husband is showing his age," Olivia said. "Do they fit?"

"Yep. Not bad. Heavy for this weather, though." He leaned back in the chair, looking around. One bunk took up most of the outer wall. In the corner was a large locker. Against the long wall was the wooden frame of a person-length bench-seat. Opposite was a desk, and the armchair. "Nice cabin. Bigger than ours."

"But only one bunk," she said. "That bench-seat can convert into a second bunk, but I don't think anyone shared this room."

Pete pointed to the rolled mattress, and the bundle of sheets. "Did he die in here?"

"I think so," Olivia said. "The cartel removed the body. Not the sheets."

"I'll give the boots a test run onto the deck," he said. "Anything else to be dumped over the side?"

"Not sure," she said. "I got distracted by his journal."

"Is that him?" Pete asked, pointing to the photographs taped to the bulkhead by the bunk. The majority showed a woman and a young girl, but a few included a man, too. Tall, lanky, balding, smiling, clean-shaven, and wearing wire-rim glasses over which he peered.

"How's your Spanish?" Olivia asked.

"*No bueno*," he said.

"His journal is handwritten," she said. "It's very detailed, very neat, and has sketches. I'm still working out what it says, but his name was Dr Umberto Tapia. He was a scientist at the university in Santiago."

"Where's that?"

"The middle of Chile, but inland," she said. "It's the capital." She turned the book around. Across a double-page was a sketch of the Americas, showing a dotted line which ran from Chile north, through the Panama Canal, and to Canada.

"That's a nice map," Pete said. "And nice birds. Lots of animals, all coloured in. I recognise penguins in the south, flamingos in the north. A polar bear. Ah, and a turtle."

"I think this was going to be a children's book," Olivia said. "He left home on December 30th, and flew to Valparaiso."

"Where's that?"

She tapped the map. "Here by the condor. Still in Chile. But it's a city on the coast."

"That's a condor? Cool."

"He gave a lecture in Valparaiso aboard the ship, but then he went ashore again. He flew north to Peru, while the ship sailed after him. After Peru, he flew to Panama, gave another lecture, and then got onto the ship."

"What was he lecturing about?"

"My Spanish is nowhere near that good," she said. "But it sounds like the ship was on some kind of science-diplomacy mission. The *Diaz Gallegos* was originally a Canadian icebreaker and it was going north for a refit and a retraining exercise. On the way, the scientists were giving lectures. Some at schools, some at universities, and some online."

"But you don't know what about?"

"Either it was the importance of climate science, or the importance of penguins," she said, turning the book around. A photographic-perfect sketch of a Humboldt penguin filled the entire page. "Dr Tapia left the ship in Miami, and caught a flight to D.C." She turned the page, this time to show a sketch of an eagle perched atop the Washington Monument.

"Did he meet the president?"

"The Sec of State and the Chilean ambassador. The ambassador accompanied Dr Tapia to New York by train. In New York, the scientist spoke at the U.N., then at a couple of schools, and gave a tour of the ship to a news crew. After that, they sailed up to Canada."

"The ship had caught up with him? What happened in Canada?"

"Six people came aboard. They did their upgrades and some training exercises. And then came the outbreak. The Canadians took the helicopter to go home. Ah, I think it was a new helicopter. That must have been the gift."

"What gift?" he asked.

"When they arrived in Canada, they were given a gift. He drew it, except what he drew is very definitely a bird." She turned the page around.

"With white and red feathers. Oh, because those are the colours of Canada's flag. He was a seriously good artist."

"He was," she said. "After the outbreak, the journal changes. The pictures mostly stop. The handwriting isn't as neat. The entries get harder for me to understand. Ah. Hang on." She flipped back to the beginning. "I get it now. He was writing this for his daughter's school class." She pointed at the photographs pinned next to the bunk. "She can't be more than eight. He was writing a journal like Darwin's, but for kids. That's why he keeps talking about *The Beagle*. I thought it was the ship's dog. I guess, after the outbreak, he realised the kids would never read it."

"What happened to the ship?" Pete asked.

"They refuelled in Halifax. That's Atlantic-Canada, isn't it? They had enough fuel to reach Chile if the canal was open. That's useful to know. It gives us an idea of the ship's range. They sailed for home. They met a lot of ships going north. Yeah, most people were going north, except those who were staying put." She flipped ahead. "They picked up a few passengers from boats which had run out of fuel. Eight in total, I think."

"Eight ships or eight people?" Pete asked.

"People," Olivia said. "He sketched their portraits. They all look so sad. Ah, but they refuelled at sea."

"Was that near Puerto Morelos?" Pete asked.

"Might have been. That could be the refuelling ship we're looking for. We better take this up to the bridge." She skipped ahead another page. "In the last entry, they saw a plane overhead, directing them to Corn Island."

Pete stood and gave his newfound boots a stomp. "Yep, these are a good fit."

"Cool," she said. "We'll come back for the clothes, but we'll take the journal to the bridge, then take these to the mess." She opened the desk drawer. It was half full of individual bags of glazed and roasted walnuts. "There should be enough for a bag each."

Like all ships, the *Diaz Gallegos* was a maze, so they made use of the cheater's shortcut by going up onto the deck where they dumped the blood-flecked sheets over the side. Tess was still at the stern, though no longer doing tai-chi. She still moved in slow motion, but now held a war-axe, which she swung at the retired soldier, Clyde Brook. He had an axe of his own with which he parried the blow.

"Now that's one honeymoon activity I *don't* want a go at," Olivia said. "Are we low on bullets?"

"Not so low you need to worry," Tess said. "But we can't risk a gun-battle aboard a fuel-freighter."

"Have we spotted a fuel ship?" Olivia asked.

"Not yet," Tess said.

"I made these axes while we were aboard the *Te Taiki*," Clyde said. "The worst kind of practice is the real thing."

"We found a journal belonging to the guy who must have been the lead scientist aboard," Olivia said. "My Spanish fails at the longer words, but it does mention something about refuelling while at sea somewhere between Florida and Corn Island."

"Take it to Leo for translation," Tess said. "You'll find him lurking in the science centre below the bridge."

The science centre wasn't a lab, but a windowless I.T. suite, with screens on the walls, and wires linking them to a central shipboard server. From there, two yellow cables ran to Dr Avalon's laptop, over which she sat, head bowed, headphones on. Dr Leo Smilovitz sat on the other side of the room, looking at a screen full of numbers. Corrie was on her hands and knees, with her head buried inside a hatch in the floor.

"Have you lost something, Corrie?" Olivia asked.

"Yep, the connection," Corrie said, rocking back on her heels. "The cartel shot up the place."

"You retrieved seven bullets," Avalon said without looking up. "It wasn't even a complete magazine, and so doesn't warrant gunfight hyperbole."

Corrie rolled her eyes while Leo smirked.

"I'm almost done," Corrie said. "Once this is bypassed, we can strip out a lot of the wiring, consoles, and most of that panelling, and dump it over the side."

"Why do we want to do that?" Pete asked.

"Weight is fuel," Avalon said.

"There's a caterpillar truck down in the hold," Pete said. "Shouldn't we dump that first?"

"Absolutely not," Avalon said. "That machine was designed to traverse the Antarctic ice-sheets. It would take us at least fifty years to relearn the technologies to build such a sophisticated vehicle."

"Do you think it'll be useful against the undead?" Pete asked.

"With a top speed of eight kilometres an hour, you would be better advised to run," Avalon said.

"The global climate was at a tipping point anyway," Leo said. "This latest blow could have pushed it over the edge. We don't know how extreme the weather will get, or where, but we might need machines capable of traversing thick snowfields. For the same reason, we must keep the equipment with which to take ice-core samples. But weight *is* fuel, so we'll get rid of everything we can replace."

"Speaking of fuel," Olivia said, "I've found a lead on the fuel freighter." She handed the journal to Leo. "It's a diary, in Spanish, written by a scientist who was aboard the ship before the outbreak and until the cartel seized it."

"It's Umberto Tapia," Leo said, after the briefest of glances.

"Um-Be?" Avalon asked, finally looking up from her notes. "He was on *this* ship?"

"You know him?" Olivia asked.

"Knew, not know. He must be dead, mustn't he?" Avalon said with disconcerting uncertainty.

"There were bloodstains in his cabin," Olivia said. "And his family photographs were still pinned to the bunk."

"Did you know him well?" Pete asked.

"In our field, the community was a frustratingly small one," Avalon said.

"He ran the project gathering data on the shift in the magnetic poles," Leo said. "Melting of the ice-sheets in the very north and south was changing the planet's weight distribution. That alters the spin, causing the magnetic fields to shift. He was trying to persuade the world this was something they should care about. We were supposed to meet him in D.C. in January, but had to deal with exposed anthrax in the permafrost."

"I'm sorry," Olivia said.

"Revenge is poor comfort," Avalon said. "But we *did* get revenge. What information did he include about fuel?"

"Oh, right, yes," Olivia said. "Near the end, he mentions they refuelled at sea."

Leo flipped through the book. "Ah, they traded information for fuel from a ship. He doesn't name that vessel, or describe it. He says information is the only real currency, but this fuel ship would also accept gold."

"Wasn't that what Puerto Morelos were accepting for fuel?" Pete asked.

"Not quite," Leo said. "Down near the Panama Canal, we found a super-yacht with a log aboard. The author, probably a teenage girl, recorded that they bought fuel for gold from somewhere *near* Puerto Morelos. Tess thinks it was from a ship at sea, and that Puerto Morelos was simply the closest spot on the chart. Captain Renton thinks it was from shore."

"What do *you* think?" Pete asked.

"We have no opinion," Avalon said, before Leo could answer. "There is insufficient data to draw conclusions."

"There, I think I'm done," Corrie said, standing up. "All the data and instrument readings here should now be accessible from a terminal on the bridge. I'll go check. Do you want me to take up that journal?"

"I'll bring it up once I've finished," Leo said. "I want to take up a summary of this data, too. The ship was running a dozen experiments before the outbreak, and kept a few going afterwards. Radiation flow is most pertinent to us. We've got a baseline for the South Pacific, the canal, and the North Atlantic prior to the nuclear exchange. We can gather more data ourselves, and from some of the same areas."

"So this is good news?" Olivia asked.

"The news will be terrible," Avalon said.

"And in your dictionary, that's the same as bad, yes?" Pete asked.

"We have the same dictionary in Canada," Avalon said.

"It will be bad," Leo said. "It was always going to be bad. When we modelled the impact of nuclear war, we assumed that cities would be the primary targets. Firestorms would hurl clouds of radioactive dust into the air, blanketing the nearby agricultural zones."

"Creating nuclear winter," Olivia said.

"No," Avalon said.

"That's uncertain," Leo said. "Nuclear winter would be the result of a firestorm in a city producing high volumes of black-carbon, which would be carried up into the stratosphere. The models required far too many variables to produce anything but arguments."

"Distracting arguments," Avalon said. "Because the agricultural zones would have been laid waste by the fallout. Famine would have wiped out our species before it could freeze. Regardless, that didn't happen. There were local fires, and some on-land explosions, but the majority of the warheads detonated in the oceans."

Pete glanced towards the door through which Corrie had vanished. "Is that better?"

"That's what I'm determining," Leo said. "This data will help me create a long-term model."

"Will it help with the weapon you're making to kill the zombies?" Pete asked.

"The weapon is immaterial," Avalon said. "Once we collect samples from New York, we'll have confirmed the parasite is, by its nature, a short-lived beast. Now we can plan for the future."

"But first, let me finish reading Umberto's diary," Leo said.

"Those two are weird," Olivia said as she and Pete made their way down the steep stairs and below decks, heading for the galley.

"Very," Pete said. "But they're a bit less weird than when I first met them in Pine Dock."

"I mean they aren't reassuring," she said. "I blame you."

"Me? Why?"

"Remember, about a month after you started working at Mrs Mathers' store, that Thursday when she went to the dentist? You said, while the boss is away, let's watch a movie."

"And you said yes."

"But you picked that end of the world film about that guy collecting books," she said.

"It was new out on the streamer," he said.

"Right, but as a result, watching apocalypse movies became our thing."

"And so we fell in love," Pete said.

"Okay, I'll give you that. But from those movies, I developed an unrealistic belief that, in scenarios like this, scientists would explain exactly how bad things could get, and how we could fix them. Instead… I mean, I'm still processing what he was saying, but it sounds like it'll take years just to gather the data to build a model for whether or not the species is going to be wiped out, and there's absolutely nothing we can do about it."

"Ah, look on the bright side," Pete said. "If we are going to be wiped out, we'll be long dead before he's able to give us advance warning."

"My husband, ever the optimist," she said.

Zach was in the galley, alone, and looking perplexed with a can opener in one hand and a screw-top jar in the other.

"Have you seen your sister?" he asked.

"Corrie? She's fixing some screens on the bridge," Pete said.

"She was supposed to be helping me cook," Zach said. "What about Nicko?"

"Sorry, no. What's in the jar?" Pete asked.

"Chillies, I think," Zach said. "There's some cans of tomato stew I was going to heat up, but I don't know if these will go with them."

"Let me see?" Olivia asked, taking the jar. "Maybe a few of them, but only a very few. How is the kitchen?"

"A complete warzone," Zach said. "Do you see the bullet holes? They shot up the fridge. The compressor's busted. Corrie said we should dump it over the side."

"What about the freezer?" Olivia asked.

"The walk-in freezer is that door, over there," Zach said. "Don't open it!" he added.

Pete paused, his hand close to the handle. "Why not?"

"There was food in there when the ship was hijacked," Zach said. "But they turned the power off, and it's gone gross. We need to empty that, too."

"Let's call that a job for later," Olivia said. "Where's the food?"

"In the pantry," Zach said, pointing to a door on the other side of the kitchen. "I've just finished putting it all away."

Pete crossed to the door. "Huh. Way more empty shelves than I was expecting."

"Yeah, we'll have to start fishing soon," Zach said. "Anything that's ready to eat and easy to carry goes on the shelves on the left. That's for storms and shore missions."

"Are those oat bars?" Pete asked. "Says they're a dollar each."

"Yeah, they're from Oz, and not for sale. I've counted them," Zach said.

"How much other food is there?" Olivia asked.

"Maybe forty days, I think," Zach said. "That's if we eat two and a half thousand calories a day, and not counting the snacks and drinks. It's not really meals, though. Most of the packaging is in Spanish, and I don't have a dictionary."

"Does the stove work?" Olivia asked.

"Only the front ring," Zach said.

"That's all we'll need," Olivia said.

9th April

Chapter 2 - Penguins and Turtles
The Caribbean Sea

Pete woke to a scream: his own.

"Pete!" Olivia said, shaking him awake.

Memories of torture mixed with visions of pain yet to come faded into the four walls of their small cabin.

"Hey," Olivia said, switching the light on. "Are you okay?"

"Sure," he said. "It was just… it was just a dream."

He stood and walked over to the porthole, pulling back the ragged curtain. Outside, the ship's spotlights battled the moon for supremacy over the waves, but a hint of brightness on the horizon suggested the sun was about to launch its daily sneak attack.

"Were you dreaming of Corn Island?" Olivia asked.

"When they caught us," Pete said. "How come you don't have those dreams?"

"Why do you think I'm already awake?" she said. "Though, for me, the dreams were mixed up with South Bend burning."

"That cop, Herrera?" Pete asked.

"I know we talked about it," she said. "I mean, it *is* a common name. And Corrie was certain Mikael didn't have any photos of him. If that cop was Mikael's son, Mikael would have had photographs. I'm sure it's just a coincidence, but that won't stop my asleep-brain from throwing his face into my nightmares."

Leaving the curtain open, Pete crossed to the armchair, sat, and stared at his hands. "For the first time in a long time, I actually miss my phone," he said.

"Me, too. Hence why I'm sketching," she said, holding up the pad.

"A penguin?"

"It was supposed to be an eagle, but something went wrong with the beak. I blame evolution." She kicked herself out of bed. "But I miss my phone. And coffee. And I could spend all day listing the rest." She crossed to the small cabinet in which they kept four glasses. "Surrounded by so much normality just brings it all home. This *is* luxury. This cabin." She opened the door to their small bathroom unit, and filled a glass from the tap. "This tap. This water." She handed it to him. "This is the best we'll get, and I doubt even the prime minister in Oz will be getting any better."

Theirs was one of the biggest cabins on the ship, and technically came with a double bed. Technically in the same way you could stick a mattress into a van and call that a double. The mattress was crammed into a shelf with barely a matchstick-width gap at the feet. It was too short for Pete. Where the foot of the bed should have been was their bathroom cubicle, which made use of the pipework from next-door's communal shower. The hiss and clank of the neighbouring pipes had been funny at first, then annoying, then forgotten for a brief few hours before becoming the background symphony to his nightmares.

The rest of the cabin was crowded by two chairs, a table, and the bags of looted clothes and weapons taken from Corn Island, and from the ship's previous passengers.

Unlike the other cabins, this one lacked closet space. Pete's opinion was that, a few weeks before the ship was due to sail from Chile, someone realised they should have an executive suite for any guests who joined them aboard for a night, so removed the lockers and tacked on the washroom.

"I've heard of worse honeymoons," Olivia said. "There was a guy in L.A. who founded of one of those cryogenics companies. He was in a car-smash. At the same time, on the other side of the city, so was someone with the exact same name, who was heading to his own wedding. There was a mix-up, and they ended up sticking the groom into the deep-freeze."

"No way. Tell me he was dead."

"Do you mean before or after they pumped him full of antifreeze? The worst bit, because it was before the ceremony, they weren't married, so the bride didn't get survivor-benefits."

"Huh. Yeah, that's rough."

She turned the sketchpad back a page. "I was thinking, when we get to Australia, we should open a spa."

"Why a spa?"

"Because we'll need jobs," she said. "We might not get a choice, but if we do, I don't want to pick between mopping and sweeping. You know those oat bars in the galley are currency, and each is worth a dollar? Zach's been collecting the wrappers. Tess said that they were going to stamp the prices on more food to regulate wages and so avoid hyper-inflation."

"Will that work?"

"Only until people get hungry," she said. "But by then, they'll have some other system. They want an economy, so they'll need things people want to buy."

"And they'll want to buy a spa-day?"

"Tell me, after a couple of months of killing zoms, you don't fancy a seaweed wrap."

"Can't say I've ever had one," he said. "But I always thought that sounded like sushi."

"Me too," she said. "Maybe not a spa, then, but we need to find something people need. A funeral home is obvious, but once we get to the Pacific, I don't want to see another dead body until I'm wrinkly. Maybe a hotel of some kind."

"Where?"

"Doesn't matter because we'll be building it from scratch. If the population in Australia has doubled, and if they don't have the ships or planes to move more than a few thousand people a month, wherever we live, we'll have to build our own house. Why not build big, and recoup the costs from paying guests?"

Pete walked into the bathroom, and refilled the glass. "Will people be able to travel? Won't they need cars and buses, or at least bikes and trains? And would they want to travel to a hotel?"

"One day, sure," Olivia said. "Ah, but maybe not any day soon. Want to see what there is for breakfast?"

It was rice, but only after they'd cooked it. Due to a translation error, it was served with condensed milk. The soldiers didn't care. The scientists didn't mind. The sailors weren't in the mess long enough to notice.

"Looking at this meal, I can see a flaw in us opening a hotel," Pete said, running his spoon through the semi-solid, semi-savoury dish.

"Just one?" Olivia said.

"What's this about a hotel?" Corrie asked.

"We were talking about what we'll do when we get to Oz," Olivia said. "But if this is the best we can rustle out of the kitchen, we should give it a rethink. What's on the job-list for today?"

"More cleaning," Corrie said. "The walk-in freezer needs to be emptied."

"Any fishing?" Pete asked.

"Not until we stop," Corrie said. "So probably not until we get to Puerto Morelos, and that won't be until tomorrow."

"The ship's slow?" Pete asked.

"The captain is taking it slow, at least until we've figured out what to do when something breaks."

"We're happy cleaning," Pete said.

"Ace. Down in the hold, there's a mountain of plastic crates with kids' art stuff in them," Corrie said. "Dump those over the side, then use the boxes for the rotten food. We won't need the crates again."

The art *stuff* was actually drawings and posters. From the detailed label on each box, the art was being swapped. Children in Chile had drawn posters for display in schools in North America, while children in Canada and the U.S. had done the same for schools in Chile. With the posters were letters in stumbling Spanish and erratic English, from one group of kids to another.

"This isn't just a cultural exchange," Olivia said, reading through an essay. "This is an action plan. Tree planting, consumption reduction, letter writing to politicians and newspapers. They've even included a list of hashtags for the social campaign. Weird to see them actually written in pen and ink."

"How old were the kids?" Pete asked.

"Too young for most to have phones," Olivia said, putting the essay back in the box before replacing the lid.

"Makes me think we should have bigger goals than just opening a hotel," Pete said.

An avalanche of optimistically hopefully posters rained from the boxes as they tipped them over the side, where they quickly vanished in the ship's churning wake. The wind caught one small piece of paper, hurling it back onto the deck. He picked it up. It depicted a penguin riding on the back of a turtle. If there was any deep symbolism to the drawing, it had been lost over the side with the rest of the class's project. Perhaps the child simply liked turtles and penguins. Pete slipped it into his pocket.

Emptying the decaying food from the walk-in freezer was grim work, with each load possessing a uniquely noxious bouquet. As he was emptying the fifth box over the deck, the foghorn sounded. The ship began to slow. Pete dumped the box, and its liquefied contents, over the side, and made his way to the bow.

On the otherwise empty ocean, ahead and ten degrees west, floated a single-sail catamaran with an enclosed cabin slung between the two hulls. Originally white, it was now a mix of cream and grey, battered and damaged by sea and storm.

"You'll get a better view from the science centre," Tess said, coming out onto the deck. "Everyone else is there."

Not the three Australian soldiers, however. They followed Tess onto the deck, armed, and tightening their straps.

"Are we going to board the catamaran?" Pete asked.

"No worries, mate, we've got this one," Nicko said.

"You can give me a hand with the winch," Tess said.

It was electrical, and only required the press of a button. The small motor launch, with the three soldiers aboard, slowly descended. The boat's engine buzzed as it sped across the waves to the catamaran, now drifting some fifty metres to port. As Clyde pulled alongside, and cut the speed, Nicko jumped onto one of the catamaran's hulls, nimbly running across the spar and to the between-hull cabin. There he crouched, one hand on a bolt, one holding his sidearm, while he waited for Colonel Hawker. When Bruce reached him, Nicko opened the hatch. Hawker entered first, Oakes, a second later. A second after that came the crack of a bullet.

"Zom," Tess said. "Must be."

Oakes re-appeared, and gave an unmistakable thumbs-up before disappearing back into the cabin. A minute later, all three soldiers were in the launch, and on their way back to the *Diaz Gallegos*.

"One zom, no survivors," Hawker said, when he climbed back onto the icebreaker's deck. "No supplies, either. I grabbed the log, and the maps. Reckon the boat sailed out of Florida."

"We'll give the map and logs to Leo," Tess said. She headed back inside. The soldiers followed, leaving Pete alone on the deck.

As the *Diaz Gallegos* picked up speed, he watched the catamaran drift with the waves. It seemed wrong to leave it. Sure, it needed some repairs, but a boat like that would have cost a fortune before the outbreak. What disquieted him wasn't the money so much as the time involved in building such a vessel. Last night, after dinner, and after losing at cards for four hands straight, he'd taken a walk down to the hold. He'd found himself walking around, then sitting inside, the Arctic caterpillar truck.

That vehicle, and that catamaran, weren't just technology, they were works of art. Irreplaceable. Irretrievable. An echo of a lost world. He patted his pocket, checking that the drawing of a turtle and penguin was still safe within, and wished he'd kept a few more of the drawings.

10th April

Chapter 3 - Gold-Standard Shipping
Puerto Morelos, Quintana Roo

"Here's another reason not to run a hotel," Pete said, as he scrubbed the char-encrusted frying pan. "Way too many dishes to be cleaned."

"And it's a reason not to opt for a life at sea," Olivia said. "Aboard a ship, you and me will always be at the bottom of the jobs ladder." She gave the broken dishwasher a kick. "I have no idea what's wrong with it, except I can't see any bullet holes, so shall we scratch appliance repair off our list, too? But pancakes for breakfast was a good idea."

"Except I need more practice in not making them burn," Pete said, grabbing the edge of the sink as the ship rocked and water sloshed over his third-hand jeans. "I must have wasted at least a quarter of that pack-mix."

"I hate to admit it," Olivia said, "but maybe we should to stick with what we know. And that's—"

Before she could finish, the speakers chimed an alarm followed by Captain Renton's voice. "Puerto Morelos is ahead. All crew to action stations."

"We're ahead of schedule," Olivia said. "Rock-paper-scissors to see which of us fetches our gear?"

"You go, I'll finish here and meet you on deck," Pete said.

When he reached the deck, he found himself alone, and getting lonelier as the inflatable sped towards the shore. Aboard were Tess, the three Australian soldiers, and Leo, with the sailor, Noel Baxter, at the wheel.

"Your wife's up in the TV lounge," Zach said, coming to join him at the rail.

"Since when does the ship have a TV lounge?" Pete asked.

"It's what Doc Flo calls the science centre," Zach said. "Leo's set up a helmet cam so he can stream live video back to the ship."

"So why aren't you watching from there?"

"Because Doc Flo keeps setting me these equations to solve," Zach said. "She calls them puzzles, but it's still homework." He pulled out a monocular and aimed it at the ship.

"Didn't you want to go ashore with the soldiers?" Pete asked.

"I wasn't asked," Zach said. "You?"

"Same," Pete said. "But I don't mind skipping this adventure. We arrived sooner than expected."

"Yeah, nah, Doc Flo says two hours is within the margin," Zach said, turning his monocular to the shore. "Doc Leo says we've got to stop counting punctuality in anything shorter than a day. You should have heard Doc Flo yell at him! Yeah, this reminds me of Tofo Beach."

"Isn't that the place in Mozambique where the zombies washed ashore?" Pete asked.

"Yep," Zach said.

"You can see zombies here?" Pete asked, shielding his eyes against the reflected glare as he peered ashore.

"Nah. But those wrecked ships are huge. Bet they're filled with zoms. Want to look?" He held out the monocular.

"Thanks."

Puerto Morelos was a small coastal town that hadn't even tried to compete with Cancun, forty kilometres further north. But it had taken advantage of Cancun's airport to lure in tourists and locals who wanted a more relaxing vacation than could be found in the bustling resort-city. Inland, there was light industry and farming. There were rainforests, jungles, and Mayan ruins. Most of that had been gleaned from maps and books left by the Chilean scientists. Those scientists had also left a helpful estimate of the town's pre-outbreak population: ten thousand.

"The boat has reached the pier," Pete said, handing the monocular back to Zach.

"Did you see any people?" Zach asked.

"Nope. No smoke. No lights," Pete said.

"There were no radio signals, either," Zach said. "I was listening most of the night. Wait, Nicko's raised his rifle. No, he's lowered it. They're moving out down the pier."

"Is it true you blew up a guy with a bazooka?" Pete asked.

"A woman," Zach said. "She was one of the cartel terrorists. She'd hidden in the coal mine in Colombia where the sisters had stashed supplies. Is it true you fought the cartel in Broken Hill?"

"Not by choice," Pete said. "I sort of ended up there accidentally, and got caught up in the war by mistake. When they start shooting, you shoot back."

"Yeah, it's not like TV, is it?" Zach said. "Wait. They've stopped by the end of the pier. I think there's a barricade or something. Here."

Pete took the monocular. "A *big* barricade. Those girders could have come from a construction site. Hang on. Here, look to the south of the town. You can see another barrier where the road hits the beach."

"Where?" Zach asked, as he took the monocular back. "Found it. Yeah, cool, so the people in Puerto Morelos barricaded all the roads leading from the beach into the town."

"They must have been worried about zombies coming from ships," Pete said.

"I told you it was like Tofo Beach," Zach said. "What does a fuel tanker look like?"

"Dunno, except it'd be big," Pete said. "Way bigger than those shipwrecks."

"That's what I was thinking. The ships are small, aren't they? Smaller than the icebreaker. Yachts, sailing boats, and— They're coming back!"

"Already?" Pete asked, leaning on the rail, standing on his toes in an attempt to see the shore party.

"Yeah," Zach said. "You go warn Doc Flo. I'll warn the captain."

But they needed no warning. Dr Avalon, Corrie, and Olivia were in the science centre, each looking at different screens showing a different cluster of corpses.

"You've caught the sun," Avalon said, after the briefest of glances. "You need to wear a hat. It was VX."

"Sorry, what?" Pete said.

"The increased radiation levels mean an increased probability of developing cancers in later life," Avalon said. "Precautions now reduce the risk. It won't eliminate it, of course, but donning a hat and long sleeves is a sensible habit to develop."

"Yes, yes," Pete said. "What was that about VX? Do you mean like you found in Colombia?"

Avalon tapped at the keyboard and brought up a still captured from a bodycam. "This was relayed live. The resolution is frustrating, but you can see this skull here belongs to a canine. This smaller skull next to it however, ironically, belongs to the heteromyidae family."

"It looks like a rodent's skull," Pete said.

"A *kangaroo* rat," Avalon said. "We are further southeast of where I would expect to find that animal. We, too, are far from home, which gives me cause to speculate the rodents have made a similar journey."

"She means the rats fled the zoms," Corrie said, even as Pete was still deciphering the scientist's words.

"Indeed," Avalon said. "And they fled some considerable distance. If we knew when the gas was released, we could learn a good deal about the world further west. If we skip forward… here. That is the remains of a vulture. A kangaroo rat is an anomaly, but we can still extrapolate a time-line. The people were murdered. The dogs died at the same time. The rats foolishly, yet inevitably, came to feast on the remains. The birds arrived last, spying the carrion from the air. The rats died in clusters, but in far greater numbers than would be expected in such a small town. It is possible they came from Cancun. That is an international city, of course, and so it wouldn't be uncommon for a non-native species to enter the local ecosystem."

"Is the VX still dangerous?" Pete asked.

"Not if it was exposed to direct sunlight," Avalon said. "In the shade, probably not. The risk remains too great for any further investigation, especially since our primary goal was to locate other survivors."

"How many people died?" Pete asked.

"Yes, that *is* the next question," Avalon said, and reached for her headphones. Music blared around the edges as she began scrawling notes while skipping back and forth through the body-cam footage.

"Hundreds died, Pete," Olivia said. "Commissioner Qwong said, over the radio, it was far more than a hundred. Did you notice how there were no shipwrecks to the north of the pier? Commissioner Qwong thinks a lot of those boats were anchored here. The plane obviously came from Corn Island, circled Puerto Morelos, and flew low, north to south. The people, and the ships, to the south, were sprayed. The survivors took to the boats anchored in the north, probably including the fuel tanker."

"So they were attacked by the cartel," Pete said.

"Must have been," Olivia said. "And the cartel must have heard about Puerto Morelos from one of those ships they lured to Corn Island."

"So if the survivors from Puerto Morelos fled from the plane, and that plane came from the south, the surviving ships would have gone north," Pete said.

"Eight hundred and fifty," Avalon said, removing the headphones. "There is a margin of error as we only saw a small part of the town. But I would say that is a reasonable estimate of the number of survivors resident here prior to the attack."

"Okay, so how many survived?" Pete asked.

"A hundred could have escaped, along with however many were already crewing the ships," Avalon said. "Two hundred is not impossible."

"Will we look for them?" Pete asked.

"That will be down to Commissioner Qwong," Avalon said. "I would advise no. From the number of corpses, and the depth of their barricades, this was their central supply depot. Based on the snippets in those journals we found, these people were very well supplied if they could afford to trade fuel for gold. Their supplies probably originated aboard the ships which stocked the hotels in Cancun. Having lost the supplies and fuel ashore, and with a threat from the air, the traders will have sought a new sanctuary far beyond a plane's operational radius."

"Maybe they went up to Georgia," Pete said. "That journal you guys found down in Panama mentioned a community of survivors in Savannah. If the journal-writer knew about them, maybe the people here in Mexico did, too."

"Possibly," Avalon said. "But if I were this group, assuming fuel and other supplies are now limited, and with a threat from the air, I would seek to get far away from here as fast as possible. I would enter the Gulf of Mexico and aim to make landfall around Veracruz, and then drive to the Pacific."

"That sounds like a guess," Pete said.

"I never guess," Avalon said. "I only posit theories based upon the best available evidence."

There was no point arguing, so Pete took his thoughts with him down to the kitchen. There were no survivors in Puerto Morelos. Did it matter that the cartel had been responsible for their deaths? Probably not. No, the key detail was that they were gone.

Chapter 4 - Flame-Seared City
Cancun, Quintana Roo

The distraction of the early arrival in Puerto Morelos meant Pete had barely finished clearing breakfast before it was time to start preparing lunch. Since no one else came to volunteer, he and Olivia had the joy of planning the menu. They opted for flame-seared chilli-rice, partly due to their familiarity with the ingredients, and partly due to a small fire in the kitchen.

"Good news, a bit of char improves the flavour," Pete said.

"Put the spoon down and grab the mop," Olivia said, returning the fire extinguisher to its bracket. "How did you make an electric stove catch fire, Pete?"

"Hey, there's a reason I live on cereal," he said.

"We'll get Corrie to take a look before we—"

The iceberg alarm sounded. The mess-hall's lights flashed red.

"Was that me?" Pete asked.

"Report to your action stations, we're approaching Cancun!" Commissioner Qwong announced over the address system.

"Make sure everything's switched off. I'll secure the meal," Olivia said.

This time, they left the kitchen together, and both headed for the science centre. They found it empty except for Dr Avalon. She sat in front of a bank of six screens, one row of three above the other. The two on the left and two on the right showed a live stream from the crane-cams, while the central pair showed stills she'd captured and was examining. Both stills came from the forward-facing camera, and each showed one half of an almost oblong cruise ship, now split in two and lying on its side. Waves foamed grey around the fire-blackened seven-storey super-structure. Around the exposed hull at the stern, the oil-flecked sea glistened and shimmered beneath the midday sun.

"What happened to the ship?" Pete asked.

"A torpedo," Avalon said, replacing the stills with the live stream, and then with a close-up of the palm-flecked, white-sand beach. "When detonated beneath a ship, a torpedo creates a pressure bubble which cracks the vessel's hull. The damage is unmistakable."

"And this is Cancun?" Olivia asked.

"Not yet," Avalon said. "Cancun is three kilometres ahead." She tapped at the keyboard, and the forward-facing mast-cam zoomed in on the horizon.

"There are more ships," Pete said.

"Indeed," Avalon said. "Hence the alarm."

"Shouldn't they be in a harbour?"

"There is no cruise-harbour in Cancun," Avalon said. "It is a resort city born in 1970, built along a coral reef which rings a toxic lagoon filled with bottle tops and coins. Building a parking lot was insufficient punishment for this portion of paradise."

"Where did the cruise ship come from?" Pete asked.

"Potentially, anywhere," Avalon said. "Most probably Cozumel."

"That's an island, isn't it?" Olivia asked.

"And far behind us," Avalon said.

Pete looked at the ships on the screen, slowly growing nearer. "Why would cruise ships come here?"

"Why would anyone build one in the first place?" Avalon asked. "These are questions beyond my expertise. You should consult a psychiatrist who specialises in serial killers and other monsters."

"We should go see where we're needed," Olivia said, and took Pete's arm, leading him from the science centre.

"She's in a mood," Pete said.

"Yep, and that's definitely what I'd class as a bad omen," Olivia said. "VX this morning, and now our pet genius is picking fights with everyone who goes into the science centre."

"There wasn't anyone else in there," Pete said.

"Now you know why," she said.

On deck, they found Clyde and Zach standing watch by the prow.

"Where do you want us?" Olivia asked.

Clyde gave each of them a once-over. "You two fought with General Yoon, right?"

"With Judge Benton," Olivia said. "And in South Bend and Michigan."

"And Broken Hill," Pete said.

Clyde walked over to the on-deck storage locker marked as containing emergency equipment. From it, he took two MARS-L assault rifles. "Spare guns and ammo are stored in the rescue-boxes fore and aft, port and starboard," he said. "Don't touch the explosives. Leave those for me and Nicko."

"For what?" Pete asked.

"For pirates," Clyde said. "Back near French Guiana we saw a flotilla of sailing ships blown out of the water. My theory is they were sunk by a civilian freighter with an on-deck torpedo system. If the cartel could buy the VX, they could have bought a few torpedoes."

"I didn't see a gunboat when we were on the island," Olivia said.

"But they didn't let you out much," Clyde said. "It doesn't matter, because around here, pirates could be any desperate survivors who see our ship as their only means of escape. If they know what they're doing, they'll have fast boats hiding behind the wrecks. They'll wait until we pass so some can get ahead, some can get behind. They'll be armed with assault rifles, and will put a lot of lead into the air, but our hull is thicker than ice, so we can take it. Keep low, and keep away from the rail. Wait until they slow, until they come alongside, then empty the magazine into their boat."

"What if they have something bigger than assault rifles?" Olivia asked.

"Like I said, leave the explosives to me and Nicko," Clyde said. "Take up station by the crane."

From the crane, they had only a limited view of the shipwrecks ahead, but a perfect view of the beautifully empty shore.

"It's so green," Olivia said. "I wasn't expecting lush trees and white sands. Are those gulls?"

"That's a zom," Pete said. "In the shallows, walking into the waves."

Below, water frothed as the ship steered out to sea, giving them a view of the hotel-dotted reef, and its new moat of abandoned cruise ships. Some were listing. Some were broken in two. Many were smoke-blackened, as were the hotels behind.

"No way was this done by the cartel," Pete said. "It's too much damage. The city was too big."

"But there must be a link between this devastation and why the fuel-freighter was operating out of Puerto Morelos rather than anywhere else," she said.

Pete mentally inserted what he could see into what little he recalled from the sales-pitch documentary about Cancun he'd half-watched while daydreaming about Olivia. "The cruise ships must have been sailing around the Caribbean," he said. "In February, there'd have been a lot of tourists enjoying the sunshine. We know Cuba was nuked."

"At least once, I think," she said.

"So other harbours might have been, too," he said. "With nowhere to go, they came here."

"That's as good a reason as any, I guess," she said.

Up close, the cruise ships were monstrous. Too big to be afloat, and made to seem bigger now they were semi-submerged, listing, or grinding their hulls against one another with a death-howl wail. They were floating hotels, floating condominiums, floating cities, though they wouldn't be afloat much longer. All had miniscule portholes in the hull and more glass than metal on the superstructure above. They also shared the red-rust and rainbow oil-stains spilling down the sides, rippling outwards in a plastic-flecked and lifejacket-dotted moat.

"There's a corpse inside that life jacket," Olivia said. "Yep, it's moving."

Pete turned his gaze upwards, scanning the nearest of these monumental floating follies. Each balcony belonged to a cabin. Each cabin had two guests. He lost count at two hundred. Double it for the other side of the ship. Double it again for the passengers in the cheaper quarters. Double that for the crew, and it was thousands. For each cruise ship. Between them, on the once-white sands of the tourist shore, were smaller ships. Mostly sailing boats. He didn't bother to count them. Beyond the boats, beyond the oil-stained sands, were bullet-flecked palms, upturned cars, and skeletal hotels, burned to steel by unquenched fires. Hotels had guests, but they had staff, too. Staff had children. Children had teachers, and they had families of their own. But all he could see was the occasional zombie, drifting down to the beach.

"No pirate boats yet," Olivia said, briefly turning away, before turning back to the ocean. "I'll never be able to enjoy *The Princess Bride* again after this."

"There's no water," Pete said. "Towns usually grow up around rivers and springs, right? But resorts get built where there's a view. There's no fresh water here. Without it, after a day, people would leave."

"Assuming they were able," she said.

The next ship lay on its side. Only a third of the vessel was above the waves, but that gave a clue as to the water's depth, or lack thereof.

A small freighter, tilted forward at the prow, had left its propeller dangling high above the waves. A wallowing yacht with tattered rigging had been anchored to a sightseeing ferry on which a zombie roamed the open deck.

"They ran them aground," Pete said. "This was deliberate. It's a wall. A wall at sea. But were they defending against zombies, or pirates?"

"People! A flag!" Olivia said, and began sprinting back to the prow.

Pete peered at the mass of vessels ahead. Sheets, hung from some of the windows, twisting in the breeze, and it appeared as if some had writing on them. Was that what Olivia had seen?

The icebreaker's foghorn sounded two long blasts.

"Pete! C'mon!" Olivia called, running back towards him, Clyde a step behind. Olivia pointed at a cruise ship, listing towards shore at a twenty-degree angle. According to the name painted on the rust-smeared bow, in what was either a cruel joke or an unfortunate oversight, this vessel was the *Siren of the Seas*.

There were two rows of portholes in the deck, and an eight-storey condo atop. Each room had an identically wide, glass-enclosed balcony. Above these narrow balconies was a ninth glass-walled deck, which jutted out over the side of the ship. It was from that top deck that a red towel was being waved.

"We're the advance team," Clyde said, as he led them to the boat. "Baxter's piloting. Me and Nicko are climbing. You and Olivia are watching our retreat. If there's trouble, give us covering fire, then get back in the boat."

"What kind of trouble?" Pete asked.

"Pirates," Clyde said. "But don't worry about them. Tess and Bruce will be ready with the second boat, or to repel boarders."

Which was easy for a former Special Forces officer to say, harder for a former carpet salesman to do.

Nicko jogged onto the deck holding two heavy bags, to which were attached four coiled ropes, and with the sailor, Noel Baxter, at his side.

"The mast-cam caught an image of a kid up there," Nicko said. "A young teen."

"Any adults?" Clyde asked, checking inside the bag before slinging it over his shoulder.

"A few," Nicko said. "Let's go count them. Don't worry, mate," he added, slapping Pete on the shoulder. "I've done this before. Of course, that was with twenty chicken-stranglers."

"Who?"

"Get into our taxi," Nicko said. "I'll tell you as we drive. Yeah, we were babysitting a sting on some pirates operating out of northern Indonesia. They were targeting long-distance sailing yachts, so we set ourselves up to look like a round-the-world race. Strewth, were they surprised when they came alongside. Should have seen their faces. Dropped faster than—"

His words were lost beneath the buzz of the engine, and before Pete learned why the pirates had been strangling chickens.

Physically closer to the sea's surface, the carpet of plastics was more clearly visible. The launch ploughed through a multi-coloured soup of cups, clips, and clothing, long brackets and bottle caps, and semi-submerged floating furniture. There was no wildlife, except for a thin, red algal bloom, already spreading up the hull of the partially capsized ship.

"We're going to do this in stages," Clyde yelled, as soon as Baxter cut their speed. "Me and Nicko'll go first, and drop the ropes. We're going up the hull, down to the deck, then we'll go up to the super-structure. You two are going to stay by the deck rail. Stay in sight of the icebreaker." He took out a small radio, and handed it to Olivia. "That's if we get in trouble."

"What do we do?" she asked.

"Whatever I tell you over the radio," Clyde said. "Don't worry. If the survivors were pirate-bait, they'd have attacked by now. We've only got to worry about zoms. Nicko, you ready?"

"No worries," Nicko said. "Last one to the top buys the beers."

As Baxter brought them close to the cruise ship, Clyde clipped a rope to a rung. Nicko took the lead, almost running up the barnacle-encrusted ladder built into the side of the ship. He had about fifteen years on Clyde, but the older man had no difficulty keeping up. In seconds, they were at the rail.

"How did they do that?" Pete asked, as Nicko jumped over, while Clyde attached two ropes, letting them skitter down the ship and to the water.

"Training," Olivia said. "C'mon. Looks like fun. We can't spend our entire honeymoon sunbathing."

"Yeah, but it'd be nice to try," he said.

"Wait," Baxter said as the boat drifted with the trash-tide. "On three, jump. Grab the ladder, not the rope. One at a time."

"Me first," Olivia said.

"One, two, jump!" Baxter said. Olivia leaped, slamming into the ship with a thud.

"Easy," she hissed, hauling herself up and out of the way. "Your turn!"

"One, two, three!" Baxter called.

Pete leaped. The metal was hard, the barnacles as rough as emery board. After the briefest scrabble, he found his footing.

"Easy enough, right?" Clyde said when they joined him at the slanting top where the hull-rail met the deck.

"Yeah, no worries," Pete said, and almost meant it.

Nicko was below them, standing on the angled deck, but he wasn't alone. An orange-brown gore oozed from the bullet-smashed skulls of three zombies, lying flush against the bulkhead wall where they'd rolled after death. Nicko walked back from the direction of the stern, his gait made awkward by the deck's twenty-degree angle. "We've got some old barricades on deck, and zoms inside."

"*Hola*! Hello!" a woman called from above. She was leaning over one of the topmost balconies, her black hair streaming in the rising wind. "*No entrar!* Don't enter. Zombies!"

"Understood!" Clyde called back. "We're coming up. Hold on." He turned to the sergeant. "What do you think, Nicko?"

"Hostile," the sergeant said, calmly raising his carbine and firing along the deck at a zombie in smoke-scorched sailor's whites. "Stairs will be quickest. We can dart back outside if we find them blocked."

"Agreed," Clyde said. "You two hold the deck here."

The two soldiers ran for the nearest emergency door.

"But didn't…" Pete began. Clyde opened the door. Nicko fired single-shots nearly as fast as an automatic burst, which were soon lost beneath the thump of corpses.

"Grab the empty mag for me, mate!" Nicko called before stepping inside the stairwell.

"But that woman said don't go inside," Pete finished, though the soldiers had already vanished. He picked up the empty magazine, and couldn't help but stare at the pile of corpses lying inside the stairwell.

The door led to a set of emergency stairs, clearly signposted for the lifeboats on deck. The down-flight of the stairs, leading below, was partially blocked with a loose net that looked as if it had come from a soccer goal. Below it was a bric-a-brac of stateroom shelves and cabin clutter, being shoved and shunted by the insatiable undead.

A tourist in a lurid red-flower shirt, and missing most of its head, tumbled down the stairs. Pete stepped back, gun trained on the doorway.

"Trouble?" Olivia asked, coming to stand next to him.

"Zoms," Pete said. "Just like the woman said."

"And there's another," Olivia said, raising her rifle, aiming it down the deck. "Just one. Hang on." She fired. "Shoulder. And again. Damn."

Inside the stairwell, below the netting-barrier, the undead writhed and pushed, causing the clutter-barricade to bang into the walls.

"Got it," Olivia said, having fired again. "I need more practice. Another's coming. I'm going to let it get close. Wait, no. There are two more."

From inside, and above, came a burst of shots, matched by two from Olivia.

"Clear!" Olivia said. "I hope. I tell you, it was bad enough doing this on land. No way do I want to do this for living."

The radio squawked. "How's it going down there?" Nicko asked.

"Zoms on the deck," Olivia said. "We got them."

"There's seven survivors up here," Nicko said. "A teenager, a mum and baby, and four adults."

A body clattered down the stairwell, landing with a sharp crack as the arm snapped at the wrist. But the figure stood, slowly unfolding until Pete fired three shots into its face.

"Trouble?" Nicko asked.

"There's zoms in the stairwell," Olivia said.

"Then we'll take the direct route down," Nicko said. "Close the door, then keep the deck clear."

With his eyes on the deck towards the stern, Pete didn't see much of the survivors' descent. Clyde came first, carrying the infant inside his backpack, but strapped to his front. On the parallel rope, watching Clyde more than her footing, was a woman Pete assumed was the baby's mother. Pete turned back to the deck, glad he had something else to occupy his attention than the perilous descent. From behind, he heard a gunshot. A thump. Then a heavier thud.

"There you go," Clyde said. "Your boy didn't even wake."

"*Gracias,*" the mother murmured.

"Pete, give her a hand up to the rail," Clyde said as the other adults began their descent. With the ship at an angle, and with the balconies for handholds, it appeared an easy climb until, two floors up, a man slipped, falling hard onto the deck. The man cursed as he clutched his arm.

"I think it's just dislocated," Pete said, helping him to his feet. "We have a doc on the ship."

The teenager came last, with Nicko just beneath her, ready to catch her. But she was as nimble as the soldier.

"Easier than rock climbing," Nicko said.

"Zom!" Pete said.

"No worries," Nicko said, firing even as he spoke. "So who fancies a ride on an icebreaker?"

Chapter 5 - *Superviventes*
Cancun, Quintana Roo

Tess was waiting for them on the icebreaker's deck, and ushered the seven newcomers below for a medical exam and a meal. On deck, Pete checked the time, and was shocked to see that less than an hour had gone by. At least half of that had been aboard the small launch.

"Here you go, mate," Clyde said, thrusting a full magazine into Pete's hands. "Plenty more cruise ships to go. Might be a few more survivors, too."

Pete walked back to the rail. Seven survivors. A mother, her baby, a teenage girl, two other women, two men. From a ship with room for thousands of passengers, in a city which had been home to hundreds of thousands.

Olivia walked over, shaking her head. He gave a nod in reply. Together, they watched the shore.

The ship's foghorn sounded again, and again. But no reply came from the wrecks. His eyes tracked from one cabin to the next, from one ship to the next, looking for life, but only finding the undead. Sooner than he'd expected, concrete was replaced with palms, and Cancun was behind them.

"All clear," came Captain Renton's voice over the ship's address. "Stand down. All free hands to the mess."

"Are we free?" Pete asked.

"I guess so," Olivia said. "And I'm definitely in the mood for lunch."

"I'll take those rifles and give them a clean," Clyde said as Pete and Olivia entered the mess.

"Come in, find a seat," Tess said. "That's Pete and Olivia, the newlyweds," she added, speaking to the newcomers. There were two of them, sitting at a mess table and tucking into the chilli-rice Pete had cooked before the alarm had been sounded. The woman was in her early forties, though she had the eyes of someone who'd witnessed three lifetimes in the last few months. Those eyes now read each face as they entered, searching each for confirmation that safety truly had been found. The man was older, though probably not yet sixty, but had the weatherworn features of someone who'd worked outdoors all his life. It was he who'd slipped while climbing down the rope on the cruise ship, and his arm was now secured in a sling.

"I guess that this is everyone who's off-duty," Tess said as three sailors found a seat, and Zach went to the galley to find a bowl. "Bring some for everyone, Zach," Tess added, before turning back to the two newcomers. "We've got a small crew, but we're all glad to welcome you aboard. Let me introduce our new friends. This is Carmen Lopez and Ignacio Morabito. Hope I didn't mangle your name there, mate?"

The older man smiled, but then winced as he stretched the recent checkerboard scar on his left cheek. "Thank you," he said. "We didn't think there was anybody left in the world except us. We didn't expect a rescue from Australia."

"New Zealand," Baxter called out.

"The Pacific," Tess said. "Renata and Ramon Mendez are down in the clinic. They're the parents to the thirteen-year-old, Pita. She's got a spot of dehydration, and a gallon of exhaustion, but she'll be right as a ray in a day or two. The new mum, Julietta, needs watching, but her son looks okay. Doc Avalon's keeping an eye on them both. She's confident there's no risk of infection, so we won't bother with quarantine. Pete, Olivia, once we finish here, can you sort out some clothes from what was left by the Chileans?"

"No problem," Olivia said.

"So that brings us to where we're going next," Tess said. "We're entering the Gulf of Mexico. In an hour, we'll turn, and speed between Cuba and Florida so we can spend the night out in more open waters. At dawn, we'll see how the baby is faring. That'll decide whether we sail directly back to Robben Island. If the kid's doing well, we'll continue north to Savannah. What we do after that will, again, depend on the infant, and on what we learn in the U.S., and from the readings we pick up along the way."

"Like radiation?" Zach asked.

"Exactly," Tess said. "Especially as we near Cuba. I know how fast rumour can fly, so I've asked Carmen and Ignacio to share what they saw, and what they know about Puerto Morelos and the cartel's attack. From what I've heard, it won't alter our mission, but it does explain a few things we've been asking each other since Colombia. Carmen?"

"*Gracias*," she said, standing briefly before sitting again. She stretched her hands across the table as if wanting to take hold of the present so as not to be lost in the past. "Soon after *la epidemia*, the navy sent the cruise ships to Cancun. The Mexican navy and the Cubans were working together. Working, I think, with the other nations in the Caribbean. The tourists were going to be sent to Cuba. The fit and able would join a militia to clear the islands to the south."

"That is what they told us," Ignacio said, his voice a low growl.

Carmen, nodded, briefly raising her hands from the table in an expressive shrug. "We think Havana wanted the ships in case they had to evacuate Cuba. They were worried about infected refugees from the north. From the United States. We spent many nights talking about this. Many nights wasted. And nearly as many as the Cubans wasted, because when refugees came by ship, they kept going. The ships went north, or they went east, to Europe. Very few went south."

"No one stayed, no one helped," Ignacio said.

"There were rumours of flotillas," Carmen said. "There was talk of millions of people aboard thousands of ships, of new fortresses, and even armies."

"*El ensueño*," Ignacio said. "The reality was hunger and fear, and then mushroom clouds."

"Did you have many zoms in Cancun before then?" Zach asked.

"*Los infectados*?" Carmen said. "*Si*. Every day was a battle. Tourists had no cars. No food. No weapons. Many were elderly. Many died. It was only the presence of the ships, and the promise of an evacuation, which kept order in the city."

"It kept the tourists from fleeing to Puerto Morelos," Ignacio said. "They didn't want more people."

Carmen nodded. "*El coronel* would refuel ships. You know this, yes?"

"Elle who?" Zach asked.

"A colonel, yes?" Clyde asked. "A colonel was in charge of things in Puerto Morelos?"

"Coronel Gorostiza," Ignacio said. "He ran a special border unit in Tamaulipas. But who was he? I don't know. Two days after the outbreak in Manhattan, he arrived in Puerto Morelos with his helicopters and declared himself in charge."

"You lived in Puerto Morelos?" Clyde asked.

"*Si*," Ignacio said. "And my grandfather before me."

"Hold on," Tess said. "Tell them about Cozumel first."

"If a ship arrived in Puerto Morelos," Ignacio said, "the coronel would refuel it, and send it on its journey. If you arrived by truck, you would be given diesel and water. No one was allowed into Puerto Morelos. No one was allowed to stay. *Almost* no one. The coronel had an oil tanker, and controlled the harbour in Cozumel. They collected diesel from Cozumel, and brought it to Puerto Morelos."

"And what happened to any refugee ships which went to Cozumel?" Tess prompted.

"They were sunk," Ignacio said.

"By the Mexican Navy?" Clyde asked.

"Mexican, Cuban, Haitian, the flags didn't matter," Carmen said.

"The cruise ships had gathered at Cancun," Tess summarised. "Warships protected Cozumel, and any passing ship was sent down to Puerto Morelos to refuel. A tanker in Puerto Morelos refuelled the passing ships, and occasionally travelled to Cozumel to top up from the storage tanks which usually serviced the cruise ships."

"How many people were in Cancun before the zoms?" Zach asked.

"A million," Carmen said. "But the locals had cars. Most left. After the bombs fell on Cuba, a military ship arrived from Havana. The captain warned us there would be no evacuation. A bomb had detonated in the harbour and destroyed every ship."

"They targeted the rescue ships?" Zach asked.

Carmen nodded.

"Couldn't you have used the cruise ships to evacuate people?" Zach asked.

"Evacuate to where?" Ignacio asked.

"The ships had no fuel," Carmen said. "I don't know why. As word of the bombs spread, Cancun became chaotic. People on the ships came ashore. People ashore went to the ships. There was no water, no power, no hope. Some people walked away, and walked into the infected."

"They came to Puerto Morelos," Ignacio said. "Tourists armed with bats and clubs. The zombies followed. We had to fight both, just to survive." As he spoke, his eyes moved from one to the other, gauging their reaction. "But within two days, it was over."

"We do not know who attacked the cruise ships anchored off Cancun," Carmen said.

"It was Coronel Gorostiza," Ignacio said.

"We don't *know*," Carmen said. "The attack was at night. They fired missiles and torpedoes. Some hit ships. Some hit the shore. At dawn, as smoke rose over the city, the streets filled with the infected. The ships were on fire. The hotels were on fire. The world was on fire. We were trapped."

"Trapped where?" Zach asked.

"My library," Carmen said.

"You have your own library?" Zach asked.

"I worked there," she said.

"Cool," Zach said. "How big was your reference section?"

"Save it for later, Zach," Tess said. "Sorry, Carmen, the kid's a bit of a bookworm."

"Book *snake*," Zach said.

Carmen smiled. "No one loots a library, so it seemed a good place to spend our nights. We knew there were still organised groups in Puerto Morelos. We planned to wait until most people had fled, and the infected had died, before going south."

"And in Puerto Morelos, we were waiting on a miracle," Ignacio said. "The coronel was harsh. Hard. Brutal. But a thousand of us were still alive in Puerto Morelos. We had a fuel tanker, soldiers, and the fuel reserves in Cozumel. When the infected died, we would be able to find other survivors. We'd sold fuel to ships, trading for information about where there were survivors, though there was nowhere like us. The coronel had plans. He would build an empire. But then the plane came with the poison gas. I was at sea, fishing, as it flew over. Ashore, everyone died. Everyone who went ashore to help, they died. I took my boat north, to Cancun."

"How did you end up on that cruise ship?" Zach asked.

"We thought the ship was empty of the infected," Carmen said. "Julietta was about to give birth. When we were quiet, the infected left us alone. A new baby can't be quiet. On an empty ship, noise wouldn't matter. So we went to the ship, but the infected were there. That is why there are only seven of us now."

"I've a few questions about Cozumel," Clyde said. "Are you saying that there's a secure harbour with a diesel supply?"

"It was never secure," Ignacio said. "*Los infectados, si*? Each time the ship arrived off Puerto Morelos, the coronel would go to the walls and recruit some of the refugees. These were the only newcomers allowed inside, but they would be sent to the tanker, and sent with it to

Cozumel. It was they who would go ashore and operate the pumps. Very few survived. You would need an army much larger than the coronel's to secure that harbour."

"I know where we can find one," Clyde said.

"Down near the Panama Canal, we found a boat that bought fuel with gold," Zach said. "Why gold?"

"If ships paid with gold, it was because gold was all they had," Ignacio said. "The coronel wanted to move people along, move them away. With Cuba gone, there was no safe refuge unless someone aboard one of those ships found it and returned. That is what he was hoping for."

"Do you know what happened to the fuel tanker?" Clyde asked.

"It had just left the harbour when the plane appeared overhead," Ignacio said. "It was sailing south, but was directly beneath the plane when it sprayed its poison. I think, because they wanted to hit the ship, they delayed when they released, and so I was saved."

"Captain Renton thinks it unlikely the ship survived," Tess said. "I'm sure we've all got other questions for each other, but I think those are the key details."

"Yeah, can we talk about your library?" Zach asked.

"I'll leave you to it," Tess said.

Two hours later, showered, changed, and suddenly finding himself at a loose end, Pete drifted around the ship until he wandered into the science centre.

"Hey, bro, come take a look," Corrie said. She, Olivia, and Dr Smilovitz were gathered around the sextet of screens.

"What are you looking at?" Pete asked.

"Footage taken by the teenager, Pita," Corrie said. "It's some photos and videos from Cancun."

"Where are the high-rise hotels?" Pete asked.

"This is proper Cancun," Corrie said. "The inland city where the locals lived."

"Is it any different from Australia or Indiana?" Pete asked.

"Architecturally, sure," Corrie said. "Though not by a huge amount. Even the barricades look similar."

"Did you want help with the dinner prep?" Olivia asked.

"There's been a coup in the kitchen," Pete said, dropping into a chair. "The dad, Ramon, was the top chef at one of the big resorts."

"Isn't that cause to be happy?" Olivia asked. "Because you're wearing your just-checked-my-bank-balance face."

"I kinda did," Pete said. "I checked the pantry. With the new mouths, we're down to thirty-three days, but I'm pretty sure I added it up wrong. Ramon's going to do a full inventory tonight."

"So we'll do some fishing," Corrie said. "I got the freezer working earlier, so we can start building up a stock."

"There'll be no fishing until after we get out of the Gulf," Leo said.

"Because of radiation?" Pete asked.

"It's risen, yes," Leo said. "But I was expecting that. The rain washed the fallout into the rivers, and they're carrying it to the Gulf. Depending on how badly the Southern U.S. was hit, and when you add toxic chemicals to the radiation, the entire Gulf will become a dead-zone. In turn, that'll have an impact on coastal ecology, bringing about extreme desertification."

"In what kind of timeframe?" Pete asked.

"The die-off has begun, but will be noticeably catastrophic by this fall," Leo said.

"That soon? Well, that puts my complaints into perspective," Pete said.

"It should be temporary," Leo said. "Within a few years, the heavy metals will have sunk to the seabed where they'll be coated in a layer of sediment. Algae, and oxygen, should return, but I can't give a time frame. We can only monitor it."

"So you think we'll come back here?" Pete asked.

"Us? I don't know," Leo said. "But someone will. Maybe this ship because it has a very long range, but probably with a warship escort. They'll want to confirm whether Corn Island is now a deserted harbour, and whether Cozumel is usable. We'll need somewhere this side of Panama as a base when we repair the canal. Cozumel is probably too far, but it's all we know of. Any bigger expedition, or resettlement, or anything beyond a survey mission next year, will have to wait until after the canal is re-opened."

"Unless we find survivors in Savannah," Corrie said.

"Or New York," Leo said.

"You still want to go there?" Pete asked.

"Don't you?" Leo asked. "I thought you wanted to hunt for Judge Benton and the rest of the Canadian army."

"Kinda," Pete said. "I didn't think we could give up the search down on Corn Island. But the search isn't really for them. It's for all the people, like those seven we just rescued. They'd have died if we'd gone back to the Pacific with the *Te Taiki*. How many others are out there, just days away from death? But tomorrow, whether we go on or not, will be decided by whether a baby needs to be raced back to a doctor."

"As it should be," Olivia said. "Isn't that the point? Isn't that what we're saying just by being here, that it's worth risking all our lives to save just one?"

"Agreed," Pete said. "I'm thinking of all the people we're leaving behind. You should have seen Ramon, down in the galley. He wasn't just grateful, he was nearly ecstatic."

"His daughter is safe," Leo said. "It must have been hell on that ship, marking time, knowing there was no way out."

"Right. No guns. No lifeboats. No hope for rescue," Pete said. "But I was looking at Ramon and a line came to me. I don't know if it's from history or a movie, *what did you do during the war*?"

"That's a recruitment poster from World War One," Leo said.

"So it was real?" Pete asked. "Because I was imagining being asked what *I* did during the outbreak, and the only answer I could think of was *not enough*."

11th April

Chapter 6 - The Better Angels
Cape Canaveral, Florida

Pete stared at the image of the empty sea captured by the mast-cam and displayed on the science centre screen. "Where are we now?" he asked.

"Somewhere between Key West and the Bahamas," Corrie said.

"No, I got that from the compass," he said.

"If you want to know exactly, I can call the bridge," she said.

"No, it's fine," he said, and turned back to the screen.

It was two hours since dawn, and they'd barely sped up from their night-time crawl.

Corrie had repurposed three flat-screen TVs into a new bank of monitors on which she watched the outbreak footage Leo had brought with him. Pete, meanwhile, watched the ocean. A sailor was doing the same on the bridge, while Olivia, Zach, and the soldiers employed a more manual approach on deck. Leo and Tess were interviewing Ignacio and Carmen on camera, one-on-one, each asking a different kind of question. Dr Avalon was with Julietta and her son, and in isolation, while the entire ship waited on news of whether they would turn south to Robben Island.

"You're being unusually quiet," Corrie said. "Is Olivia okay?"

"Oh, sure."

"Did you have a fight?"

"Nope."

"Is it because Ramon has taken over the kitchen?" she asked. "No offence, mate, but you're no more a cook than I am."

"No argument," Pete said. "Breakfast was good, even if it was more like dinner. Birds," he added, leaning forward to look at the screen. "A flock. Maybe a hundred. Heading…" He checked the compass. "Heading away from Florida. That's not good. What did Leo say about the readings last night?"

"He mumbled a lot," Corrie said. "But he kept us sailing slow, so it can't have been that bad."

"I guess not," Pete said.

"It's the baby, right? We'll know soon, but Doc Flo's been down there for hours. If there was a problem, it'd have been obvious, and we'd be sailing at full speed for Cape Town. Nope, I'd put my money on us going north."

"To Savannah and New York," Pete said.

"Depending on what, and who, we find along the way," Corrie said, and returned to the footage of New York, uploaded in those early few days before the world's final collapse.

Pete turned back to his own screen. Ignoring the gulls, he looked at the floating wreckage. There was a lot, though nothing that could be called a raft, let alone a boat.

It hadn't been spoken loudly or often, but the New Zealand sailors hoped for a repeat of Mozambique. An enclave. A bastion containing thousands of survivors. It was slowly sinking in that there *had* been one: Cuba. The bombs had destroyed that hope, while the cartel had wiped out the most likely successor settlement of Puerto Morelos.

"Me and Olivia were talking about what we'd do if we found thousands of survivors, like they found in Cape Town," Pete said. "Not everyone in Cuba can be dead, surely. Some must have survived the bombs. But unless we hear them on the radio we won't ever know."

"What did you settle on?" Corrie asked.

"For what?"

"If we found survivors, what would you do?" she asked.

"If they were ashore, sail straight for Robben Island. If they were on a ship, tow them to a source of fresh water, then sail for Robben Island."

"Good plan. Is that what's getting to you?"

"Not exactly. But in Cuba, the nuclear bomb was detonated in the harbour, on top of the evacuation fleet."

"According to Carmen," Corrie said. "We don't know how many mouths and ears the news passed through before reaching hers."

"But an evacuation fleet wasn't a target picked months ago," Pete said. "It wasn't part of some old Cold War plan. Someone made a deliberate decision to destroy the ships, ensuring that no more lives could be saved."

"Probably a sub," Corrie said. "But they could have been aiming for Havana and missed. There's a huge margin of error when you're firing ballistically."

"I guess there's more than one kind of evil in the world," Pete said. "The compass is wobbling. Oh, I can feel the engines. We're changing direction. North. We're turning north."

"Yep, but don't read anything into that," Corrie said. "If we're going to Robben Island, we'll head north until we're beyond Grand Bahama, then turn east. There'll be less debris on the open sea."

"Less chance of finding survivors," Pete said. He turned to the map, found the island of Grand Bahama, and then traced a line across to West Palm Beach on the Florida shore. From there, he traced a line south, picking out the names he remembered from the news, books, and TV. "Mrs Mathers moved to Florida," he said.

"Do you want to go ashore to look for her?"

"I can't remember where she moved to," Pete said. "Olivia would know. But I don't want to ask her. It's been so long since the outbreak. Too long. We *could* go ashore. I think Tess would be okay with that. I don't think it would do any good."

"That's what's eating you up?"

He glanced at the door, and then lowered his voice. "Kinda. Back in the outback, you went online. Didn't you reprogram the missiles?"

"No," she said, her voice equally low. "I just tweaked a bit of code I wrote years ago. It was embedded in the GPS, and the other similar positioning systems. It should have been obvious that the satellites weren't working properly, so no one should have launched."

"But they did, and the bombs landed in the oceans," Pete said.

"Not all, but some. Hopefully enough. Hopefully not too many. What of it?"

"Can you undo it?" he asked.

"Not without a time machine," she said.

"I mean un-break the satellites?" he asked.

"Nope. They were bricked. Not all the satellites would have been affected. There are some small science experiments up there that should still be running. With the right equipment, I could grab control of some of them. They'd be low-power, probably without cameras, and maybe not even in orbit around Earth. But they'd be designed to send data back to Earth, so we could use them to ping messages back and forth. But if we really want satellite coverage, it'd make more sense to launch a few new rockets. The Pacific launch-sites would have been destroyed by the tsunami, but we can always build a launch platform in the outback. Finding the rocket components will be difficult. Some were made in Australia, so we'll have to see what we can piece together."

"It sounds like you've given this some thought," Pete said.

"Leo and I were discussing it yesterday. We think we can launch two or three comms satellites in a few months. That'll give us a really basic link to New Zealand, to Indonesia, and the seas between. There are a couple of places in Australia that make satellites, but building rockets is a different story. Once we've used up existing stock, we'll need eighteen months to build enough for a proper satellite communications network. Could be two years. Next issue is going to be debris from all the old satellites, so we'll have to get used to launching regular replacements."

"You say rockets, I hear missiles," Pete said. "But that's cool. The scientists wanted to go to New York to find patient zero. You're going through the footage. Do you know where it began?"

Corrie shrugged. "I have a hunch where the Manhattan outbreak began, but I reckon there were multiple outbreaks, globally. Since the virus was manufactured, that should be expected. Once the corrupt politicians decided to use the pandemic as a weapon, they deliberately deployed military forces away from the hot-zones to help speed up the spread. If they're willing to do that, why not infect a few people in more remote places to give the apocalypse a push? But that doesn't matter to us, not if they're right about the peach-zom."

"The who?"

"The zombie in the peach pantsuit," she said. "The woman who you see get infected, die, and then come back."

"It's three separate video clips, right?" Pete asked.

"Yep, but we know where she is. That's why we'll go to New York. We'll find her, and get proof the zoms have been dying from the start. That'll be good news to share back home. Better even than news of survivors, though I hope we can bring back both."

"Home," Pete echoed. "I guess it was for you."

"It was," she said. "It wasn't a bad life there."

Pete returned to his screens. He, Olivia, and Corrie had all given their own videoed interviews to Tess. Some might be used in the trial of the two cartel gangsters on their way back to the Pacific aboard the *Te Taiki*, but that trial was part of the story, too. Call it news. Call it propaganda. Call it morale boosting. Call it history. It really was *just* a story. Part of a truth, but not its entirety. It was that part which people needed to hear in order to struggle on for a year or two more. It was that realisation which gnawed at his soul. The story wasn't complete fiction, but it wasn't the complete truth, either.

"Carpets," he said, decisively. "We need to focus on carpets."

"On the ship?"

"In the Pacific," he said. "When people can shop for a new carpet on a Saturday, and have it laid on a Monday, that's when we'll know we're back to a more normal world."

"You really did like your old job, then?" she said.

"More than I realised," he said.

"Excuse me." It was the teenager, Pita, who stood by the door.

"Hiya," Corrie said. "Lunch was great, thanks. Are you looking for someone?"

"Paint," she said. "Do you have paint?"

"I saw some in a locker a couple of decks below," Pete said. To which Pita frowned in incomprehension. "Um... *por qué quieres... pintura*?" Pete tried.

Pita smiled. "For my father," she said in far better English than his Spanish. "He always wanted his own restaurant. I want to paint a sign for him."

"In the mess?" Corrie said. "Cool idea."

"We should check with the captain first," Pete said.

As the ship turned north, shadowing the Florida coast, his mood improved. However much of this new history was fiction, it *was* the past. His future would be with the woman he loved, and he found her perched on a gun-locker beneath the shade of the deck-crane.

"Did you hear the good news?" Olivia asked.

"No, but I want to," he said.

"Baby Angelo is doing well," she said.

"Angelo? He has a name? A good name, too."

"Julietta wanted to call him Angel, but Doc Flo wouldn't allow it."

"Since when does she get a say?"

"It's *her*. Of *course* she gets a say. The baby's fine. Mom and child are going to be kept in isolation for a few more days, but they can have visitors just as long as we scrub up first. Want to go say hi later?"

"That'd be nice. Angel's a good name. More of a girl's name, though."

"You think?" she asked.

"Or is it tempting fate? You know, if you call your daughter Angel, she'll turn out to be anything but."

"Nice to know where your head's at, Pete," she said, leaning in close.

"Yep, I'm focused on the future. Isn't that supposed to be Florida over there?"

"On the other side of the ship, Pete," she said. "Florida is depressing. The glimpses I've seen are as bad as Cancun. What was the radiation like as we were sailing near Cuba?"

"Not sure," Pete said. "I was helping Pita paint the mess-deck."

"Why—" Olivia began, but was interrupted by the iceberg alarm.

They ran to the rail, each turning north then south, before sprinting around the crane, and almost straight into Zach.

"Boats!" the Australian said. "Lots of them on the radar. Where's your guns?"

They retreated back to the on-deck locker, both collecting carbines and ammo before heading back to the ship's side, where Clyde had appeared with an armful of metal brackets.

"Hold this for me, mate," he said. "Built this after Cancun. Looks like I finished just in time."

"Zach said there were ships," Olivia said.

"Yep, there could be trouble," Clyde said.

"So why are we slowing down and turning towards shore?" Olivia asked.

"Because we don't want trouble to catch up with us after dark," Clyde said. "Nah, better we chase them off in daylight. Hold that bracket. Good on ya."

"What are you doing?" Pete asked, as Zach staggered onto the deck with a machine gun nearly as long as he was tall.

"We're setting up a machine gun mount," Clyde said.

"We didn't do that in Cancun," Olivia said.

"Because I hadn't finished building it," Clyde said. "We didn't spot boats on the radar back then, but we have now. Fast boats. Speedboats. They're darting into range, then away. It's the kind of probe and feint pirates do, but this lot, they've underestimated the range of our radar set. We've counted twelve boats, operating in three packs. One's shadowing us from in front, one's keeping closer to shore, the other's headed out to sea. That's why we're moving closer to the beach. We want to encourage the attack at a time and place of our choosing. There, she'll do." He patted the now-affixed machine gun, before swivelling it left, then right. "Trigger is that button on the handle. Two hands at all times, when you're operating her."

"Aren't you going to operate the gun?" Pete asked.

"At first, but not if they get aboard," Clyde said. "They'll attack from the front, because they don't want any of their bullets to damage the engines. But they'll try boarding from both sides, to spread us out, so they can overwhelm us. If we've got the gun here, they'll divert, attempt to board on the starboard, where Nicko has a few surprises ready for them. If any boats make it alongside, just empty your magazine into them. Zach, report to the med-bay."

"Don't you want me here?" he asked.

"No, mate. You're protecting our precious cargo. Go on. Quick now."

As Zach hurried away, Ramon and Renata came onto the deck.

"Rifles?" Renata asked.

"I'll show you," Olivia said.

"Then you three go report to Nicko at starboard," Clyde said. "Pete and I'll guard here."

The speedboats were small. Dots at first, approaching from shore. Four. All red. As fast as a car, but a nightmare to turn, ploughing a crescent as they turned back towards land while the icebreaker carved onward.

"Gasoline-powered cigarette boats," Clyde said. "That's good. They've got a terrible range. Tells us we're dealing with amateurs."

"They might not have much experience, but they're not giving up," Pete said. "Here they come again."

The boats sped towards the ship, now nearly side on, but again slowed while still well beyond rifle range.

"Do you want me to fire next time they do that?" Pete asked.

"Not yet," Clyde said, peering after the boats. "They're too far out, and we don't want to give them any warning."

His radio squawked. "They're using an encrypted radio channel," Avalon said. "Corrie is hacking it."

"Figured they might be," Clyde said, lowering the radio. "They've got organisation, leadership."

"Could they be friendly?" Pete asked.

"Could be," Clyde said. "We're about level with New Smyrna, just north of Cape Canaveral. There's a lake of fuel stored beneath the space centre, and in tanks designed to withstand ground-level explosions. Good site for survivors to group."

The radio chirruped. "Expect an attack."

"Well, that's a shame," Clyde said.

The four boats that had been close to shore approached once more, but this time, two boats pulled ahead. There were two seats at the front, and benches at the back, but these craft weren't really designed for passengers. Despite that, Pete counted five people in each of the two lead boats, and on each, someone was waving a white flag.

"They look friendly," Pete said.

"So does a dog until he bites you," Clyde said.

The closest two speedboats were now less than two hundred metres out. The other two were about the same distance behind. The lead boats leaped ahead, halving the distance before slowing again, now running parallel to the icebreaker.

"Any second now," Clyde said. "They're expecting us to cut our speed. When we don't, they'll attack."

To Pete, they didn't look hostile, not until the boats leaped forward again, cutting the distance to fifty metres. Two people in each boat raised their hands, opening fire. The machine-gun crack of the bullets was barely audible over the whine of their engines, and the rumble from the icebreaker.

"Head down, mate," Clyde said. "Told you. Machine pistols. Utterly useless from one moving target to another. On three, get ready. Two. One."

Pete stood, just as the lead speedboat was replaced by a fountain of water, wood, and plastic in an explosion which rocked him back on his heels.

"What was that?" Pete asked.

"Nicko," Clyde said. "I told you we brought some surprises from the *Te Taiki*."

The other three speedboats broke off, turning towards shore, slowing, but clearly having abandoned pursuit.

"You keep watch," Clyde said. "I'm going back to the machine shop to see about some armour shields to give us a bit more cover to fire from."

"Do you think they'll follow?"

"Ask me again in an hour and I won't have to guess at the answer," Clyde said.

Chapter 7 - The Land Jaguars Once Ruled
Mayport, Florida

After one circuit of the deck, Pete met Olivia coming the other way.

"If I said jaguars rule, can you guess where we're going?" she asked.

"Jacksonville?" Pete said. "Why?"

"Well, almost to Jacksonville," Olivia said. "There's a military base called Mayport which is on the Atlantic coast. We're heading there."

"What about the speedboats?"

"This is *because* of the speedboats," Olivia said. "But don't ask me why. I heard about Mayport from Renata when she handed me Ramon's rifle to give to Clyde because Pita had summoned Ramon back to the mess to cook a meal now in case we can't later." She took a theatrically deep breath. "Ah, gossip, I did so miss you." She tapped the rifle still slung on her shoulder "The slide's jammed, so it needs a fix. Do you know where Clyde is?"

"In the machine shop making metal shields for us to stand behind. Do you have any gossip about those speedboats?"

"Nope. But if we're cooking meals when we can, I'm guessing we're in trouble. I'll see what Clyde knows. Back in a bit."

Pete continued his lonely patrol of the deck, trying to recall where Jacksonville was on the map, but that didn't help him work out how far away it was.

"Still keeping watch? Good on ya," Clyde said, when he returned to the deck, a bag in hand. "You can give me a hand with these brackets for the machine gun. We'll place one on each side of the ship. We've only got the one machine gun, but she's not too hard to move."

"I thought you were going to make some metal shields."

"Ignacio's prepping the materials," Clyde said, "but I finished these this morning. They're not polished, so mind out for sharp edges."

"Sure. Did we win?" Pete asked.

"We didn't lose," he said. "It wasn't really a fight. They didn't stand a chance, because they didn't know how vastly outgunned they were. Next time, against them, it'll be tougher."

"They were using radio, right?"

"Yep, with civilian encryption. Your sister had it unwrapped in seconds. Even Avalon was impressed."

"Corrie used to be a hacker," Pete said. "But she retired from all that."

"In these times, we've all got to take our swords out from under the bed. You hold the bracket there, I'll do the bolts."

"What did the pirates say?"

"Pull back," Clyde said. "Not you," he added. "That's what they were saying. They had orders to scare us off. Those orders were being relayed to one of the boats from someone ashore."

"But they attacked."

"Two boats didn't hear the orders, or ignored them."

"Did we try talking to them?" Pete asked.

"We did. They didn't want to talk back."

"If they follow us, and attack, can we sink them?" Pete asked.

"No worries, and long before they get alongside," Clyde said. "But we've only brought the weaponry to stop one proper attack. Once it comes, we're turning around."

"Oh. I didn't realise there were contingencies."

"A bloke still on active service might be insulted by that," Clyde said. "Nah, we didn't want to spread the gloom. The whole point of us going north is to find survivors. Implicit, but unspoken, is that we bring those we find safely back to the Pacific. So we can sail on for another two thousand kilometres, or for another fifteen days, or until one sustained attack, or the loss of two lives. Bet you're wishing you'd not asked."

"Pretty much," Pete said. "But we're heading to Jacksonville?"

"To the naval base in Mayport," Clyde said. "And partly because of those people near Cape Canaveral. Mayport is one of the major Atlantic naval bases. It's a logical hub for survivors to gather, and for any U.S. ships to return to if they were at sea during the crisis. To be blunt, if we don't find any ships there, we won't find them anywhere in the Atlantic, and we know they're not in the Pacific."

"How far away is it?" Pete asked.

"About two hundred and seventy kilometres. We're going slow right now, but we'll speed up near dark. Radar will tell us if the Floridians are following. If they are, we'll skim out into deep water. But Bruce has a theory. They weren't looking for a fight, just to scare us off. They're not pirates, just survivors trying to protect their supplies. If there are ships in Jacksonville, the only reason the Floridians wouldn't have taken them is because those ships had crews willing to fight for them, but who didn't want to chase down a few hungry survivors because that'd be murder."

"Do you think it's likely?" Pete asked.

"Nah," Clyde said. "But Bruce is right, we've got to look. That'll do. Let's fix the next."

With the brackets in place, Clyde returned below to his workshop. With no one telling him not to, Pete went back inside, but only as far as the utility closet from which he took a mop, seeking comfort in a simple and familiar chore. After having spoken with Clyde, he finally understood the anxiety gnawing at him since the euphoria at rescue, and marriage, had waned.

Yes, some of it was the uncertainty that everyone aboard shared. The uncertainty over when they would turn around, and whether any more might die before they reached the safety of the Pacific. For him, added to it was the realisation that he had power. *Real* power with which to effect real and lasting change, the like of which few emperors had ever had. He'd pitched the idea of going north without much thought. If Tess had said no, then, in all likelihood and after a conscience-salving debate, he, Olivia, and Corrie would have stayed with the New Zealanders. But they *had* gone north. They *had* found seven survivors, and the Floridian pirates. If they found a military ship in Mayport, a second expedition would certainly be dispatched. The canal would be repaired. More survivors would be found in North America, while others, elsewhere, would die because resources were so limited. Some would live, others would die, and a future would be written because of him. Not just him, true. But that was power. Real power. And it was unsettling.

"There you are," Olivia said. "I thought you'd fallen over the side. Why the mop?"

"Someone has to clean," he said.

"Better you than me," she said. "Pita wants everyone in the galley for the grand opening."

"The grand opening of what?"

"The Mendez Muncheria," Olivia said. "Zach helped with the name. C'mon. We get to eat afterwards."

It was a small turnout, with only about half the ship's complement present. Avalon was there, though Leo wasn't. Nor was Tess, but

Captain Renton had come down from the bridge to cut the ribbon. That was a nice touch, Pete thought. It helped confirm that the newcomers were now part of the crew. Before Renata and Ramon had finished their welcoming speech, Tess's voice came over the address. "Radiation is rising. Captain to the bridge."

"Carry on, eat," Renton said as he hurried to the stairs, but was overtaken by Dr Avalon.

About half the room took a step towards the door.

"Yep, we should eat," Pete said. "If trouble's coming, I'd rather face it on a full stomach. Looks great, Ramon," he added.

"*Gracias*," he said. "I phoned the supplier to send us more stock. Until it arrives, we must make do."

"Looks like we're making do with a feast," Olivia said, with forced cheer.

The meal was a distinct improvement on Pete's own efforts, or the irregular scraps they'd had while confined, and the just as irregular meals they'd had on the road before then. But he barely noticed what he was eating. His eyes watched the wall-speaker, waiting for another announcement. When it came, it was of the worst kind.

"Radiation readings have spiked," Tess announced. "Everyone is to remain off the deck. We're detouring out to sea. We believe Mayport was the target of this bomb. We'll aim to approach land near Savannah, and take readings again."

Olivia leaned forward, keeping her voice low. "If Mayport was targeted, Jacksonville will be gone, too."

"I guess so," Pete said. "But we made the right choice." He looked over at the serving counter where Renata and Ramon were quietly reassuring their daughter. "We definitely made the right choice."

12th April

Chapter 8 - Lookout for Land
Savannah, Georgia

Pete woke in a river of sweat.

"Same dream, hon?" Olivia asked from the chair by the porthole where she'd been reading.

"Same dream," Pete said. "Did I wake you?"

"I'm surprised *I* didn't wake *you*, clambering over you to get out," she said. "From now on, you've got the wall-side."

"Fair enough. It's hot, right? That's not just me?"

"The air is off," she said. "Corrie knocked on the door. She woke me."

"Why? What's wrong?" Pete asked, sitting up.

"Radiation," Olivia said. "It spiked so we went out to sea."

"Spiked? Again? That's… that's bad." He shook his head. "Where are we?"

"North of Mayport, South of Savannah," Olivia said. "We're not travelling fast, because Leo's been collecting readings."

"Ah. So where was hit?"

"He thinks Mayport was the principal target, but they threw multiple warheads at it to make sure at least one hit. That's according to Corrie. We're still heading for Savannah. Go have a shower. You'll feel better. Oh, but water's limited. One minute. I'll time you."

Twenty seconds of tepid water gently sprayed from the nozzle, barely long enough for his skin to decide whether it was hot or cold before Olivia reached in and switched it off.

"Time," she said. "Soap."

The shower cubicle was skin-scuffingly cramped. Elbows and knees banged into the sides as he sloughed soap everywhere. Forty seconds of rinsing, and he felt damp rather than clean, but he was awake.

"What time is it?"

"About two a.m.," Olivia said. "Tess has the bridge, but she didn't want to wake Angelo by using the alarm. Corrie and Leo were sitting watch with her."

"Right. And Jacksonville was bombed, but there are pirates in Cape Canaveral."

"One caused the other, I think," Olivia said. "The pirates are trapped between Cuba and Jacksonville. If radiation is spreading east from Mayport and Jacksonville, into the sea, it must also be drifting west, inland."

"South, too," Pete said, opening the locker to hunt for clothes.

"Sure, but west is more important. A band of radiation going west from Jacksonville would cut Florida off from the rest of the country. The pirates were using gasoline in their boats, Pete. Leo says you'd get forty times as many miles per gallon in a car, and then had a big fight with Doc Flo about how fallen bridges and the odds of smashing into a zom would affect fuel economy."

"They've been fighting a lot," Pete said.

"Zach says more than usual," Olivia said.

"Clyde said the pirates were trying to scare us off," Pete said.

"Right, which makes sense if they have nowhere else to go. They've got a lot of fuel, but limited supplies otherwise, and they don't want to share."

"Maybe we should try talking with them," Pete said.

"They shot at us," she said. "But it's not up to you and me. Savannah is the priority. Although, I wonder if that's where the pirates came from. I guess we'll find out later today. Want to try to go back to sleep?"

"I don't think I could."

"Then a movie?" Olivia said, holding up a memory stick. "It turns out that footage of the outbreak in New York wasn't the only thing Leo downloaded before the internet went down."

"Nothing apocalyptic," Pete said. "I think you and me need a new favourite genre."

"Good news there, then," she said. "The best way to describe Leo's collection is movies Doc Flo won't yell at. There's a lot of biographical stuff, and movies so old, they might have originally had a contemporary setting but they now count as historical. He recommended a movie about Madame Curie, but I think there's one about Darwin."

"I'll take the animals," he said.

He dozed through the movie, and they both dozed afterwards, sleeping fitfully in the stifling cabin. When the fans came back on, they both got up, luxuriating in the feel of circulating air.

"A house near a river," Olivia said. "That's what we need. Lots of water, lots of breeze."

"And a view," Pete said. "It's still dark out there."

"The clock says it's six," Olivia said. "What time's dawn?"

"I was going to ask you that," Pete said. "But it should be around now, right?"

They quickly dressed: trousers, boots, t-shirt, holster. The guns, nine-mils, had been salvaged from Corn Island. They were growing into a familiar weight, but each time he did up his belt, and checked the gun's position, he got a brief echo of his old life when he'd check his pockets for phone and keys. Outside, they met Corrie coming down the corridor towards them.

"Perfect timing," Corrie said. "You're on lookout duty."

"Looking for what?" Olivia asked.

"Land. We've sailed into a fog bank, so land must be close, but we don't know precisely how close. Go up onto deck, and watch for rocks."

On deck, they couldn't see much. Even the blinking light atop the crane was lost in the stultifying shroud engulfing the ship, but they did see Clyde, pacing the rail. "You've come to help? Good on ya," the soldier said. "Bruce is at the stern. Nicko's at the bow. You can help watch seaward."

"For rocks?" Pete asked.

"Pirates," he said. "The boss is watching the radar, but you can never be too cautious."

The couple crossed the deck. Pete leaned over the rail. "I can just about see the waves sloshing against the hull," he said.

"From here, I can't even see the crane's hook," Olivia said.

"Seen any crocs?" Zach said, appearing so quietly, Pete jumped. "Ah, sorry mate, almost made you go for a swim."

"Any word from the bridge what's causing the fog?" Olivia asked.

"Georgia," Zach said. "Doc Leo said it'll clear now the sun's up. The captain thinks we're off Sapelo Island."

"Where's that?" Pete asked.

"You tell me," Zach said. "But there's at least another fifty kilometres to go before we get to Savannah."

"Anything on the radio?" Olivia asked.

"Just the Big Bang," Zach said, and sauntered aft.

"I assume he means static," Olivia said.

"I dunno, the year we've been having, maybe the sun's blown up," Pete said.

As the fog lifted, and visibility improved, the engines came on, and the restaurant opened.

"Now this is more like what I was expecting from a honeymoon cruise," Olivia said. "A restaurant with table service. Thank you."

"You're welcome," Pita said, placing a bowl in front of her, and then Pete.

"Enchiladas?" Olivia asked.

"Not really," Pita said, with a shrug. "But it will do until we get better supplies."

"Made from wheat flour, I think," Olivia said, as the teenager headed back to the kitchen. "What, are you upset it's not cereal?"

"Hmm? Oh, always. But I was thinking it was missing cheese. The sauce is good."

The echo of normality barely lasted the time it took to eat, and was drowned by an announcement that land had been sighted.

"Back to work," Pete said.

"Where is that?" Olivia asked.

"The deck, I guess," Pete said.

"Meet you there," Olivia said, disappearing through the other door, but caught up with him on deck, now carrying a monocular. "Tess says we can watch from the science centre if we like."

"I'm going to enjoy the fresh air while I can," Pete said. "I *can* enjoy it, right?"

"Leo's still collating the readings from last night, but he says we're okay."

"So where are we?" Pete asked.

"Near Savannah," Olivia said. "Hopefully somewhere to the south. Here."

He took the monocular, and trained it on the shore. "Small town. Usual mess of small ships on the beach. Very small. Nothing huge at all. Maybe even some usable boats. Can't really tell from here. Wait. No, I think that's a zom."

"Let me see?" Olivia asked. She took the monocular. "Yep. Zom. Oh. Hang on. I know where we are."

"Where?"

"Like I told you, near Savannah," she said, and handed him the spyglass before running to the stairs leading up to the bridge. Pete raised the monocular again. The shoreline conurbation looked bigger than Puerto Morelos, but was still a vacation spot with sea-view condos and beachfront houses. To the north, where the town met a wide estuarial river, was a short lighthouse that seemed to grow taller as the ship turned into the silt-laden river.

"Don't you remember the lighthouse?" Olivia said, as she returned a lot more sedately than she'd left.

"Pretty sure I've never been here before," Pete said.

"But you've seen it," she said. "*That* is Tybee Beach, and *this* is the Savannah River. Remember *The Keeper at the End of the World*? We watched it Memorial Day weekend."

"Oh, sure," he said. "Mrs Mathers paid us overtime to come up, but she should have paid some customers to come in instead. We only booked three fittings."

"You remember that but you don't remember the movie?"

"No, I remember. There's a woman who thinks she's the last person alive. She's travelled across America and comes to a lighthouse. She turns on the light, hoping someone will spot it. But that movie was set on the Pacific coast."

"Yes, but they filmed it here," she said. "Tax breaks."

"Ah, gotcha. So if that's the Savannah River, the city must be ahead." He passed her the monocular. "Take a look, but I can't see anyone at the lighthouse. If it were me, and if I were in the city, I'd station someone there."

"Maybe they did, and maybe they're watching, wondering if we're friendly," she said. "We're not far from Cape Canaveral. But no, I can't see anyone, either."

The ship juddered. The engines switched from a whine to a burr.

"Have we hit something?" Pete asked, gripping the rail, peering down.

"We're turning," Olivia said. "C'mon."

She ran to the deck-door, leading to the science centre. He followed, and found Leo, Carmen, Zach, and the bottom half of his sister, one foot balanced on a ladder. Her head, arms, and chest were buried deep inside a partially dismantled air vent.

"What did we miss?" Olivia asked.

"A cargo ship is blocking the river," Carmen said.

"We caught it on the mast-cam," Leo said. "It's at anchor, but listing. That journal we found down near the Panama Canal said they found their yacht in Blackbeard Creek, but that they were refused entry to Savannah. I guess the cargo ship is, or was, partly how they kept visitors away."

"Are we worried about an attack?" Pete asked.

"Not yet," Leo said.

"This place looks like French-America," Zach said.

"Do you mean New Orleans?" Carmen asked.

"French Guiana," Zach said. "That place was full of crocs until the zoms chased them away. Yeah, this reminds me of Dégrad des Cannes. Not the beach, or the town. The trees are stubbier, and the green leaves are more brown. The bushes are thinner, I think. But, you know, otherwise."

"I can see a road," Pete said, pointing at the screen.

"Savannah was built on… ah, *pantano*," Carmen said. "Wet land."

"A swamp?" Zach asked.

"Marshland," Leo said.

"What's the difference?" Zach asked.

"Fewer trees," Leo said.

The ladder clattered to the deck.

"You okay, sis?" Pete asked, picking it back up.

"No worries," Corrie said, climbing back down. "But I'll leave the rest until the rollercoaster stops."

The door to the bridge opened, and Tess appeared. "Zach, go find Clyde, tell him he's stretching his legs."

"Are we going ashore?" Pete asked.

"We'll take the inflatable up the Wilmington River," Tess said. "That river meets the sea a bit further south. Nicko and Bruce will stay aboard because we're not one hundred percent sure this place is deserted, but it does feel it."

"We'll come," Olivia said.

"I'll need another few hours to fix the air con," Corrie said. "I can do it now, or later."

"Finish the repair," Tess said. "If we do go ashore, I doubt it'll be for long."

"I'll come," Carmen said.

"Good on ya," Tess said. "Grab your gear, and meet on deck in five."

They were all there in three, but it took another half hour before the ship reached the entrance to the Wilmington River. Tess, Zach, Carmen, Clyde, Olivia and Pete held on, enjoying the view while Baxter piloted the reinforced inflatable through sparse tidal flats dotted with scrub-coated mud-dunes, waist-high salt grass, then increasingly tall trees. Palm trees were replaced with tupelo, and then moss-covered oak. As the trees grew denser, marking a more solid footing for their roots, a house appeared: a low cabin. Deserted, but with a narrow wooden jetty jutting out into the slow-moving river. Its neighbour, a four-storey wood-clad apartment, was close enough to cast a mid-morning shadow across the boundary line.

"No zoms," Pete said.

"No birds," Olivia said.

"Too many mozzies," Zach said, slapping at the buzzing cloud which had settled above him. "Yeah, this is way too much like Dégrad des Cannes. It'll be crocs next."

The river curved, but the saltmarsh continued, while the clusters of trees grew denser, older, with a gently curving slope to their canopy, betraying marginally higher ground to the north. Along the riverbank, an uneven tangle of flotsam marked a late-spring flood. He could identify umbrellas, deck chairs, tables, probably from some waterfront bar, but had they been deposited by the sea, or by the river?

"Croc!" Zach called, pointing to the south.

"Log," Tess said.

"It's moving!" Zach said.

"With the tide," Tess said.

Pete wasn't sure, but the croc-log *was* moving away from the boat, so he turned his gaze back to the shore. Again, the trees grew denser still, while the rooftops lurking behind the canopies grew more numerous. A few apartment balconies towered above the trees, but they were as deserted as the mansions whose manicured lawns were already returning to wilderness.

The river curved, and curved again, so it was travelling almost south-to-north when a bridge came into view. Just before it, they sailed past a string of small, empty marinas, once catering to the semi-professional sailors.

"Cut speed," Tess said, as they neared the bridge. She didn't need to explain why: a five-metre-span in the middle of the bridge was missing.

Wooden boards had been hung over the side near the western bank. On them was painted: *No Entry, Wait Here for the Harbor Master.*

"That's a professional demolition job," Clyde said. "They've taken out the roadway between two supports. We can get through, closer to the shore, no worries."

"That looks like a barricade up on the bridge," Tess said. "And I see zoms behind it on the further, more easterly bank. Take us back to the marina. We'll go ashore on the other bank and see if we can find any traces of their last harbour master."

Chapter 9 - Paint It Blue
Thunderbolt, Georgia

The marina had once been a bustling dock. Dozens of concrete jetties curled into the river. Each was supported by towering pillars, rising over two metres above the current water level. Pete forced himself to do a mental reset from Australian back to American, and reframed that as seven feet, stretching to eight. Each of the mast-like supports was topped with a vivid blue ring of paint. While that would act as a warning to boats if the river rose above the jetty, it also matched the colour scheme of the shore-side buildings. They appeared deserted, though a welcome committee of brown-skinned frogs watched from the steps leading up the flood-defence riverbank.

By the time the boat's passengers had clambered onto the jetty, the frogs had bounded up the steps, and disappeared into the knee-high weeds at the riverbank's top.

"Is it a good sign when the frogs didn't jump in the water?" Zach asked.

"Ask Doc Flo when we get back to the ship," Tess said. "Clyde?"

"Looks clear," he said. "But you know what they say about looks. The tall building must be apartments. That low roof could be some kind of service building."

Pete looked back towards the barricaded and broken bridge, now a good hundred metres away. He couldn't make out any of the undead trapped on the other bank. When he looked directly across the river, he only saw windswept marsh-grass ringing an ancient grove of oaks. But the smell of death hung heavily over this sultry swamp, and it was ready to drop.

"Guess what this place is called," Zach said, reading a sign affixed to the nearest cement pillar.

"Savannah," Olivia said.

"Nope, you lose. This is Thunderbolt," Zach said. "It's the Bahia Blue Marina in Thunderbolt. Good name."

"Must be a suburb," Tess said. "The sign on that bridge proves they had a garrison here recently."

"I'd place a sentry atop that apartment block," Clyde said. He'd detached the scope from his carbine, and had aimed it up at the building. "I'd stay inside. Top floor. On the balcony at the southern end. Looks empty." He re-attached the scope, then waved. "I'm trying to look friendly."

"Good call," Tess said. "Baxter, call in our position, then wait at the top of the steps. Listen for boats. Clyde, Zach, scout the outside of the apartments. Don't go in. Pete, Olivia, find the main road. Look for signs of battle or escape. Don't go onto the main road. Carmen, you and I are hunting for fuel." She tapped the sign screwed to the cement pillar. "Gas and diesel are apparently available here, so we'll find where. If anyone hears a single gunshot, stop what you're doing. If you hear two shots, come back to the top of those steps. That's our rally point. Leave any rescuing to Clyde."

"What if he's the one who needs help?" Zach said.

"Then I'll never live it down," Clyde said. He walked back to the boat and picked up two of his self-made boarding axes. He handed one to Tess, then held one out for Pete. "Avoid unnecessary shots, but avoid risk more. The cemetery is already crowded with heroes."

Ash coated the steps leading from the jetty, and shaded the dark grass atop the embankment. To the south and west were balconied apartment blocks; to the north was the main service-complex. In the middle was the parking lot. Soot stained the lower balconies facing the parking lot, but the smoke had come from a long row of cinderblock and chicken-wire barbecues recently built along the car park's northern edge. Everywhere else, there were mismatched tables. They'd been upturned, as had the chairs.

"No bones," Pete said, using the axe to push at the layer of litter scattered among the discarded furniture. "No bodies. No blood."

"Not many flies," Olivia said, as they picked their way around the upturned chairs and so through the parking lot. "Those cars form a wall, don't they?"

The automobiles had been pushed and dragged to the far edge of the parking lot, creating a wall around the marina's buildings. The gaps between the cars had been filled with furniture, spilled sandbags, and a jungle of pipework secured with nylon sailing rope.

"Whatever they were barbecuing, they dumped the ash and trash in the river," Olivia said. "This place is far from clean, but it's not nearly as filthy as a refugee camp should be."

"Do you think that's what this was?" Pete asked.

"Maybe," she said. "The sign on that bridge sort of implied this was as far as strangers were allowed to come. And there was that tanker blocking the Savannah River. Maybe this was all part of a deliberate attempt to keep newcomers away from the main settlement like they did in Puerto Morelos."

"The wall of cars has no gate," Pete said.

"That's it!" Olivia said. "There's no road-exit. To get out of here, they must have used boats."

Pete walked up the barricaded driveway. "So this was a holding-zone for visitors. A quarantine camp, maybe."

"The Panama-journal said visitors weren't welcome," Olivia said. "That entry described events just after the bombs. But maybe visitors were tolerated before then, or after, as long as they didn't mingle with the locals."

Pete held up a cautioning hand. He'd been concentrating on the abandoned truck on the far side of the vehicle-wall, so it took his brain a second to realise the sound came from much nearer. A sound that was far too familiar. A rotting palm slapped against rusting metal. Then came the leathery swish of flesh brushing against battle-scarred paintwork. Pete pointed to the far side of the vehicular barricade.

Olivia held up a hand with one finger.

Pete nodded, raised his axe, and pointed at the car's hood.

Olivia raised her rifle.

Pete shook his head, but as he stepped up onto the bumper, it snapped along a concealed fracture, clanging to the ground while he jumped back to firmer footing. From the other side of the vehicle, the slow slide-slap turned into a thumping beat.

"So much for being quiet," Olivia said.

"No shots if it's just one," Pete said, this time jumping up onto the hood. The car groaned and creaked beneath his feet, shuddering beneath the drum-roll beat of the zombie's fist.

"No way is that quieter than a bullet," Olivia said.

"It's fine," Pete said, seeing his foe. A girl. A child. He jumped down the other side. The zombie rolled away from the car, towards him. Her legs were shattered, below the knees. Shreds of sinew trailed beneath the hem of her blood-drenched pink dress. The white bows, already stained black and brown, trailed through the dry mud as she dragged herself towards him on forearms which ended in ash-matted stumps.

As her small mouth snapped open and closed, her neck-length plaits swung like a pendulum, left and right, left and right.

"Why did it have to be a kid?" he murmured as he swung the axe down onto her leaf-flecked crown. "Clear," he said, stepping back and turning around. "Yeah. It's clear."

"A kid?" Olivia said, stepping up onto car's hood.

"Yep." Pete looked away from the dead child, scanning the undergrowth, forcing his brain to focus on the undead, not on the life lost before it had been lived. His eyes settled on the large truck parked in the road almost immediately outside the barricaded entrance.

The six-wheeler was obviously a military vehicle with a cab-over-engine design he'd seen on the news, but usually in places where the soil matched the sand-yellow paintwork. The tarp covering the back was a dark shade of desert, but neither could be called camouflage in this urbanised marshland.

"U.S. Army?" Olivia asked, as they walked around the vehicle, to the cab.

"Dead zom," Pete said. It lay buried beneath the front left tyre, but someone had added a merciful bullet to its brain. Up close, the truck's paintwork was marred with dents, scratches, and dark plumes of dried blood.

"The cab's facing the Atlantic," Olivia said. "So it came from the direction of Savannah."

"Or the broken bridge," Pete said. "Skull there. A few bones. Definitely human."

"Cab looks empty," Olivia said. She opened the door. "There's some paper down in the foot well."

"You check that, I'll check the back," Pete said, though he first bent down to check beneath the vehicle. He nearly jumped when he heard a rustle in the low bushes on the far side of the road. Axe raised, he stepped wide, around the cab, scanning the bushes. Beyond the trees was a hint of lawn, then a house. Dark. Empty. Forbidding.

A roar came from behind. This time, he did jump, raising the axe even as his brain shouted *engine*.

"The truck works," Olivia called, as she switched the engine off. "Tank's half-full, and the battery is buzzing. How's the back?"

"Watch the bushes," Pete said before walking around to the back of the cab. "Empty," he called after the briefest glance. "A few shoes and bags. Refugee stuff that was left behind."

Olivia climbed back down. "Let's go tell the commish."

"Yeah, hang on," Pete said, and grabbed a thin blanket, woven with blue stars. "Was there a map?"

"Didn't see one," she said. "If the tank's half-full, what's the range, do you think?"

"No idea, but Clyde will know." He draped the blanket over the dead girl before climbing up onto the barricade, and back into the car park.

Tess and Clyde were waiting by the barbecues.

"We found enough food to open a fete," Tess said. "Carmen, Zach, and Baxter are carrying some down to the boat."

"We found treasure, too," Olivia said. "There's an army truck on the road. The tank's half-full. From the way it was facing, it came from Savannah."

"Looks like an FMTV," Clyde said, climbing up onto a picnic table to get a better view. "Bit of a workhorse in the U.S. Army. If the tank was half-full, it could manage another two hundred and fifty kilometres before running dry. Did you see any bullet casings or bones?"

"Some, sure, but not so many you'd easily notice," Pete said. "A couple of zoms. A few skulls."

"But no sign of a real battle, right?" Tess asked. "It's the same here. The evidence points to them being able to leave at a time of their own choosing. They had patrols and guards, and had to shoot a few zoms, but there was no desperate last stand. They were rushed, but not panicked. And when they left, they didn't take everything with them. Maybe they ran out of space, or maybe they had all they needed. We found food, and fuel in the shore-side tanks. Diesel *and* petrol."

"Were they trading it?" Olivia asked.

"Can't say yet," Tess said. "This began as a quarantine camp, but with the Savannah River blocked, and that bridge down, it became a way-station for people visiting the city. It's possible they were trading fish for fuel, but they left behind enough canned food for a small army."

"When did they leave?" Olivia asked.

"I'm used to a drier climate," Tess said. "But I'd guess at days not weeks. I'm going to take another look around the service buildings to see if I can't find a more definitive answer."

"We could drive to Savannah," Olivia said. "We can take the truck, and be back in an hour."

"And bring the zoms back with us," Tess said. "Maybe later, but only if we can't find the answers here, and only after we've loaded up a bit more of the food."

"Me and Pete could take a walk," Olivia said. "Maybe not to Savannah, but we could check out a few houses, look for more trucks. Maybe go as far as the bridge."

"You sure?" Tess asked. "Because I need Clyde on guard duty here."

"We came looking for people," Olivia said. "We haven't looked hard enough yet to say we can leave with a clear conscience."

Tess took out a small map. "I found this in the office. It's not to scale, but it shows the marina, and what's nearby. That includes a town hall, so Thunderbolt is more than just a suburb. We're a good eight-k from Savannah, and I don't want you going anywhere near as far. But check out the bridge. See if they left any equipment with which they could quickly repair that missing section. Look for a guard post. Go there, come back, and be back here within an hour."

"Swap," Clyde said, holding out his suppressed MARS-L assault rifle. "You'll want to keep the noise down until the boat's ready to go."

Chapter 10 - Thick-Skinned Locals
Thunderbolt, Georgia

When they again reached the car-barricade, Pete paused. "In all those horror movies we saw, when is it ever a good idea for people to split up?" he asked.

"Hang on," Olivia said, and turned around. "Nope, I don't see a camera crew following us, so I think we're okay. Besides, I want to us to be sailing north before nightfall."

"You actually want to go to New York?"

"I want to go to Australia," she said. "If we're really going to New York, the sooner we get there, the sooner we'll leave. If we piece together everything we've seen since Corn Island, and what Tess and her team found since they left Perth, chronologically, it's the story of collapse. Everywhere, it's the same. People held together as long as they could. They fled or died. Or they became pirates like in Cape Canaveral. Maybe Judge Benton has held something together up in the farthest north. Maybe there are others like her. To find them, we'll need a lot more than just this icebreaker. We'll need a fleet. An air force. Maybe satellites, and definitely an army."

Pete climbed up onto the hood of the car, and looked down at the blanket-shrouded body. "We have found survivors," he said.

"Exactly," she said, following him up. "That's exactly what I mean. We weren't too late to save Pita and Angelo, but how many others are a few miles inland? We'll never be able to save them all travelling like this. But the Pacific can save some, here, and in South America and across Asia, but only if we get back, and persuade them it's worth the risk and the resources."

"I doubt they'll listen to us," Pete said.

"They'll listen to Doc Avalon, and to Leo," she said. "Anna Dodson will listen to Tess, and she sounds like one of the most influential people down there. I'm not saying we were wrong to come north, but I think we've seen enough. From now on, we're just going to be witnesses to horrors similar to these. So let's go see what horrors we can see at the bridge, then get back to the ship. Agreed?"

"You mean no shore mission to hunt for Judge Benton just before the ship turns south?" Pete asked. "No, agreed. I'm glad we came north. We didn't give up, not even after Corn Island. But we've done all we can. Well, almost." He reached into his pocket and pulled out a phone.

"I think we're out of service," she said.

"I got it from Corrie for music, but the camera can work for video."

"Okay, but mute the mic," she said. She jumped down from the car. Rifle raised, she walked around the truck. Pete hurried to catch up, then walked alongside.

"The map says this is River Drive," he said. "We'll follow it north until we get to East Victory Drive, and the bridge will be on the right."

As they strolled north, she scanned left and right, and he kept turning forward and back, watching for movement, but listening for slithering limbs, cracking branches, and breaking undergrowth.

"For all Zach said this reminded him of the South American tropics, it reminds me of Canada," he said.

"Those are palms, Pete," Olivia said. "Pretty sure you don't get those up beyond the maple-line."

"That's an oak tree," he said.

"Dripping with… oh, what's it called? Oh, I should know this. Spanish moss, that's it! And the way those junipers are locked in a death-struggle with manicured boxwood hedging doesn't remind me of Canada, but it kinda reminds me of home."

"This does *not* look like South Bend," he said.

"More like the home I dream of having," she said. "Somewhere where, just beyond a property's boundary, wilderness is lurking, ready to return."

"That's pretty much everywhere these days," he said. "I'll take anywhere you can see straight to the horizon."

Beyond the marina-complex, the houses were of an achingly familiar style. One storey, occasionally made of salmon brick, but most were painted white. The wide lawns had few fences, but always with a strategically planted tree shading the house. Yes, it was different from the Midwest. Different, but close enough. Even the damage was similar. Broken windows, ajar doors, bags left in the empty driveway when the owners had fled.

"I can see the river," Olivia said, pointing east, across the tufted grass.

"That's an island on the other side of the bridge," Pete said, pulling out the map. "That island is White Marsh. Wilmington Island is further west. Hutchinson Island is on the Savannah River, just north of the main city, and has a four-star golf club. Could be a good place to look for survivors."

"But there are zombies on the island-side of that bridge," she said.

Feeling as if they were only going to confirm the worst, they walked on, towards the nearing junction.

From between two small, white-painted houses, both with shallow ramps leading to the porch, and mobility assistance bars by the front door, came the sound of fists beating against wood.

Olivia walked wide across the road, rifle raised, Pete at her side, until the undead came into sight. There were four. Three wore civilian jungle-patterned trousers and tunics. The fourth wore a flower-patterned dress whose dark stains and mud smears made it as effective a camouflage as the other three's hunter garb.

"Trying to get to someone," Olivia said, raising the rifle. "No, can't get a shot. Watch my clock."

The front door shattered, splintering outwards as a shape charged through. A survivor, but not a human one: an alligator.

Zoms fell onto the back of the un-evolved dinosaur as the beast charged from the house, shaking, twisting. The undead slapped, punched, and broke their teeth on the scaly armour of a monster nearly three metres in length. The gator's tail came free of the door; it swished around, smashing the lintel, before swinging again, splintering the jungle-green legs of an undead hunter. The alligator lumbered on, the other three zombies still beating against its armoured hide until the beast was in the drive. As it swung its tail, it jumped. Momentum pivoted the gator nearly a hundred and twenty degrees, scattering the zombies about the driveway. The monster's jaws clamped around the skull of the creature in the sundress. With a wet pop, the gator bit down, and the zombie's head burst. Its tail whipped around, knocking the last hunter from its feet. The backswing crushed its skull. The other two zombies crawled on as the gator slowly padded around, turning its head from one approaching zom to the other. A lunge, a snap, and both were dead. Finally, the gator turned its baleful glare to Pete and Olivia.

"Back away," Pete said.

"Don't move," Olivia said, her rifle aimed at that scaly head.

The gator turned and stalked back into the house.

"Please tell me you were videoing that," Olivia said.

"Oh yes."

"Wow," Olivia said. "The gator went back into the house. It must have a nest there, or nearby. It's protecting its territory."

"So we go on to the bridge?" Pete asked.

"We go back to the marina," Olivia said. "There's no way people live anywhere near that monster."

But as they backed away from the house, they heard an engine. The army truck which had been parked by the marina was now speeding towards them. Behind the windshield, the passenger was unfamiliar, but Tess was driving.

"Get in the back!" Tess called as she slowed.

"Gator in that house, be careful," Olivia said.

"Survivors," Tess said. "Get in!"

Clyde was in the back of the truck, alone, legs braced, barrel aimed back along the road. He reached down, hauling Olivia, then Pete, up and inside. Before Pete had a chance to sit, the truck began speeding along the road.

"What's happening?" Pete asked, dropping to a knee before he fell.

"The passenger up front says he's the mayor," Clyde said. "The last group of survivors in the city is trapped at a self-storage facility just up the road and inland. He set off at dawn to grab this truck. It's only a couple of miles, but it took him hours just to reach the bridge. Sounds like he was chased. But when he got to the bridge, he saw our boat. So he jumped in the river and swam to meet us, and nearly got shot by Zach."

"If he'd waited another minute, he could have saved himself the swim," Pete said.

"Ah, but that'd make him a fortune-teller," Clyde said. "Weapons ready. Mind if I borrow mine back, Olivia? Good on ya. Remember not everything with two legs is a zom. We've got about twenty friendlies to collect. The mayor's got a plan, so we'll listen to that, but you two will follow my lead."

The truck spun left and right, veering, accelerating, braking. Each time they slowed, Pete thought they were there, and made ready to jump out. Each time, Clyde shook his head.

"Easy, mate, easy," the old soldier said.

The truck sped on, smashing into abandoned cars, and through the undead, leaving a trail of bone and brain, and the occasional crawling zombie, in their wake.

Again, the truck braked. This time, Tess yelled, "Out! Out!"

"On me," Clyde said, as he jumped down. His rifle swung left, right, and around the truck, angled low as he stepped wide, clear of a crawling zombie which managed one ankle-level swipe before Clyde put a bullet in its skull.

Pete jumped down. Olivia slipped down next to him. Clyde fired as he walked, aiming across the road at a loose pack of the undead, lurching between the fire-singed oaks lining a U-shaped strip mall.

Tess had jumped out of the cab and was running the other way, to the closed-roller gate in a blue and white wall.

"Pete, Olivia, on me!" Tess called.

"Go," Clyde said, between shots. "I've got our six."

Pete ran, sprinting until he saw them, when he juddered to a halt. Beyond the gate were hundreds of the undead. From the signage, it was a self-storage facility with low garages in the west, and an enclosed tiered building in the east.

"Not good at all," Tess said. "Do you see them?"

"The roof! They're on the roof," the passenger said. About six-foot, with a near white streak through his greying, scissor-cut hair. His olive-green shirt and swamp-coloured jeans were still damp from his swim, while the trainers were dry enough to be hasty loot from the marina.

Beyond the zombie-infested loading dock, atop the tiered rooftop where a one-storey building met a second, a small crowd waved caps and shirts.

"We're clear!" Clyde called, running to their side.

Attracted by the truck's engine, a zombie clanged into the roller gate as its arms stretched through the gap in the vertical bars.

"No worries," Tess said. "We'll drive the truck back up to that bit of wall nearest the roof. We'll make a bridge between the wall and the roof, and the survivors can climb across. We'll need a distraction. Pete, Olivia, you're up. Kill the zoms here."

"No suppressors," Clyde said, pulling a flare gun from his vest. He handed it to Olivia. "If you have to run, find high ground as close to the river as you can. Fire this off, and we'll come fetch you."

"You stay with them, Mr Mayor," Tess said, handing him the pistol from her holster. "Clyde, drive."

"Distract the zoms, no worries," Olivia said, and fired through the railing. Thanks to the truck's engine, there were plenty of targets.

About a quarter of the horde were now heading for the gate. "Nope. No worries."

The passenger, whom Tess had addressed as Mr Mayor, took up position by the railings a metre from Olivia. "Much obliged for the assistance," he said. "Shall we say that everything to the left of that warning sign is mine, everything to the right is yours?"

"Cool," Olivia said. "Pete, you've got our six."

"Why's it not eighteen?" he asked, turning around. "Zom. Twenty seconds out, coming from central Savannah."

But his words were lost beneath the barrage from the mayor and Olivia, a sudden roar from the engine, then a patter of gunfire further along the wall. He didn't look, but raised his sidearm, taking aim at the creature lumbering towards them. Tall. Wide shoulders, narrow hips. An athlete. Or he had been. The t-shirt was shredded, as was the skin beneath, leaving a checkerboard of gore that bubbled with each erratic stride.

Pete squeezed the trigger, and was so shocked he hit his target he almost fired again. The zombie collapsed, and he let his field of vision widen. Two more approached. He shifted aim, rushed the shot, and missed. The bullet slammed into what looked like a fold-up scooter still tied to the pack the zombie carried on its back. The leaf-matted long hair was white at the tips, but black at the roots, and the face was recognisably human. This was someone only recently turned, surely one of the mayor's people, infected during the stalled escape. Pete fired. Hit. The zombie fell.

"Don't suppose y'all have a spare magazine?" the mayor asked.

"Sure," Pete said, pulling one from his pouch. As he turned to hand it over, he saw the wall of dead behind the gate. While he'd shot two, Olivia and the mayor had killed at least ten times that number.

"Obliged," the mayor said.

"No worries," Pete said.

"How's Tess doing?" Olivia asked, taking a step towards the wall, and so away from the four-body-high mound in front of her previous position.

"They've made a bridge from the roof to the wall," Pete said. "I think they're using a ladder."

"They're crossing?" Olivia asked.

"Yep. Tess is sitting on the wall. Can't see Clyde."

"Huh," Olivia said, concentrating on the undead. "Gate's beginning to bulge."

"When it breaks, we can walk our way over to the police department," the mayor said. "That's directly opposite. We can go up the fire escape at the side, and down the other at the rear. Lead the zombies there, and I can lead you back to the river."

Pete turned around. Three zombies approached from the north, and one from the south. No, four from the north, but the nearest was still twenty metres from the first zombie he'd shot.

"I'd say two minutes and this gate will break," Olivia said.

"Y'all aren't from Australia, are you?" the mayor said.

"South Bend," Olivia said. "Hi. I'm Olivia Guinn, that's my husband, Pete."

"Mayor Jak," he said, even as he fired into the undead beyond the gate. "No c, no e. Ex-mayor," he added. "How bad was Indiana? I have a friend who moved to Osceola."

"It got pretty bad," Olivia said. "But there was an evacuation in the early days. Some people made it to Canada."

"Well, then there is hope for her," Mayor Jak said. "What more can we ask for in life?"

"How about a regiment of SEALs?" Pete said. "We've got another twenty inbound, travelling in a pack, approaching from right across the road."

The mayor glanced around. "Ah, that's the direction of the police station. Could I trouble you for some more bullets?"

"I'm down to my last mag," Pete said.

A loud crack came from the gate's upper-left hinge, but it was drowned by the sound of the truck's engine.

"Wheeled salvation," Mayor Jak said. "Please, after you."

They jogged rather than sprinted, matching the mayor's limping pace, reaching the truck a few seconds after it had stopped on the road. The back was crammed with people sitting and standing. Arms reached forward, hauling in Mayor Jak, then Olivia, then him.

By the time Pete had disentangled himself from the heap of desperate humanity, they were already speeding down the road. Not as fast as they'd come, and with far more shudders and bumps as the truck collided with the undead.

"We lost three," a woman said. Short. Exhausted. Wearing a long t-shirt, but combat trousers beneath, and military boots below that.

"Who?" the mayor asked.

"Patsy, Jeb, and Cyrus," the soldier said. "The ladder fell."

"God have mercy on them," Jak said.

"The zoms didn't," a young man said, and was shushed by his neighbour.

At the marina, the truck skidded to a halt. Bruce Hawker jumped from the barricade, sprinting past the truck. Clyde jumped out of the cab, running to his side.

"All out, everyone out!" Tess said. "Anyone without a gun, down to the river."

"You heard her," the mayor echoed. "One last dash to safety!"

Pete found himself on top of the car, helping people up, while Olivia, in the compound, helped them down. Soon, too soon, they were alone.

"Pull back!" Tess called. She, Bruce, and Clyde retreated from the road, back to the barricade. From the shore, Zach and Nicko sprinted towards them, along with the mayor and the soldier in the t-shirt, both now holding carbines.

"We'll fall back," Bruce said. "Right back to the waterfront. No one runs. Watch the flanks. Slow now."

"Twenty-three survivors," Olivia said, as she and Pete fell into place at the left of the slowly retreating line. "Only two kids, though. Look to be about Pita's age."

Pete nodded, looking back along the road, and at the approaching undead, and their nearly recognisable faces. Once again, they'd almost arrived too late, but it had clearly been too late for so many more.

Chapter 11 - All Aboard
Thunderbolt, Savannah

Twenty-three survivors climbed aboard the *Wenceslao Diaz Gallegos*. It should have been twenty-six. If the ship had arrived yesterday, it would have been more. Some of the newly rescued wore an expression of terrified exhaustion. A few, like the soldier and the mayor, were warily watchful. The two children, girls about thirteen years old, looked around with curious interest, while the woman standing between them, possibly their grandmother, looked nearly catatonic.

"Zach, mate," Tess called. "Can you take the kids straight to the med-bay to see the doc? Anyone have any injuries that require immediate treatment? Anyone got any gunshots, stab wounds, anything like that? All right, listen up, please. You're all going through a decontamination shower. After that, we'll get you some clean clothes, and you'll go down to the mess for a meal. You have questions, *we* have questions, so we'll all have a chat. The key thing, the important thing, is that you're safe. In a few days, we'll be heading south, and back to the Pacific where there are millions of survivors. You can come with us if you want, or we'll drop you off somewhere a bit safer than this. It'll be your choice. Two lines, please, behind Olivia and Pete here. They'll show you the way to the showers. Trash can go in the bin. Any clothes and blades go into one of the red boxes. We'll get them cleaned, though I'll be grateful for a volunteer to give me a hand."

"You want us to hand over our knives?" a young man asked. Lanky and lean, his face was as tense as the muscles on his bare arms. No more than twenty years old, he stood with a group of three others, about the same age, though his companions looked as surprised as everyone else at the sudden outburst.

"We've got a baby aboard," Tess said. "Zombies aren't the only virus we've got to worry about. Everything that was ashore gets bleached."

"Now, Elijah, don't let a hot head cause a hot meal to grow cold," the mayor said, laying his hand on the young man's shoulder. "I'm certain none of us want to go ashore *here*."

"Guess we're having a wash, then," Pete said, undoing his holster, and handing it to Clyde.

"Reckon you got the long straw this time, mate," Clyde said.

It took him about three minutes before the absurdity of the situation struck him so forcefully, he couldn't help but laugh. He was naked, and leading a group of similarly naked men through a shower whose purpose was to see if any had recent bite marks.

"Life took a truly weird turning a few months ago," he muttered.

Battling exhaustion, grief, and a little embarrassment, his group of survivors didn't say much while washing, and then dressing. Most of the questions were to confirm there were survivors in the Pacific, and that Australia was the ship's ultimate destination. As to their *next* destination, Pete merely said it would be down to the captain.

Olivia and her group beat his to the mess. The women were already seated, half eating, the other half waiting on the bowls Olivia had balanced on her tray.

As the Georgians found seats, Pete headed to the serving hatch. Renata had been demoted to server, and placed a tray in front of him. On the tray were six bowls.

"Where's Pita?" Pete asked.

"In the hospital with the new girls," Renata said. She wore a holstered sidearm at her hip. So did Ramon.

"Best front-of-house smile, Pete," Olivia said. "Remember, we work for tips. Renata, can I have some water? Thanks."

Pete took the bowls over. "Ramon's one of the top chefs in Cancun, so I promise this will be good. Does anyone have any allergies we should know about?"

"Zombies," the soldier said. "Staff-Sergeant Nikki Temple. Sixty-Fourth Armoured out of Fort Stewart, before Mayor Jak persuaded me I'd be happier running his bar. Where were you stationed?"

Olivia laughed. "Sorry, I shouldn't laugh, but the two of us were selling carpets at the beginning of the year. We did serve with General Yoon up in Canada."

"Canada?" Temple asked. But before she could ask any more, Tess entered the mess, with Mayor Jak at her side.

"G'day," Tess said. "In case you missed it earlier, my name's Tess Qwong. I'm a commissioner with the Australian Federal Police, and we're here in the Atlantic as part of a group hunting the people responsible for the outbreak. We came here in a New Zealand warship, which is why quite a few of our crew are Kiwis."

"Excuse me," Temple said, raising a hand. "Do you mean to say you know who was behind the zombies?"

"Yep, it was a cartel and some politicians," Tess said. "We're still working out the fine details, but I'll share all the evidence we've gathered. In brief, they tried to stage a coup down in Oz, but we put paid to that. Over in this ocean, we destroyed their supply base. We took out a large number of their reserves, and we arrested a few prisoners. Those suspects went south, with our warship. They'll stand trial. We're about to pull anchor and head north. New York is our next, and final, destination. There are a couple of scientists aboard who want to grab a bit of data lost during the outbreak. They think it could bring this crisis to an end. We'll go into that later, too. After New York, we'll head back to the Pacific. We'll probably return to Savannah to grab some more grub, so we'll be happy to drop off anyone who wants, here, or up north. Just ask."

She paused, while everyone looked at everyone else, but there were no volunteers. Not yet.

"If you've not heard," Tess continued, "there are a hundred million survivors in the Pacific. I won't lie and say life will be like it was, but we have schools and hospitals, and you'll have homes and salaried jobs. Longer term, once the zoms are gone and we can spare the ships, anyone who wants to return to the U.S. can. For now, you're safe, so it's time to do a bit of research on the place that'll become your new home." She switched on the large screen to the left of the door.

Everyone leaned forward, curious. So was Pete, and he wasn't the only one who laughed when *The Lord of the Rings* title screen appeared.

The mayor walked over to Temple, and spoke quietly with her. She followed him to the door. Tess, though, came over to Pete and Olivia.

"Here," she said, holding a zipped first-aid bag. "There're handcuffs inside. If anyone exhibits symptoms, secure them. The time they spent on the rooftop should be enough of a quarantine, but I want to be certain. Renata and Ramon are armed, and I'll send down Nicko just as soon as we're certain we're not being followed."

"By whom?" Pete asked.

"The pirates from Cape Canaveral," Tess said. "We're pretty certain they know about the supplies in the marina. I'll tell you about it later, but I've got to speak with Sergeant Temple first."

13th April

Chapter 12 - Four Days
The Northwestern Atlantic

Before Bilbo had left the Shire, Corrie and Zach entered the mess deck with the first mattress. By the time the Fellowship had formed, half the Georgian survivors were asleep. Nicko came in at midnight, but it wasn't until four that Corrie returned with the welcome news their shift was over.

"Doc Flo's given them the all-clear," Corrie said. "We're going to give them breakfast, sort out cabins, more showers, and then allocate some light chores for the day. You two can get some sleep."

"Were there signs of pirates?" Olivia whispered.

"None," Corrie said. "We sailed into deeper water where they can't follow."

Olivia took Pete's hand. "Then we'll go and enjoy some time off before we get volunteered for something else."

They trudged their way onto the deck, and to the narrow bench by the crane that Pete was beginning to think of as *their* spot. Above, the sky was inky black, swept with dark velvet clouds, dotted with shimmering diamonds.

"It's chilly," Olivia said.

"I was thinking that," Pete said. "It finally feels like we've left the equator behind."

"For now," she said. "Tess mentioned returning to Savannah for food."

"Oh, sure, but New Zealand and Australia have upside-down weather, so we'll be arriving in time for winter."

"How much longer do you think we'll call it Down Under, and describe the weather as upside down?" she asked. "The next civilisation will be born there. Maybe they'll make their maps with south at the top, and the ruined north at the bottom."

"The symbolism would work," Pete said. "Paradise at the top, with hell beneath."

The horizon glowed as the racing sun caught up with them. "Twenty-three souls," she said. "Let's go to bed."

When Pete woke, he found the bed empty. He opened an eye. Olivia sat in the chair reading a book.

"What time is it?" he asked.

"About eleven," she said. "We'll be in time for lunch if we help clean the mess-deck first."

"Do we have to get up?" Pete asked.

"You know the rule: if you're awake enough to form a complete sentence, you're too awake to sleep."

"Since when is that the rule?" Pete asked.

"A clear set of rules makes for a happy marriage," Olivia said. "Mrs Mathers told me that. She also said to be sure I'm the one who makes those rules."

"I bet she did," Pete said. "Did we get any coffee from Savannah?"

"There's an easy way to find out," Olivia said. "But maybe put some clothes on first. I'm going to see if I can find out a bit more about what happened in Georgia. I'll meet you for lunch."

Ten minutes later, he stepped outside, and into a damp corridor where two of the Georgian survivors were mopping the deck.

"Sorry," Pete said. "Morning," he added.

The pair muttered a good morning, and stood aside. One was the young man who'd objected to having his knife taken away, though he was carrying it again. The other was similarly armed.

"Elijah, right?" Pete asked, before turning to the other. "Sorry, I didn't catch your name yesterday."

"Spence," he said. "And… ah… yeah, thanks for helping us," he added, slightly abashed.

"Thank you," the other said.

"Ah, no worries," Pete said. "You'll get to do the same for someone else soon enough."

He left them to continue their cleaning, and headed down to the Mendez Muncheria where he found the other two jocks, similarly on cleaning duty. One scrubbed the tables, the other was cleaning the floors. Ramon was in the kitchen, examining a clipboard.

"I came to see if you needed a hand cleaning up," Pete said.

"I have new staff," he said. "They volunteered. The tall one, he wants to set up a franchise when we get to New Zealand."

"I thought they were on punishment," Pete said. He looked at the two men, not that much younger than him. "What did you say?"

Ramon shrugged. "What could I say? Renata said this would be a trial. A test. But a franchise? A restaurant with paying customers, and which can pay suppliers? It is a fantasy, but the work will help them heal."

"Did they talk much about what they saw?"

"Only enough for me to know they need a distraction."

"Did we pick up any coffee in Savannah?" Pete asked.

"Enough for two cups per day for two weeks," Ramon said.

"What about food?" Pete asked.

Ramon handed him the clipboard. "We now have meals for twenty-six days."

"So we picked up just enough to feed the newcomers? That's not too bad."

Ramon shook his head. "When did you last eat fresh fish?"

"I'm not sure," Pete said. "But not since we came aboard."

"Exactly. When we have had the opportunity to fish, the radiation was too high. We must find better opportunities, or better waters."

Coffee in hand, and looking for work, Pete made his way up to the science centre where he found Corrie running a circuitry class for Pita, the two children from Savannah, and Zach.

"Did something break?" Pete asked.

"Welcome to the School of the Sea," Corrie said. "Fixing electronics will be a must-have skill in the years to come. Take a seat."

"Yeah, you can tell us about that gator fighting the zoms," Zach said. "I can't believe I missed that."

"I thought we got it on video," Pete said.

"Not all of it," Zach said. "I was saying we need a proper camera rig."

"And I said we're not a documentary crew," Corrie said. "Want to learn how to build a motion sensor?"

"Everyone's going to want them back home," Zach said. "Even in the outback."

"And I've got Corrie to build them for me," Pete said. "I'm sure I should be doing something. Where's Tess?"

"She was interviewing the newcomers," Corrie said.

He went below, and found Tess, Mayor Jak, and Sergeant Nikki Temple, sitting next to a camera aimed at a man who was on the emaciated side of thin, and sagging in his seat.

"I think that's enough for now," Tess said as Pete entered. "Sergeant, can you take Mr Washington back to his cabin? I think you need a bit of sleep, mate. You'll feel better in a few days."

Pete stepped aside so Nikki could help the man to the door.

"It's radiation sickness," Tess said after the two had gone.

"From Savannah?" Pete asked.

"From about five miles east of White Springs," Tess said.

"That's in Florida," Mayor Jak added. "Due west of Jacksonville."

"Oh. So near Mayport?" Pete asked.

"But it had to have been a different bomb," Tess said. "Mr Mayor, would you mind getting…" She looked at her notes. "Rita Ryan. I think we should speak with her next, to see what she has to say about Atlanta in case we've got any follow-up questions for Mr Washington."

"Of course, but please call me Jak," the mayor. "Just Jak. No c, no e."

"He's an odd fish," Tess said after the mayor had left. "But the odd ones are usually honest. Were you looking for me, Pete?"

"Just to find out where I can make myself useful," he said. "I'd be cleaning, except the Georgians have stolen my mop."

"It's good for the newcomers to keep busy and there isn't much else for them to do," Tess said. "Trust me, there'll be work enough for you when we get to New York. So until then, rest up. Or you can sit in on these interviews if you like. I'm stitching their stories into a tapestry which has death woven throughout. You might be able to add some depth to the details."

"Do many of them have radiation poisoning?" he asked as he took a chair.

"Probably. But we're only immediately worried about Mr Washington," Tess said. "There appears to be a band of radiation sitting across the north of Florida. If you were a sub captain whose targeting systems had been reduced to a compass, you might view cutting off the Florida panhandle as a good use of your missiles. *Good* being used as a synonym for bloody evil."

"Could it have been that Russian sub who chased you in the Atlantic?" Pete asked.

"Sure," Tess said. "Or it could have been the British boat that sank the Russian sub. We've come across far too much damage for all of these missiles to have been launched by a single submarine. At this stage, I'm no longer interested in *who* fired, but what their targets were. Mr Washington's story might interest you. They were organising an airlift in Atlanta after the bombs fell, and he left the city after the planes flew north."

"Were they trying to link up with General Yoon?" Pete asked.

"They were trying to get civilians to safety," Tess said. "He doesn't know much about the airlift, except the final destination hadn't been set. Rumours swirled around Atlanta about a Pacific Alliance, and about a Canadian general, though he didn't know her name, or even that she was a her. He knew there was a debate among the pilots as to where in Canada they'd be able to land, but he was just another survivor at the airport. He had no say in the destination, or the planning."

"Why didn't he catch a flight?"

"He wanted to look for his daughter," Tess said. "Sergeant Nikki Temple heard about the Atlanta airlift from a trucker who'd decided wheels were safer than wings, but that bloke's attempt at driving west backfired, and he ended up in the east, in Savannah, where he died a week ago. Infected."

"Oh. How many planes were in this airlift?" Pete asked.

"Hundreds. They were all civilian aircraft, grounded after the outbreak. Someone had flown north to make contact with the general, but hadn't returned before the bombs fell. Mrs Rita Ryan, whom we're speaking with next, was apparently near Atlanta when the planes took off, and actually saw them in the air. We know they flew north, but don't know whether they went towards the Pacific, the Atlantic, or somewhere between."

"The Canadian northeast was hit," Pete said. "But so was Vancouver, wasn't it?"

"The city, yes, but not Vancouver Island," Tess said. "At least, I don't think it was. Messages were getting few and far between before the bombs fell, and they got worse afterwards, but we did get a request for help. If they had a hundred passenger jets there, they'd have sent them south."

"So this airlift went towards the Saint Lawrence, and General Yoon," Pete said.

"Probably," Tess said. "However, we don't need to guess at the aircrafts' fate. A small group had agreed to stay behind in Atlanta to gather their family members and other survivors who didn't arrive in time. A plane was supposed to return for them. Ms Ryan told them no planes ever did, but I want to double-check that with her."

"Where did he get exposed?" Pete said.

"His sister-in-law lived in Savannah, so he headed there, by bike. Zoms made him take a detour, and he ended up spending three days hiding from a large group of them. Doc Flo thinks the water he was drinking was contaminated because, the next day, he drove right into a crater."

"Will he make it?" Pete asked.

Tess shook her head. "Doc Leo's not a physician, but he is a world expert. Mr Washington has about four days."

"To live? Oh," Pete said, and sat silent for a moment, taking that in. "He didn't look that sick. Is that how it is? There's nothing that can be done?"

"Nothing," Tess said.

"Did he find his family?"

"Nope. We'll add Florida to the list of irradiated zones along with Vancouver and the Canadian northeast. I never heard it confirmed, but the suspicion was California was hit by a tsunami, while the borderlands were waiting on supplies lost at sea. South Africa, Brazil, and Cuba were bombed. We didn't pick up any radio signals in the Caribbean, probably because the cartel heard them first. We can infer that Europe is gone from the lack of any contact. Madagascar was overrun. You remember how some ships went east from Puerto Morelos? None returned, and I'm inclined to blame the subs which also plague the southern Atlantic."

"So many places. So many people," Pete said. "Is there any chance those passengers are alive?"

"It's slim," she said. "They flew into the unknown. Even if they didn't land in a hot-zone, they had to locate a runway without any guidance systems. Let's say they did, and that the runway was free of debris, each plane had to land without wrecking the runway, and be towed out of the way before the next plane came in. The first few planes might have landed safely, but sooner or later there'd be a crash. But you can look at this another way. The only chance they *did* survive is if they picked up a beacon set up by Judge Benton. Looking at the time frame, she had a couple of days to move some people north before the planes left Atlanta. You said General Yoon was using helicopters and planes, so it makes sense the judge would secure an airport and operate a long-range radio beacon to guide in any survivors from the combined army. If these people from Atlanta flew north, they could have picked up that beacon, and so, yes, could have survived. But before you ask, we don't have the resources to look for her, either."

"We'd need a helicopter, I guess," Pete said.

"More than one," she said. "We'd need fuel and the supplies to keep the ship's crew alive while they flew. We'd need more ships to carry the survivors. But we don't have them, or a helicopter. It's just us, and we're running out of food."

"Ramon says twenty-six days," Pete said.

"That's only if we don't pick up more survivors," she said. "What if we get engine trouble? Ah, this is why I left Broken Hill for the big city. I hate these types of decisions. Sure, I'd read too much Sherlock Holmes and fancied myself a detective. But I also wanted to get away from the pile-ups in the never-never. You can only do CPR on one person at a time, and I hated having to choose. That's what we're dealing with now. There'll be other survivors out there, north and south. We have a real chance of being able to resupply and reinforce a community in Chile and Argentina. Up here, we can only evacuate them, and I don't think we have the resources. No, we'll go to New York, but afterwards, we're heading home, and not with the news I wanted."

"You stopped the cartel," Pete said. "That was your mission, wasn't it?"

"Only part of it," Tess said. "But I hoped we'd find a group of survivors as large as in Mozambique. False hope is never any help, so the grim news we've learned will help in the long term, but the short term is looking pretty dark. We're going to become a police state, no two ways about it. It'll be a challenge preserving knowledge, let alone democracy. But we've got to try. That's why we're going to New York. We need some good news to spread among the refugees. A photograph of this dead zom in Manhattan should keep the peace for a bit."

"If the zoms are dying in New York, won't they be dying in Australia, too?" Pete asked.

"By now, I hope we've killed all the infected in Oz," Tess said. "But yes, there should be rumours of them dropping dead wherever the front line now is. Rumours get twisted. We need some facts in an official report to justify the privations, while also establishing how long the draconian conditions will remain in place. That report has to come from Doc Flo, and based on data from where the outbreak began. That was a good job your sister did, nailing down where that was. Doc Flo seems confident that hospital is where we might find patient zero. I don't know what real data we'll get from that, or from this subject we're calling the peach-zom, but the video will be invaluable as propaganda."

"You're worried," Pete said. "Really worried. Sorry, I haven't known you long, but I've never heard you sound so… well, uncertain."

Tess smiled. "Mate, I'm anything *but* uncertain. I know *exactly* what's going to happen next. Before we left Australia, I was given a warrant signed by the new secretary general of our new United Nations. That U.N. is made up of the ambassadors who were stationed in Oz before the outbreak. You've seen for yourself what happened to the world. Those countries they represented are gone. Those ambassadors have no mandate. Oz, New Zealand, Papua, parts of Indonesia, maybe the Philippines, maybe Malaysia. I really don't know how many old nations will have survived, but I bet it's less than ten. We'll probably have an election. We'll certainly have some kind of combined Pacific administration, at least for a few years. We might even have an Australian Empire, but we're also going to have unrest. We'll have terrorism. We'll have uprisings. That's assuming that the spreading radiation doesn't mean we all end up like poor Mr Washington."

14th April

Chapter 13 - No C, No E
The Northwestern Atlantic

Pete and Olivia lay in the dark, watching the stars through their porthole window. They weren't waiting for dawn, because they knew it would come regardless.

"New York won't be any better than Savannah," Pete said.

"It won't be any better than South Bend," Olivia said. "Australia will be, even if it's a police state. Which is worse, that it's inevitable, or that there's no other way?"

"No, the worst bit is knowing, even if the Pacific is run like a military camp, the radiation, or climate, or zoms, might still kill us all," he said.

"Yep, no way am I getting back to sleep now," she said. "What time was Ramon opening the restaurant?"

"Six."

"Ah, that's an hour away."

"Are you hungry?"

"No. I just want to hurry up and get to New York so we can leave again," she said. "Because the worst bit, the soul-gnawing terrifying bit, is not knowing whether the Pacific has collapsed while Tess has been away. Even when we get back to the Pacific, we'll be at the beginning of the crisis, and we'll remain there until the zoms are all dead. It'll be the work of a lifetime to rebuild. Ah, but I guess that means we'll have plenty more years to talk about it, so let's not think about it now. Want the shower first?"

"You go," he said. "I'm going to get some air."

Still thinking of New York, rather than what would come after, Pete went for a pre-breakfast run around the ship. He wasn't the only person up early. He found Mayor Jak on deck, and by the rear rail.

"Can't sleep?" Pete asked.

"I always get up early," the mayor said. "While in office, I learned to be awake before the journalists, a habit I've been unable to change. I'm much obliged to you for what you did."

"No problem," Pete said. "I only fired a few shots."

"I'm thanking you for going to Canada after Australia, for your efforts in organising a relief effort."

"It didn't come to much," Pete said. "Besides, I was looking for Olivia. Any other good I did was utterly unintentional."

"Actions always count for more than intentions," he said. "I understand the Kiwis fought pirates off Madagascar, and zombies in Mozambique. The police officers stopped a coup in Australia, and destroyed the cartel's supplies in Colombia. If there'd been more like you, acting like you, we wouldn't be wallowing neck-deep in disaster. I blame myself for not doing more when I could."

"You're the first group of survivors we've found since Florida, and they were pirates," Pete said. "I'd say you did a fair job. You were the mayor of Thunderbolt?"

"The *former* mayor of Savannah. I left office at the last election. But I served for twelve years before that. The greatest honour of my life, but increasingly filled with regret. Mayor Jak. No e, no c."

"You've said that before. What does it mean?"

"Oh, it was a slogan from my first campaign, which became another of those habits it's hard to kick. During my first television interview, the producer called me Rick while the journalist kept calling me Richard. If the press can't remember a name like Adam Richardson when it's written in front of them, how's a voter expected to remember it when they see it on the ballot? A gentleman from the north came to see me the next day. Very peculiar sort, with the most peculiar accent, as if he were an Iowan impersonating an Englishman pretending to be a Kennedy. Tom didn't have much experience, but he offered his services for free because he'd taken a personal dislike to my opponent, a man called Trowbridge who, sadly, went on to greater things than I."

"You ran against Trowbridge?" Pete asked.

"Ran and won. You've heard of him?"

"Yep. Met him once," Pete said. "Can't say I liked him much."

"Don't think anyone did except the donors," the mayor said. "When did you meet Trowbridge?"

"Oh, up north," Pete said, and decided it was best to change the topic. "So this slogan won you the election?"

"It certainly helped. Jak was a family name from the old country. No c, no e. No compassion, no economy. No curriculum, no education. No charity, no expansion. We had a dozen of them. All meaningless, when you thought deeply about them, but they looked good on a billboard, better on TV, and sounded perfect on the radio. I won. And won re-election. So, yes, I suppose it did help me win, right up until social media arrived. The slogan became a meme and I became a joke. I called up the old pollster, but he was too busy running presidents to bother with a small-city mayor. Ah, the world turns, and some of us old rocks are too slow to turn with it."

"Three terms is an accomplishment most presidents would be envious of," Pete said.

"Ha! I knew I liked you, son," he said, giving Pete a skin-bruising slap on the back.

"So you weren't in charge of Savannah during the outbreak?" Pete asked.

"No one was," Mayor Jak said. "Glen, my successor, was away on one of his fact-finding missions to a five-star resort. The National Guard was ordered to protect the interstate near Florida. They must have been wiped out by those nukes. The police were ordered to Atlanta. Not all went. But too many did. The infection arrived only hours after Manhattan, but it took us days just to organise an emergency administration. Took us a good week to regain some measure of control. We put up barricades, told people to guard their homes, to stay put. Help would come. But it was only refugees who came. If they came in boats, we'd give them fuel, give them food, give them shelter for a night, but we sent them on. It sounds uncharitable, but we'd have done them an ill service by allowing them to stay."

"It sounds similar to Puerto Morelos," Pete said.

"It does. I'd wager you'd hear a similar tale all across the world. In times like these, you can't fool yourself that safety is measured by the power of a gun, or the number of your supporters. It's the depth of your pantry. Perseverance requires resilience, and that doesn't come merely from strength of character. Few of the passing ships would accept new passengers, so those in Savannah who fled did so by land. They had no choice, even after the nuclear bombs fell. We left it too late," he said, slapping the rail.

"To leave?"

"To organise," the mayor said. "If we'd had just a few hours more, we'd have saved thousands. Without the bombs, we'd have saved millions. But one morning, a few weeks back, we looked around and realised there were only a few hundred of us left."

"But you had boats of your own?" Pete asked.

"A few, but only at first. We knew the food supplies wouldn't last forever, so we kept a small fleet for fishing. It turned out, when it was needed, to be too small, but that was my salvation. We were down to one central community, one garrison at Thunderbolt, and a few roaming patrols. The islands were overrun. The fresh water was polluted. We needed a temporary bastion. Something with thick concrete walls and a flat roof on which we could collect rain. We knew northern Florida had been hit, but thought we could find a harbour to which we could ferry everyone before heading into the Gulf, and up the Mississippi. The boats left. They never returned. Seems likely, now, they were captured by those pirates off Canaveral."

"Did the pirates ever come north for supplies?" Pete asked.

"No. So maybe I'm wrong, and we were abandoned to die, but I take greater comfort in assuming they died honest and loyal, since they surely are dead."

"Why weren't you based in Thunderbolt?" Pete asked.

"Without any ships, the marina was just a storehouse, and we had a larger one on Hutchinson Island. A week after the National Guard were sent away, a plane arrived with their supplies. We kept those on Hutchinson, well away from where they might be stolen. The zombies proved to be a bigger threat. The bullets ran out long before the food did. Now we're twenty-three souls who'll be twenty-two when Mr Washington dies."

"How many lived in Savannah before?"

"Counting the greater metropolitan area, four hundred thousand."

"I'm sorry," Pete said.

"Gone isn't the same as dead, and so we can still hope," he said. "You're proof of that. You found your sister; you found your wife. You're together now. Perhaps we might be, too, in good time. This ship is an ark. It's salvation. The last salvation. I never was much of a gambling man. Always used to think you made your own luck. But, now, I truly don't know." He tipped his hat. "But we are alive thanks to you, so I'll thank you again, and let you finish your run."

Pete nodded, and jogged a few steps along the deck, but soon slowed to a walk that came to a stop as he completed a circuit. The mayor was correct, Pete had truly done all he could to offset the apocalypse. More than he'd ever have dreamed possible six months ago. It hadn't been enough, but it was time to close the book on the past. That left the question of how someone like him could prevent the past from repeating in the future.

Part 2
New York, New York, So Good They Destroyed It Twice

New Jersey, New York, and the Delmarva Peninsula

15th April

Chapter 14 - The Harbour Sea
New York Harbour, New York

The icebreaker raced the dawn to shore, but the sun won.

"Is that New York?" Zach asked, leaning against the rail next to Olivia and Pete.

"That's New Jersey," Pete said. "Captain Renton said the current dragged us too far to the south. Doc Flo then began a lecture on vectors, at which point, I fled the bridge."

"So that's *not* Long Island?" Zach asked.

Olivia reached across, and turned over the folded map Zach held. "That's the side you want," she said. "We're just about to reach Sandy Hook. Once we pass that, and Fort Hancock, we'll enter New York Bay."

"That's Sandy Hook?" Zach asked. "Should be called Rusty Hook."

On the eight-kilometre-long spit at the very north of the Jersey Shore, mast-forests rose from oil-slick sands. As the wind rose, torn sails flapped against rain-washed hulls. A grey freighter turned soot-black as a white cloud rose and then circled, looking for somewhere else to roost.

"Strewth, that was birds!" Zach said, as the gulls settled on beached craft further south.

"Must be migrating," Pete said. "I read that volcanic eruptions can alter migration patterns. Bombs must be the same. There are no boats."

"There's tons," Zach said. "I can count a million wrecks."

"But no one fishing," Pete said. It was his turn to point to the map. "If you had a sailing boat, Sandy Hook would be perfect. The narrow part can't be more than a few dozen yards across. There's plenty of metal in those wrecks to make a barricade, and the homes of twenty million people nearby to loot."

"Yeah, but remember Tofo Beach," Zach said. "Where you get shipwrecks, you get zoms."

"Oh, true," Pete said. "Pity."

"Wouldn't be much fresh water around here," Olivia said. "Wouldn't be many fish after those ships begin leaking oil."

"The radiation isn't that high, right?" Pete asked. "It's not, no?"

"Guess not," Olivia said. "Or we'd get a warning."

"All you'd have to do is last a few weeks more, and outlast the undead," Pete said. "And if it began here, it'd end here first, too."

"But would you try clinging on if you didn't know that for sure?" Olivia asked. "I wouldn't. Looks like the locals didn't, either."

"Where's the Statue of Liberty?" Zach asked.

"Miles away," Pete said. "Still hidden by the curve of the Earth."

"I'll get my camera," Zach said. "Oh, wait, no. Clyde wanted you."

"He did?" Olivia asked.

"Yeah, sorry. I was supposed to come find you. He's in the armoury."

"I was about to send out a search party for you two," Clyde said. "Where's Zach?"

"Sightseeing," Olivia said.

"He's got curiosity in his veins, that one," Clyde said. "Here's your gear for the shore-mission."

"We're wearing camouflage?" Pete asked.

"Naval fatigues," Clyde said. "We're all wearing uniform ashore, and body armour. Don't call it a bulletproof vest because it's not. It won't stop everything, and will only protect the bits it covers. Helmets have a light here. There's another light on the vest, and there's a bodycam which will be recording everything. Sights and sounds," he added. "Day *and* night."

"Gotcha," Olivia said. "But I thought we were only going to be ashore for a few hours."

"We'll plan for delays, because the moment darkness comes, we'll take shelter. We don't know what we're going to find, so we'll be moving slow and sure. Tess will give you the details. One Glock 17 nine-mil pistol with a suppressor and four mags. You two are taking the shotguns. White shells are beanbag rounds. Red is for breaching. The others are standard slugs."

"Beanbag rounds?" Pete asked. "Is Doc Avalon hoping to capture a zom?"

"We've picked up a bit of radio chatter broadcast over shortwave," Clyde said. "It sounds like a sit-rep from a civilian. That's why we're in uniform, wearing the armour, and why we're bringing the beanbag rounds." He patted his left hip. "And why I've got a Taser."

He added two of his long-handled boarding axes to the pile.

"We have to carry those as well?" Olivia asked.

"They'll be handier than a crowbar," Clyde said. He reached down and picked up two small packs. "Water, rope, med-kits. There's a bit of food in there, too. Just the oat bars, walnuts, and dried apricots."

Pete picked up a bag. "That feels like a lot of food."

"You're carrying some of the docs' gear," Clyde said. "They've got their instruments and tools to bring. Get changed, bring this up to the science centre. Our team will meet there prior to departure."

"When will that be?" Olivia asked.

"When we drop anchor," Clyde said.

The science centre now doubled as a multi-generational classroom, and buzzed with competitive chatter from the two teams engaged in a child versus parent graph-off. At one table sat Pita and the teenagers from Savannah, Chloe and Divine. At the other table sat their guardians, Renata and Kathleen. The wall screen had been split to mirror both workstations where the graphs were still being constructed.

From the hurried muttering from both teams, winning was more important to them than the invisible horror the data revealed. As a spreadsheet flipped to a graph, then back again, Pete caught sight of the curve.

"Are those numbers current?" he asked.

"Shh," Pita hissed. "He's a spy."

"*Si,*" Renata said. "The last figures taken this morning."

"Great, thanks," Pete said. "It's dropping, then?"

This got no response. He turned to Olivia, but she was watching a different screen on the other side of the room, next to Dr Smilovitz. Pete walked over.

"Is the radiation dropping, Leo?" he asked.

Leo briefly glanced up before returning his attention to his own screen. "To say it's dropping would be incorrect usage," he said, in an unintentional imitation of his colleague. "The current, the tide, and the rain are transporting radioactive particles into the ocean. From that, we can infer that the coastal conurbation wasn't bombed. However, contrasting the discrepancy between atmospheric and at-surface readings tells us that at least one bomb was dropped upriver."

"How far upriver?" Pete asked.

"That's impossible to tell at present," Leo said. "We'll need to gather more data from inside the bay before drawing a conclusion. If you'll excuse me, I must speak with Tess."

As he hurried away, Pete finally let his eyes settle on the screen Olivia was watching. "What's that?"

"The Verrazzano-Narrows Bridge," she said. "Or it was. Leo said the damage was done by a missile strike. Conventional, though."

Nearly a kilometre and a half in length, the suspension bridge had linked Staten Island in the south with Long Island in the north. Now, it was a ruin. The two supporting towers were shattered and smoke-blackened. From each tower jutted a stump of road, leading downward to the surging waves. Stray cables dangled like tentacles probing the estuary, and gathering a growing mat of flotsam.

"Can we sail through?" Pete asked.

As if to answer, the ship shuddered as the bow-thrusters came to life.

"Oh, I hate this," Pete said, grabbing hold of the bolted-down table as the ship began a steep turn, but the ship settled into its new course too swiftly for them to have turned south.

"Change of plans," Tess said, even as she bounded down the ladder from the bridge. "Who's here? Good. We're taking the icebreaker to Great Kills Bay. Nicko and Bruce will take one of the boats first to scout for a dock. We're not going to wait for them. Our team is taking the other boat, and we're going to motor right up to Manhattan. I reckon two hours to get there, one hour to reach the subject we are, against my objections, calling the peach-zom, and an hour to return to the launch. We'll sail back as night falls. Bruce and the mayor's people will look for supplies around the harbour, and we might get out of New York with the first tide tomorrow. Where's Zach?"

"Clyde went to find him," Olivia said.

"Well, you find them both, and meet me at the boat," Tess said.

The air hummed with chatter as the Georgian survivors mingled on deck. Now armed, they were lookouts, ready to defend their floating refuge. Louder still, though diminishing with each second, was the buzz of the smaller launch, cutting its way towards Staten Island, with two sailors, Clyde, Nicko, and Sergeant Temple aboard.

"Anyone know who they killed here?" Zach asked, as they waited for the other launch to be lowered into the water.

"Who killed whom where?" Avalon replied.

"They're going to somewhere called Great Kills Bay," Zach said. "Who got killed, and who thought that was great?"

"Ah, a common misconception," Avalon said. "Kills is actually an Anglicisation of a Dutch word for creek. That the English settlers opted for the bloodier name provides a useful insight into the mind-set of the early settlers and, indeed, into their descendants."

The small launch was now a speck, disappearing towards the urban shorefront sprawl. Concrete. It was everywhere, except where there was water or sky. Immediately to the west, and a large arc to the north, was Staten Island. Further north and east, beyond the ruin of the Verrazzano-Narrows Bridge, lay Long Island. To the south was New Jersey.

"Everyone ready?" Tess asked, though the question was addressed to Clyde who was walking through the small group, inspecting their gear.

"Ready enough, Boss," he said.

"Why aren't we waiting on Colonel Hawker to confirm there's a safe harbour?" Olivia asked as they lined up to board the boat.

"Because our treasure is not to be found on Staten Island," Avalon said.

"There *are* people here," Tess said. "We don't know who they are, where they are, or whether they're aware of our presence. A ship like this is hard to miss if they're watching the harbour, but it'll take them time to get organised. Maybe they'll miss us, or ignore us, but if they want to be pirates or seek rescue, they'll make their approach around dawn. Whether it is before or after will tell us whether they're friendly or not. Either way, we need to be ready to go, with those samples aboard. Even if they're friendly, we can only take a maximum of seventy with us."

"What if more come?" Olivia asked.

"We'll work something out," Tess said, "but getting those samples, the children, and what we've learned, back to the Pacific is our priority."

"How many people do you think might be here?" Pete asked.

"Modelling from Cape Town, Savannah, and Cancun would suggest thousands," Avalon said.

"Wow," Pete said. Then he remembered the twenty million who had lived in the region before the outbreak. "Wow."

There were eight in their shore-party: Zach, Tess, and Clyde, Corrie, Olivia, and himself, and Leo and Avalon. Everyone had a gun, a camera, and wore a uniform. The two scientists carried large, though empty, first aid bags to store the samples. Corrie had a radio. Leo wore a tool-belt with what looked like a bone-saw next to his holster. Tess wore a watch she checked as they boarded the boat, and again as Clyde began motoring them north.

The small launch was noisy due to the engine and made noisier still with Avalon listing what she considered the tourist highlights, and Zach interrupting her with pop-culture footnotes. Pete tuned them out.

The water through which they ploughed might not be as radioactive as the deeper ocean, but it was definitely toxic, foaming grey and green in their wake. Staten Island's South Beach was, like Sandy Hook, covered in wrecks, but here they were cars, driven onto the sand after their owners had run out of road.

Those cars were now roosts to gulls which rose and circled, collectively shifting up, then down the beach. Their flight was elegant. Beautiful. Serene. Until he saw the reason behind the pattern: the small pack of undead, lumbering slowly back and forth after the flocking birds.

As the bridge neared, his ears whistled with relief as Clyde cut their speed. The water grew rougher, churning wildly as they carved through the semi-submerged wreckage: parts of cracked hulls, plastic furniture, clothing, toys, bodies. One moved its arm as it rolled with the current, but was dragged beneath a fibreglass pontoon before Pete could ascertain if it was undead or a true corpse. That pontoon had belonged to a seaplane, the remains of which were still tied to the bridge, but there were no signs of the pilot, or of why they had landed here.

Clyde cut their speed again. The wreckage grew denser, topped with a colourful mat of river-rinsed clothing, spilled from the bags of refugees who'd been on the bridge when it was destroyed. Just when Pete was wondering if they would become entangled in the multi-patterned debris-quilt, Clyde opened the throttle, and they accelerated north.

All around them, the skyline filled with cement and steel, but not enough glass. Few buildings had survived the apocalypse unscathed. Many were smoke-blackened. Many more had sheets hanging from those broken windows, all making an unheard plea for help. It was a cry echoed by Lady Liberty, whose eyes cried soot-black tears from a missile strike which had dented her crown.

Clyde slowed. "Didn't you want a photo, Zach?"

Zach simply shook his head.

They circled around Liberty Island, and turned west, then northwest, entering the East River. Where the Upper Bay had been brisk and chill, the East River foamed grey, like the waters of the Atlantic.

"Do we need gas masks?" Tess asked.

"If we did, it would be too late now," Avalon said.

"We're fine," Leo said, having dropped a sensor over the side. "And the radiation's still low. Just no one drink anything unless it's in a bottle."

"Why's it that colour?" Olivia asked.

"It's probably just ash," Leo said, with a rare hesitancy as disturbing as the devastation.

Now sailing the narrower, though still kilometre-wide, waterway between Manhattan and Long Island, they found the surface littered with storm-dragged debris from the war-torn shores.

"Break out the paddles!" Clyde called as they approached the white-water rapids where the old Brooklyn Bridge had once stood. Like at the Verrazzano Narrows, the bridge had been destroyed, and the towers had become a magnet for clothing and signage, plastic and wood.

With no warning, Clyde throttled the engine up to full. A flat bang echoed from below as Clyde slalomed them over the crashing white-water, and didn't slow until they were long past the bridge.

"Bullet!" he called. "Fired from the Long Island side of the bridge."

"Keep going!" Tess said.

No one shot at them from the ruin of the Manhattan Bridge, nor from the Williamsburg Bridge, but Clyde didn't slow until Leo called out. "There! We're here. That's the U.N. building. Take us ashore."

Chapter 15 - Where Nightmares Come True
Manhattan, New York

Clyde docked the launch at the northern side of the East 34th Street Ferry. As Corrie secured the boat to a rung of a barnacle-encrusted ladder, Clyde bounded up, pulling himself over the chest-high safety-barrier.

Between the unfamiliar weight of the helmet, and the impossible devastation to the storybook city, Pete hadn't noticed the clouds gathering overhead until, as he looked skyward, a raindrop landed on his cheek.

"Looks clear, Boss," Clyde called down.

"Everyone up," Tess said, taking the lead. "Who shot at us?" she asked even as she climbed.

"Two people, one shooter," Clyde said, pointing south while keeping his gun trained forward, towards Manhattan. "They were on the Long Island side of the Brooklyn Bridge."

"Yeah, it was only two of them," Zach said, looking at his phone.

"Did you get a picture?" Tess asked.

"A video," Zach said, handing his phone to the commissioner.

"Looks like they were camped atop a flat-bed truck," Tess said, watching, pausing, and then re-watching the clip. "They've got chairs, but no shelter, except maybe inside the truck's cabs. Chairs mean sentries. So they're watching the river. If they were hoping for rescue, they wouldn't have shot at us. Sentries don't stand guard for themselves, so they're not alone. Clyde, how much danger is the icebreaker in?"

"Depends on whether these people have boats," Clyde said. "If they do, they'll come after us before they explore where we came from. We've got about three hours until dusk, four until dark. Assuming they have a boat, and the people to come hunting, it'll take them a couple of hours to find us. They won't go searching for a large ship until dawn at the earliest."

"Then we'll stick with the plan," Tess said. "Corrie, radio the ship. Warn them there are hostiles on Long Island. We'll make contact in two hours. If we fail to make contact in four, they're to implement plan-Adelaide."

"Pete, Olivia, hide your bags among the luggage," Clyde said. "Doc, same goes for you. Anything you don't absolutely need stays here."

"But hidden," Avalon said. "You believe we're in danger?"

"That's what gunfire usually means," Clyde said.

"Any idea what plan-Adelaide is?" Olivia asked as she and Pete pushed and kicked a gap in the abandoned luggage.

"There's only two things it could mean," Pete said. "Either leave, or mount a rescue. Neither bodes well for us. Did you see who fired?"

"I was too shocked by what I could see of the city," Olivia said. "I was expecting… I suppose I *wasn't* expecting it to look like a warzone. Here will do."

The abandoned luggage had been stacked beneath a fixed awning next to security gates leading to the rest of the ferry concourse: suitcases, holdalls, school backpacks, designer gym bags, even a few handbags. They were all full, and while a few had been searched, jutting from the phone-pouch of a delivery-driver's over-the-shoulder bag was the bright orange pistol grip of a flare gun. Inside the bag were plastic-wrapped t-shirts.

"Let's move," Clyde said. "They could have a boat and could have followed us here. Pete, Olivia, beanbag rounds in the shotgun, but you two are at the rear. Avalon, this is your turf. You tell me the way, but I'll lead."

The pier's gates were closed, though not secured. A mound of litter and mulch marked where a debris-drift had gathered, then been pushed aside when the gate was recently opened.

"Someone's been here before," Pete said.

"Don't say that," Olivia said. "And don't you dare say you've got a bad feeling, either. No tweaking fate's beard with lines from horror movies until we're back on the ship. Careful," she added. "Skateboard."

"Where?" Zach asked, turning around before looking down. "Cool!" He ran back a step to pick it up. "Slot it in my bag, mate."

"You are *not* using it on the ship," Tess said. "Not inside, or out."

"Yeah, no worries," Zach said, "but I still want a souvenir."

Outside the pier, twenty corpses had been dragged into a pile by ropes tied to limb or neck, but at least twice that number still lay where they'd fallen, amid a sea of rain-rinsed brass bullet casings.

"Movement," Tess said, pointing beyond an upturned limo, lodged across the on-ramp leading up onto the elevated FDR Drive.

Pete saw nothing, until he looked down. A column of rats scampered out of a drain, becoming a dark river, flowing across the road, disappearing behind the limo and up the on-ramp.

"Gross," Zach said.

"Entirely natural," Avalon said. "Without power to the pumps, the sewers and subways will be flooding. The rodents are seeking safer ground."

"Aren't we all?" Corrie said.

"Nah, bet they were fleeing from gators," Zach said. "That's why I'd go to Roosevelt Island."

"Where's that?" Olivia asked.

"I thought you were locals," Zach said.

"Local to two thousand miles away," Olivia said.

"Roosevelt Island is in the middle of the East River, just north of here," Leo said.

"Mayor Jak said that was the most likely place to find people," Zach said. "Boss, why didn't we bring Mayor Jak with us?"

"Because he'll do what Bruce tells him, and the Georgians will do what the mayor tells them," Tess said. "Right now, they're being told to keep watch for trouble, and you should do the same."

"Which way?" Clyde asked.

"Straight ahead to First Avenue, then north until we reach East 40th Street," Avalon said.

Clyde set a steady pace while his rifle metronomically pivoted in time with his steps: left, up, right, down, left. Pete kept his shotgun aimed down as he trudged a path through the inch-thick sludge shimmering with broken glass, discarded brass, and far, far too many bones. Some of the small skulls clearly weren't human, but were too big for rats. They had to have belonged to pets. Killed by the rats, or the undead, or by hunger, just like the people who'd once loved them.

Here, more than anywhere else he'd been, he saw the truth of the outbreak. It could have been stopped, but the quarantine had come too late, long after the virus had become global. Destroying the bridges had simply turned the island into a death camp, the inhabitants sentenced to the cruellest and most unusual end.

At the junction with First Avenue, a fire truck and bus formed a V-shaped barricade outside a brick-clad tower block's main entrance.

Outside and atop both vehicles were coils of razor wire, coated in snagged strips of cloth and wind-dried flesh. The fire engine's ladder was extended, leading up to a fourth-floor window. But was that an entrance or had it been last used for an escape?

"Crawler!" Zach called, nearly as quickly as Corrie fired a hasty shot, and then a more measured, and more accurate, bullet.

"Close up!" Clyde called.

A second zombie snaked around the bus's partially deflated tyres. What remained of its clothing was fluorescent orange. What remained of its left arm was unnaturally bent downwards above the elbow while its stump swung left and right with each lurching step, until Clyde fired.

"Stay close," Tess said. "Doc?"

"Straight on," Avalon said.

An animal roar echoed along the canyon street, its origins impossible to pinpoint.

"No way was that a zom," Zach said.

"Or a human," Corrie said.

"It is the aptly named *Ursus arctos horribilis*," Avalon said.

"A grizzly," Leo said. "They imprisoned a pair at the Central Park Zoo."

Regretting that the shotgun was loaded with a beanbag, Pete began checking behind as he brought up the rear. "Think I'd rather face gators," he said.

The next skyscraper had smoke stains ringing the entrance, but the fire hadn't spread beyond the lobby. Across the road, a mound of dead zombies lay heaped against an ambulance. As they neared, the vehicle began to shake, causing the pile of corpses to shudder.

"Hold fire, hold your fire," Clyde said calmly, jogging ahead to look through the grime-smeared windshield. He raised his rifle, and fired twice. The ambulance went still. "Clear. Move on."

For Pete, New York was a place from the TV. A place from the movies. Attacked by terrorists, plagued with serial killers, and destroyed by aliens. A place to find love, fame, and friends, and a place to lose them, too. A place to dream of leaving, and a place to leave one's dreams behind. A place of history and myth, and he wasn't sure which was which. But it was now a place without a future. A place of darkness, dirt, and decay. A place of broken glass and fallen stone, blocked drains and flooded streets, twisted lampposts and abandoned cars. A place of decaying bodies and still-living corpses. There was no hope, no life, no love, only the promise of destruction as the foundations flooded, and the towers fell.

A howl came from the north.

"Did they have wolves at the zoo?" Pete asked.

"Let's assume it was a dog," Olivia whispered.

"Dunno if that's much better," Pete said, as a very familiar sound bounced off the clad stone.

"Single shot, came from the south," Tess said.

Pete reflexively looked behind him, though he was uncertain which way was which.

Clyde whistled softly, pointing them on.

They were getting close. They had to be. Nearing the end. Nearing the point they'd turn around. Never had he so wanted to leave a place behind. But if First Avenue had been depressing, walking down East 40th Street was terrifying. On either side were moon-scraping towers, which created a desert canyon the sun would rarely reach. Beneath his feet crunched glass fallen from the gaping windows above. Far more forbidding, on either side, were dark caves marked as below-building parking structures. These were perfect places for the undead to hide, as proven when the shadows moved immediately to Pete's right. Less than four metres away, a trio of damp and dripping undead staggered up the ramp.

He only had to raise the shotgun a few degrees, and fired reflexively but on target. The beanbag round slammed into the chest of a woman wearing a hedge-fund suit and designer diamonds. She skidded backwards, into the dark cavern.

"Hold fire," Clyde said even as he raised his weapon. A headshot. A second. "Eyes on the perimeter," he said, as he stepped forward, and fired a third shot into the zombie Pete had felled. "Clear. Move on. Don't forget to reload, mate."

Pete loaded another beanbag round, but then slung the shotgun, and drew the boarding-axe instead.

Beyond the cavernous entrance to the parking lot was a hotel so nondescript as to be almost be invisible. A nameless green awning jutted halfway across the sidewalk. There was no name plaque outside the looming redbrick skyscraper. The plate-glass windows on either side of the door were opaque. From how they were dented, though unbroken, they were clearly made of reinforced glass.

The police car was stopped almost immediately outside the entrance with the front left tyre on the kerb and bones on the driver's seat. From the shattered skull, the driver had been shot in the head.

"This is it," Avalon said. "This is where the outbreak began."

Chapter 16 - Where It Began
Manhattan, New York

"What is this place?" Olivia asked, as they stepped inside, through the unlocked door.

"It's a hospital and, technically, an embassy," Avalon said, turning on a flashlight.

"Looks more like a bank," Zach said.

There was barely any furniture, and no ornaments, paintings, racks of newspapers, or signs to a bar. There wasn't even a reception desk, just a freestanding lectern by a pair of metal-grey elevator doors.

"It's through there," Avalon said.

"What is?" Clyde asked, as he pushed the door closed.

"The building is owned by the United Nations," Avalon said. "Traditionally this is where dictators and their families would come for medical treatment if they weren't technically allowed onto American soil. Obviously this would come with a quid pro quo. In recent years, other nations saw the cost-effectiveness of medical diplomacy, and so the patients here were more likely to be dissidents than despots."

"Stick close, lights on, barrels low," Clyde said. "Expect zoms. Which way?"

"Through here," Leo said, indicating the elevator doors.

"We've got to go up?" Tess asked.

"Not exactly," Leo said.

When Avalon turned the mechanical override key, and Leo pushed the doors apart, it was to reveal a carpeted corridor with an opaque white glass wall on the left. There had been a similar glass wall on the right, but it had been shattered, revealing a bank of monitors for thermal and X-ray imaging, and a metal door held open by a corpse. The black-suited body had an obvious shoulder holster, but the gun was missing, as was most of its skull.

"If this was a hospital, they didn't bring stretchers in through here," Clyde said.

"No," Leo said. "This was the visitor entrance for diplomats who had meetings with patients. Obviously no weapons were allowed, but nor was any recording device. There is a separate patient emergency-entrance, and another for staff."

"Why didn't we come in that way?" Zach asked.

"Because we don't know where that is," Leo said.

"We came here twice," Avalon said. "Both times, for the same case of dioxin poisoning."

"A journalist?" Tess asked.

"The primate of the Russian Orthodox Church," Leo said. "We were asked to advise whether it could have been accidental."

"Wow," Tess said. "Was it?"

"Not even slightly," Avalon said.

"Save the yarn for later," Clyde said. "Let's keep moving. With that storm gathering, night will come early, and we really need to be gone by dawn."

The security station had been raided. The weapons locker had been ripped open. The door beyond led to a reception desk for a hotel lounge, though one from a different millennium.

The ceiling was three storeys above them, supported by marble columns. The floor was a mosaic. The space between was filled with leather armchairs placed in sets of two or four. At the rear of the room was a broad staircase, sealed at the top with a faux-marble wall. That same dark grey stone ringed the perimeter of the lobby except around the entrance through which they'd come, and around two double-width opaque glass doors. One set of doors was near a reception desk. The other door was in the far corner of the room, near where the stairs began.

"This is weird," Zach said.

"That was my reaction on first coming here," Avalon said. "But this is merely a waiting area for visitors. The door by the staircase leads to the bathrooms. Inside, there is another door which leads to the service-side of this hospital. It is from there that they brought my coffee. It was most unsanitary considering this was supposed to be a medical facility. Through those double doors is an elevator which leads to the wards on the upper floor."

"The doors also lead to some conference rooms," Leo said. "We met a politician there who tried to make us sign an NDA before we were taken up to a secure ward on the fifth floor."

"Is that where we're going?" Tess asked.

"No, we want the old ballroom," Leo said. "Corrie?"

"Probably," Corrie said. "The decor matches. I think this is it."

"Very old-fashioned clothing for a hospital," Tess said, picking her way between the bones. "No scrubs. Too many ties. And no way you could properly clean these sofas."

"Who are the bodies?" Pete asked. "White coats are staff, but who are the suits?"

"Bodyguards and dignitaries," Leo said, picking a path between the skeletal corpses, and towards the furthest set of opaque doors.

"You say dignitary, I say parasite," Avalon said. "Gold braid belongs on Halloween costumes, not on someone's work clothes."

"That's a zom," Olivia whispered as they followed Leo to the doors. "And there's a gun still in the holster. Someone shot the zom but didn't take the gun. Who doesn't take the ammo?"

"Someone fleeing in a hurry," Pete said.

"Sorry, it was rhetorical. I don't think they were fleeing," Olivia said. "I think someone came this way before us. Obviously, they had no more need of ammo than us. They weren't simply survivors."

Pete and Olivia were at the back of the loose column as it entered the pitch-dark corridor. Lights from helmets and body armour bounced off the crystal-effect glass fittings, the elevator's brass buttons, the key-card readers next to the closed mahogany doors, the ceiling-mounted CCTV cameras, and the fire-axe embedded in the wall.

"Bones, bones, bones," Pete muttered, trying to distract himself from the smell. Somehow it was unpleasantly chemical, while also being unnaturally inhuman.

"Gun," Olivia said. "Shotgun. Yep, we're not the first people to come here."

It was a theory confirmed when they reached the improvised ward.

There had been twenty-eight gurneys lined up in rows next to medical monitoring equipment. Most had been overturned. On a bed which hadn't been upturned, a partially decayed corpse lay with its head crushed by an ECG machine. More bodies lay scattered among the wires and stainless-steel trays. Some wore patients' gowns. Some wore uniforms. Others wore suits.

"Well, this is disappointing," Avalon said.

"We came to the wrong place?" Tess asked.

"Absolutely not," Avalon said, crossing to the patient with the crushed skull. "Leo, the drill. We'll take samples from this patient.

Corrie, I want any data which has been stored on any of these machines."

"So this *is* where it began?" Zach asked. "This is where the first zom came alive?"

"No," Avalon said. "The agent was developed in a lab. This wouldn't even have been the location of the first *test*. This is simply the location of the first test that broke beyond their containment procedures. *Very* primitive procedures, as you can see for yourselves. We'll need a few minutes to gather samples."

"How did you know to come looking here?" Clyde asked.

"Deductive elimination, and a lead from Ms Guinn," Avalon said.

"What lead's that, Corrie?" Clyde asked.

"The pattern on the mosaic floor matches one of those bits of early footage from the outbreak," Corrie said. "Doc Flo pieced the rest of it together."

Pete walked back to the room's entrance. He wasn't sure how much Corrie had learned about the development of the virus before it was unleashed. He didn't know how much Lisa Kempton had told her afterwards. He wasn't sure how much his sister had guessed. Even if the bodycam hadn't been recording, he didn't want to ask. Not here, not now, maybe never.

"Every hard drive is gone," Corrie said. "There's a tripod over there, and the camera's been removed. Someone beat us to it."

"It could have been the CDC," Leo said.

"Hold the light steady," Avalon said. "Give me the saw."

"Got a soldier over here, Boss," Clyde said. "French Army. A colonel. And this civilian has an I.D. She's a deputy director in the Indian Intelligence Bureau. Both were shot in the head."

"Bag the I.D.s," Tess said. "And hurry it up, Doc."

Pete did his best to ignore the whine of the drill and the burr of the bone-saw as Avalon and Smilovitz worked.

"No more horror movies," Olivia said.

"Or hospital dramas," Pete said.

"That will do," Avalon said. "We can leave."

"Will this help?" Tess asked.

"With which task?" Avalon said. She walked around two of the fallen gurneys, and pointed at a silver suitcase. "That is a pressurised case, designed to withstand falling from a plane after it has been blown out of the sky. It is conjecture, but I would contend it contained samples which were injected into patients strapped to these gurneys. This outbreak was manufactured. It was a demonstration for the French colonel, the Indian spy and whichever officials managed to escape. I suspect some were infected. Some survived long enough to spread the infection beyond this hospital. Do you wish to confirm it?"

"Can we find out where the samples came from?" Tess asked.

"You are the police officer," Avalon said. "By all means, search for clues."

"We don't have much time, Boss," Clyde said.

"We're done," Tess said. "Half done, anyway. We're heading to that coffee shop where we'll find the peach-zom, then we'll radio the ship and make our way back."

Chapter 17 - A Bark in the Daytime
East 36th Street, New York

Back outside, Pete kept his gaze low, watching the gaps between the abandoned cars, so it was an entire block before he noticed the vehicles barricading a building's entrance. The glass crunching beneath his boots was from upper-floor windows, broken to provide air and rain to the survivors inside. After the island of Manhattan was quarantined, the trapped locals had attempted local quarantines of their own. Like the city, the state, the nation, and the entire world, this quarantine had failed, and those towers were now empty, with the survivors having either fled, died, or joined the ranks of the undead.

The further they advanced down Madison Avenue, the more barricades they found, and the bigger they got, blocking side roads and alleys, often containing buses, trucks, and even military vehicles. At the junction with East 36th Street, the easterly branch-road was blocked with a trio of NYPD Bearcats. Between, and partially beneath, the APCs was a secondary line of crushed cars, ringed by a low wall of sandbags. As Zach headed towards the armoured vehicles, Corrie a step behind, Leo took an abrupt ninety-degree turn.

"We're here," Leo said. "This is the coffee shop."

"It can't be," Avalon said. "The body should be lying in the doorway, propping the door open."

"It's been a while," Tess said. "Bodies rot, looters close doors."

In the distance, the bear growled. Nearer, the wolf howled.

"Hold position," Clyde said, while he stepped out into the road, turning north, then south, before his gaze settled on the APCs. "Corrie, Zach, step back. Slowly." The soldier crossed the road, moving with care.

"What is it, Clyde?" Tess asked, taking a step after the soldier.

"Those sandbags can only be there for one reason," Clyde said.

Pete had no idea what that reason could be, but Tess clearly did as she followed the soldier across the road to the militarised armoured police trucks.

"Bones don't rot," Avalon said, reaching for the cafe's door.

A hand smashed through the glass, grabbing Avalon's vest, tugging her forward. Leo grabbed Avalon, pulling her backwards. Pete ran, swinging the axe up, hacking it down on the desiccated arm in a blow that sliced diagonally through the pale orange cloth and rotting flesh, severing enough tendons that Leo was able to tug Avalon clear.

The zombie followed, and Pete was now right in front of the door. Gore flecked his cheeks as the monster thrust its shattered arm towards him. He stabbed the axe back in return, and with far more force, punching the axe-head into the zombie's face. The creature stumbled. Pete roared, punching the axe-head forward again as the zombie raised its foot. Off-balance, the impact knocked the creature from its feet. It fell backwards, shattering the remains of the glass door. Long shards of glass pierced through its pale orange coat, puncturing its stomach. The wound tore as the zombie rolled. Coils of intestines spilled onto the doorway, releasing an eye-watering vapour as they split. Pete stepped back, just as Olivia stepped forward, pistol raised. She fired, once.

"Yep, I'm sticking with guns," she said.

Pete breathed out, and regretted the foul breath he then inhaled, but the stench cut through the dark fog of anger and rage which had overtaken him.

"I need more practice with this axe," he said. "Looks empty inside."

"Are you okay, Flo?" Leo asked.

"Perfectly," the scientist said, brushing herself down. "Honestly, Leo, you do make a fuss."

"Um, Doc, wasn't that zom you wanted to take samples from wearing a peach pantsuit?" Olivia asked.

"Apricot rather than peach, but yes, one of the summer fruits," Avalon said. "Can you see her?"

"Absolutely," Olivia said, pointing at the corpse she'd just shot. "Isn't that a peach pantsuit?"

Avalon and Smilovitz stepped into the doorway.

"Ah," Avalon said.

"It could be her," Leo said.

"No," Avalon said after a moment's reflection. "It absolutely *is* her."

"Trouble?" Tess asked, coming back over, though not with Clyde.

"This is her," Avalon said.

"The peach-zom? Ace," Tess said. "Take your samples, and we'll get out of here, because this is the last place we want to be."

"The peach-zom was alive," Pete said. "Olivia just shot it."

"Oh," Tess said. "That's not good, is it?"

"Two minutes," Leo said. "We only had two minutes of footage covering half an hour of events."

"Stop providing captions for the hard of thinking, and give me a hypothesis," Avalon snapped.

"In the footage, the zom was stunned," Leo said. "A blow to the head scrambled the brain enough to stun it, but not to kill it. We saw it fall, but after the recording ended, the zombie stood up. Without re-examining the footage, that's the best I can come up with."

"That'll do for me," Tess said.

"Time to clear out," Clyde said, jogging over with Zach and Corrie behind. "The barricade won't hold. They heard the shot."

"Who?" Pete asked, though he could guess the answer.

"There are zoms on the other side of those Bearcats," Clyde said. "At least fifty. But the pier is down that road beyond them, so we'll need to take a detour to get back to our boat."

"Only fifty zoms?" Olivia said. "We can use the Bearcats as shooting platforms, like we did in Canada."

"We can't," Tess said. "They rigged C4 to the front. The explosive has been removed, but the detonators remain. If one of those goes off next to you, it'll do more than throw off your aim. The wiring's intact, and leads up to an upper window in that tower over there. Add it all together, the explosives had been placed there as a trap. They planned to lure the zoms here, blow them up, and hope the APCs' armour directed the explosive outwards. Clearly the zoms came from behind to overwhelm the defences."

"They're doing it again," Clyde said, pointing north down Madison Avenue. "Six hostiles south, twelve to the north, one minute out, all heading this way."

Tess peered into the cafe. "There's a backdoor in there. Probably leads to a stockroom. There will be a rear door, an alley, and a different road. Everyone inside. Corrie, first chance you get, radio the ship and tell them the peach-zom was alive."

"I don't have a code for that," Corrie said.

"Send it unencrypted," Tess said. "It won't mean anything if it's overheard. Pete, Olivia, check the stockroom for a backdoor."

The coffee shop's interior was achingly familiar. The tri-tone green pastel trim, ignorable art, faux-oak, and un-ironically complex menu was as common a sight in South Bend as in Sydney, though he personally preferred his coffee to cost less than an entire day's food.

The stockroom, too, was familiar from his own brief stint working as an underpaid kettle back in the long-ago era before he'd met Olivia. Neat metal shelves, each with an alphanumeric label, organised according to how early in a day they might run out. Boxes, unopened from a delivery the day of the outbreak, filled the relatively clear space close to a rear door.

"Is it locked?" Pete asked.

From outside, came a pop-pop-boom louder than gunfire. Then came a blast far more powerful than a detonator. The shelves shook, the floor shuddered, dust fell. Inside the cafe, the glass was blown from the window.

"Sound off!" Clyde called. "Anyone injured? Anyone hurt."

"On your feet," Tess said, as they picked each other up. "Does the stockroom have a rear door?"

"Yes," Olivia said.

"Then everyone move!" Tess said, her voice ringing with urgency, even as she wiped away the trickle of blood from a glass-shard cut above her brow.

Across the road, the cloud of smoke and dust coalesced into crawling shadows as the shrapnel-ridden undead scrummed through the explosion-shattered APC barricade.

"C'mon, Doc," Corrie said, hurrying the scientists into the stockroom.

"Door's locked!" Olivia called.

"Do we fight?" Pete asked, looking back at the undead spilling through the smoke cloud.

"Traps. Bears. Zombies," Tess muttered. "Who'd want to live in New York?" She followed him into the stockroom. "How's the door coming, Clyde?"

"It's reinforced metal," Clyde said. "A breaching-round won't do the trick."

"I'm working on it," Leo said. "I need ten seconds with the drill."

"No worries," Tess said.

"Does saying that help you mean it?" Pete asked.

Tess grinned. "Sometimes."

Pete leaned against the shelf, thinking about fire escapes until he saw the boxes. "Hey, that's coffee."

"It *is* a coffee house," Tess said. She grabbed a box, and stuffed it into his bag. "At least the day wasn't a complete bust."

"Done," Leo said. "We've got an access corridor here. Sign for a laundry. Another for a fire exit."

"That's us," Tess said. "Clyde, lead the way."

Before she pushed the door to the shop closed, Pete's last sight was of the first rank of shrapnel-flecked undead tumbling over the broken window frame.

The corridor led to another, and then to a fire-door which exited into a squalid, sunless courtyard at the centre of the block. On all four sides, broken windows towered up to the cloudy sky. The splendid veneer of the more famous streets to the south was utterly absent in this dank quad, which was heaped with the undead. Scores of bodies lay atop one another in a broken-limbed writhing mass, uncoiling as they crawled across broken glass and the shattered window frames.

"Back!" Clyde called as he fired. "Let's give door number three a try. Go."

Pete, at the rear, now took the lead, opting for the last direction available. The battered sign said they were heading to a laundry, but it led them into an apartment lobby. The elevator doors were open, but the lift-car was lodged half a floor above. The stairwell was blockaded with furniture. The front doors were completely missing.

"Take a breath, everyone," Tess said, peering around the doors. "Corrie, did you get the ship?"

"There was no signal," Corrie said. "It might be the buildings, but the handset's rattling. I think a wire's loose."

"No worries," Tess said. "The mission's over. We're going to aim for the boat. We'll stick together. Jog, don't sprint. We'll go south, then east, back to the river, then back to the boat." A crash came from deeper inside the building, setting off a metallic tremor in the elevator. "And that's our cue," Tess said.

Outside, the street immediately in front of the building was empty, but there were zombies angling westward across a junction forty metres away.

"Where are we?" Tess asked, as they jogged along the road, falling into two rough lines with Avalon, Leo, Clyde, and Tess in front, Corrie, Zach, Olivia, and Pete behind.

"Fifth Avenue," Avalon said.

"We're seeing all the sights today," Olivia said.

A muted gunshot reverberated off the decaying skyscrapers.

"Brooklyn Bridge," Pete muttered. "I forgot about them."

"Mrs Mathers warned me about New York," Olivia said. "Boy, I wish I'd listened."

Clyde set the pace, an unintentional jog-walk-sweep-jog as he slowed to check the interior of a broken-windowed shop, or to give an upturned car a wide berth.

Pete no longer had eyes for the city, only for the road ahead, and just as frequently behind as he turned to check how many undead were following. Each time he looked, there were more. Traipsing from alleys, from broken doorways and smashed shop fronts, even falling from the apartments above with a wetly thudding slap.

Another distant gunshot. Another howling bark. What sounded almost like another explosion, and only a few streets away. Above it, always, was the sound of shattering glass, of air hissing from dead lungs, and the increasingly loud footsteps of a growing army of the dead,

"We're getting near," Clyde called. Ahead was the raised FDR expressway. Behind it was the river.

"Survivor!" Zach called, pointing up at the elevated roadway.

"Down!" Tess called, dragging on Zach's arm as a bullet shattered the wing mirror of a car a metre to Zach's right. Clyde fired. Two shots, angled upwards at the bridge. "Back to the alley!" he yelled as he fired again. "On the right!"

Olivia broke right, spotting the alley before Pete. He followed while she opened fire, her gun aimed low, her bullets peppering the two zombies crawling through the ankle-deep mud-drift.

"Everyone here?" Tess asked as they gathered in the alley.

"Yes, as shall be our undead pursuers in under thirty seconds," Avalon said.

"No worries, plenty of time," Tess said. "Who was shooting at us?"

"Windbreaker, body-armour, cap, single-shot rifle with a scope," Clyde said. "Had a second shooter up there. Maybe a spotter. Must be the people from Brooklyn Bridge."

"Any chance we can try talking with them?" Olivia asked.

"Fifteen seconds," Avalon said.

"No," Tess said. "They found high ground from where they could snipe, so they found our boat. They aren't interested in talking. We're going to get clear of here, and then make our way to the other side of the island. We'll radio the ship to pick us up there, and be back in deep waters before midnight. If that doesn't pan out, we'll default to plan-Adelaide."

"Please tell me that's a plan for Nicko to bring up another boat," Zach said.

"Nope," Tess said. "Plan-Adelaide is that they leave without us."

There was no time to worry that the radio might not work as they were moving again. This time, running.

At the end of the alley, Clyde pointed across the road. "Over there!"

As Pete tried to see what kind of safety the soldier had spotted, his gaze was caught by a ball of golden fur, bounding towards them.

"Wolf!" Zach yelled.

But no wolf wore black booties on its feet and an FBI harness on its back.

The dog slowed as it neared, stopping next to Olivia, yipping before running behind, pushing at her legs.

"Rufus?" Olivia asked. "Rufus!" She knelt, while the dog yipped with irritated impatience.

"Who's Rufus?" Tess asked.

"A friend," Olivia said. "*My* friend. Steady, boy."

"Come with me if you don't wish to die twice," a woman called, stepping out from a narrow apartment doorway.

"Lisa?" Corrie said.

"I am as surprised as you to meet here, though is it really surprising?" Lisa Kempton said. "We can talk momentarily, when we are secure."

She pulled a smoke grenade from the pocket of her ankle-length coat.

"Rufus, do *not* fetch," she said, and threw it out into the street.

Chapter 18 - The Best Safety Money Can Buy
Manhattan, New York

Lisa Kempton led them through the building to another exit, another alley, and then into another apartment block.

"I believe we will be safe here," Lisa said, "though safety is relative, and belief rarely offers physical security."

"Clyde, watch the front," Tess said. "Pete, Olivia, secure that door to the stairwell. Don't open it. Corrie, we need that radio fixed." She finally turned to the bedraggled billionaire. "You're Lisa Kempton?"

"I could claim I was in disguise," Lisa said. "The reality is that we have all fallen on hard times and I had much further to fall than most. You have the advantage of me."

"Commissioner Tess Qwong, Australian Federal Police, but originally out of Broken Hill."

"Ah. I see. Since you, the Guinns, and Ms Preston are here, I assume we are pursuing the same goal?"

"It's Mrs Guinn, now," Olivia said. "We got married."

"Congratulations," Lisa said. "I shall blame the postal service for losing my invitation."

"What goal?" Tess asked. "Why are you here?"

"I am in pursuit of the cartel," Lisa said.

"The cartel's here?" Tess asked. "That's who shot at us?"

"Then I take it that's not why you came to New York," Lisa said.

"We were looking for data on where the outbreak began," Tess said. "But mostly because we thought we'd finished with the cartel down in the Caribbean."

"Did you find the sisters?" Lisa asked. "I assume you know who they are?"

"Yes, I know of them," Tess said. "We didn't find them, but we killed the brother, and destroyed the cartel's supply base in Colombia."

"Mikael's dead? Wonderful," Lisa said. "From that, we can infer that their redoubt in Miami has fallen. Well, that will save me a trip."

"How did you end up here?" Tess asked. "The Guinns said they found you in Canada. You went off to hunt for the sisters. But they're not here, right? So who is?"

"There are between two and five thousand survivors on Long Island," Lisa said. "They are being led by Governor Pruitt from Michigan, one of the cartel's pet politicians."

"There are five thousand cartel gangsters here?" Zach asked.

"No," Lisa said. "Governor Pruitt arrived a week after the nuclear exchange with ten loyalists. Her first act was to broker a peace between two rival armies, the convicts on Rikers Island, and a civilian militia clustered around La Guardia Airport. Under her leadership, the two groups became one, and became a magnet for every survivor nearby. As both prison and airport were uninhabitable, she relocated this new, and formidable, group to a few blocks around the Barclays Center, the Atlantic Terminal Mall, and One Hanson Place, a skyscraper she currently calls home."

"Did you know Pruitt was here?" Tess asked.

"No," Lisa said. "I arrived here ten days ago and was shocked to find order and peace, of a kind. You've heard the saying that every society is one meal away from anarchy? In this case, Pruitt provides that meal to every survivor. One meal, each day. There is cold water, a free clinic, and a school for every child under seventeen. The younger adults are given safer jobs within the Green Zone. Additional food, clothes, hot water, electricity to recharge phones, and a good deal more can be bartered for in their markets. Thus, survivors have become scavengers who roam Long Island, killing the undead."

"Zoms inbound," Clyde said. "Two. Walking east."

The group went quiet, listening for the all-clear while watching Kempton, except for Corrie who was peering at the circuitry inside the radio.

"Clear," Clyde said.

"Who is Pruitt?" Tess asked.

"Most recently, she was one of the cartel's candidates for the presidency," Lisa said. "Ten years ago, she was involved in a hit-and-run. Her licence plate was captured by the cameras outside a bar. She was arrested, but the body in the morgue was re-examined and found to be a forty-year-old vagrant who'd died from hypothermia, and who showed no evidence of having been in a car crash. Pruitt was a lawyer, and running for the state senate. An FBI investigation resulted in the arrest of two members of the state police, and the medical examiner. They were all found to have vast gambling debts, and to have received a cash pay-off from her opponent's campaign to frame her for murder.

All three committed suicide before going to prison, though this was after Pruitt had won the election."

"Which part of that did the cartel arrange?" Tess asked.

"The cover-up," Lisa said. "She really did kill a student. Roberta Gomez, nineteen years old. She was a budding photographer, taking pictures of night-time wildlife. Messages from Ms Gomez were sent to her parents from L.A., and then from South America, implying she had run away to photograph far more exotic animals. Six months later, she was reported dead in Colombia. However, my investigators found the glass from her camera lens mixed with the mud at the kerb. It was very specialist glass, not the kind you'd find anywhere in an automobile."

"The cartel arranged all of that to get Pruitt elected?" Tess asked.

"Indeed, and she was far from their only candidate. Once in office, Pruitt pushed for improved funding for the state's forensics capabilities, including the construction of a body farm."

"What's that?" Zach asked.

"A place where cadavers are observed as they decay, often in the open," Tess said.

"If you control the records system," Lisa said, "it is the perfect place to dispose of a body. The cartel owned the new medical examiner, and a good percentage of the police. There was even an incident, about six years ago, when some unconnected murderer dumped their victim there in the misguided belief it wouldn't be noticed. The institute was lauded for the swiftness with which they identified the errant addition and then solved the murder. Pruitt pushed for funding for better science education, and for more policing, and easily won the governorship. Better policing, better education, a better state. It was a clever campaign funded, of course, by the cartel. The governorship set her up for a presidential run, but Mr Clemens scuppered her nomination."

"Tom?" Corrie asked.

"Who's he?" Tess asked.

"Another grey knight like myself," Lisa said. "I was not the only person who realised, with the authorities having been infiltrated, an alternative approach was required to save civilisation. We both failed, of course, but that's another story."

"It is indeed," Tess said. "So let's cut to the end of this one. You arrived ten days ago to find that Pruitt's running this place, and keeping people alive?"

"Alive and safe," Lisa said. "There is even justice, albeit a rough kind. A week after she arrived, three rapists were executed. One was a member of her own staff. After that, she allowed people to leave. As a result, they have few boats, and little diesel, but the people who remained did so willingly. I don't know if they would die for Pruitt, but they *would* fight alongside her. New York is a logical destination for both refugees and scavengers, thus her numbers will inevitably grow. However, as those desperate survivors will be drawn here regardless, better they find some measure of organisation and justice than lawless chaos."

"You're saying that you originally came here to kill her, but you've decided not to?" Tess asked. "I'm happy not starting a war. So we'll leave them be, and return in the autumn with a freighter full of fruit, and a warship armed with soldiers. We can arrest her then, if Canberra still cares. But I'd guess, once Baker's trial is over, they'll want to close the book on the past."

"There's to be a trial?" Lisa asked. "I believe there is a lot for me to catch up on."

"Another zom," Clyde said. "This one's coming *from* the river." Again, an expectant silence settled until Clyde announced, "Clear."

"You are Doctor Florence Avalon and Doctor Leo Smilovitz," Lisa said.

"You know us?" Leo asked.

"Indeed," Lisa said. "My wife is a fan of your fiction, Doctor, while I am a fan of your joint work together. Indeed, I was one of your principal backers. I know of your reputation, so find it intriguing to see you both here. From what has been said, I infer the Pacific hasn't collapsed."

"Pretty much everywhere else has," Zach said.

"When we left, there were a hundred million survivors in the Pacific," Tess said. "Hunting the cartel was part of our mission, so was finding survivors, and finding out what had become of the world. If you came here ten days ago, and decided not to kill Pruitt, why are you still here?"

"Partly vanity," Lisa said. "Partly because of what happened five days ago. A ship arrived. It is currently anchored at the absurdly named Dumbo Pier, which lies in the shadow of the Brooklyn Bridge. The newcomers keep to themselves, but the rumour is they come from a bunker in Pennsylvania called Raven Rock. But that was my previous stop before coming here. It is only full of the undead."

"Could they be the people who shot at us?" Clyde asked.

"That is one possibility," Lisa said. "The other is that you were shot at by scavengers afraid of being caught. Pruitt has issued a ban on scavenging on Manhattan as she wishes all efforts to be focused on clearing Long Island. However, when I saw you, and your uniforms, I initially assumed you were these newcomers. Rufus, fortunately, realised otherwise. A rogue scavenger wishing to avoid detection would be foolish indeed to attack these new arrivals."

"Hostile," Clyde said. "Human. One shooter. Opposite. Two buildings down. No, he's gone. Whoever they are, it looks like they're hunting for us. Darkness is coming, Boss. We need to move while we can."

"Wherever you intend to go, may I suggest you use the subway?" Lisa said. "Day or night makes no difference down there."

"Aren't there zoms down there?" Olivia asked.

"Aren't there gators?" Zach asked.

"Yes to zombies, no to alligators," Lisa said. "But it is far safer than the surface streets."

"Can the subway get us to the other side of Manhattan?" Tess asked.

"Some areas are flooded, others are blocked, but there should be a way through," Lisa said.

"How's that radio, Corrie?" Tess asked.

"I just need another minute," Corrie said.

"We'll call the ship, and tell them to send the other boat to pick us up at the other end of the island," Tess said.

"What about the people on Long Island?" Zach asked.

"We're going back to the Pacific and we'll return with an army, doctors, and food," Tess said. "We've done everything Canberra wanted, and more. Now we've a duty to return, and to report, even if we didn't find what we were looking for."

"What was that?" Lisa asked.

"The records from the initial outbreak," Avalon said.

"In the U.N. hospital?" Lisa asked.

"You know of the place?" Avalon asked.

"I went there," Lisa said. "It was my first port of call, and the reason I came to New York. Like you, I found the hospital empty, because it was also Pruitt's first port of call. When she arrived, she collected the hard drives. The food is guarded. The ammunition is guarded. The fuel is watched from a safe distance. But the hard drives were just dumped with the paintings and artefacts rescued from museums. I broke in at night, climbed up the residential elevator shaft, located her treasure room, and made myself a copy of all I could find."

"You have a copy?" Avalon asked.

"The *only* copy," Lisa said. "I used a magnet to wipe everything before leaving her lair. If Pruitt realised, no mention has reached the survivors at large."

"I need those files," Avalon said.

"Why?" Lisa asked.

"I imagine for the same reason you made a copy *before* destroying them," Avalon said.

"I doubt it," Lisa said. "I made my copy out of habit. I wanted a bargaining chip. For what, and against whom, I didn't know then and don't know now. It was not to *use* the data."

"We need it to make a weapon," Leo said.

"A biological weapon targeting the undead?" Lisa asked. "That is my very worst fear."

"Mine, too," Leo said. "There are a hundred million survivors in the Pacific. There's a government. There are politicians. One of those politicians pretty much promised the people that a weapon would be developed. That's why Flo and I are here. We didn't want to make a weapon. We hoped it wouldn't be necessary. Before the internet went dark, footage was uploaded which we thought showed someone being infected, turning, and then the zombie just dying. We were wrong. That zom wasn't dead, and nearly took a chunk out of Flo an hour ago. While we still suspect the undead *are* dying, we have no proof. Without proof, when we return to Australia, the politicians will demand we work on a weapon. If not us, someone else. Someone worse."

"You need the data because giving it to you is the least worst option for humanity?" Lisa asked. "There was a time I thought I occupied that place on this marble. I was wrong, but my time is done. I know of your work, so perhaps you are correct. I'll give you the data, but it won't help. The virus wasn't made here. When it was clear that this outbreak was out of control, the cabal of politicians sponsoring this project decided to help it spread further, and so use the chaos to gain power. They failed. But so did I. Perhaps you will have better luck if I pass you the baton. I keep the files in the subway. It's where Rufus and I have been living. We can collect it as you leave."

"As *we* leave. You're coming with us," Tess said.

"Am I under arrest?" Lisa asked.

"The world doesn't need that particular trial," Tess said. "But we need a longer talk than we've time for here."

"There is still the matter of Long Island," Lisa said. "The community here is on the brink of collapse. How long will it take to bring a rescue fleet to New York?"

"Two months, minimum," Tess said.

"They do not have that long," Lisa said. "These newcomers are lying when they say there is safety in Raven Rock. Or perhaps it is Pruitt who is lying, in the hope the lie will hold long enough for her to flee aboard that ship. False hope in a rescue which won't come, or in a refuge which isn't there, will only hasten this group's collapse. Killing Pruitt to stop her from leaving would, obviously, be counterproductive, but I can warn Commander Dewhurst. I can inform him who Pruitt is, and warn him there is no safety in Raven Rock. May I suggest a compromise? I *will* come with you to the Pacific, and I *will* give you the data from the hospital, but I will need eighteen hours to warn Dewhurst."

"Clyde, what do you think?" Tess asked.

"That it looks clear out there," the soldier said. "Now's the time to move."

Chapter 19 - Fighting Retreat
Manhattan, New York

"Everyone ditch your extra weight," Clyde said. "Anything we carry out of this building, we're taking all the way to the boat. We're not leaving a trail for the enemy to follow. Boss, if you can watch the front, I'll scope a rear exit. We'll move in three minutes."

"I can't believe I got you back," Olivia said, bending down to give Rufus a hug. "First Pete, now you. It's fate."

"Fate comes in weird shapes," Pete said. "Because I was just thinking the same thing about Kempton and the cartel."

The cartel *hadn't* been destroyed. That was more of a shock than literally running into Lisa, especially since she, and the two scientists, had wanted the same data from that first outbreak. It wasn't that much of a surprise the cartel was here, either. Some of them, anyway. They'd been in Canada and Australia, Minnesota, West Virginia, and Corn Island. They were a global plague before the real outbreak began, infesting every corner of the globe, but especially those places with wealth and power.

"Let's move," Clyde said. "Ms Kempton, you're with me. Pete, Olivia, take the rear, and load breaching rounds in the shotguns. If we take fire, we'll take cover in the nearest building, find the rear exit, and be long gone before the sniper can change position."

"What do we do if we get separated?" Zach asked.

"We won't," Clyde said. "We stick together, in a pack. Everyone take a breath, And in not much longer than that, this will all be over. Let's move out."

He led them through a corridor reeking with sweet-smelling damp, and to a fire exit at the side of the building. A neat stack of un-mortared cinderblocks, fresh from a construction site, were ready to barricade that exterior door, speaking of the desperation of the survivors living here after the city had been quarantined. The door led to an alley wide enough to be called a road, which had proved too narrow to be called a bus-lane for the single-decker lodged between the buildings, though it had a ladder placed against the cab.

Almost covering the windscreen was a strip of sheet metal. As Pete waited for his turn to climb the ladder to the roof, he bent low and peered inside the bus. He saw crates and bags, boxes and tools. Was it someone's stash? Or had the supplies been abandoned after the bus had been turned into a barrier?

"Can you get up there, Rufus?" Olivia asked. "Clearly yes. You next, Pete."

Leaving the mystery frustratingly unanswered, he climbed up to the roof. At the other end of the bus was another ladder, secured in place with a tight coil of wire. Had the ladders had been placed there by Lisa, or could other survivors still lurk among Manhattan's ruins? But Lisa was too far ahead to ask, already at the end of the alley with Clyde and Tess, planning the next leg of their escape.

He clambered down, and raised his arms for Rufus, getting splashed with muddy rain as the dog jumped and nearly knocked him over.

"You've been eating well, then?" Pete said, brushing himself down.

Rain had been falling infrequently all day. The tactical helmet, and encircling danger, had made it an ignorable irritant since they'd come ashore, but the rain was now growing into a storm. At the alley's end, the rain pattered into a slow-moving river, covering the road, flowing south towards a stagnant swamp at the next intersection.

"Be careful of rapids," Lisa said. "They usually betray the presence of a sinkhole. Rufus, show us the way."

Rufus gave a resigned growl and bounded through the shallows. The rain began pattering harder as they followed Rufus. They zigged and they zagged before the dog settled into a straight-line dash along the left-hand side of the road.

Pete watched the ripples. He watched the stalled cars. He listened for movement, and jumped when a car window shattered.

"Take cover!" Clyde called.

Pete ducked around the car, uncertain where the bullet had come from. Then came a machine-gun roar of a fully automatic rifle discharging an entire magazine. The shallow rainwater river became a wall of spray as bullets impacted and ricocheted. Tess ran out into the street. Clyde stood and fired three-shot bursts upwards at the towering skyscrapers.

Tess bent down to pick up Zach. Pete hadn't even realised the young man had been shot. Tess began dragging Zach back towards the line of cars. Avalon dashed from cover, meeting her halfway as Leo joined Clyde firing back and up. Pete raised his shotgun, looking for a target, but only saw windows. Thousands, stretching up to the cloud-filled sky, any one of which might conceal the hidden shooter.

"On me!" Clyde called, from three cars ahead. "Two shooters, got one," the soldier added, as Pete and Olivia reached him. "Assume more. Watch the road."

"Can you hear me, Zach?" Avalon asked. She and Tess had positioned him just in front of a stalled taxi.

"No worries," Zach said. "It hit my vest. Ow, gerrof!" he added as Avalon pulled him forward, roughly examining his back.

"Don't squirm," Avalon said. "Leo, hold him still."

"What are you doing?" Zach asked.

"You've been shot. You're bleeding. Antiseptic," she added, speaking to Leo. "The bullet was deflected by your armour, but it's lodged beneath the muscle. The good news is you'll regain full movement of the arm once we remove the bullet. This will require us getting back onto the ship."

"How far are we from the subway?" Tess asked.

"Two hundred metres," Lisa said.

"Pete, Olivia, you take the lead with Kempton," Tess said. "Clyde and Corrie, cover us. Up you get, mate," she added, helping Zach back to his feet. "Time to get you home."

Their race through the street became more urgent, but it also became slower as they splashed, then waded, through the increasingly flooded streets.

"Zoms ahead," Olivia said, swinging her shotgun towards the trio fighting each other to escape a restaurant's rear door.

Kempton slipped a hand into her coat, drawing a suppressed handgun, firing even as they ran. "Mr Guinn, watch the doorway," she said, as they reached it.

Pete levelled his shotgun, aiming the barrel into the pitch-dark void beyond the door. Somewhere amid the darkness, metal clattered and banged.

"On you go, mate," Clyde said, reaching him. "We've got zoms on our six, but I think we've lost the shooter. It's a straight race for the finish line, so take the baton and lead the way."

Pete ran to catch up with Olivia, as Lisa led them on. The water level dropped from knee to calf to ankle, becoming a waterfall down the steep steps to the subway station. A gate sealed the entrance, but it wasn't locked.

Once they were inside, Clyde pulled the gate closed. "Keep moving down to the platform," he said. "Wait for me there."

"How are you doing, Zach?" Pete whispered, having swapped with Tess as they moved into the dank cave which had once been the subway's ticket concourse.

"Yeah, fine," Zach said, his voice low, but weak rather than a whisper. "Did we miss the Empire State Building?"

"I guess so," Pete said.

They clunked down the motionless escalator. The steps grew increasingly dry, as the waterfall river had found an easier path to the lower depths. At the bottom of the escalator were dumped bags, more bodies, and a rustle of movement as something scampered away.

"Where are we?" Tess asked.

"Twenty-third Street and Park Avenue," Lisa said.

"That doesn't mean much to me," Tess said. "Where's that in relation to the shore?"

"The shortest distance west is one and a half kilometres," Avalon said. "But that's if we travel above ground. Following the tracks, we'll have to go south to Union Square, pick up the L to go west, and still have to trek above ground to get to the waterfront."

"If you know the route, you don't need me," Lisa said. "I will pick up the data gathered from the hospital outbreak, then travel on to Long Island. You can collect me there, tomorrow at dusk. This will give me time to warn Commander Dewhurst as to Pruitt's identity, and to Raven Rock's fate."

"I can't promise we'll be able to make that rendezvous," Tess said.

"And if I miss it, what have you lost?" Lisa said. "Do I have your permission to make the attempt?"

"You're actually asking?" Tess said.

"We need that data," Avalon said, once again bending over Zach.

"Then go," Tess said.

"I have become well used to managing on my own, but the assistance of another would guarantee your receipt of the data you want," Lisa said.

"You need help?" Tess asked. "Fine. I'll join you."

"While there are so many survivors on Long Island that many are strangers to each other, your accent would make you stand out."

"I'll go," Corrie said.

"Us, too, then," Olivia said. "Family sticks together. But you take Rufus with you. Rufus, watch Zach."

Tess nodded. "Okay. We'll pick you up tomorrow at dusk on Long Island. But where?"

"Coney Island," Lisa said. "There is a pier jutting into the Atlantic. We'll shine a light after dark to guide your boat in."

"If we're not there, if we've had to move, get down to Thunderbolt," Tess said. "We'll wait there for one week from today, if we can. You guys sure you want to do this? You know this could be a one-way mission?"

"We kinda have to," Pete said.

"That truly is the spirit, isn't it?" Lisa said.

Chapter 20 - Too Late to Turn Back
East Manhattan

"Are you wishing I didn't volunteer us?" Olivia asked as they trudged through the subway tunnel, heading away from Tess, from Zach, and from Rufus.

"You're reading my thoughts," Pete said. "But no, it's right we go. It's right *I* go. I mean, I started all of this, didn't I?"

"If I may offer a correction, Mr Guinn?" Lisa said. "A sociopath using power to mask engrained inadequacy *began* this. I brought you into it. There is, however, little danger. I don't intend we should fight. And I *do* intend you catch that ship."

"And do *you* intend to come back to the Pacific with us?" Corrie asked.

Lisa didn't reply.

Despite the nearly solid stench of damp, the tracks here were dry. The air felt cold and smelled stale. Ahead, and behind, they heard scurrying. The rats were evolving, learning anything on two legs was now more likely to attack than scream.

Though it was an exhaustingly long trek, it didn't take them long before Lisa pointed ahead to a platform. "This is us," she said. "One more set of stairs, one corridor, and we'll have time for a proper reunion. Wait." She aimed her light low, onto two parallel wires running across the stairwell leading from the platform.

"Is that a bomb?" Corrie asked.

"Just a guide-wire to show whether any undead have been up or down these stairs since I was last here," Lisa said.

The final climb sapped the last of Pete's strength, and so he was more than glad when they reached the station's security office.

"Welcome to my latest home," Lisa said, opening the door. Inside, she switched on a lantern. "Bolt the door, please."

She carried the lantern over to the far wall, and pulled the breaker-lever atop a freestanding battery pack. No other lights came on, but six laptops did, each placed in front of the security office's original monitors. In front of those laptops was a chair, next to which were a nest of blankets, and a bowl.

"This is where you and Rufus have been living?" Olivia asked.

"While it lacks the view I had from my apartment's balcony, it has the benefit of less traffic noise," Lisa said. "Truthfully, I rarely used my penthouse. I preferred living aboard Tamika's ship. When that wasn't an option, I had my mansion on the Delmarva Peninsula. In recent years, I spent more time in hotel rooms than anywhere I would choose to call home. But a Manhattan address was *de rigueur* for my public persona."

"Are these laptops broken?" Corrie asked, taking the chair in front of the screens.

"Dark, not broken," Lisa said. "I repurposed some home security cameras, but there is little to see in an underground tunnel at night when there are no lights. The cameras have a light-and-motion sensor. If they activate, we know we have company. Whether we can see that company or not will indicate whether it is of the undead variety."

"Are there many still on Manhattan?" Corrie asked.

"Zombies? Yes."

"What about survivors?" Pete asked.

"A few, I believe, but they do not wish for company. Nor would they invite it by attacking a group such as yours which they would surely assume came from Long Island. Pruitt has issued a moratorium on scavenging from Manhattan as looting is synonymous with killing the undead, and she wants that effort focused nearer to home. While there are rowing boats on Long Island, there are few larger craft and a shortage of fuel. That is why I suspect those who shot at you are more likely to be these newcomers than from among Pruitt's group. More likely, but not certain."

"What do you know about these boat-people?" Olivia asked.

"I have counted sixteen on their crew," Lisa said. "Nine male, seven female. All with police badges and military uniforms. Their vessel is a civilian twin-mast sailing ship, though they arrived under power of their diesel engine. They do have a small motor launch, which is another reason to suspect them to be the ambushers. Their ship is docked at the Dumbo Pier on the Long Island side of the Brooklyn Bridge. They keep sentries atop the bridge, and on the access roads to the pier. With so many guards, I thought they had too few to send any out on a hunt, which begs the question, if it was them who shot at you, why was their first instinct to open fire?"

"I'm guessing that's a rhetorical question," Olivia said.

"Indeed," Lisa said. "While they claim to have come from Raven Rock, I am certain they did not. Why they made such a claim is less important than what that lie allows them to do. They can leave, saying they intend to return to their base, taking supplies with them. It is no great leap to assume that they are, or were, being pursued. By whom and why is a question Dewhurst might be able to answer."

"Do you have a boat?" Olivia asked.

"For crossing the river?" Lisa asked. "No, I use the tunnels. They are far safer than you might suppose as an attack can only come from ahead or behind, and rarely from above or below. There is a station near the pier, but I see little purpose in making a direct approach, at least initially, since it will be difficult to trust anything these newcomers say. Commander Dewhurst ran an emergency response unit for the city prior to the outbreak. He is a good man. Honest, but lacking in charisma and inexperienced in long-term planning. When Pruitt arrived, he saw her, an elected official, as being the rightful authority and handed over control."

"And you said the other group is basically convicts?" Olivia asked.

"From Rikers Island, yes," Lisa said. "Soon after the outbreak, they established a new hierarchy, and eliminated the more erratically unreliable and universally undesirable elements. Pruitt won them over through negotiation. It is unclear what she offered, though seeing how the combined community is relatively stable, and relatively peaceful, I would guess she won control due to cautious self-preservation. The prison leaders understood how close they were to death, how old routes to power were gone, and how money was worthless. Survival was everything, and it could not be done alone."

"Can I just be clear on something?" Olivia asked. "We're going to speak with Dewhurst, yes? We're not killing him?"

"I intend him no harm," Lisa said. "Dewhurst is the only viable successor to Pruitt, though nor do I intend any harm to her. No, at two-thirty a.m., we will leave here, traverse the tunnels, and should arrive at the Atlantic Avenue Subway Station at four-thirty. We will wait in the tunnels until five minutes to five, then make our way up to the market where we will barter for breakfast, and for shower tokens, and then linger. Commander Dewhurst is a man of routine. He collects breakfast at the same stall every morning at a quarter past five, takes it to his office, then opens the shower block at a quarter to six. We shall walk with him from the market stall to his office. There, we will put a gun in his face, and march him to the pump room just beyond. We will ask our questions, and give him some answers, tie him up, and then make our way down to the tunnels. We'll leave our long arms down there, and collect them before heading south, having told Dewhurst we are going to Manhattan."

"That's it?" Olivia asked. "It's not very complicated."

"Complicated is what I've been doing for the past five days, and it's got me nothing but blisters," Lisa said.

"What if he doesn't talk?" Olivia said.

"He only has to listen," Lisa said. "I shall tell him who I am, and who Pruitt is, and who these newcomers are. And when he says he doesn't believe me, I shall show him proof." She patted her pocket. "I shall show him video of Raven Rock. It was a mountain fastness in Pennsylvania, a bunker designated as a control centre for the entire northeast. That was my stop before this."

"You can't sail a ship to New York from the mountains," Corrie said.

"Indeed, the deluge has not yet been that complete," Lisa said.

"No, I mean they could be telling the truth," Corrie said. "They could have set off weeks ago, and spent another week looking for a ship."

"That is one scenario, yes," Lisa said. "It is about two weeks since I was there, and no one had been alive there for weeks before that. Yes, it is *possible* that these people were stationed there at the beginning of the outbreak. After a long and roundabout journey, they believe there are survivors there still. However, it is unimportant. All that matters is that we do all we can to prevent this community's collapse. Once Dewhurst knows the truth, what he does will depend upon what Pruitt has told him. As to what *that* is, we shall find out in a few hours. However, we will need some trade goods."

"Do you mean like bullets?" Pete asked.

"That would generate too much interest. Long Island is already low on ammo. All rounds are supposed to be handed in to the authorities, and are only issued to their sentries. Medical supplies or batteries would work best. Food works better, but it is getting harder to locate. To the New Yorkers, I am Eliza Keynes, a former travel agent, who become a mortician's assistant. The work was mostly administrative, though I did assist in clearing the homes of those who died without heirs. I also helped with the at-home clean-up of those whose bodies were not discovered for some time. Subsequently, Eliza has a natural talent for finding her way around the homes of the dead. If you will give me an hour, I will see what I can gather."

"I've got lots of these oat bars," Corrie said, opening her bag. "They came from Oz, and were our emergency stash if we ended up stranded here."

"Perfect. We will say we found them in the home of an Australian celebrity, the location of which we will not divulge as this represents only a fraction of the stores we found there. That will give us reason to linger in the market while we wait for Dewhurst. If something goes wrong, we'll improvise, which is why I asked the ship to collect us at dusk rather than midday."

"Pete, what do you think?" Olivia asked.

"That we should have talked this through before we split with Tess," he said. "We'll tell Dewhurst who Pruitt is, but what if he decides to arrest her, and that starts a civil war?"

"That is why we will tell him in private and leave immediately afterwards," Lisa said. "Our presence, and mine in particular, would only bring greater agitation. They would not accept me as dictator, nor would they accept your commissioner. I suspect your commissioner wouldn't accept me as dictator here, either. They trust Dewhurst. If, as I suspect, Long Island is on the verge of collapse, there is no one else who can lead them towards safety, and there is nothing we can do to help them reach it other than provide them with the best information we have. You, however, *will* have to reach Coney Island." She walked over to a locker marked with a first-aid kit. She picked up a small purse and handed it to Corrie. "This is the data on the Manhattan outbreak I collected from Pruitt."

Corrie unzipped the coin-purse. "One thumb-drive? That's all?"

"I had time to collate it," Lisa said. "It contains video of the event, stills of those present before they were infected or fled, and the raw data."

"I bet Doc Flo is expecting more," Corrie said.

"I told her she would be disappointed," Lisa said.

16th April

Chapter 21 - Dressed for Shopping
Long Island

Pete slept deep, and woke to the glorious scent of coffee gently bubbling atop a camping stove.

"Honestly, Lisa, I'm kinda disappointed," Olivia said as she sorted through the suitcases. "Despite all those designer stores upstairs, these clothes are distinctly practical."

"I didn't pack the bags myself," Lisa said. "I found them on the platform. My theory is that they belonged to a group of survivors who lived in one of the buildings above, but decided to flee through the tunnels after the bridges were blown. There is evidence to suggest the bags were abandoned after their owners were attacked by the infected. What they left behind provided an easy supply of trade goods when I crossed the river. The green bag contains some packs of pressed dates and some crackers. Vitamin supplements are in the camera case."

"You've been living on dates, crackers, and coffee?" Olivia asked.

"And vitamin tablets," Lisa said. "My diet has barely changed. I will sometimes take a meal on Long Island, though only when I'm certain of the ingredients. If you'll excuse me, I will change into my costume."

"Since Lisa's got a cover-identity, I thought we should have one, too," Olivia said. She held up two near-matching red plaid shirts. "We'll be Mr and Mrs Guinn, two carpet sellers from the Midwest who've spent the last couple of months doing their best to stay alive. Jeans, and a plaid shirt for us both, and you can keep your boots. I've found a couple of jackets that'll keep us dry in anything other than a hurricane, and they'll hide our handguns."

"Nice jeans," Pete said as they changed in the relative privacy of the adjoining locker-room. Where his trousers were straight cut, hers were straight from a bedazzled nightmare.

"They were the only pair that fit," Olivia said. "You know, I think these might actually be diamonds. That's what I'm going to pretend, anyway. Turn around. Let me see your holster. No, it's hidden. Cool."

"After this, no more volunteering," he said.

"After this, Australia," she said. "There was something I read once. It must have been by Mark Twain, because most things are. The world is full of big people who have big adventures and little people lucky enough to lead little lives. But beware when the little people tire of being dragged into the big people's war. For us, the social order was upended by the apocalypse, not a revolution. Leo and Doc Flo, Tess and Colonel Hawker are the big people now, maybe even Clyde and Zach. It's not Lisa and the cartel. Not anymore. It's a brand-new day, Pete, even if it is absurdly early. Shall we?"

Corrie had opted for the near camouflage of grey utility clothes that had been someone's work gear, and probably not someone who lived in the mansion-apartments upstairs. Lisa had changed into a long skirt and longer coat. She collected a blue canvas bag from the locker and slung it over her shoulder. "My worldly possessions," she said, before pulling on a large-brimmed hat and picking up a four-foot-long cane with metal reinforcements at both ends. "But there is a pleasing symmetry in leaving New York with as little as that with which I arrived."

"You came here with Rufus," Olivia said.

Kempton pulled the breaker-lever, then switched on her flashlight. "I was referring to when I first arrived in New York. This way." She led them outside, and to the steps leading down to the platform.

"A bank balance counts as a worldly possession," Olivia said. "I read your bio when you bought out Mrs Mathers. You were born in Kolkata, were adopted by aid workers who died in a plane crash in the Himalayas. You went to an orphanage in Switzerland, and—"

"A lie," Kempton interrupted. "A useful lie, but a fabrication nonetheless. I was a runaway, and it was one of the best decisions of my life. At fourteen, I ran here. I lived here, in the subway. Ironically, it was one of the safest parts of the city for a young girl who didn't want to live on anything but her wits. This was…" She sighed. "We shall just say it was some time ago. We follow the tracks to the right," she added.

"Hold up a minute," Corrie said, sweeping her light up and down the tunnel. "No, we're clear."

"You really lived down here in the subway?" Olivia asked, as the quartet began trudging along the tunnel.

"Perhaps it would be more truthful to say I spent a lot of time *lurking* down here," Lisa said. "Not in tunnels used by the trains, but there is a honeycomb-maze beneath Manhattan. New York is mostly built on old ruins, sealed up and forgotten until a new cable, or new pipe, needs to be installed. I learned the engineer's codes which act as signposts, and which allowed me to navigate Manhattan without straying up to the surface. I hid down here. I escaped *to* here. I slept down here and learned that, in a world without sunlight, there is no such thing as day and night. But I spent time above ground, and increasingly in computer cafes. The early days of the internet were a fascinating time. Users were so much more trusting, and security was so much more lax. All those cables, hastily run below ground, all so easily accessible, so easily hacked. That is how I went from being a runaway to a millionaire who needed a new identity."

"You stole money?"

"Technically, I stole information," Lisa said. "Specifically, corporate data on expected mergers. I was somewhat limited in what information I could access but my primary resource was a group of overly gossipy lawyers who dealt with hostile acquisitions. Shh."

Ahead, hidden beyond the gentle curve of the track, a foot stumbled across a rail while an arm thumped into the tunnel wall.

"Mine," Corrie said, aiming handgun and flashlight ahead. The creature's skin was ashen in the harsh electric light, there and gone in a second as Corrie fired. "Wait," she added. They all listened. "Clear."

"So you played the stock market?" Olivia asked, as they continued following the rails.

"No, I sold tips," Lisa said. "I pretended to be the go-between for a lawyer who was a terrible gambler, but had an expensive habit. I made ten million before I turned sixteen."

"Ten?" Olivia said.

"Sixteen?" Pete said.

"I was reckless, and lucky," Lisa said. "The collapse of a Ponzi scheme covered most of my tracks. Bribes and a fire did the rest. I bought a new identity, and invested in secure data centres, and secure data transmission. I made sure that no one could hack *my* clients' data."

"No one but you," Olivia said.

"Precisely. It was an unfortunate, but inevitable, consequence that I should attract a less than scrupulous clientele. Thus, it was equally inevitable that, in time, I learned something which forced me to act. Be careful what you wish for, because I wished to know what was really going on in the world. When my wish was granted, what else could I do but devote the rest of my life to pursuing that knowledge to the very end?"

"Zom," Corrie said. "Behind us. We better pick up our pace."

They hurried through the tunnels in silence, ears pricked for the sound of approaching pursuit, eyes scouting ahead for moving shadows, but Pete's brain was replaying what Lisa had said. He didn't believe her any more than he'd ever believed the puff-piece biography. He got the sense she was reinventing her past once more, one last time, to better suit the ending.

As the tunnel reached the river, they reached the flood. Water lapped at their boots, then rose an inch with every metre walked, forcing them to crab-crawl along a narrow lip at the tunnel's edge. The water rose further, frothing grey, pocked with iridescent bubbles that released an eye-stinging vapour as they burst. He began sweating, and not just from exertion, while his clothes were additionally drenched by the putrescent slime exuded from the tunnel roof.

"It's getting worse," Lisa said, when they reached a damp, but relatively dry section of track. "New York is sinking so much more quickly than I expected, and yet not more quickly than we were warned."

"It won't sink for a few hours yet," Corrie said. "Good thing we're not coming back this way."

"I know you said Long Island was on the verge of collapse," Olivia said. "I didn't think you were being literal."

"It is not the most immediate problem," Lisa said. "Only one of many, and it is because there are many problems that the fate of New York, and her inhabitants, is inevitable."

The curve of the tunnel forced them to walk single file. The placement of the rails and sleepers, and occasionally flooded sections, forced them to walk unnaturally slow. Time lost all meaning. So did distance. Only when they came to a station's platform did they get a clue as to how much further they had to go. But when they next heard footsteps, it came with the reflection of a light, and the echo of a voice.

Chapter 22 - The Terminal Market
The Atlantic Terminal Mall, Long Island

As the voices grew nearer, Kempton led them into a conduit-tunnel bursting with forgotten wires and damp pipes. Outside, the voices began to fade.

"We're safe," Lisa whispered. "Leave the long arms here."

"What about the axe?" Pete asked.

"Blades are expected, but a shotgun would bring questions and we are the ones seeking answers. This way."

Near the end of a tunnel, they squeezed through a metal door with a twisted frame and into a cracked-tile corridor forgotten for at least half a century, judging by the antiquity of the plastic food wrappers littering the floor. After two more rat-ridden corridors, and one forgotten staircase, they stepped into an equally dirty service corridor. One last door led them out onto a narrow staircase.

"I told you it would be easy," Lisa said, as she pushed the door closed. "We're in the Atlantic Terminal Mall. Our first stop is breakfast, and we'll find that upstairs. Ah, wait."

Bickering voices rose in volume as feet descended down the narrow stairs towards them.

"Don't tell me you're taking a day off, Jilly?" Lisa called up before the people had appeared.

"Is that you, Eliza?" came the reply, echoing around the corner, and was followed by a woman wrapped in enough layers for the Arctic, accompanied by a man half her age, and who carried a rifle. "I missed you yesterday."

"I was nearly trapped by the infected up by Prospect Park," Lisa said. "Didn't get back until late. You know what they say: slow and steady keeps us safe. You remember Corrie? We're combining forces."

"There's safety in numbers," Jilly said, giving a smile of assumed recognition to Corrie.

"Come on, Mom, I've got to be on patrol in two hours," the younger man said.

"You're busy? I won't keep you long," Lisa said. "We've stumbled across some treasure. It's quite a haul. I thought we could discuss a deal."

"Show me this afternoon," Jilly said. "We're running late and Jim is waiting for us."

As mother and son headed down the stairs, Lisa sighed.

"Problem?" Corrie asked.

"Not necessarily," Lisa said. "The Jim she referred to is Commander Dewhurst. She and he have been dating. More pertinently, it sounds as if his routine may finally have been disrupted. No matter, he gets his breakfast from Mustafa, so he is our next port of call. Come."

On the first floor of the mall, the exterior windows of a denim store were reinforced with the signage from a dozen fast-food franchises. A coffee-kiosk filled where the doors should be, with more salvaged signs blocking the view of inside. Currently, that kiosk was empty, at least of people. A cat dozed on the out-jutting lip of a *Cleopatra Coffee* sign. From behind the stall came the smell of frying meat.

"That can't be bacon," Pete said.

"No, it can't," Lisa said. "I advise against asking questions before accepting any food."

On the counter was a radio-frequency doorbell. Kempton pressed it. A distant dong sounded. The cat leaped down and darted behind a trio of delivery-cages filled with water barrels.

The door at the back of the coffee shed was opened by a tired man who was trying to hide his age. His thinning hair had been inexpertly dyed leaving a blotchy stain on his balding scalp. His white shirt was brand-new and still bore the crease-marks from the packet, while his high-end suit had been tailored for a man with longer arms and a smaller chest.

"Good morning, Mustafa," Lisa said.

"Mrs Keynes, it is always a good morning when it begins with you. Where's your dog?" he asked.

"With the rest of my team," she said. "We've found a very interesting stash."

"These are your people?" Mustafa asked, taking in the trio. "I wondered when we might see you here."

"Oh, you must remember Corrie," Lisa said. "And I know you remember Pete."

"Ah, that is a very impressive axe," Mustafa said. "How much do you want for it, or will you trade some gossip?"

"That would depend on the gossip," Lisa said.

"Hang on, it's *my* axe," Pete said.

"I've heard something good about those people from Raven Rock," Mustafa said.

"The newcomers from the boat?" Lisa asked. "What did you hear?

"Give me the axe, and I'll tell you," Mustafa said.

"We're here to sell something far more valuable," Lisa said. She pulled one of the Australian oat bars from her bag. "We can bring you five thousand of these."

"Five thousand?" Mustafa asked, taking the bar. "Looks artisan. Only a dollar a bar? That's under-priced." He opened the door behind him, tore the packaging, and dropped pieces onto the floor. A squad of cats emerged from beneath one of the laden tables, and came to investigate the crumbs.

"Ah, I see we have achieved the whisker-lick of approval," Lisa said. "I'll take fifty percent of the sale price."

"Ha! Be serious."

"We've sufficient quantity to open a store of our own," Lisa said.

"And if you were serious about that, you'd have done it already," he said. "Five percent."

"Now *you're* not being serious," Lisa said. "Forty percent, and a twenty-percent discount for a month."

"And watch you get fat while I starve?" he asked. "I'll give you ten percent. Nothing more."

"Twenty-five," Lisa said.

"Twenty," he said.

Lisa made a show of debating the deal. "Twenty, *and* the gossip." She opened the bag, dumping the contents on the counter. "I'll give you this as a down payment."

"And as a sign of good faith," Mustafa said, "I'll give you each a ticket for the showers, for breakfast, and for the recharge-station."

"Deal," Lisa said.

Mustafa swept the oat bars into a cardboard box, taking them with him through the door at the rear of the cabin before returning with a stack of rectangular wooden squares. Each was hand carved and half the size of a slim paperback. He handed over four with a duck in a bath, four with a duck holding a knife and fork, and one where a duck was holding a phone.

"What's the gossip?" Lisa asked.

"The ship's captain served with General Yoon up in Canada," Mustafa said, then misread Olivia's surprise as confusion. "You haven't heard of General Yoon? She led an army being supplied from the Pacific. They brought in mining machines from Australia to use as tanks."

"Oh, that can't be true," Lisa said.

"The ship's captain served with her," Mustafa said.

"Does that mean this general is in Raven Rock?" Lisa asked.

"That I don't know," Mustafa said. "But that's where the sailors came from. They are Canadians and Americans, and some Australians who were driving the earth-moving machines, or so I heard."

"And from whom did you hear all of this?" Lisa asked. "Was it our illustrious commander?"

"I never reveal my sources," Mustafa said. "But I *do* hear we'll be getting a lot more customers very soon."

"Oh, come, you must share a little more than that," Lisa said, clearly trying to drag out the conversation.

The sound of footsteps made Pete turn. It was the young guard who'd been on the stairs with his mother.

"Solomon!" Mustafa said.

"Hey," he said, and gave a nod to Kempton. "Good morning again, Mrs Keynes. The commander wants me to pick up his breakfast. And his lunch."

"He is breaking with his routine?" Mustafa asked. "Ha! I told you good things are coming, Mrs Keynes."

"They are indeed," Lisa said. She nodded her goodbyes, and led the team away.

"He was using cats as food-testers," Olivia said, when they were beyond earshot.

"I have a related question about what he was cooking," Corrie said.

"Through here," Lisa said, indicating a corridor ending in a small service door. "We'll take the long route around, and cross via the roof."

"General Yoon can't be in Raven Rock," Pete said.

"And we were the closest thing to Australians serving in her army," Corrie added. "But it was a big army."

"You believe him?" Pete asked.

"It depends on how much the rumour got twisted between the ship and that man's mouth," Corrie said. "Some American soldiers could have helicoptered to Pennsylvania after the bombs fell, fled Raven Rock after a couple of days, and spent the last month trying to reach here."

"This rumour neither proves nor disproves anything," Lisa said. "Though if we could ask one of these newcomers ourselves, I expect you could quickly discern if they were lying."

"Is that what we'll try now?" Olivia asked. "Because I'm sensing that didn't go as planned."

"No, we must adapt," Lisa said. She led them up the stairs, and to the roof, which had now become an open-air garden. Metal troughs and plastic trenches had been filled with soil and surrounded by thick sheets of transparent plastic, supported by tent-pole scaffolding. As Lisa led them between the aisles of this skyline garden, Pete noted the obvious thing missing: green shoots.

Lisa led them to the edge of the roof, and to a pair of leaking above-ground pools being used for rainwater storage. "They originally attempted to farm inside the Barclays Center," she said. "There wasn't enough light so they used generators, and burned through most of the fuel. They've begun again here, in the daylight."

"Where are the farmers?" Olivia asked.

"Where are the people?" Corrie asked, stepping back from the edge of the roof. "I can only see a few sentries, but farmers wake with the dawn, and the sun's already up."

"The work day is nine to five," Lisa said. "We are on the roof of the Atlantic Terminal Mall. Immediately to the east is the Atlantic Center. Do you see the two green-painted sheds? Between them is the rooftop walkway. We'll make use of that when we go to the showers, but they won't open for another thirty minutes. In this mall are the traders and some storage. In the other mall is the school, the repair shop, an electricity supply, the showers, and the new clinic."

"Where was the old clinic?" Corrie asked.

"In a care home, one block to the south," Lisa said. "There was an outbreak, two weeks ago. Injured scavengers were infected, but claimed to be immune."

"Don't they have a quarantine?" Pete asked.

"No," Lisa said. "Few people actually live inside this Green Zone. If you look north, that skyscraper is One Hanson Place. That is where the administrators live. Pruitt, too. A few of the traders like Mustafa live in their stores. Everyone else lives beyond the barricades surrounding these few blocks. The children arrive for school at nine. Their parents sometimes take work here, or they go out scavenging. Everyone can claim one meal a day, in the evenings. Parents eat with the children after school. Everyone else eats after that. The clinic is free. Everything else has to be earned. Including the showers."

"That's what these ducks are about?" Pete asked, holding up one of the carved wooden rectangles.

"It's what Ms Sosa could carve. She runs the school. Think of this as a castle, under siege."

"By the zoms?" Corrie asked.

"Under siege by the survivors," Lisa said. "One meal a day, rudimentary plumbing, safety for the children, and an ill-equipped clinic ensure that the gangs don't take over. That is what the scavenging teams have become. It is what many of them were six months ago. Pruitt governs not out of strength but because no one else wants the trouble that goes with leadership. Think of this less as a community than an island of individuals without a raft. The original theory was that people would split into village-sized teams, setting up colonies across the island. They would clear their territory, and then secure the land between themselves and their neighbours. If there had been sufficient ammunition, perhaps it would have worked. Instead, this is place is one disaster away from collapse."

"Which isn't our problem," Olivia said. "We came for Dewhurst."

"He didn't collect his breakfast," Lisa said. "That is the first opportunity lost. Since he sent for his lunch as well, he is operating beyond his usual routine. We can use these tokens to gain access to the shower block, and see if he's in his office. If he's not there, we'll resort to plan-B."

"Is that heading back to the ship?" Olivia asked.

"I honestly don't know," Lisa said. "I only went to Raven Rock because another of the cartel's politicians had taken refuge there. She was dead. Yet here, in New York, we find another corrupt politico, and mention of Raven Rock. It shouldn't be a coincidence, but perhaps it is."

"Let's go see if Dewhurst is in his office," Olivia said. "If he isn't, *then* we can discuss a plan-B."

They followed Lisa over a rickety scaffolding bridge and into the opposite mall. Inside, the decor was noticeably brighter, if not cleaner. Hand-painted signs pointed the way to the showers, the school, and the recharge station. From the faltering letters and bright colours, the signs were the busy-work of children. An early-rise labourer mopped the floor, but did so with eye-stingingly concentrated bleach, suggesting a relative scarcity of water.

They followed the signs to the ground floor, and to the showers. Outside, a stall bore a handwritten sign for soap and towels. It was closed, and so were the doors to the gym, outside of which a modest crowd had gathered: twenty-five adults, and two pairs of children who clung close to their guardians. There was a little morning chatter, but it was still too early for most people to be properly awake.

"Is this normal?" Corrie asked, keeping her voice low as they lingered near the back of the crowd.

"There's fewer than usual," Lisa said. "Ah, the man approaching with Solomon is Dewhurst."

Pete stretched as an excuse to turn his head. Dewhurst was in his late fifties, exhausted, and had a stooping limp, while his ill-fitting FBI body-armour did double duty as a corset.

"Morning, Mrs Keynes. I was hoping to see you here," Dewhurst said, forcing bonhomie through evident exhaustion.

"And I am always glad to see you, Jim," Lisa replied. "I wondered if we could have a word. We've discovered something which will be of most interest to you."

"Sorry, Eliza, it'll have to wait," Dewhurst said. "Listen up, everyone," he added, pitching his voice to the small crowd. "We've got a crisis and an opportunity. By now, I'm sure you all know we've got some guests docked at the river."

"From Canada?" called out a woman in a red NYU hat, a dirty grey leather jacket, and carrying a crossbow on her back.

"From Pennsylvania," Dewhurst said. "From a military bunker at a place called Raven Rock. There are more survivors there. They've got supplies. A *lot* of supplies. We're not alone. Hold your cheering. That's the good news. There's a complication. To get there, we've got to cross a lot of water and a lot of land. Driving is no safer than walking, and you all know how dangerous that can be. Sailing would be safest of all, so we need fuel. Specifically, a thousand gallons of diesel. With that, we can run a ferry across to New Jersey. We'll use gasoline to drive to the Delaware River. We'll take the river to Back Creek, cutting above the Delmarva Peninsula, then we'll sail up the Susquehanna."

"Diesel isn't much use without the ships," the woman in the NYU cap said.

"We've got the ferry for the first leg," Dewhurst said. "Our new friends know where to find ships for the rest. Now, they don't know what state the engines are in, so I don't want people getting their hopes too high. This won't be a quick trip, and it won't be an easy journey, but it'll end with enough supplies to keep us all fed for a decade. You probably heard our diesel supply's been contaminated, so it's down to you. Find us diesel. There are bicycles out front."

"And if we say no thanks?" the woman with the cap asked.

Dewhurst shrugged. "Then you'll still have to go out scavenging today and tomorrow and next month, until there's nothing left to be found. But with a few gallons of diesel we can all reach a government bunker with enough supplies to keep us alive until the zombies are long gone."

"We're in," Lisa said. "Where are these bikes?"

"Follow Detective Demarkos," Dewhurst said. "No kids," he added. "Just the adults."

"Yeah, c'mon, I want to be done before lunch," Demarkos said. Like Dewhurst, she wore jeans and a plaid shirt, but her body-armour was marked *Police*, and around her neck was a badge.

Dewhurst remained by the entrance to the gym, while the young guard, Solomon, fell in at the back of the group.

"I think Dewhurst is staying here," Olivia whispered.

"When the villagers gather outside the castle, better to be the one selling them pitchforks than the person raising the drawbridge," Lisa said. "For now, I believe it's best if we follow the crowd."

Chapter 23 - Burning Pitchforks
Long Island

At the Atlantic Avenue entrance to the mall, the main doors and glass windows had been removed. In their place was a chain link barrier which had been folded back, though a shotgun-carrying guard stood by the gate, presumably ready to close it should an alarm be sounded. Outside, rows of city-bikes were already being claimed by reluctant volunteers. Opposite was Old Man McDonald's Indoor Farm, according to the spray-painted name, though *Barclays Center* was visible beneath. From the laden wheelbarrows left outside, it looked as if they were mostly farming dirt.

"They really tried farming inside there?" Corrie asked. "Why not plant in the parks?"

"Rats," Lisa said. "The fields at Prospect Park were chewed to the roots. It would make more sense to relocate the entire group to somewhere with more grass. The rooftops are the compromise solution."

"People don't want to move?" Corrie asked.

"Moving means leaving the relative safety of this block," Lisa said. "In order to raise a search party to find diesel, Dewhurst has had to conscript early risers who still insist on a morning shower. That should give an indication of how difficult it is to persuade people to work beyond an illusory nine-to-five, let alone move to somewhere new."

They claimed a bicycle each and wheeled them to the back of the small group. There were only twenty, not counting Solomon and Demarkos, though there were enough bikes for four times that number.

"Does anyone want to make this easy and just tell me where we can find this diesel?" Demarkos called out. "No? Figures. Then saddle up, and follow us. We'll take you where you're supposed to search, but all we care about is getting this diesel. The sooner we get it, the sooner that ship can sail. Anyone? No? Typical."

"Where is Dewhurst?" Pete whispered, looking around.

"Recruiting more scavengers," Lisa said. "Inferring from the number of bicycles, we won't be the only search party dispatched today. But forget Dewhurst for now. We'll question Solomon when we stop, then slip away as soon as we can."

As they wheeled their bikes to the Green Zone's new and imposing gates, Pete took in the rest of the unwilling volunteers. Their clothing was mostly high-end, and shop-clean. No one wore body-armour, but zombies didn't shoot. A few had helmets, the kind once worn by stunt-bikers or skateboarders. Most wore gloves. A few had knee and elbow pads. Everyone had weapons: hunting knives, hammers, fire-axes, a samurai sword, crowbars, tyre-irons, baseball bats, and long metal bars. Make-do weapons, carried by conscripts who were paid in food. Was this a proto-dystopian dictatorship, or just a group of survivors, muddling through as best they could?

At the junction with Sixth Avenue, a roller-gate sealed in this quasi-secure Green Zone. A sentry stood guard in the basket of a cherry picker, raised above the gate. Pete looked back and up at the garden rooftops. He'd seen no sentries there, no armed patrols, or even a guard post with soldiers ready to respond to an alarm.

Nor, though, were there any undead outside the gate. There were three empty handcarts, stained black with blood, then bleached grey with disinfectant. The flies didn't seem to mind the chlorine, and rose in a cloud that followed them for a hundred metres as they cycled south.

The detective led from the front, setting the pace, with Solomon gamely keeping up. No one followed at the rear. Demarkos never even looked back, and only stopped when she had to shoot the undead. Twice.

Finally, Demarkos braked, just before a cluster of school buses almost blocking the road. She raised the rifle and fired two shots, then a third. Behind the buses, blocked from view, Pete heard a thump.

"Solomon, go check on Zed," Demarkos said, lowering her weapon, but not turning around.

"Seriously, Leah? Do I have to?" Solomon asked.

"Worst case, he's alive," Demarkos said. "Go on."

"Where are we?" Pete asked.

"The corner of Fourth Avenue and 9th Street," Olivia said, reading from the road sign.

"Yeah, but where's that?" Pete asked.

"I want to know why they didn't barricade this street," Corrie said, her voice low.

"What do you mean?" Pete asked.

"Didn't you see all those alleys and side streets?" Corrie asked, gesturing behind them. "Most of them were sealed."

Pete turned around to look. "Like on Manhattan?"

"More so," Corrie said.

"No luck," Solomon said, coming out. "He's still alive."

"There you have it, people, Zed's not dead." She raised her foot as if to kick off, then changed her mind. "Ah, this'll do. You lot know where it's hidden, so bring back some diesel, and bring it back by lunch. You coming, Solomon?"

Demarkos pushed off, cycling back towards the Green Zone. Wobbling as he struggled to keep up, Solomon followed.

"Do we follow them?" Olivia asked.

"Too many witnesses," Lisa said as the rest of the scavengers, in twos and small groups, peeled off and away.

"Now what?" Pete asked when they were finally alone.

"Hold that thought," Olivia said. "I want to know who this prisoner is."

"It's a zombie," Lisa said. "They keep a zombie chained up in there so as to know when the outbreak is over. When that zombie dies, others might do the same."

"That's sick," Olivia said. "And smart. But still sick. So what went wrong there, Lisa? We're on the wrong side of the fence, without our rifles, and without Dewhurst."

"It's the inevitable consequence of a barter economy," Lisa said. "To avoid devaluing their trade goods, scavengers only bring back the smallest quantity of items to trade for what they immediately need. Not wishing to leave the trading post with excess weight, they exchange the rest for services. Especially a hot shower. Thus, when you need to find a scavenger, the best place to wait is outside the shower block, first thing in the morning."

"That's not really an answer," Corrie said.

"But it is context," Lisa said. "Dewhurst appears to know someone has found diesel. Since it is only purchased by the central authority, the price is fixed. It is thus not worth bringing back to the settlement when other goods could fetch a higher price. Essentially, we scavengers have been told to reveal the location of our fuel stash. Since we didn't do it back at the settlement, we were punished by being brought out this far."

"Do *you* have a diesel stash?" Pete asked.

"No. Nor do I know who does," Lisa said. "Nor, clearly, does Dewhurst, or he wouldn't have bothered bringing us out this far."

"Which will be fun for us to discuss back on the ship with Doc Flo and Leo," Olivia said. "It feels like we've failed, so it's time to cut our losses and head to Coney Island."

"When presented with potential failure, I always find it best to redefine the conditions for success," Lisa said. "I wanted to question Dewhurst, but warning him of Pruitt and Raven Rock is more important. That can still be done by leaving him a message. A video message, along with the video from Raven Rock."

"Then we're cycling back to their base?" Olivia asked.

"Ah, could we make one small detour?" Lisa asked. "While I don't think it will be possible to ask the questions of Dewhurst, we could still go to the source."

"Do you mean the boat at the pier?" Olivia asked. "You want to take one of the boat people hostage?"

"No, we will simply say we have found a large stash of fuel, and offer them the address. That will provide an opportunity to ask two or three questions. The difficulty now is deciding which will produce the most illuminating answers."

Chapter 24 - Archangel
Brooklyn, Long Island

This time, as they cycled through Brooklyn, Pete *did* notice the barricades, the bullet-holes, and the bones. He noticed them even more after they crossed beyond the cleared streets and into the nowhere land behind the improvised walls.

The barricades must have gone up during the early days of the outbreak; the Long Islanders hadn't wanted the same fate as their neighbours on Manhattan. But their attempts at self-salvation had been counter-productive, dooming even more to a brutal death. The barriers across the side roads were more than just a way of keeping the undead away from community block-fortresses, but of funnelling the roaming infected into a murder-zone. When the ammo ran out, those defences had become a prison. When the undead got in, they became a tomb.

Fleeing rats scampered ahead of the undead lumbering out of alleys and crawling from beneath cars. The Family Guinn swerved left and right, but didn't stop. Low-rise bodega-basement towers were replaced with high-rise glass and steel apartment-offices. Aspiring or affluent, the plague didn't care in this city whose streets were paved with bones.

"It's ahead," Lisa said, slowing though not stopping.

"We're here already?" Pete asked, looking back the way they'd come, checking for any of the undead they'd woken during their cycling sprint.

"The pier is just beyond the tank," Lisa said.

The abandoned Abrams MBT was parked on Furman Street, but its cannon was aimed upward at the eastern tower of the Brooklyn Bridge.

"We'll leave the bikes by that fire escape," Lisa whispered. "We'll go upstairs and inside and take advantage of an elevated position to survey our target before we approach."

The fire escape belonged to the recent extension of a brownstone. Just as recent was the new gate and thick concrete wall. More recently still, and possibly when that tank made its way to the waterfront, the wall had been knocked over, and now partially blocked the already narrow one-way Doughty Street.

Broken baseball bats and chair legs lay at the base of the fire escape's metal staircase. There were few bones, though, suggesting they'd not been dropped in battle, but after they'd been proven ineffective weapons against the undead. One of those zombies lay at the top of the stairs, an antique brass candlestick still embedded in an eye socket. The other of that pair of candlesticks lay in the doorway, keeping the fire door ajar.

"Have you been here before?" Corrie whispered, as she pulled the door open. The hinges squeaked louder than her words.

Before Lisa could answer, Olivia tugged on her arm, then Corrie's, then pointed upwards. Quickly, and as quietly as they could, they stepped inside. The smell of burning tobacco drifted down from above.

They were in a dark, dank hallway. When Lisa turned on her light, Pete counted three doors, and a junction at the far end.

"Sentry on the roof," Corrie whispered, as she drew her sidearm. Slowly, she affixed the suppressor. "Might have seen our bikes. Stick close. Coney Island's the rendezvous. Lisa?"

"This way," she said.

The apartment doors, though pulled closed, had all been forced. At this stage, it was impossible to know who had broken in, or how many times the rooms had been searched. It was a near certainty that the ship-borne newcomers had come hunting for clothes. But had they come looking for beds to sleep in?

At each door, Pete listened, but heard nothing, yet someone had kept that fire door propped ajar. At the end of the corridor, Lisa led them left, and to the last apartment. Like the others, the door had been forced. Unlike the others, it was kept open by a slowly decaying zombie. Its head had been split open either by the dumbbell, the hammer, or the foot-long wooden pulley lying among the decaying putrescence of its corpse.

They entered a broad hallway where the alcove on the left had been repurposed into a galley kitchen. There were only six cupboards, and each was open. On the right of this odd hall, and beyond an antique coat stand, were three doors. Lisa made a beeline for the furthest. Pete followed, while Corrie ducked into the kitchen, taking position by the fridge-freezer where she had a clear shot at the entrance. Behind him, Pete heard Olivia open the door to the bathroom, but when he turned, she motioned him on, so he followed Lisa into the living room.

The apartment's owner had nautical aspirations but a pedestrian's budget. Old ships sailed across every wall, though the prints were new and the frames were cheap. The half-height bookcases were filled with second-hand maritime paperbacks, while the battered Civil War globe was a reproduction. The astrolabe was a replica, the barometer was digital, and the ornaments were kitsch. The sofa looked comfortable, and as well-used as the armchairs. The cup-rings on the coffee table, and the stack of board games beneath, suggested frequent visitors. The dust, the damp, and the dead zombie in the doorway suggested no one had lived here for some time.

A tripod stood next to the corner window. Though the telescope had been looted, the window still offered a perfect view of the now-broken bridge, the river, the pier, and the yacht. It was definitely a civilian boat. Twin masts, but with a drinking deck at the rear. Not a racing yacht, nor a fishing boat, but someone's toy, onto which two people loaded small red fuel cans.

The pier itself was a match for the boat, as much an open-air drinking space for a wood-framed bar-restaurant as a place for sailors to dock. He couldn't see any signs, or buildings, offering refuelling ship-services. A defensive wall ringed the pier, built out of yellow taxis and parts of the semi-dismantled wooden bar. There were no tables or chairs on the pier close to the ship, so if the crew did come ashore to cook or sit, it would be in the remains of the bar.

"Intriguing, isn't it?" Lisa said.

"I don't know what to make of it," Pete said.

"As I say, intriguing," Lisa said.

"There's no one here," Olivia whispered, joining them in the living room. "This place is the definition of well-looted."

"I'll go swap with Corrie," Pete said, and headed back to the entrance.

"Nothing yet," Corrie said.

"The ship's there," Pete said. "They're already loading fuel. Go take a look, and I'll keep watch here."

He'd barely settled into position by the fridge, when he heard a hiss from Olivia.

"Pete! Come here!"

When he got back into the living room, Corrie wasn't standing at the window, but sitting on the sofa.

"What is it?" he asked. "Are you okay?"

"It's the *Archangel,*" Corrie said. "That's Mikael's boat."

"Are you sure?" Pete asked.

"I'm positive," Corrie said. "He had a thousand photographs of it. The squares and lines on the side are a stylised form of Cyrillic he invented for himself when he was a child. He used to pray to the Archangel Michael to save him from his life. He'd write out prayers in his made-up language until his father found them. Mikael got a beating. He got a lot of those, until his older sisters stopped their father for good. He gave his boat that name as a reminder that he was his own guardian angel. That's the story he told me. He certainly loved the ship more than he did his son. The boat was pretty much all he'd happily talk about. But the boat was left in Miami after he was extracted."

"He was a prisoner within the family," Lisa said. "An honoured prisoner, and kept away from most of the business, but he knew too much to be allowed any real freedom. His house in Miami was used as a meeting place, and he was used as the host and occasional figurehead."

"He's dead," Corrie said.

"Yet the cartel are clearly here," Lisa said. "I confess I didn't recognise the boat, but it is too great a coincidence for it, and Pruitt, to both be here. In fact, I would speculate that she came here because this is where she expected to be collected." She patted her bag. "No matter. We will stop her."

"What do you mean?" Olivia asked.

"As I told you, this bag contains my worldly possessions," Lisa said. "The most burdensome of which are four kilograms of plastic explosive and a remote detonator."

"You always planned to blow up the ship?" Olivia asked.

"Prepared rather than planned," Lisa said. "But I did consider it as an eventuality."

"You and me are going to have a long talk about openness and secrets when we get to the icebreaker," Olivia said. "But are we agreed we should blow up that boat?"

"Absolutely," Corrie said.

Pete shrugged. "I'm not voting one way or another until I hear how we get a bomb aboard, and how we'll get away afterwards. We've got a sentry on the roof above us, and there's one by that taxi-wall, and at least three inside the wall or on the boat."

"Shh," Olivia said, pointing towards the far wall.

From outside came the low burr of an engine, rising in volume, approaching from inland.

A small tanker stopped by the barricade. A passenger jumped out, armed with a rifle, and ran to the rear of the vehicle, seemingly aiming at the road down which they had driven. A second passenger climbed out of the cab, waving to the people inside the pier-barricade while the driver climbed out, turned around, but stayed by the door. The passenger now at the rear of the tanker fired a shot. A second. A third.

"Must be zoms," Olivia said, stepping closer to the window, though staying flush with the wall. "I can't see them."

"The woman who just ran to the barricade is Pruitt," Lisa said.

Pete stepped over to a different window, carefully moving the slatted blind so he could see. She was peculiarly dressed by the standards of any era, wearing a grey pantsuit, combat boots, and a military belt with a sidearm at one side, a long bayonet at the other. Her scissor-cut hair ruffled in the breeze as she gesticulated for people to come help. And they did. Four of them, from inside the bar.

"You said there were sixteen of them on that ship?" Pete asked.

"At least," Lisa said. "Though I doubt there would be many more. Dewhurst is the tanker driver and… yes, I see her now. Demarkos was the shooter."

The police officer had walked to the front of the tanker to stand next to Pruitt, her rifle at the low-ready.

"It can't be diesel in that tanker," Pete said. "Not so soon. It must be fresh water. And they're loading some individual fuel cans already, so they're preparing to leave."

Using a ladder, a trio of sailors climbed over the barricade, and ran to the rear of the tanker. Now it was their turn to open fire.

"They aren't short of bullets, are they?" Olivia said.

"If I had a rifle, I could kill Pruitt now," Corrie said. "I don't know if I can make the shot with a handgun. What kind of detonator do you have? Maybe we could throw the explosives close enough."

"We'd have to break the window first," Lisa said. "Or at least open it. That would give them too much warning. Destroying a water-tanker would slow their departure, but only by a day."

"Does anyone have binoculars?" Olivia asked. "Quick!"

"I've got the optical scope," Corrie said.

"Thanks," Olivia said, taking it. She aimed the scope towards the ship. "That's him! Look! The ratty guy in the red coat, now standing on deck. The one not working."

"Who?" Lisa asked, taking the scope.

"That's Herrera," Olivia said. "The cop from South Bend who burned people alive. That's him!"

"On Mikael's boat," Corrie said, stepping forward.

"Keep back from the window," Lisa said. "Are you sure it's him?"

"Absolutely positive," Olivia said. "Pete, want to give a second opinion?"

He took the scope. "Yep. That's him."

"He *must* be Mikael's son," Corrie said. "There's no other explanation for him being aboard that ship."

"Lisa, you must have come across him," Pete said.

"I knew the nephew was being groomed for leadership, but that he'd been sent out to make his own way in the world, to prove himself worthy. As such, he had very little to do with the running of the sisters' empire, and so wasn't of major concern to me."

"If only we had a rifle," Olivia said. "But we don't, and he's on the boat. No one could throw that bag far enough."

"The gunfire is slowing," Pete said. "Looks like we've got two targets. We can go for Pruitt, or the nephew."

"Three targets," Lisa said. "There is still the ship, and it is not impossible the sisters are aboard."

"It's only about twenty-five kilometres from here to Great Kills Bay," Corrie said. "If we can find a working radio, I could call the icebreaker and get them here in a few hours. They could sink the ship."

"How long should we hunt for a radio?" Lisa asked. "If they are loading water, we can assume they intend to depart as soon as the fuel arrives. If they spy the icebreaker coming, the yacht could put to sea, go north, and disappear up the Hudson River. Even if they can't outrun your icebreaker, they can go ashore, and disappear in the ruins."

"There's a rifle on the roof," Corrie said. "We kill the sniper, take it, shoot Herrera and Pruitt."

"We'd get one, not both," Lisa said. "But I might have an alternative."

"Does it involve any of us dying?" Olivia asked.

"I hope not," Lisa said.

Chapter 25 - Ambush
Dumbo Pier, Brooklyn

Handbrake, seatbelt, mirrors. Pete ran through a mental refresher course for his part in the plan. Corrie, being their best shot, would be the sniper. Olivia, because Herrera might recognise her, was Corrie's spotter. Dewhurst and Demarkos would recognise Lisa, so she had to be the one to make the approach. Pete would be the getaway driver, assuming everything else didn't go fatally wrong. It also assumed the keys had been left in the water-tanker's ignition. His other role was to carry the axe, thus implying he didn't carry a gun, and so, by implication, nor did Lisa.

Handbrake, seatbelt, mirrors. Repeating the words helped dispel his rising anger as he and Lisa walked towards the taxi-barricade. His fury wasn't just due to the proximity of Herrera and Pruitt, but that this task had been left to him. Indeed, before the outbreak, it had been left to people like Lisa Kempton to battle these evil forces. Power corrupts, sure, but that explanation was small comfort when these murderers might be about to escape. Yes, it was a good thing he held an axe in his hands; if he'd held a gun, he would already have opened fire.

They'd left the apartment building the way they'd entered, then split up. He and Lisa had looped around the block to obscure in which direction Corrie and Olivia now lay in wait. It had taken less than ten minutes, but the gunfire from Demarkos and the sentries had completely ceased. As they approached, Pete counted a dozen dead zombies on the road and four living people by the water-tanker. Pruitt and Dewhurst were talking with one of the cartel-sailors, though it wasn't Herrera. Demarkos stood guard at the rear of the tanker. The other cartel-sailors had returned behind the barricade where they were loitering. One was drinking soda. One had begun to strip his rifle. A third was pacing.

The sailors by the ship had finished loading the small fuel cans, and they too were waiting, presumably on the outcome of the conversation with Pruitt. A conversation that Herrera was not taking part in.

Back when Olivia had first met him, Herrera had been the junior partner in a pair of roadside brigands using their police badges to kill and loot fleeing motorists. She'd reported he'd occupied a similar position during the battle at the University of Notre Dame. There, he'd been a killer, not a leader. Was that still the case now? Was the bald man talking with Pruitt the captain of this ship?

For that matter, how had Herrera got here from Canada? No, Pete realised. How wasn't nearly as important as why. None of those questions was as important as whether the keys were still in the tanker, and he'd learn that answer very soon, because he and Lisa had been spotted.

Dewhurst pointed towards them. When Lisa raised a hand, Dewhurst raised his in reply. Demarkos gave them a glance, but returned her attention to Old Fulton Street, along which the brief battle had been waged.

"Commander, Governor!" Lisa called out, as they drew near.

Dewhurst began walking towards Pete and Lisa, but stopped when a shot rang from the rooftops. Pete was watching Demarkos. The detective looked up at the roofs, raised her rifle, aiming along the street, but lowered it again without a shot being fired. Good, no one was using radio. With no coordination between those on the ground and those on the roofs, confusion would be their friend when it came to escape.

"Mrs Keynes!" Dewhurst called. "I didn't expect to see you here. Is there trouble?"

"My cup filleth with trouble, and spilleth with tribulation," Lisa said. "But I have some good news to splasheth about." She patted the bag she'd brought with her from the subway locker. "I know where we can find diesel. All the diesel we could possibly need."

"I knew someone had a stash," Dewhurst said. "But I didn't expect you had a part in that hydroponic weed farm."

"I know nothing about that," Lisa said.

"You've got diesel?" Pruitt called out, taking a step towards them.

Dewhurst shrugged, and walked back a step, turning so he could address both groups even as Lisa kept walking, Pete at her side. "Governor, this is Mrs Eliza Keynes. She's one of the scavengers."

"We've met, Governor," Lisa said. "Long ago."

"We have?" Pruitt asked. "Forgive me, I don't recall the occasion."

"My appearance has changed somewhat," Lisa said.

"Whose hasn't?" Pruitt said.

"You said you'd found diesel," Dewhurst said.

Lisa reached into her bag and withdrew a phone, which she handed to Commander Dewhurst. "On there is the location of the fuel. Enough diesel and gasoline to equip a small army. Just press play."

"It's a video?" Pruitt asked as Dewhurst pressed play. The two of them watched the screen. There was no sound, so Pete had only the governor's face to judge her reaction as she watched the recording Kempton had made in Raven Rock. Pruitt's face crinkled into a frown.

"I don't think this is the correct video," Dewhurst said. "All I can see are zombies. A lot of them."

"But you note the vehicles?" Lisa said. "And do you note the name on the wall behind them?"

"Name? What…" Dewhurst's mouth hung open, the rest of the sentence unfinished.

Pruitt's face had frozen, the blood slowly draining from it.

"The people on that boat work for the Herrera sisters," Lisa said. "Their captain is the sisters' heir and nephew."

"Him?" Pruitt asked, shock re-animating her, as she turned around

"I was with General Yoon," Pete said, addressing Dewhurst. "That guy on the boat burned down a hospital in South Bend and destroyed the refugee camp at Notre Dame. He's as evil as they get."

"He said…" Pruitt began, and again shook her head. She thrust the phone back at Kempton before turning to Dewhurst. "Commander," she began, but a gunshot echoed from the rooftops. Pruitt jumped.

Pete gripped the axe, waiting for Lisa to raise her hand. That would be the signal for Olivia to sprint up the road yelling that zombies were coming. When Olivia appeared, Corrie would open fire on Herrera. In the confusion, they were going to push Pruitt to cover in the tanker. Pete would then drive her away. It would be an abduction, followed by an interrogation, and then an execution.

But Pruitt did something unexpected. She drew the gun from her holster, and opened fire at the sailor standing by the tanker. "Traitors!" she yelled, firing as she ran for the barricade. The sailor fell, while Pruitt screamed a nearly incoherent battle cry. "Traitors! They're traitors!"

Demarkos turned around, gun half raised, and clearly uncertain who the target was because the barrel swung towards Pete until the detective saw her leader charging the barricade. The detective shifted aim, and opened fire. Dewhurst had drawn a gun of his own, and though he hadn't fired, he ran after the governor.

"Our side has been chosen," Lisa said, and followed Dewhurst.

Pruitt had already reached the taxi barricade, and fired wildly at the ship over the roof of a cab. Demarkos dragged Pruitt down behind the taxi as the cartel returned fire.

Bullets cracked glass and tore into metal, but the sailors were sprinting back to their ship rather than taking the time to aim. Burdened by exhaustion, Dewhurst ran slowly. Pete was level with the man when the commander collapsed. Pete skidded to a halt, dropping to the man's side. He'd fallen, face first, with blood spreading from his lower back. Pete dragged him to cover between the tanker and the taxi-barricade.

"Detective!" Lisa called. "The roof!"

Demarkos spun around firing, but the sniper didn't return fire, having already fled their post. "What the hell is going on?" Demarkos asked.

"Does anyone have a bandage?" Pete asked, attempting to stem the bleeding with his hands.

Lisa pulled a small med-kit from her bag.

"I'll ask again," Demarkos said. "What's happening?"

"It's them," Governor Pruitt said. "They're the cartel."

"Raven Rock's been overrun with zombies," Pete added, as he pushed a dressing against the side of the worryingly quiet Dewhurst. "General Yoon's army was right beneath a nuclear bomb. It's gone. What you were told was a lie."

"They want our fuel and supplies," Pruitt said.

Demarkos reared up, firing, before ducking back into cover while a barrage was launched at the wall.

"The rooftop sniper has fled," Lisa said, dropping in front of the tanker's cab. "Their ship is preparing to leave."

"They haven't got the diesel," Demarkos said.

"They have sails," Lisa said.

Pruitt had crossed to Dewhurst's side. "He's dying," she said. "We need to get him to the clinic."

Demarkos glanced down at Dewhurst. She shook her head before rearing up and firing an angry burst.

"I know you used to work for the cartel, Pruitt," Lisa said. "I know they engineered your election. First to the state house, then to the governor's mansion. Roberta Gomez," she added. "That is the name of the student you killed in the hit-and-run. A student they claimed ran away to Colombia where she disappeared."

Pete drew his gun, moved along the barricade, and fired a shot at the ship, before ducking back down. He'd barely aimed, and knew he'd not hit, but he wanted a gun in his hand for whatever came next.

"You know?" Pruitt asked. "How do you know?"

"They wanted you to be president," Lisa said.

"That might be what others wanted, but not me," Pruitt said. "It was a dark night. I'd been drinking. I shouldn't have been behind the wheel, but I was. I killed a child, and I was ready to confess. But they replaced the body without asking me."

"What body?" Demarkos asked. "What are you two talking about?"

"The victim," Pruitt said. "While I was sitting in a cell, they switched the bodies in the morgue, then framed a couple of cops and the medical examiner, and made it look as if they had taken a bribe from my opponent. I was never asked. Never. Not until it was done. I never wanted any of this, but I had no choice. Not until the world came to an end."

"As long as we're alive, we have a choice," Lisa said.

"Believe me or not," Pruitt said. "I *know* the truth."

Demarkos fired over the barricade so Pete did the same.

"There's only one sailor on deck," he said, just before that sailor opened fire, emptying an entire magazine at the barricade. At least one bullet made its way through, cracking the tanker's passenger-mirror.

"Raven Rock fell months ago," Lisa said. "It is full of supplies, especially diesel, and those trucks you saw on the footage, but it is also full of the undead. Manhattan is flooding except where it is sinking. The Canadian army was destroyed by a bomb. Whatever else those gangsters told you, it can't be believed. But the cartel has otherwise been destroyed. Their supporters are dead. They cannot help you, nor does it appear as if they wish to."

"No, they're just robbing us," Pruitt said.

"They didn't tell you who they were?" Pete asked.

"They said they were from Raven Rock," Demarkos said. "They said they were the last remnants of the Canadian army, and they were sheltering in that bunker. Governor?"

"That is what they told me," Pruitt said. "If they'd said otherwise, would I have fired just now? Would I not have opened fire before? Are you telling us there are no survivors in Raven Rock?"

"No," Lisa said. "Though it is filled with supplies, it is also home to the undead."

"The ship's leaving," Demarkos said. "They had two snipers on the bridge, and one on that rooftop. We've got to hunt them down."

"Do you have a radio?" Lisa asked.

"In the tanker," Demarkos said.

"Then you take care of Dewhurst, we'll stop the ship," Lisa said. "Take shelter. We'll take the tanker, and if we're successful, we'll return in two hours. If not, you'll find us by following the smoke. Pete?"

It took him a long second to understand, but he then sprinted for the truck, and jumped into the driver's seat.

"Keys? Yes. Handbrake... done."

"More haste, more speed," Lisa said, closing the passenger door.

Pete reversed a few metres, before heading south down Furman Street.

"The ship's pulled anchor," Pete said.

"Yes. It's departing," Lisa said.

"Is it going south, or should I turn around?"

"Forget the ship," Lisa said. "But let's not forget your sister and wife. Ah, there they are. I would also advise you not to forget the undead. At least ten were approaching the barricade. While they cannot possibly catch us, we should expect similar danger ahead."

Pete slowed as two figures ran out into the road, stopping so Corrie and Olivia could jump aboard.

"What happened?" Olivia asked.

"Pruitt started shooting," Pete said. "But not at us. She fired at Herrera."

"I think I winged him," Corrie said, squirming to find space in the over-capacity two-person cab.

"Herrera?" Pete asked.

"Zombie!" Olivia said, pointing ahead.

Pete swerved.

"Careful!" Corrie said as the tanker clipped the zombie's shoulder, sending the creature spinning to the roadside.

"You shot Herrera?" Pete asked.

"I got one sailor for definite," Corrie said. "And I at least winged him. Maybe killed him. It was hard to be certain from a distance."

"Did you kill Pruitt?" Olivia asked.

"No," Lisa said. "But Detective Demarkos knows the truth now. It will be down to her to decide Pruitt's fate."

"Assuming she's not cartel, too," Olivia said.

"If she was, she would have killed us at that barricade," Lisa said.

"Pruitt didn't hesitate," Pete said. "When you showed her that video of Raven Rock, she pulled a gun pretty quickly. Maybe too quickly."

"Perhaps so," Lisa said. "But that ship has left. Pruitt has no way to leave, and so she must lead. It is not the method I hoped for, but we have achieved the best possible outcome."

"Not quite," Pete said, slowing to drive around a car barricade, then speeding up as the zombies behind it tried to break through. "What about the *Archangel*? How exactly are we going to stop it?"

"We aren't," Lisa said. "Our destination is the rendezvous at Coney Island, but I was getting tired of cycling. There should be a radio aboard here somewhere, Corrie. See if you can use that to contact the icebreaker."

"We're letting the cartel escape?" Corrie asked.

"We are on land, they are at sea," Lisa said. "There is little we can do. Yet whether Pruitt was acting or not, she shot at the cartel. They will not return here, and so will neither have the diesel they were waiting on, or the drinking water in the back of this tanker. They left behind at least three of their number, and lost at least two. It is unlikely they will find a more welcome harbour elsewhere."

"Watch out!" Olivia said.

But Pete sped up, slamming into the zombie staggering towards them. Gore flew up, while the body was dragged down, beneath the wheels.

"Found the radio," Corrie said, holding up a small handset. "I can't guarantee it has the range to reach Staten Island, but I can't even try until we're clear of these buildings."

"Start looking for directions," Pete said, as he leaned forward, gripping the wheel tight, keeping his eyes on the road ahead.

"We've got zombies behind," Olivia said, leaning out through the window. "A lot of them."

"Then get ready to jump and run," Pete said. "We probably should have stuck with the bikes."

"Get ready to turn," Lisa said. "The road ahead appears to be blocked."

"Yep, seen it," Pete said.

He turned hard left away from the bay, then right just as quickly as the way ahead was blocked by the undead, and found himself driving down a narrow alley. The tyres crunched over abandoned bags. The cab grated against brick as he drove too close to the left-hand wall. It screeched against metal as he over-corrected and knocked into a too-low fire-escape landing. The alleyway litter gave way to a flood. Mud sprayed the windscreen, mixing with the gore, and nearly obscured the view.

"Try the wipers," Olivia said

"They're broken," Pete said.

"This *is* fun," Lisa said.

"Seriously?" Corrie asked.

"Absolutely," Lisa said. "Don't tell me that you didn't wish you were able to do such things back before the outbreak. Life is for living, Ms Guinn, even now. Ah, and it looks like rain."

"And the way out," Pete said as the alley met a road.

"And a sign," Corrie said.

"Seen it," Pete said, pulling them onto the on-ramp for the elevated road where one and a half lanes had been cleared by some previous, and heavier, traffic.

"Did anyone else just hear a gunshot?" Olivia asked.

"I think that was the engine," Pete said.

Chapter 26 - Do Zombies Dream of Infected Sheep?
Coney Island, Brooklyn

As muddy sand pattered against the blood-smeared window, Pete stopped the already slow tanker. "That's it," he said. "We won't get any further down this road."

"I swear I heard another gunshot," Olivia said.

"Probably the engine," Pete said. "Does anyone know where we are?"

"Close enough to walk," Lisa said. "There is ocean sand mixed with the mud, and we crossed the high-tide mark four blocks north."

Pete opened the door, jumping out, his boots leaving Armstrong-prints in the sandy deposit covering the road. Apartments towered all around them, except to the west where there was a fenced high school. But if he looked where the road had been, he saw broken stumps of roadside trees, upturned cars, cracked fragments of plastic hulls, lengths of rope, and scraps of sail.

Between the trees, around the apartments, or on either side of the school's fence, there must surely once have been grass. Now there was red-brown mud, dotted with an occasional pool of greenish water.

"Tsunami?" Pete asked.

"Flooding, certainly," Lisa said.

"Well deeper than my head-height," Olivia said. "Imagine…" She trailed off as her eyes tracked up to the towering apartment on the far side of the junction, where scraps of white sheets hung from the topmost floor. Now sun-faded and storm-drenched, none were legible, but by taking a letter from one, then another, it was probable all had read *Help*.

"Do you smell that?" Lisa asked.

"Rotting sea, rotting land," Corrie said.

"Gasoline," Lisa said. "I don't believe this is a water tanker."

"That's something I wish I'd known before we played dodgems," Pete said.

"I'm glad we didn't," Olivia said. "Gasoline, though, not diesel?"

"I believe so," Lisa said. "One assumes Herrera wanted it for the land-leg of his journey so as to save the diesel for the ship. Of course, that does raise the question of where he was trying to reach."

"We've got zoms coming," Olivia said, pointing west. "Over there, from that… I guess it's an apartment. Big wall, tall fence above, broken in the corner."

"Seen them," Pete said. "Let's—"

This time, he heard the gunshot, and reflexively ducked behind the cab.

"Where did that come from?" he asked.

"Wrong question. Are they shooting at us?" Olivia said, looking up at the tower blocks.

"Ask nothing and run before a spark ignites the gas," Corrie said. "Head for that cement mixer just behind the fishing boat." She dashed behind the rear of the tanker, and was gone long enough for another shot to ring out. "Go!" she yelled.

Except for an occasional rain-filled pool, wind and storm had smoothed the muddy silt into a desert. In some places Pete's boots sank to the ankle. In others, there was barely an inch of dark sand concealing some sturdy piece of wreckage. Running was nearly impossible, and Corrie didn't try. Instead, she walked backwards, with her pistol initially aimed up at the distant rooftops. By the time Pete reached the cracked hull of the rusting fishing boat, Corrie had both her hands raised above her head.

"What are you doing?"

"Showing we give up," Corrie said, finally ducking behind the fishing boat. "Don't stop, though. We've got to get to the pier first."

"First?"

"Before those zoms," Corrie said. "And before whoever's shooting at us, *and* before the *Archangel*. At least three cartel killers were left behind and they've got radio with which to arrange a pick-up."

Near the landlocked boat, the drifts grew higher, and higher still around the neighbouring cement mixer. Their pace slowed to a trudge as they waded over to the apartment block where the towering buildings had acted as a breakwater. The drifts of mud were replaced with piles of flotsam. Pete caught sight of a two-metre-long wooden spar, reinforced with metal at one end. When he picked it up, he saw a scrap of cloth still attached to the point, on which sat a single white star in a field of damp blue.

"Flagstaff? Good enough until I can get another axe," he said. Olivia was just behind him, Lisa now just ahead, but Corrie was out on the road, jogging down the middle. "What's she doing?"

"Just keep moving," Olivia said.

"Zoms?" Pete asked.

"Yes, but people, too," Olivia said.

Pete didn't hear the gunshot, but the explosion was loud enough to be heard back on Manhattan. A spark had finally ignited the gasoline vapour, setting off an earth-shaking blast. Shrapnel sprayed in every direction, hitting the cement truck, the buildings, and the undead. Glass fell from windows, raining down as slicing rain. Olivia sprinted over to Lisa. Pete ran to where Corrie had been thrown to the ground.

"Sis!"

"I'm fine," she said, as he picked her up. "I think I am. We can check later. That worked better than I hoped."

Pete looked back to the burning fuel truck. He didn't know how many, or how close, the zombies had been prior to the explosion, but dozens were dead. Dozens more, some already aflame, crawled through the burning pools of fuel. Of their shooting pursuer, there was neither sight nor sound.

"You planned that?" Pete asked.

"Kinda," Corrie said. "Couldn't think of another way to get rid of the shooter."

"Did you see who it was?"

"Nope. Nor whether they survived, but they've got a hundred zoms between us and them."

It would soon be more. Woken from their peace-less slumber by the explosion, the undead emerged from shattered doorways, from between-block alleys, from inside cracked hulls, and from beneath upturned cars. They fell from broken windows. They rose from the deeper mud drifts. Hundreds. Thousands. Most headed towards the explosion, but some changed direction, angling towards the four running figures. Pete kept his eyes ahead, focusing on the giant sea-tanker lodged across the road ahead, leaning against two apartment blocks. Surely there couldn't be any other buildings between it and the sea. But the undead were getting nearer, closer. Too close.

He lunged with the flagstaff, but aimed too low. The pole hit the zombie's chest, ripping cloth and skin as it tore across its sternum. But the impact knocked it back, while it brought Pete to a halt.

"Right! Go right!" Corrie called.

Pete sprinted after the other three. There were just so many undead. As many as the grains of sand, as many as the stars. And then, seemingly, there were none.

Ahead was a mudflat. To the right, shipwrecks rested against the stumpy remains of sea-wrecked apartments. To the left lay a wreckage-strewn beach, and then the sea.

"They were asleep," Olivia said, as all four slowed their jog to a walk. "The zombies were asleep."

"Do they dream?" Corrie asked.

"I do hope not," Lisa said. "Look for a skeletal red metal tower. It is the old parachute jump from Steeplechase Park, and directly opposite the pier."

"I can't see it," Olivia said.

Sun-dried seaweed hung from crooked streetlights. Occasional wooden slats jutted from the sand; grave-markers for the boardwalk which had once run along the beach. Ropes clacked, and metal creaked as the tide rattled the wreckage in the shallows.

"Zoms ahead," Olivia said.

"And lots behind," Corrie said. "But we've got time. I can see the pier ahead, and it looks mostly intact. We'll be trapped there," she added. "I haven't been able to reach the ship. If it doesn't come, escaping from that pier will be hard."

"I trust Tess," Pete said.

"Me, too," Corrie said. "That doesn't mean she'll come. The zoms are following us. That explosion woke up a legion. I don't know if the blast killed all our pursuers, but that pier is the obvious place for anyone to be picked up. That's why they were pursuing us, not just for the fuel, but because they wanted to come here to board the *Archangel*. By truck, we outpaced the boat, but that ship will arrive within the hour. If we shoot at it, maybe it'll go away. Maybe they'll shoot back."

"We've got a lot of zoms on our heels now," Olivia said. "I say we run."

"I think I can manage a fast walk," Lisa said. "My knees say no to a run so I'll take my chances on the pier, though the choice is yours."

"We'll stick together," Pete said.

"Okay, but we *will* have to run if we're going to beat the zoms to the pier," Corrie said.

The boardwalk had run along the beach, joining the pier as it lazily rose above the sea, jutting two hundred metres into the bay. While the concrete pillars serenely stood as proud as before, the wooden-slat walkway had been ripped asunder. The steel support struts remained, and offered the only way to get off the beach, and to the questionable safety above the sea.

As they'd neared, they'd slowed, but the undead hadn't. The nearest, a zombie snagged in a fishing net, lunged. Pete launched the flagstaff at its face with all the strength his fury could muster. The reinforced wood smashed through skin but the pole lodged in bone, and was ripped from his hands as the zombie fell.

"C'mon!" Corrie called, running onto the shattered boardwalk. She fired a shot, another, walking achingly slow as Pete drew his own sidearm, and followed Olivia and Lisa.

"I think we're clear," Corrie said. "But watch your footing."

Large swathes of the wooden floor had been ripped apart by the tumultuous sea. A narrow walkway remained along the eastern edge of the pier. In some places, it was only a metre wide, but that was more than wide enough for them. It would be more than wide enough for the undead. At the second artificially narrow section, Pete paused. Below was the sea. Inland were the undead. Already there were hundreds, but they were milling around, woken by the explosion, but uncertain, as yet, where to go. Ashore, smoke rose above the towers, marking where the tanker had blown up. At sea, there was no sign of any ship.

"We're clear," Corrie said, jogging back to them. "Someone used this pier before us, recently. They left their bags behind. No clue where they went."

"Does the radio work?" Olivia asked.

"I think so, but I've had no reply from Tess," Corrie said.

"Then I'm going to see if there are any weapons in those bags," Olivia said.

"I still have the plastic explosives," Lisa said. "We could easily blow up this last section of walkway. We would be safe from the undead then."

"But the explosion would summon the undead to the beach," Pete said.

"They will come anyway," Lisa said.

"Not all of them," Pete said. "If the ship doesn't come, we've got to find our way back through them, because I don't fancy swimming. How many did you shoot, Corrie?"

"On the pier? Four," she said. "Speaking of which, I'm down to my last mag."

Pete handed her his only spare. "We should keep the explosives for the *Archangel*," he said.

"If we can wait that long," Corrie said. "Two zoms have just found the pier."

"I found a sabre," Olivia said, holding it up as she walked back to them. "And a sledgehammer."

Pete took the sledgehammer, and took in the approaching foe. One of the undead had fallen through a yawning gap in the boardwalk. Since, at that point, it was over sand, it had landed on its feet, with its hands reaching up through the hole. The other zombie continued on. But only for another two metres before it, too, fell through a gap in the boardwalk.

"I'll find us some more weapons," Corrie said.

"And I shall look for some flotation devices," Lisa said.

"So that was Brooklyn," Olivia said, as they watched another pair of the undead creep towards the pier.

"That was New York," Pete said. "Can't say it lives up the hype."

"What did you make of Pruitt?" Olivia asked.

"The more I think about it, the more I'm suspicious," he said. "I think she might have recognised Lisa. When Lisa showed her the video of Raven Rock she immediately started shooting at the sailors. I guess if she were genuinely shocked and confused, she'd have asked more questions, but maybe I'm being cynical."

"I suppose it doesn't matter what she knew, just what she'll do now," Olivia said.

Pete took a reflexive step forward, half raising the sledgehammer, but relaxed as the nearest zombie slipped, and tumbled down into the shallows.

"She's an effective leader," Olivia said. "There was a school, a clinic, showers. It's not a bad start."

"Doomed, though," Pete said. "There'll be a riot when she tells people Raven Rock was overrun."

"Unless she doesn't tell them," Olivia said. "Okay, that doesn't look good. We've got a pack heading towards the pier now. At least fifty."

"You think she might tell the people that Raven Rock is real, and the ship has sailed off there?" Pete asked.

"Maybe," Olivia said. "It would buy her time. Trouble is, if she does that, how will she stop the New Yorkers from wanting to go to Raven Rock?"

The pack of the undead were scrumming and pushing, and shoving each other into the larger gaps, but for every zombie that fell, another found its way to the narrow walkway running along the eastern side of the pier.

"I'll go tell Lisa we might need that explosive," Pete said. As he turned around, his gaze fell on the sea, and on a pair of masts. It was a ship. The *Archangel*.

"So that's what it means to be caught between the devil and the deep blue sea," Pete said. "Corrie! Ship!"

Both Lisa and Corrie paused in their scavenging, and looked out to sea. Pete turned back to the approaching undead. There were twenty on the broken walkway, pushing their way forward in a loose line. Occasionally, one behind would catch up with one in front, and either knock it, or themselves, off the edge. There was no doubt that most would make it to the narrow pass.

"Smoke!" Corrie called.

A cloud rose from the ocean, nearly white in colour. Not emanating from the *Archangel*, but further out to sea. A moment later came a chattering roar of machine gun fire.

"They're getting close, Pete," Olivia said.

He turned back towards the undead. "Go get Lisa and the explosives," he said.

"You go," she said, raising the sabre.

"Boat!" Corrie called.

"We know," Pete said.

"No, *our* boat!" Corrie called.

Again, Pete looked around. He couldn't see what Corrie was pointing at, but he could see the icebreaker emerging from the artificial cloudbank while its machine gun sprayed the yacht.

A boat *was* approaching the pier, but it was the icebreaker's small inflatable, piloted by Mayor Jak. He gave them a wave as he brought it alongside. "Someone call for a taxi?"

Chapter 27 - Movie Endings
Hudson Bay, New York

"There were no survivors," Tess said, meeting them on the deck as they disembarked from the small launch. She was armed, and armoured, and rubbing her side. "No survivors, but no dinghy, launch, or other small boat. If anyone fled, they didn't do it around here. The rest couldn't flee, so chose to fight. It was a bad choice."

Pete turned back to the *Archangel*. Smoke billowed from the seams and flames licked up the mast. "How did you know to attack them?" he asked.

"We heard Corrie's message saying they were cartel," Tess said. "I reckoned you couldn't hear our reply, but it worked out in the end. One of our bullets hit something flammable. Three of them were still alive when we went aboard, but they didn't want to surrender. The ship was already burning. I grabbed what intel I could, and we came back here. So that's our story. What's yours? Are we heading back to Long Island?"

"Back?" he asked.

"Did you take photos of the people on that boat?" Olivia asked.

"We've got bodycam footage," Tess said. "Why?"

"That was Mikael's boat," Olivia said. "His son, the heir to what's left of the sisters' empire, was on the boat."

"I shot him when the boat was at the docks," Corrie said. "But I might have just winged him."

"It sounds like we've a lot to discuss," Tess said. "But I'll ask again, are we heading back to Long Island? Nightfall isn't far off. If we're heading south, and if we reach open water before dusk, we can sail through the night."

"I bet everyone on Long Island would want to go to the Pacific," Olivia said. "But there's too many to fit on this ship. Let's get back to the Pacific, and send a rescue fleet."

"Anyone else got anything to add?" Tess said. "No? Great. Then if you could come with me, Ms Kempton, I'll find you a shower, some new clothes, and something to eat. Then we'll have the first of what I'm sure will be many *very* long chats."

"I am at your service," Lisa said, and followed Tess off the deck.

"I'm going to find the bodycam footage," Olivia said. "I'll sleep better knowing Herrera is dead."

"Then I get first dibs on the shower," Pete said. But he didn't go immediately below. Instead, he joined Corrie by the bow, where she was watching the burning ship. "Hey, sis. What's up?"

"This is where my movie ends," Corrie said.

"Wow, that's super-bleak," Pete said. "We didn't get torn apart by zoms on the pier, or drown as we tried to swim away from them. That tanker truck could have blown up during the drive, or Pruitt could have shot us or… well, we're alive, and we found more survivors than can fit on the ship. We did what the Pacific wanted, what Judge Benton wanted, and we found Olivia, Rufus, and Lisa, too."

Corrie laughed. "Exactly. Don't you ever think your life is like a movie?"

"No, because up until recently, it was way too boring," he said. "Oh, I miss those days."

"Movies are abbreviated stories, right?" Corrie said. "They end on a happy note, after everything appears to have been resolved. This moment, now, is my resolution. I didn't get to see Mikael die, but I've seen his boat burn, with his son either choking on the fumes below or dead on that pier back in Brooklyn. And yes, we looked for survivors. We didn't give up. We found Olivia. We found Lisa. We found Rufus. So, now, I'll walk back to my cabin, while the camera will pan out and up, taking in the ship, the bay, and a school of whales frolicking in the depths. And that'll be it. That's how the movie ends. On a happy note."

"Can we have a post-credits scene where the ship sails into an Australian harbour?" Pete asked. "Or we could do that thing where there's a fifty-year time jump to reveal you've been retelling the story to your grandkids?"

"Sure," she said. "As long as they're *your* grandkids. Ah… no more adventures, Pete. I've been living this one too long."

Pete turned his back on the burning wreck, and the ruin of New York. "We did all we could," he said. "And you did more than anyone else. If there's a future for any of us, it's because of what you did. But speaking of futures, want to see if ours has a meal in it?"

An hour later, he'd showered, changed, and visited the galley. He returned to his and Olivia's cabin with a tray in hand. "Room service," he said, pushing the door closed.

"Champagne and caviar?" Olivia asked, her head emerging from their almost-person-sized shower cubicle.

"Close," Pete said. "It's a chicken tortilla which has a fancy name in Spanish, and there are grape pancakes for dessert."

"Wow, they found chicken on Staten Island?" Olivia asked.

"I think it's from a can," Pete said. "There's a new sign in the cafeteria telling you not to ask questions, so I didn't."

"Ooh, ominous," Olivia said. "I suppose that means I shouldn't ask where they found grapes, either. Are there any dry towels?"

He put the tray on the desk and checked their small closet. "No towels, no. Best I can offer you is a t-shirt. It's clean."

"That'll have to do. Put towels on our shopping list for when we get to Savannah. Did you see many people in the mess?"

"Pretty much everyone who isn't on the bridge," Pete said. "Corrie's telling them what happened. Zach was there, and Rufus."

"How is Zach?"

"Well enough to complain," Pete said. "I think he'll be fine. Rufus was a bit grumpy, but I think that's due to an abundance of attention from the kids. I guess he's used to his alone-time. Did you check the bodycam footage?"

"I did," Olivia said, as she began a hunt for clean clothes. "Boots!" she added as Pete dropped onto the bed. "You best get into the habit, because when we get to Oz, we're having a shoes-off-at-the-door policy."

"Tell that to the spiders," Pete said, pulling them off.

"If I see a spider wearing boots, I will," she said.

"Was Herrera among the dead?" Pete asked, as he stretched out.

"No. I didn't recognise any of them," she said. "Maybe he died back on the pier. Or maybe there was a mutiny and he was thrown over the side. I don't think it matters, because even if Pruitt *did* know who he was, *and* if he survived, she can't let him live. Besides, the cartel is clearly defunct, and he was basically on the run. Ah, but I'd feel happier if I had proof he was dead. What did they say Staten Island was like? Any sign of survivors?"

"Nope," Pete said. "A load of bags had been left on the pier, and that's where they found the food. It sounds like what we saw at Coney Island, or a bit like that pier near the U.N. on Manhattan. I guess there wasn't room for the bags when the ship took the survivors away. At least, that's the story I'm going to tell myself."

"Was it a lot of food?" Olivia asked.

"They're still doing a stock-check," Pete said. "Ramon thinks it'll amount to a couple of days, but most of it had spoiled, which is why I don't think that chicken really is chicken."

"Don't say that until after I've eaten it," she said. "We're still going to Savannah?"

"Yep. Then the Pacific. And then… who knows?"

"Hopefully somewhere with a bigger bathroom," Olivia said, lifting the warming-dish from the plate. "Was this for us to share, or is this all for me? Pete?"

She looked over, and saw that he was asleep.

17th April

Chapter 28 - The Leader's Choice
The Atlantic

Pete was halfway to the mess for breakfast when Pita dashed along the corridor.

"The commissioner needs you!" she said, tugging at his arm.

"Both of us?" Olivia asked.

"No, just Pete."

"Sounds like you're in trouble," Olivia said.

"It does, doesn't it?" he said.

Aboard a rigidly stratified military ship, the room would have been the officers' mess. Instead, it was a seminar room used for video-conferenced lectures during the ship's diplomatically educational voyage north. Tess had used the room to interview the survivors. First, the three Guinns, then the Mexicans, and then the Georgians. Those first-hand accounts would be broadcast in the Pacific as a sad missive to the public, and to the exiled politicians, that the old order had been washed away.

Like in most of the ship, the room's walls were panelled in green-shade vinyl, but here they were covered in vibrant prints of near-extinct animals of the Andes. The long, wood-effect table in the centre of the room had been riddled with bullets during the massacre of the original crew. The table, and the quarter of the flooring which it had proven impossible to scrub clean, had been thrown over the side. There were no tables now, just two rows of chairs, one facing the other.

"G'day, mate, have a seat," Tess said, indicating the row opposite herself and Colonel Hawker.

"Am I in trouble?" Pete asked.

"Not a bit of it," Tess said. "We're discussing what to do about Long Island, and wanted your input."

"I thought we were going to Savannah, then the Pacific," Pete said.

"We are," Hawker said. "When we get home, Canberra will want a report, and recommendations on what we found in New York."

"We were given a broad remit for this mission," Tess said. "I'd say we've done more than we were asked, but we need to decide what to do about Long Island."

"I still don't follow," Pete said. "I guess, if we went back, we could pick up a few of the kids to bring back with us, but I'm not sure we have space for them all."

"Kempton's assessment is that Pruitt will do what she can to keep the people there alive," Hawker said. "Do you concur?"

"I guess so," Pete said. "Pruitt didn't seem evil, not like the cartel. I'm still going back and forth on whether she recognised Lisa or not, whether she knew whether the *Archangel*'s crew were cartel. But whoever she was, and whatever crimes she once committed, I think she's trying to repent. She's kept the Long Islanders alive so far. Plus, now the *Archangel* is sunk, she has no easy way to escape. Either she leads those people, or lets someone else do it, and I can't see her handing over power."

"That's not a ringing endorsement," Tess said.

"Sorry, but I met her for less than five minutes," Pete said. "Most of that time, I was waiting for gunfire."

"But during that time, Kempton told Pruitt there were supplies in Raven Rock, and that the facility was empty except for the undead, yes?" Hawker asked.

"Yep, and Lisa showed Pruitt a video of Raven Rock so she could see it was abandoned."

"Do you think Pruitt might go to Raven Rock?" Tess asked.

"We told her not to," Pete said. "I think we did. Although, actually, no, I guess we didn't. We just told her that *wasn't* where the cartel sailors had come from, but that there were supplies and zombies there. Even so, it's a long way by sea and road."

"When we return to Canberra, we'll give them our recommendations," Tess said. "We could ask them to send a rescue fleet here. Say two cruise ships, plus a couple of warships, and a fuel tanker. Assuming they agree with our recommendations, and the ships are available when we roll into harbour, it'll be a month before we get home, and another month before that rescue fleet sails into New York. Will Pruitt and her people still be there?"

"I see what you mean," Pete said. "I can't really speak for Pruitt, or any of her people, but if it were me, and after that gun battle at the pier, I'd want to leave. The rats ate their first effort at farming, and all they're growing now is dirt. They've got walls, but they're running out of bullets. We stole, and then blew up, a tanker filled with gasoline, and that must have been a large portion of their reserve. They were using gasoline generators for electricity. Maybe they can set up some solar or wind power, but I wouldn't hold my breath. Without electricity, cooking food and boiling water will become increasingly difficult."

"They're running a barter economy, is that right?" Tess asked.

"Yep. You can trade loot for hot showers, hot food, and power to charge up phones and the like. Medicine, too. I'm sure they were selling other things we didn't see. Without electricity, they'll have nothing to sell, so there'll be no reason for the scavengers to bring their loot to the market. Someone was already stockpiling diesel. They haven't handed it in yet, and I bet they won't now. I guess whoever that is could use the fuel to bargain for a position of authority, except why would anyone want to when they can use the fuel to flee?"

"Exactly my point," Hawker said, nodding to Tess. "Where else can they go, but Raven Rock?"

"Pete?" Tess asked.

"Hmm. I think they know that Canada was hit with bombs, so going north is out. South, along the coast, is just as urbanised, and you'd want to get into the countryside as quickly as you could. They know there are supplies at Raven Rock. Pruitt knows the cartel *aren't* there. She also knows they don't have many boats on Long Island. I think they have a ferry, but it can't be big enough for all of them at the same time. If the mood is that they should leave, then she'll need to lean into it, organise an exodus before the last ships are stolen and she's trapped there. She'd ferry the people to the mainland, then drive the rest of the way. Everyone together, so that no one can jump ahead and lock them out of the bunker. And once she realises that's a possibility, she'll have to act quick or not at all."

"And if you were living there, would you take that risk, Pete?" Tess asked.

Pete drummed his hand on the chair's arm. "Whether Pruitt was lying to us or not, she's in trouble. Dewhurst is probably dead, and certainly incapacitated, but he was leading one of the largest factions. Pruitt's been shown to be weak. Except, I don't think she can simply quit. Whatever she tells people about Herrera, she'll need to give them a plan. Detective Demarkos knows about Raven Rock, too. But if Pruitt's killed her to hide her link with the cartel, and if Pruitt dies in a coup, everyone else will still believe Raven Rock is full of survivors. Huh. Okay, sure, now I think about it, and if *they* think about it, Raven Rock is the only option other than staying put."

"Let's say there are five thousand on Long Island," Tess said. "It's more than we found in Cape Town, but less than were in the African Union convoy that departed from Inhambane. It's a *lot* less than were being evacuated from the Andaman Islands, and there are a thousand populated islands a lot closer to Australia than that. There is a very good chance that the resources can't be spared to help these people."

"Each life is finally worth the same," Hawker said. "We'll save more if we start looking closer to home. The decision won't be made by us," he added. "But parliament will listen to our recommendations. Do we recommend anyone will be here in two months' time?"

"We could go back to Long Island and tell them about the Pacific," Pete said. "But it wouldn't be fair to give them false hope if we couldn't also promise help was on its way. What about a plane? Didn't you guys run an airlift from Mozambique?"

"We had an African Union army protecting the runway," Tess said. "We could fly a jet from Auckland. Maybe a 777, and certainly there are a few small jets with the range. It'd be a one-way trip. To guarantee the runway remained secure, we'd have to leave a team behind."

"We don't have the ammo," Hawker said. "It sounds like the Long Islanders don't, either."

"And we don't know if the runway at JFK is in a usable condition," Tess said. "More importantly, we don't know if that plane will ever be sent. If it is, it's still one plane which, almost certainly, can't refuel. We can send supplies, and soldiers, but only if a fleet is on the way. If the ships aren't available, we risk stranding our people on Long Island, and we'd have wasted a month or two of those survivors' time and supplies which could be used to get them to Raven Rock."

"We could go back and tell them to leave," Pete said.

"They might try to take the ship," Tess said.

"After their experience with the *Archangel*, they might try to sink us," Hawker said. "Anyone who stays is being left behind."

"Oh. Well, it's not like I want to, but yeah, okay, I'll do that," Pete said.

Tess laughed. "Kind of you to offer, but we're not asking for volunteers."

"Nicko and I would stay behind if we thought it would help," Bruce said. "But for it to help, we've got to go in with a plan, and be certain it represents their best chance at survival. That brings us back to whether or not they should leave."

"I really couldn't say," Pete said.

"No worries, because Lisa Kempton had a suggestion for us," Tess said. "She says she owns a converted cruise ship that she dispatched to Europe to pick up some of her people. Honestly, the more I hear about what she did, the more I want to lock her up. I'd say the charges are treason, except she was proved to be correct. It's going to be a real mess when we get her back to Oz."

"And it'll be someone else's mess," Hawker said. "She says her ship went to Europe to pick up her people. She doesn't know when, or if, it might re-cross the Atlantic because her plans, like the cartel's, didn't include zoms. She has a mansion on the Delmarva Peninsula. She thinks some of her people might go there, and that maybe this ship will dock nearby. The captain's her wife."

"Tamika," Pete said. "I met her. She was driving the limo which took me to the airport in South Bend."

"Tamika has a sister, Loretta, who was in the FBI," Tess said. "This FBI agent was last seen heading to D.C. Not on orders from Kempton, but out of duty to her oath, to her country, and to her conscience. That mansion is somewhere this FBI agent might go, bringing other survivors with her. Maybe the ship's already gone, or maybe it never arrived. But it could be her people went there. Lisa wants us to look. If they're there, she'll lead them to New York to help the Long Islanders."

"Help them to stay, or to go?" Pete asked.

"That would depend on whether the ship's there or not," Tess said. "But maybe the peninsula is a more defensible location than Long Island. Maybe these people of hers know of another redoubt."

"What do you think?" Hawker asked.

"I know she stashed guns and gear across the world," Pete said. "But it was small amounts to help her escape the authorities."

"And what do you think of us taking a detour to the Delmarva Peninsula?" Tess asked.

"I guess it's worth a try," Pete said. "That's all it is though, right? The chances of us finding anyone are slim."

"They are," Hawker said. "My opinion is that we'll find no one, because if there was anyone there, and if they had the ability to travel, they would have gone to New York. However, Naval Station Norfolk is on the Virginia mainland, south of the peninsula. The odds of finding any survivors, or ships, there is no greater than of finding them on the peninsula, but there could be some supplies left behind, and a naval base would make for a more defensible redoubt than Long Island. It is possible we could send a team to New York, and tell them to move there."

"The stay-behind team would be Bruce, Nicko, Sergeant Temple, and Mayor Jak," Tess said. "I want you to keep an eye on Kempton for me. On the ship, and on the shore. If she wants to vanish, let her. But I don't want anyone else vanishing with her."

"You don't trust her?" Pete asked.

"Considering what she did to you and Corrie, I'm surprised you do," Tess said.

"Me, too, sometimes," Pete said. "When do we arrive at the peninsula?"

"Tomorrow," Tess said. "We'll make our approach at dawn."

18th April

Chapter 29 - Rising Danger
The Delmarva Peninsula

The Delmarva Peninsula was a massive almost-island, nearly two hundred miles long, and seventy miles wide, sheltering some of America's most famous cities from the worst of the Atlantic storms. North of the peninsula lay Philadelphia. To the west, across the Chesapeake Bay, were Baltimore and Washington. South of the bay was the city of Norfolk, and the U.S. naval station that was to be their first port of call. But as Pete looked west through the binoculars, he saw an obvious and immediate problem: the Hampton Roads Bridge clearly wasn't tall enough for a sailing yacht, let alone the icebreaker.

An alarm sounded. "Radiation warning," came the crackly voice of Captain Renton. "All crew inside."

Pete took one last look at the bridge, catching a lurching movement between a pair of abandoned cars, before heading inside, and to his secondary station.

They'd run drills yesterday for what to do in the event of a fast-boat pirate attack. Everyone who knew how to fire a gun had been given a station on deck, but now they were gathered in the corridors, looking as anxious as when they'd been rescued from Savannah.

The Georgians had brought few firearms with them. The New Zealanders had brought enough MARS-L assault rifles and Benelli M3 shotguns for the original crew, while the Australians had a crate of well-travelled M4-carbines rescued from a runway in Perth. A few souvenirs from Corn Island rounded out the armoury, leaving half of the Georgians armed only with Clyde's boarding axes.

Pete's station was in the science centre, where the cameras, and multiple doors, would provide quicker access to any part of the deck. When he arrived, he found it empty except for Corrie.

"Where's Doc Flo and Leo?" Pete asked.

"On the bridge with Tess, the colonel, and the captain," Corrie said.

"And Mrs Guinn?"

"Walking Rufus around the hold," Corrie said. "He was getting antsy stuck in here."

"How bad is the radiation?" Pete asked, taking a seat next to his sister. She'd redesigned the layout of the screens again. Four monitors each displayed a different compass-point-view from the mast cameras. Next to each screen was a shaded silhouette of a ship, indicating whether it showed port, starboard, aft, or forward.

"Atmospheric is up one point," Corrie said. "But it's the below-surface reading which is rising fast. It's probably due to radioactive run-off from shore. We're safe, but somewhere inland isn't, and around here, there's one obvious target."

"Naval Station Norfolk," Pete said.

The door opened. Mayor Jak entered. "Mind if I sate my curiosity?" he asked. "People are getting restless. I thought I might take them some tidings, one way or the other."

Corrie waved her hand at the screens. "There's not much to see, not yet," she said.

"Is that movement?" the mayor asked, pointing at the monitor showing the bridge.

"Zom," Corrie said. "I think it's following the ship. Wait, no, that looks like a new one. Must be, unless a zom learned how to put on a hat."

There were vehicles stopped on the low bridge. Mostly cars. Mostly abandoned. Mostly at odd angles, and covered with silt and grit. Between them trekked the undead, heading southward, as had the cars until the drivers had abandoned them.

"I saw a documentary about aircraft carriers," Pete said. "It was mostly about life on board, but they're way too big for that bridge."

"Now there's an understatement worthy of a Hoosier," Mayor Jak said. "I served aboard the *Truman*. Five years with a spatula in hand."

"I didn't know you were a sailor," Corrie said.

"I was little more than a fry cook with a very expensive uniform," the mayor said. "But to allay your fears, the crossing is about eighteen miles long, and is mostly bridge, but there are two mile-long tunnels. Look for the towers. And there it is. That's the artificial island where the tunnel begins."

"Is that a hand-painted sign?" Corrie asked. "Hang on, let me zoom in."

A tangled plastic sheet dangled over the side of the bridge, hanging from one rope, at a point where a bus and a truck had been parked against the bridge-barrier in a near V.

"I can't see movement," Pete said. "Wait, no, I can. Zom."

One solitary zombie remained from this last desperate redoubt where stranded survivors had hung a sign, hoping for a rescue which hadn't come until much too late.

The ship's foghorn sounded.

Pete's eyes skipped from screen to screen, hoping to catch sight of a flag, flare, or any other hint of a survivor. But there was nothing, and so the ship sailed on.

"First the radiation, now that," Pete said. "I don't like our odds of finding survivors on the peninsula."

"I wouldn't rule it out yet," the mayor said. "The peninsula was traditionally a gardener's paradise, growing produce that could survive a slow ferry crossing to the markets of Washington, Philadelphia, or Richmond. With a canal in the north, I would describe it now as an island."

"So it's the kind of place people might head to?" Pete asked. "People from Washington, Richmond, and Philadelphia? People, bringing the infection."

"And how many brought Geiger counters?" Corrie asked. "I'd be seriously worried about the ground water around here. And the rain. And the sea. The northern shores were flooded. Hang on, let me bring up the footage. There. Look for the rooftop."

On the screen, water brushed the shingles and swirled around a satellite dish. In what was probably the front yard, the drooping branches of a dying beech rose and fell with this new tide. "Why haven't the waters receded?" Pete asked.

"Elsewhere, they have," Corrie said. "That's just the most striking image. I'm collating them for distribution when we get back to Oz. Still images with a voice-over will be lower data, and more easily adapted to print. Tess wanted a package we could distribute on USB and DVD, but is that really the best use of discs? Every old house might have multiple TVs, but do they still have electricity? Power probably won't be an issue where population is densest, but for rural areas, and the new towns, I thought we could make the news a travelling show aboard a van with a projector."

"And then show them a comedy afterwards," the mayor said. "It reminds me of the mobile theatres they had during the Great War."

"Oh, so you served in the trenches before you went to sea?" Pete asked.

The mayor laughed. "Mockery might be the preserve of the young, but age finds us all, sooner than we expect. People will want to see this footage. People like us. Refugees who need to be shown that there is no alternative to hard labour beneath an Australian sun."

The ship's address system crackled. "Radiation levels are still rising. We think Norfolk was hit. We are continuing north to the naval academy at Annapolis. Remain inside."

"So Norfolk is gone, too," the mayor said. "Do we have images?"

"We didn't get close enough," Corrie said, quickly cycling through the footage. "They must be making the decision based on the radiation data."

Pete had picked up the map. Annapolis was on the Washington D.C. side of the Chesapeake Bay, some two hundred miles north of Norfolk by ship. Between Annapolis and the Delmarva Peninsula was about three miles of water and Kent Island. Further north of Annapolis was Baltimore. But almost due east, on the peninsula, was the town of Centreville, near where Kempton had built a mansion.

"Annapolis is only thirty miles from D.C.," Pete said. "If Norfolk was hit, surely D.C. was."

"It wasn't nuked," the mayor said. "A couple of ladies who'd worked in D.C. reached us in Savannah. Gail was a lobbyist. Ruby was a cleaner. They'd been part of a much larger group who'd banded together after the city collapsed."

"Did they mention anything about the peninsula?" Pete asked.

"Only that they considered going east until they found themselves on a clear road heading west. Initially, they were aiming for the mountains, but too many roads were blocked, and they ended up coming south. By all accounts, theirs was a fraught journey, a hard road along which they left most of their friends. By the time they reached Savannah, only those two remained."

"The rest were killed by zoms?" Pete asked.

"Some were, yes," the mayor said. "For the rest, it was radiation, and those two ladies died soon after they arrived. They never saw a crater, and stayed away from towns and cities. I'd speculate they drank contaminated water. But not in D.C., and they never went to Norfolk."

"It must have been the result of some random bomb," Pete said. "Like in Brazil. Like in South Africa."

"Why should this nation be any different?" the mayor said. "I should go spread the word, such as it is."

"I know what you're thinking, but it's not your fault," Pete said after the mayor had gone. "You didn't push the button."

"I could have done more," Corrie said.

"I can't think what," Pete said. "If you'd told the world, no one would have believed you. If they had, they'd have rebooted the satellites or something. If the bombs had gone off in the cities, the death toll would have been worse."

"The deaths would have been quicker," Corrie said. "Leo's already mapping the spread of oceanic dead zones. He's predicting complete ecological collapse."

"Predictions can be wrong," Pete said. "As long as we're alive, there's still hope, and we're only alive because of you."

She said nothing, and returned to her screen.

"Where is everyone?" Tess asked, when she came in from the bridge.

"Still at action stations," Pete said.

"Didn't you hear the all-clear?" Tess asked. "There must be something wrong with the wiring."

"I can take a look," Corrie said.

"Leave it until we get back from shore," Tess said. "We're making good speed, but there's no way we'll get back to the open sea before nightfall. The radiation level has fallen away. We think a bomb was dropped somewhere inland of Norfolk, but so far, Leo thinks that was the only one in this area. We'll drop your team off in a boat, and you'll go ashore on the peninsula. Meanwhile, we'll continue on to Annapolis. If we go ashore, it'll only be for an hour. We'll be back to pick you up around dusk. We'll wait in the channel until dawn, and make our final decision about Long Island tonight."

"Are you still undecided?" Pete asked.

"I'm hoping for a miracle," Tess said. "Short of that, we've no choice but to leave the New Yorkers to their fate."

Chapter 30 - The Withered Garden
The Delmarva Peninsula

Pete was still swallowing half his lunch when he boarded the boat. The other half had been eaten by Rufus as a consolation for being left behind. Olivia had wanted Rufus to join them, and so had Lisa, vocally extolling the benefits of a watchful companion. The issue, however, was radiation. More specifically, the logistical difficulties in decontaminating a dog.

With Zach confined to the ship, and Tess needing most hands for Annapolis, there were only six on their team. Lisa Kempton was their guide, while Dr Avalon was there to collect samples. Of what, and why, Pete hadn't asked because he suspected the reason, like with this mission, could be summed up as desperation. Clyde was in command while he, Corrie, and Olivia filled the ranks, and nearly filled the small launch as it slowly buzzed up the Wye River towards Queenstown, where they would hopefully find wheels. It wasn't how he'd have planned the mission, but though his opinion had been sought, his advice had not.

The peninsula's shoreline was nothing at all like New York's, so he found himself comparing it to Savannah. Here the greens were deeper, though less vibrant. The trees were more dispersed, with more land cleared for farming, though much of that was now semi-submerged. Old metal poles jutted from the languid river marking where land had once been, while beached rowing boats and raised jetties showed where the original riverbanks had burst.

The zombies, trapped beneath drifts of brush and silt, explained why no survivors had come to claim the boats. Slipways, houses, farms, occasionally a road; but always the undead. Not as many as Savannah, not yet, but the day was still young.

"Do you see that? Slow down!" Lisa said.

"What is it?" Clyde asked, as he cut their speed. The boat rocked as everyone turned to look ashore. Parked on a swathe of lawn wide enough to be a field was a helicopter.

"Take us to that jetty," Lisa said, slipping back into her familiar role of command.

"Why?" Clyde said. "We're still ten klicks from Queenstown, so about thirty from your mansion."

"Which is nothing when flying," Lisa said. "The helicopter arrived after the flood, and so it must work."

"Must it?" Clyde asked, scanning the opposite shore, and then the swollen river ahead. He returned his gaze to the helicopter. "Corrie, radio the ship. Tell them we're detouring to inspect a helicopter."

As they approached, Pete realised the jetty belonged to the house, as did the field-sized lawn on which the helicopter had landed. Except it wasn't just a house. The waterfront building was a brick boathouse, twice the size of Corrie's cabin. Behind it was a mansion. But even that was a dollar-bill description for a bullion-priced building. Four stories tall, counting the narrow windows in the eaves. Built of a pale yellow brick that must have been imported, though they'd saved on mortar by making the windows massive. Ten on each floor, in neatly regimented lines. Each window had ornamental shutters, half of which were closed, and a quarter of which hung loose or had been ripped clear.

"Weapons hot, barrels down," Clyde said as the boat bumped against the jetty. The waters here were high, or the ground had sunk, making it an easy step down to the nearly flooded walkway.

Corrie climbed off first, but Clyde quickly overtook her. "Kempton, Doc Flo, with me," the old soldier said. "Guinns, see if there's a car in the drive or in the garage."

"I guess the garage would be at the front of the house," Corrie said. "There's a path over there."

Pete, once again, carried one of Clyde's ship-made axes, though this had been modified with a spike next to the head. "Anyone know much about helicopters?" he asked.

"Not how to fly one," Corrie said. "But Lisa does, doesn't she?"

"It didn't look big enough for all of us," Pete said.

"That's good, because I'd be happy never flying again," Olivia said.

The path meandered through a screen of wilting bushes, and to a swimming pool. The water was black with patches of green on the surface.

"Fancy a swim?" Pete asked.

"Look at the pool house," Olivia said.

"I never understood those," Pete said. "You've got a real house just over there, why not change clothes inside?"

"If you want to get on your soapbox, ask why you'd need a swimming pool when there's a perfectly good river at the end of your yard," Olivia said. "But I was talking about the roof. Those are solar panels."

"One set of panels, one solar water heater," Corrie said. "Mind the path, it gets slimy."

"This would be the perfect refuge," Olivia said. "But it's clearly deserted, so where did the helicopter's pilot go?"

There were fewer windows at the side of the house, but they were as dark as the building's river-facing rear. Beyond another dying shrubbery, they reached the front of the house, and a circular drive with a fountain in the centre and a cavernous garage in the north.

"I knew there'd be a fountain!" Olivia said. "Pete, if Lisa ever gives you your back pay, we're buying a house like this."

"I think I'll need a few more zeroes in my paycheck," he said. "Main gate's open. Can't see any tyre marks, for all that tells us."

He rested the axe on his shoulder as they strolled over to the garage. The main doors were electronic and locked. But the small door at the side of the garage was open.

Pete turned on the small light pinned to his vest before pushing the door. "Hello!" he called. A paint can rattled. A falling broom clattered. Pete stepped back. "Hey," he said. "Are you alive?"

"Gator," Olivia whispered, aiming her shotgun low.

"Maybe a dog," Corrie said.

A desiccated palm slapped into metal as a figure in yellow-trimmed blue overalls padded heavily towards them.

"Just a zom," Pete said.

Olivia raised her shotgun, and her light, shining it on the zombie's face. Pete lunged forwards, spearing the axe's sharpened point into its eye.

"Careful!" Olivia said. "You nearly signed off on a shotgun-divorce."

"Sorry," Pete said, pulling the axe-point clear as the zombie fell. "Just one, I think. And there's a car inside. Big car, too."

"Okay, but let's be careful," Olivia said, "because someone infected that mechanic."

"I don't think he was a mechanic," Corrie said. "That uniform looks familiar."

"Check the doors," Pete said, shining his light beneath the one vehicle still in the garage. There was room for four, though the monstrous SUV took up nearly as much space as two.

"Keys are in the ignition," Olivia said. "There's a handgun on the seat, and a bag in the footwell. A couple more bags in the back." She opened the trunk, and then a bag. "Food, clothes, soap, and toilet paper. Maybe looted from the mansion. It's like he was ready to go."

From outside came a mechanical burr, there and then gone as the helicopter's engine was shut down again. Pete opened the driver's door. When he turned the keys, he got a mechanical roar of his own. "Battery is fine, and the tank's full. We better tell Clyde."

"You found a car?" Clyde said. "Show me."

"We could fly," Lisa said.

"I'm not convinced you can," Clyde said.

"Ask Rufus, he will attest to my skill," Lisa said.

"There's a limited amount of fuel," Clyde said. "We won't waste it when we might need it to survey the harbours down in South America. A car will get us to your mansion quick enough."

"There's a zombie, too," Pete said, as he led them down to the garage. "Or there was."

"Capital. I'll gather a sample," Avalon said.

"Later," Clyde said. "We'll have a wait while we load that helicopter onto the ship. Big garage, isn't it?" he added as they neared.

"Big house," Pete said.

Lisa broke into a run, overtaking them, and coming to a halt by the corpse. "Jorge LeMarck," she said.

"You know him?" Clyde asked.

"He was an employee of a sort," Lisa said. "About twelve years ago, Tamika and I were having a row about whether I was squandering my wealth, how I was wasting it on this battle with the cartel, and their politicians. How I should be doing more. Out of spite, really, I picked up a newspaper, and picked the first medical condition I found a mention of. It was multiple sclerosis. I donated a hundred million to various research projects. Jorge's brother was part of the first trial on the first treatment the money funded. The patient's quality of life improved, but not the outcome. Yet Jorge was grateful. He was also a pilot for a news station in D.C."

"That's his helicopter?" Clyde asked.

"Of his former employer," Lisa said. "He insisted he owed me a favour. So I said, one day, I might ask him to fly me out of the capital, no questions asked. He agreed. I never had a need to take him up on the offer until the outbreak. That Mr LeMarck is wearing one of my uniforms is proof he fell in with some of my people. But the only one who knew of him, and who might have called upon him and his helicopter, is Loretta."

"That's your FBI agent sister-in-law, right?" Clyde asked.

"I never dared get institutional sanction for our relationship," Lisa said. "But yes, Loretta is family."

"She must be at the mansion," Clyde said.

"Must she?" Lisa said. "The helicopter didn't land there, and the pilot was infected."

"They took the boat," Pete said.

"What boat?" Lisa asked.

"The boat that's not here," Pete said. "Why else leave a helicopter behind?"

"Then everyone get in that car," Clyde said. "We'll go to this mansion to confirm it."

Chapter 31 - Strange Meetings on Stranger Roads
The Delmarva Peninsula

Pete drove. Clyde rode shotgun, though armed with an assault rifle. Everyone else was in the back. Even so, the SUV had room to stretch. For the first few miles, it was wonderful to be behind the wheel again. The open road, overhung with brown-mottled trees, was a tonic compared to the panicked sprint through Brooklyn. Until a zombie stepped out from behind a stalled milk-tanker.

Pete braked, but not quickly enough. The truck slowed, but not enough. He swerved, but not enough. The undead soldier hit the front right corner, and was dragged beneath the tyres. The SUV rocked.

"Sorry," Pete muttered, half to the soldier, half to the passengers.

"Stop," Avalon said.

"Keep going," Clyde said.

"A uniformed soldier must have been infected close to the beginning of the outbreak," Avalon said. "The sample would be invaluable."

"Then we'll get it on the way back," Clyde said.

Pete glanced in the mirror. Behind them, the undead soldier was trying to put weight on its now broken limbs.

"At least put on the radio," Avalon said.

"No stations will still be broadcasting," Lisa said.

"How do you know?" Avalon asked.

To the soundtrack of static as the radio cycled through frequencies, they drove on.

The road gave way to mud, then to rain-rinsed asphalt, and then to birds. Thousands, not just on the road, but in the fields on either side, and all recently dead. The storm-drenched fields had been turned grey and black, and occasionally red, with a blizzard of feathers.

"Could it be VX?" Olivia asked.

"Radiation," Avalon said. "Keep going."

"Are you sure?" Olivia asked.

"I've had my suspicions since the bushes close to the shore," Avalon said. "The birds carried the radiation on their feet, their beaks, their wings. The decay at the shoreline was the opposite of what one would expect. Most of the plant life is struggling, which is understandable after a flood laden with toxins, but the grass showed signs of recovery, while the trees were showing signs of cellular decay."

"That's why your people left, Lisa," Olivia said. "Who'd want to stay here?"

"Tell us about this mansion," Clyde said as, once again, the tyres found solid ground.

"It was camouflage," Lisa said. "A billionaire is supposed to own mansions, so I had one built. I invited in a television crew so they could show the world I lived just as lavishly as was expected."

"Modest piety would have been a more cost-effective camouflage," Avalon said.

"Car!" Clyde cut in. "Approaching from ahead."

The vehicle came into view as they neared a junction. A tow truck whose back was filled with fuel cans and rolls of barbed wire. Pete slowed, while the other vehicle braked sharply, stopping at the edge of the junction from where the driver had a choice of escape routes. One driver, no passengers. Pete stopped the SUV on the other side of the junction.

"Everyone stay put," Clyde said, as he opened the door. "G'day!" he called out, as he raised both of his empty hands up into the air. He stepped away from the car. "Major Clyde Brook. Australian Defence Force. Can we talk?"

The driver wound down his window. He didn't get out. "D'you say Australia?" he yelled.

"That's right, mate," Clyde said. "We're looking for survivors. Haven't found many so far."

"Won't find them here," the man said. His words were slurred.

"The road back there was full of radioactive birds," Clyde said.

"Yep," the driver said. "Came in a while back. Flocked together, died together."

"Together? Fascinating," Avalon said.

"Shh," Olivia said.

"Do you want to come with us, mate?" Clyde asked. "Or do you know of anyone around here who might? We've got room on our ship."

"If you're looking for people, you won't find them," the man said. "Not here. They're all gone. Went weeks ago. You should do the same while you can."

"What about you, mate, will you come with us?" Clyde asked.

"I was born here. I'm going to die here," the man said. "There's no help for me, so do yourselves a favour, and leave."

He wound the window back up, and drove off, taking the junction south.

"Safeties off," Clyde said as he got back in the truck. "Corrie, see if you can reach the ship. Warn them there are survivors on the peninsula, and I think they're hostile."

"He didn't sound hostile," Corrie said.

"It's a feeling," Clyde said. "A very bad feeling."

Pete tried to keep his eyes on the road, but they kept straying to the mirror, only being dragged back with a muted left or right from Lisa, or a communal warning of a zombie straight ahead.

"Stop here," Lisa finally said.

"This doesn't look like a mansion," Clyde said.

Pete pulled up outside a split-level ranch with a rose-garden and sheltered porch from which a flag-pole jutted at a forty-degree angle.

"Count the stripes on the flag," Lisa said.

"Hard to do from here," Clyde said. "Is this it?"

"My estate is on the other side of the road, beyond that wall and fence, and what will be the most wonderful forest in a century's time."

"I shall add a reminder to my calendar," Avalon said.

"The flag is a signal," Lisa said, opening the door. "The number of stripes is the message."

She began walking over to the flag, until Corrie yelled a warning.

"Zom!" she said, aiming her carbine at a rustling bush, from which a four-legged, white-faced ball of brown fur scampered, fast, disappearing beneath the porch.

"A possum," Olivia said. "That's something to tell Zach."

Clyde tapped the camera on his body-armour. "He'll see it for himself. What's this about the stripes?"

"A moment," Lisa said, picking up the damp fabric. "Fifteen stripes." She let the flag drop. "If a flag is flying, it means danger. This one has fifteen stripes. That was supposed to be used if the FBI had the house under surveillance. It is the signal to scatter. In retrospect, I should have used flags with a rigid frame that would have been easier to see from the road. Ah, but there was so much to do, much was overlooked."

"Never mind that now," Clyde said. "Why did we stop here?"

"Because we found Mr LeMarck and his helicopter at the shore," Lisa said. "This flag isn't a message for me. As you will know from the death of my pilots in Broken Hill, I suspected my organisation had been infiltrated and *knew* the FBI had. This flag was a signal to warn people away. Clearly, the FBI aren't a danger, and so it must be the undead who now occupy my mansion. Yes, I believe my people have gone, and most likely by ship."

Clyde looked at the flag, then the high wall, then the length of the road down which they'd driven, finally settling on the solitary zombie staggering towards them. His gaze returned to the high wall. Well above head height, it was impossible to see what lay beyond, but they could hear it. "We've got zoms on the other side of the wall. We shouldn't have stopped here, but we have, so is our mission done?"

"Can you hold this position for ten minutes?" Lisa asked.

"What for?" Clyde asked.

"There is a tunnel between here and the mansion," Lisa said. "If one were to be accurate, it is an escape tunnel leading *from* the mansion. I won't need long, but I would like to see if Tamika left a message for me. I could say that, if she did, it would contain invaluable data on Europe, but for me this is a personal quest, driven by love."

Clyde looked at the wall, then at the approaching zombie. He raised his rifle, and fired. "Show me this tunnel."

At the back of the house, overlooking a mature orchard, was another porch, this one far wider than at the front.

"Who lived here?" Olivia asked.

"John Clayton," Lisa said. "My first secretary. He retired here. I offered to buy him an island, but he said a bushel of apples was all he desired." She took a step towards the backdoor, before shaking her head. "There are some things best never known."

In the corner of the porch, a section of the decking was hinged and already raised up. Inside was a metre drop to a metal hatch set in concrete.

"Looks like we're not the first to use the tunnel," Clyde said. "It runs straight, right? Just two ways in and out?"

"Like a pipe," Lisa said.

"Then she and I will go into the mansion," Clyde said. "Everyone else, stay here. Two here, two by the car."

"Absolutely not," Avalon said. "I don't know what data might be found in that house, but there is none here."

"I'll stand guard," Olivia said. "Pete, you watch Doc Flo."

"Family sticks together," Pete said.

"So I'll stick with Olivia," Corrie said. "Ten minutes, right? So hurry back."

"I'll go first," Clyde said. "Then Lisa, then the doc, then Pete. Keep your lights on, and a fighting space between you and whoever's in front. Leave your bags here."

"I'll need mine if there are samples to be collected," Avalon said.

"Whatever," Clyde said, sounding uncharacteristically irritated. "Let's just get this done."

Below the hatch, a ladder led down. Pete stopped counting rungs at twenty, and gave up estimating depth at thirty yards, but when his boots hit firm concrete, he guessed he was about fifty below the surface.

They were in an antechamber, slightly wider than the tunnel leading from it, and down which Clyde was walking, though Lisa was levering open an electrical junction box. It clunked loudly, swinging ajar to reveal nothing, not even any wires.

"It's a dead drop," Lisa said.

"An apt choice of words," Avalon said. "Did you ever consider the effort you put into this subterfuge could be better spent?"

"Many times," Lisa said. "Though since we are currently using a tunnel to avoid the undead, I would say it would have been better spending *more* money."

"Move up," Clyde called.

"Go on," Pete said.

The tunnel was just taller than a person, and just wider, with a pair of drainage trenches, either side. It ran utterly straight for as far as Clyde's beam reached, though the light didn't reach the tunnel's end, instead glistening off an occasional spider web which Clyde broke as he passed.

"How long does it take a spider to spin a web?" Pete asked.

"That would depend on the spider," Avalon said. "Though usually a few hours. But yes, we are the first to come this way in some time."

In his next life, there'd be no more tunnels, Pete decided. No tunnels, no subways, no billionaires.

After what seemed like an aeon in the dark, they reached another antechamber with another ladder, and with a pair of electrical junction boxes. Lisa opened the bottom box. Inside was a tablet.

"No power to the cameras," Lisa said. "They had a thirty-day battery." She lifted the tablet out, looking behind. "No message, either."

"What's above us?" Clyde asked.

"The mansion," Lisa said. "The ladder leads to a tunnel which runs between the ground-floor rooms. Think of it as a servants' passage from the Victorian era, but which has a few concealed access points. One can hardly ask an architect to include an escape route in the official plans. A servants' passage was a useful disguise."

"Shh," Clyde said, as he put a foot on the ladder. "Quiet from now on. Quiet, and listen."

The higher they climbed, the clearer the sound became. A whisper of cloth. A distant thud. An echoing clump-clump of dragging feet. Unmistakable, and when they reached the narrow ledge at the ladder's top, seemingly coming from all around.

Pete, still on the ladder, looked up at Lisa and Clyde pantomiming and pointing at the blank walls. It took him a moment to figure out that Lisa was uncertain how to get the concealed door open from this side. Finally, Lisa found the recessed lever. The door clicked open, and a brief gust of air shimmered across Pete's face.

Clyde waved him up, and into the ground-floor corridor. This corridor was narrower than the tunnel. Darker, despite the lights from helmets and body armour, though the end was obvious. Obvious, and not an end but a T-junction.

"Left," Lisa whispered.

Pete heard a dry whispering gasp in reply, and coming from the other side of the wall, only a few inches of plaster away.

After the turning, the tunnel ahead was much shorter, ending in a wall after only a few yards. Clyde motioned them to wait. Lisa, again, searched for the latch. Avalon's bag clanked into the wall as she attempted to turn around. That clank had an echo.

Pete made himself thin so he could more easily turn. At the far end of the corridor, beyond a right-angle junction, a zombie fell forward, slamming into the wall. A second zombie fell on top, pushing the first down, even as both struggled to get to their feet. Old paint rose in a cloud as the pair thrashed their way upright.

"Hurry," Pete said, meaning Lisa and Clyde, though it was the undead who seemed to heed him. He raised his axe, getting ready to stab it forward. Above and behind him, the pattern of light changed.

"Harriet?" Lisa said.

"Move!" Avalon said, tugging on his arm.

Pete walked backwards, not daring to turn, not trying to run, and moving not nearly as fast as the three undead. Another arm grabbed him, pulling him aside with much greater force than Avalon. Clyde, gun raised, fired three shots into the tunnel.

"Move! Close that door!" the soldier said as Pete stumbled out into a massive hall. He saw Lisa, clutching her arm.

Avalon had dropped her bag, and was rummaging inside. "I've bandages here," she said.

"What happened?" Pete asked.

"I said move," Clyde said, grabbing the scientist and pulling her to her feet. "The stairs, go! Pete, get her upstairs."

Pete grabbed Avalon's arm, while Clyde took Kempton's. Together, they ran up the broad staircase, pausing only when they reached the top.

"Where's the exit?" Clyde said. "Lisa? Lisa, are you okay?"

"A scratch from that knife," she said. "Nothing more. I was distracted when I saw Harriet. I apologise, we appear to have walked into a nightmare."

"Right, and we need a way out," Clyde said. "The tunnel's no good. Is that front door our exit?"

"There's a balcony down which we can climb. It's this way," Lisa said, moving off along the corridor.

"My bag," Avalon said, leaning over the balcony.

"Is it important?" Pete asked.

Avalon checked her uniform, before patting her hip pocket with relief. "No. No, I have Leo's book here, so there's nothing inside which is irreplaceable."

"Then let's go," Pete said, pushing her after Clyde and Lisa.

A wide corridor filled with gilt-framed paintings ended in another concealed door which led into a sparsely furnished suite. What little Pete had seen of the mansion had fit every billionaire stereotype. A staircase wide enough for an elephant, and a hallway tall enough for a giraffe. More brass and glass light fittings than a small town, and more marble than a quarry. These private quarters, however, were spartan: a kitchenette with un-matching crockery, and an ancient set of appliances, a bedroom barely big enough for the pair of throne-like chairs and the empress-sized futon. The bathroom was high-end, but still functional rather than decadent. It was a glimpse, though only a brief one, behind Lisa's life-long facade.

"Clear," Clyde said, finishing his quick sweep. "Let's see your arm, Lisa."

"There should be some bandages in the bathroom," Lisa said. "On the far side of the bed, there is a drawer. Remove the drawer, remove the panel beneath. There is a dead drop. Tamika will have left a message there."

"I think she left it on the bed," Pete said. "There's an envelope and a tablet."

"Let me see," Lisa said.

"Let *me* see your arm," Avalon said.

"They were here," Lisa said.

"Your people?" Clyde asked.

"The cartel," Lisa said. She'd opened the envelope. From it, she removed a thin slip of card, then let the remaining contents fall onto the bed. "Rose petals for the Rosewood Cartel."

"What does the card say?" Clyde asked.

"The Mountain View Motel, Sutton, West Virginia," Lisa said. She picked up the tablet, and switched it on. "No password. Not much power. It's a video. Paused." She let it play for a few seconds, then stopped the playback.

"What was it?"

"Harriet, being injected," Lisa said. "She was the zombie down in the hall."

"Did you recognise anyone else in the video?" Clyde asked.

"I will watch the rest when we are back on the ship," Lisa said. "The message is clear, because there is one other person I recognised, the person holding the syringe. It was Margalotta Herrera."

Chapter 32 - Captured on Camera
The Delmarva Peninsula

Quarantine! Again! Pete raged. He fumed, but he did so quietly inside the med-lab's transparent observation room from where he could observe Avalon examining the samples taken from shore. He'd not even noticed the cut on his neck, and had no idea how, or when, he'd got it. He was next to certain it hadn't come from a zombie, but it had been spotted by Sergeant Temple when they'd returned aboard, and so he'd been sent to quarantine. He assumed Lisa was in quarantine somewhere else, because it wasn't in the med-bay.

He knew he was immune. Avalon knew it. But Tess had said it was important to maintain procedures. Let them slip now, and they'd be harder to re-implement on the long voyage home.

He looked up as the door opened. Olivia entered holding a tray. Her mouth opened as she silently, and exaggeratedly, formed words.

"The walls aren't soundproof," Pete said.

Olivia grinned. "Ah, foiled. Dinner?"

"Please."

"Did you bring two?" Avalon asked.

"Just one for the patient," Olivia said.

"He's only been lying there," Avalon said. "That hardly warrants room service." She grabbed her notebook, and left the lab.

"She's in a mood," Olivia said.

"We had a fight," Pete said.

"Why?"

"It's about Leo's next novel. He wants to set it aboard a spaceship, but she thinks it'd be technically impossible for his survivors on that moon to build one. I clearly didn't agree with her vociferously enough."

"How's the neck?" she asked.

"Itchy and stingy and sore," he said. "But I'm fine, just a bit antsy. Why's Lisa not here?"

"She's in quarantine next door, in the office, talking with Tess and the colonel, and has been pretty much since we got back. You eat, and I'll catch you up."

"Have I missed a lot?" he asked.

"Not really, but we're staying here tonight. It's because of the helicopter. I think they've decided it's too dangerous letting Lisa try landing it on the deck, so we're not going to bring it with us. There's enough fuel to fly it a few hundred miles, so that would cover D.C. and Norfolk and then back."

"If we're staying here overnight, Leo can't be worried about radiation."

"We wouldn't reach open water tonight anyway," Olivia said. "Which I think means it's something he *is* worrying about, but I really don't want to."

"What did they find at Annapolis?"

"It's a real disaster zone," Olivia said. "A big explosion tore chunks from the buildings. There are zoms everywhere. They didn't even go ashore in the end. But it looks like there were a lot of military vehicles gathered nearby, as if they'd been readied for some kind of pushback which never began. Oh, and the bridge to the peninsula was demolished. It'd be difficult to get a ship, even one like the *Archangel*, through the wreckage. I don't know if that helps decide things or not."

"Do you mean because of the video left for Lisa? Did you see it?"

"You can, too," she said. She took a small tablet from her pocket. "It's not good, Pete."

The screen was paused, but showed five seated people, cuffed and bloody. Two wore Lisa's blue and gold-trim working uniform, two wore military fatigues, while the fifth wore battle-stained jeans. Behind them were two guards in black coats, both holding baseball bats.

"Does Lisa know them?"

"Just the woman on the left," Olivia said.

"Harriet? Right. Yeah, Clyde had to shoot her," Pete said.

The chairs were ornate, with hand-stitched fabric and curving white frames, while the room the prisoners were held in had silk curtains and gilt wallpaper. The windows had been boarded with plyboard. Illumination came from somewhere behind the camera.

"Are you going to press play?" Olivia asked.

"I was just thinking that room's the kind of place you'd sign a peace treaty."

"Or start a war," Olivia said. "You didn't see the room?"

"We saw a tunnel, the hall, and then her bedroom. It was very minimalist. Ah, I'm stalling." He pressed play.

A man stepped forward, into the frame. He was about fifty, balding, clean-shaven, tall and large but with the flab of someone who prized steak and beer over cardio. He wore military camouflage, but he didn't look like a soldier. At his belt were knives, but no gun. In his hand was a metal case which he placed on a walnut side table. Opening it, he withdrew a syringe, filled it from a vial, then placed it on the table. He repeated the action, carefully, deliberately, four times, until five syringes were on the table. He glanced back at the camera before stepping aside, then walked behind the row of prisoners.

"There's no sound," Pete said, as the torturer opened his mouth.

"No," Olivia said. "We think this was recorded on the tablet, but the videographer had their finger over the mic. Corrie's trying to recover the sound, but I don't think we need it."

An older woman stepped into the frame and walked to the table. There, she turned around, speaking to the camera. At least sixty, though possibly older, her hair was jet black, pinned into an iron-firm bun. She was short, with bony arms, and a wrinkled neck. She wore a long black skirt, black short-heeled boots, and a black, waist-length coat. It was funeral attire, and from a different era, except he'd bet she dressed like that every day. She picked up a syringe, and walked over to the first victim, Harriet.

Harriet squirmed, stretching against the bonds, clearly aware of what was in the needle.

The large man grabbed her shoulders, pushing her down into the chair as the funeral-clad woman stabbed the needle into Harriet's thigh. The woman returned the syringe to the table, and picked up a second, walking over to the next victim, even as Harriet slumped forward. As the second victim was injected, Harriet thrashed and bucked, rocking the chair, obviously undead. The killer didn't slow, nor did she speed up; she returned the spent needle to the table, and collected a third.

Five victims, five injections. Harriet and the young man in jeans turned immediately. The other three didn't. The black-clad woman paused to look at the camera, then walked out of shot. The large man did the same, followed by the two guards. Just as one of the soldiers slumped, and as the undead Harriet fell to the floor, breaking the arm of her chair, a sixth prisoner was brought before the camera. Old, small, terrified, bruised, and bloody. He was there for a moment, then led away. The camera lingered on the undead Harriet, who'd managed to rip a hand free. Her legs were still pinned, as she rocked and rolled towards the so-far still human soldier, but the camera went dark before she reached him.

"That's it?" Pete asked.

"That's it," Olivia said. "That vile woman who won runner-up for worst witch costume, that was Margalotta Herrera."

"One of the sisters," Pete said.

"And where one goes, so does the other, or so Lisa says," Olivia said.

"The sixth guy, who was that?"

"The old man? John Clayton. Lisa's first secretary. The guy who retired to the house with the orchard and tunnel. Did Lisa show you the card that was left with the video?"

"It had an address in West Virginia," Pete said.

"Exactly," Olivia said. "Remember where that plane which took us to Corn Island refuelled? Now look at the time stamp."

"It's the same day?"

"The day before," Olivia said. "Clearly, the sisters came to the mansion looking for Lisa, but gave up waiting. I don't know how long they held these people prisoner, but it must have been for ages. Clyde thinks that some of Lisa's people made it to the mansion, and so did some soldiers, and who knows who else. They defended it, and lived there, at least for a while, until the sisters came."

"Then the sisters left for West Virginia, but if they ever arrived, wouldn't they have flown to Corn Island?"

"You'd think," Olivia said. "Meanwhile the nephew ended up in New York aboard a ship from Miami. The only explanation I can come up with is that, whatever they had planned, it fell apart weeks ago."

Pete watched the clock. His neck burned, which was probably a sign it was healing, but it added to his irritation as he watched the minutes tick by. Twelve-thirty. He'd tried reading, but couldn't concentrate. He couldn't help but think of the people in that video, and whether that had been the fate intended for him.

"You awake?" Tess asked, entering the med-bay.

"Just about," Pete said. "Is quarantine over?"

"More or less, sorry about that," she said. "There was a bit of friction after Annapolis. Some of the Georgians took this detour poorly. Sticking you in isolation was a way of showing we've still got rules and will apply them to everyone."

"Sure, I understand."

"Good on ya. Mind if we talk?" She held up a flask. "I brought tea. No one needs coffee when you can't tell if it's breakfast or bedtime."

"Is something wrong?"

"You saw the video from the mansion, right?"

"Olivia showed me."

"Good," Tess said. "So you saw that bit with the old man at the end?"

"John Clayton, Lisa's secretary, yes. They didn't kill him on screen."

"Lisa had a hunch, and Corrie cleaned up enough of the audio to confirm it," Tess said. "He was taken to a motel in Sutton, West Virginia. That's the address left on that card on the bed. Herrera challenged Lisa to come get him before it was too late. She wants to take the helicopter and go see if he's still alive. I'm inclined to let her since she's our only pilot, and we don't have any spare fuel. The helicopter doesn't have the range to reach Sutton, but Lisa has a vehicle stashed somewhere to the southwest. She's going to fly there, then drive the rest of the way. We're heading on to Thunderbolt to refuel and re-supply, but we can't stay there long. At dusk, in five days, we'll sail south."

"How far away is Sutton?"

"From here? About five hundred kilometres, due west."

"How far from Sutton to Thunderbolt?" Pete asked.

"About nine hundred kilometres," Tess said.

"That's not too far," Pete said.

"Maybe a year ago," Tess said. "Pete, Lisa's making a one-way trip. I'm next to certain the sisters never reached West Virginia. I'm just as certain Lisa won't reach Thunderbolt before we leave. Lisa presents a problem to me, a problem for the Pacific. I don't know whether we can charge her with anything, or whether the public, or the politicians, will want to. Her leaving solves a lot of problems. That doesn't mean you have to go with her."

"But you're asking me anyway?"

"No, I'm telling you how it is. You've done your part, mate. So have I. So has everyone on this ship. We were tasked with destroying the cartel, and we did that in Colombia, and on Corn Island, and when we sank the *Archangel*. I feel no compunction in ignoring this lead. The sisters didn't get to Colombia, so they probably died on their way to

Sutton. Mr Clayton is dead, and it will never be known how. You don't have to go with her."

"But you can't spare anyone else? Pete asked.

"I can't spare *you*," Tess said. "We'll need you down in the Pacific."

"But maybe Mr Clayton needs help," Pete said. "Who else is going to help him, but us?"

"Clayton's dead, Pete," Tess said. "Kempton can manage well enough on her own. You don't need to go with her."

"But you don't really need me on this ship," Pete said. "I was a prisoner, and you saved me. I've got to do the same. How could I live with myself if I didn't?"

"I want you to understand this really is a one-way trip," Tess said. "We'll endeavour to remain in Thunderbolt for five days, but I can't guarantee it. If the marina has been overrun, we don't have the ammo to clear it, so won't have the supplies to linger. After Savannah, there's no knowing when, or where, or *if*, the next ship will come. This is it, Pete. I'd like to promise different, but I can't."

"No, I understand," Pete said. "We've got to make the most of the days we have, and live them the best we can. I think I have to go."

"Your quarantine's over, so talk with your family before making any final decision," Tess said.

He found Corrie, and Rufus, waiting with Olivia in his and his wife's cabin.

"I really want to see kangaroos," Olivia said. "What do you say, Rufus? Want to chase some 'roos?"

The dog growled sleepily.

"Lisa can't go to the Pacific," Corrie said. "She knows it. At best, she's facing house arrest. So am I, when the full story gets told."

"If it gets told," Olivia said.

"I told Tess," Corrie said. "I'd told her most of it before, and I think she'd worked out the details I omitted. Leo worked it out on his own."

"It doesn't mean they'll tell anyone," Pete said.

"They have to," Corrie said. "You can't build a society on secrets and lies. We can't risk a revolution, or an uprising, or even discontent. Have you seen Leo's mapping of oceanic dead-zones? The world's on the brink. Leo doesn't know if it has a future, but he's not worried about the zoms anymore; that's a clear sign of how bad things are. I don't want to make it any worse. I'll go with Lisa."

"Then we'll come too," Olivia said. "Family sticks together."

"You don't have to," Corrie said. "And I don't want you feeling that you have to."

"I *do* feel I have to," Olivia said. "It doesn't have anything to do with Lisa, but how could I possibly live with myself if we left that poor man to die?"

"That's what I said to Tess," Pete said. "We'll go because someone has to, and there is no one else but us."

Part 3
Jam Today, a Future Tomorrow

Virginia and West Virginia

19th April

Chapter 33 - The Billionaire Biker Gang
Amelia Court House, Virginia

"She's about ready, mate," Clyde said. "I'm expecting a good yarn next time we meet. Thunderbolt, five days."

"Thunderbolt, sure," Pete said. "See you there."

"Remember rule one," Tess said. "Do take care, until we meet again."

"Until then," Pete said. He watched Tess and Clyde walk back to their launch, then turned his back on the water, and walked to the helicopter.

Corrie had rigged a camera to the cabin which would broadcast images as they flew west. When the helicopter was out of receiving-range, the icebreaker would depart.

"Having second thoughts?" Lisa asked.

"Absolutely," Pete said. "Doesn't mean I'm changing my mind."

"I would understand if you did," Lisa said. "There's no need for you to come with me."

"If we all left the tough jobs to other people, we'd end up with... well, with a world filled with zoms and radiation," Olivia said. "One apocalypse was enough, thanks."

Corrie raised her carbine and fired. "One zom. That's our signal to get aboard," she said. "If we see another, it's time to take off."

Five minutes later, they were in the air.

As they flew, it was impossible to hear anything but the roaring motor and churning blades. Outside, it was impossible to see any hope for the future of humanity. The devastation was so extensive, so complete, so much more obvious from above. Branchless trees, glass-less homes, lifeless bodies, some of which slowly lumbered beneath them. Entire forests had been felled. Whole suburbs had burned. A town had been completely replaced with a crater. It wasn't Norfolk, but without the map, he couldn't identify it. He bowed his head, thinking of the world he'd known. It hadn't been such a bad place, all things considered. Not bad enough to deserve this.

Far sooner than he'd expected, and much sooner than he was prepared for, Lisa began their descent. As the helicopter set down on the branch-strewn highway, an avalanche of grit pattered against the cabin, while a jungle of leaves were shredded by the rotors. Something much heavier was dragged into the turbine. The helicopter shuddered, just before it thumped to a heavily final landing on the woodland highway.

Pete grabbed his bag and carbine, and opened the door. Before he could step outside, Rufus leaped, disappearing into the cloud of dust. Pete followed, keeping his head well below the slowing, but smoking, blades.

"Haste is always a fugitive's ally," Lisa said, as Rufus returned. He circled around them warily, before settling his gaze, and ears, on the road behind.

Lisa grabbed her bag from the helicopter.

"Where are we, Lisa?" Corrie asked.

"And where are we going?" Olivia said. "Guess I should have asked that sooner, right?"

"Unfortunately, I believe we landed a few miles short, but behind us, in the east, is the town of Amelia Court House. We are about a hundred and eighty miles south-southwest of Annapolis."

"Sutton was due west of the peninsula," Pete said.

"Indeed, and then we want to travel a lot further southeast in order that you should catch the last ship leaving this hemisphere. We need a vehicle, and this is the nearest location where I concealed one. If we follow this highway west, we will soon reach a motorbike showroom and garage."

"Oh, that's right, your bio said you love riding your bike across the country," Olivia said.

"That was another lie," Lisa said. "Between the bugs and the noise, I would much rather travel by car if I have to, plane if I had the choice, and ship if I had the time."

"Yeah, that was a nice plane," Pete said, as he slung the bag over his shoulder. "So why lie to the journalists about liking motorbikes?"

"So there were no questions as to why I would own a showroom and garage," Lisa said.

With Olivia by his side, he followed Lisa and Corrie, who now followed Rufus, along the highway away from the helicopter. Without the rotors' thunder-burr, the world became artificially quiet and apparently empty. But the ocean-roar of silence quickly subsided. A crack and crackle came from the woodland on either side. The trees, though young, were densely planted, with a fern and bracken barrier between the trunks and the roadside. On the southern edge of the road, the verge was raised in a rain-channelling berm, while in the north it had been dug into a deep gulley. With as much ash as rain having fallen in recent weeks, that gulley was more sludge than water, which churned, grew, rose into a two-legged swamp-monster as a zombie stood.

"Leave it," Olivia said, at the same time as Pete.

"Jinx," he said, while the zombie stumbled, tripped, and splashed back into the brackish ditch.

"If," Olivia said, "you ever wonder when precisely I began to have misgivings about the wisdom of leaving the ship, it was now. Corrie, did you check the radiation when we set down?"

"We're fine," Corrie said. "Just don't drink the water."

"Very serious misgivings," Olivia said, glancing back at the still-splashing zombie.

Pete had never adjusted to how relentlessly fast the icebreaker could move, despite often seeming glacially slow. Now, he felt like a snail, and his shell grew heavier with each step. New York hadn't been like this, nor Thunderbolt or Delmarva. But they'd no home to return to this time, and the backpack was hardly a protective castle into which he could retreat.

Drawing on memories of New York, Delmarva, and Thunderbolt only brought forth memories of Corn Island. There'd not been much walking there except to go outside for an occasional torture. It was mostly psychological, thanks to Corrie, and even fake executions can become routine.

"The zoms are ignoring us," Olivia whispered. "No, don't look. Oh, I suppose it doesn't matter. Look south, at the far edge of the trees, they're heading towards the helicopter. I don't think they've seen us."

Pete looked up at the trees, back at the still visible helicopter, then at the road ahead. "Any who are on the road will be heading straight towards us," he said.

"Ah. Guess we should hurry," Olivia said.

"That doesn't look promising," Olivia said, as the motorbike showroom came into view.

The roadside signage had given them a clear early warning their destination lay ahead. The giant poster showed Lisa herself astride a low-rider beneath the slogan: *Freedom Is for Everyone*.

Part showroom, part gas station, part repair shop, it was completely wrecked. The showroom's floor-to-ceiling windows had been smashed, the stock taken. From how a manual crank was inserted into the pump, the fuel was gone, too.

"We won't find any wheels here," Corrie said, giving a discarded and split tyre a kick. "Not which are still attached to an axle."

"No, and I don't plan to," Lisa said. "A track runs north into the woods from just over there. Two kilometres away is a shack. There is a car parked inside, and fuel buried beneath. But first, I need to give Mr and Mrs Guinn their wedding gift."

"A wedding gift?" Pete asked. "I don't think this is the time."

"Surely the lesson from the last three months is that we must sometimes make the time, because none of us know how much of it we have left," Lisa said. "This way, it won't take long."

Rufus gave a warning growl.

"Yes, I've seen it," Lisa said, picking up a discarded pitchfork from among the debris. She stabbed it down into the skull of the zombie crawling across the broken glass. It was far from the only body outside the showroom, and there were even more inside, but no others moved.

At least a dozen, all zombies, all dead, had fallen increasingly close together in a line leading to a rear door. Around them lay discarded shotgun shells, but far more tools to suggest a hard-won victory for any survivors.

"We appear to be alone," Lisa said, walking through the showroom and to the garage behind. "Rufus, do you agree? Good."

"Escapees from the town," Pete said, turning a slow circle, looking for more of the crawling undead. "You'd stay at home as long as you could. But after the bombs, you'd know no help was coming. You'd want to go west, to the mountains. You'd remember there was an out-of-town showroom, so you'd come here hoping to grab some more fuel and wheels."

"Exactly," Lisa said, stopping by the sump. "But to go where? There is no purpose in flight without a destination. Corrie, would you mind using that hook to lift the grate?"

"Unless they were fleeing radiation," Olivia said.

Kempton descended the five short steps into the recessed pit. She drew her knife and attempted to use the blade as a screwdriver to remove the redundant sign warning people against a naked flame. "Ah, this won't do. Can anyone see a crowbar?"

Corrie passed one of the discarded, and bloody, tools down to her. With a loud crack, the sign split in two. With a little scraping, Lisa found a groove into which the knife fit. With an even louder crack, a concealed panel popped out revealing a mechanical keypad behind.

"The code is 1776," Lisa said. "My little joke."

After tapping it in, the entire floor at the base of the sump began to retract, slowly clicking into the wall. The drift of leaves and oil dripped down onto stairs that continued down into darkness.

"Another tunnel? No way," Pete said.

"Not a tunnel, no," Lisa said, taking a flashlight from her belt. "It's a cellar. You will want to see this. Please."

"Best do it," Corrie said. "It'll be the quickest way out of here."

The tunnel led into a low-roofed, cement-walled cellar, barely two metres high, but five wide, and ten deep, running underneath the showroom. The chamber contained boxes, but Lisa made for the largest, just over two metres long, and one and a half tall, but only half a metre deep. She pressed a catch at the top, and the front of the box swung down. Inside, was a long, tall, and thin transparent Perspex box. Inside the box, a desperate crew of sailors struggled to save their ship from a tumultuous storm.

"It's a painting," Olivia said.

"It is Rembrandt's *The Storm on the Sea of Galilee,*" Lisa said.

"This is a weird place to keep pictures," Pete said.

"Would it be so weird were I to tell you they were stolen?" Lisa said. "Here, you will also find Van Gogh's *Poppy Flowers*, Vermeer's *The Concert*, and a few other missing treasures. They are now yours."

Pete shone his light on the picture, but between the gloom of the cave, and the reflection off the plastic, it was hard to make out more than a few brushstrokes. "Thanks," he said uncertainly.

Kempton closed the box. "Now, they are no more, or less, valuable than any artwork hanging in any museum. However, I suspect these will be easier for you to recover in good time."

"Corrie, do you want to come see?" Pete called up.

"Nope. I want to find some wheels," she said.

"A wise choice," Lisa said.

Outside, Kempton tapped four zeros on the keypad. The gate swung closed. She returned the grating to the sump. "I doubt anyone will come this way again, and if they do, what will they find?"

"So why bring us?" Olivia asked.

"Can we talk as we walk?" Corrie asked. "The day is already getting away from us."

"Certainly," Lisa said. "There's a track on the other side of the road. Come."

Pete picked up his bag. "Those paintings are all stolen?"

"Indeed," Lisa said.

"By you?"

"I would prefer to describe my actions as recovering and preserving them. I owe all three of you more than I can possible repay, but I must try."

"They're big paintings, so I guess we should start shopping for a big house," Olivia said.

"At least Australia isn't short on room," Pete said.

"I doubt Ms Qwong will allow you to keep the paintings," Lisa said. "However, when you return to Australia, you should tell the press that you know the location of the world's most famous missing art work. You should publicly demand an expedition to retrieve them so they can be put on display. That is your gift."

"That's an odd gift," Pete said.

"Where's this track?" Corrie asked. "You said there was a track leading to a cabin."

"Just beyond that tow-truck," Lisa said.

"Careful, there's a zom beneath the tyres," Olivia said.

The zombie was *mostly* beneath the tyres, but already ripping its guts to shreds as it pulled and twisted, trying to reach the warm-bloods. Pete hacked the axe down in a vicious overhead swing, and missed completely. The blade dug deep into the dirt. He jumped sideways, out of its reach, adjusting his aim before stabbing the short spear point into the pinned zombie's skull.

"Next modification should be to flatten the underside of the blade, and widen it, so you can stamp down like on a shovel," he said.

Though the truck's keys were in the ignition, the fuel cap had been removed. Presumably after the zombie had been run over, which begged the question of why the driver hadn't finished the pitiful creature.

They followed the rutted track away from the highway. Last night's rain glistened on the shaded ferns huddled beneath the overgrown canopy.

"Someone's driven this way recently," Corrie said, pointing at a dusting of leaves and twigs ripped from a zealous thicket encroaching onto the track.

"Yes, that was a possibility," Lisa said.

"How many people knew about this fuel stash?" Corrie asked as ahead, Rufus paused, before dashing on a few feet. Corrie dashed after him, but waved them to follow.

"Around twenty knew of the fuel," Lisa said. "Realistically, there are only three who might have used it, John, Loretta, or Emma-Lee."

"John the hostage? And Loretta was the FBI agent, right?" Olivia said. "Who was Emma-Lee?"

"The owner of the showroom, and my agent in these parts," Lisa said. "She knew nothing at all of my wider plans, but was simply a guard for those paintings who would ensure, when the time came, they were revealed to the world."

"Okay, so explain that," Pete said. "And the paintings."

"They are your get out of jail free card," Lisa said. "When we get to Australia, assuming it hasn't collapsed, journalists will be sent to gather your stories. Yours in particular, Mr Guinn. It is inspiring, even aspirational, in that it will give hope to many that their loved ones abroad might still be alive."

"I wouldn't call hiking through zom-land aspirational," Pete said.

"But it won't be your words they print," Lisa said. "The journalists will use hyperbole and bombast to create a readership-boosting narrative, probably serialised and stretched over many weeks as a preventative against they themselves being sent out to find a new story. But what happens when your tale is told?"

"We tell them about the paintings," Olivia said. "I get it. It's propaganda. It's a fable. Coming to rescue some famous paintings is a pretty good sequel."

"Those paintings aren't just famous," Lisa said. "They were famously stolen and missing for decades."

"Seeing the trouble they had sending that one ship, I can't see them sending another just for some pictures," Pete said. "Not even if a newspaper tells them to."

"Really?" Lisa asked. "You underestimate our need for gossip, myth, and legend. And it won't be a newspaper. It will be the radio. Perhaps the TV, depending on how tightly rationed electricity becomes. Wood and linen will be too scarce to turn into paper when sanitary, medical, and building demands will be so much higher. That is what life will become in that final bastion of our species: unsanitary, of poor health, and poorly housed. We shall all be cold in the winter, baking in the summer, and exhausted all year round. Radio will once again be a worker's lifeline to a world beyond factory and dormitory, a pictureless window to a world they will never again visit. Yet they will want something more. They will settle for a story, but it will have to be a compelling one, and this is the best I can provide. Because it is *your* story, you three will accompany the expedition. You will be the heroes when it returns, and so there will be no repercussions for any association you had with me."

Rufus paused, eyes narrowed at the sprawling undergrowth.

Corrie raised a cautioning hand, then shook her head. "Squirrel," she said and trudged on.

"And what happens to you?" Pete asked.

"House arrest, I imagine," Lisa said. "Until my ship comes in."

Pete mulled that over, as they trudged on, and uphill. "So why are the paintings hidden there? Why did you steal them?"

"They were stolen to order, and not by, or for, me," Lisa said. "But I stole them from the crooks who'd paid for that original theft. The heist was a whim. Call it a manifestation of my mid-life crisis. Or call it revenge, but it was surprisingly enjoyable. I will save the specifics until we have time to enjoy them, as it is definitely a tale worthy of the details. Having acquired the paintings, I was then at a loss as to what to do with them."

"You could have returned them to their proper owners," Olivia said.

"Yes, and I might have done that had events transpired otherwise," Lisa said. "I navigated a narrow crevasse between the cartel and the authorities. A wrong move would have led either, or both, to fall on me. If I were arrested, I would have been dead before dawn. But death doesn't have to mean defeat. Whatever story the cartel and their pet politicians told, it was essential to prove it was a lie. How to ensure that? By gaining the attention of journalists, and so the public, from across the world."

"By letting them think you were an art thief as well?" Pete asked.

"I *am* an art thief," Lisa said. "But art of that infamy requires authentication. I was reasonably confident the FBI's art crime division was of no interest to the cartel. Nor were any of the major galleries, and every single curator would want to view those paintings. Amelia Court House has a well-funded local newspaper. They would ensure the story of the paintings' discovery was printed."

"Did you fund the local paper?" Olivia asked.

"Indirectly, yes," Lisa said. "But questions about the paintings would lead to questions about this escape route I so obviously organised. It would lead to questions about Denmark."

"What's in Denmark?"

"That is *another* story for another time," Lisa said. "But questions would lead to answers, and perhaps to the exposure of the cartel and their plot. I believe we're here."

They clearly weren't the first.

The track led to an almost derelict cabin with a garage of about the same size, set inside a clearing.

"You said there was a car here?" Corrie asked, stepping out of the empty garage. "It's gone. But I'm pretty positive that's what drove down the track. Where did you keep the fuel?"

"There should be a concealed storage area hidden beneath a junction box," Lisa said.

"We'll keep watch," Olivia said, though she turned her eyes to Rufus who sat on the cabin's porch, watching the way they'd come.

"Here," Corrie said, exiting the garage a minute later with a red plastic fuel can in her hands. "We can use that to refuel the tow truck at the bottom of the hill, then bring the vehicle up here for the rest, if it'll work."

"We've got fuel?" Pete asked.

"Enough for a thousand miles," Corrie said. "We'll be able to reach West Virginia, but not Savannah."

"One problem at a time," Pete said.

Chapter 34 - Jam Today
Cumberland County, Virginia

By the time they had the truck fuelled, three more corpses lay on the road, while above, the sun was already approaching its zenith.

When it came to sharing out driving duties, Pete won. As each mile slipped by, he wondered if he'd lost, and was just chasing a memory of happy days from a world which was gone. Slipping into his very-careful-load posture, he gripped the wheel tight, leaning forward, eyes flitting between the rear-mirror and the one remaining side mirror. Lisa shared the rear bench-seat with Rufus, while Corrie rode shotgun, and Olivia sat beside her, cycling through the radio stations.

"Just static," Olivia said, finally giving up and switching the radio off.

"There are some Johnny Cash CDs back here," Lisa said.

"Not here," Olivia said, picking up the map. "Not yet. It's about two hundred miles to the trap. I guess we could make that tonight."

"Doubt it," Pete said, slowing to navigate around another open-door car, abandoned on the road.

"We shouldn't try," Lisa said. "We'll stop in two hours. Tomorrow, we'll make our final approach, but stop about ten miles out. If possible, tonight, we might look for at least one bicycle. Otherwise, tomorrow, we'll hike the final distance on foot, and cross-country. We'll spend the afternoon surveying the trap, as you call it. We'll make our move at night. The deed will be done before dawn, leaving you two full days to drive to Savannah, with one day to spare before the ship departs."

"And what will *you* be doing?" Corrie asked.

"That will depend on who and how many we find in West Virginia," Lisa said.

"We should have asked Tess for more time," Olivia said. "But okay, so what happens when we get to the trap?"

"We spring it," Lisa said. "We have gasoline. We have carbines. We'll use an explosion, or a fire, to draw them out, then we'll shoot them. Beyond that, until we can see what awaits us, we can't plan the details."

"Two hundred miles," Olivia said. "Pete, we're going north now. We need to be heading northwest."

"Blame the road builders," Pete said.

"There are no straight roads in Virginia," Lisa said. "It is the indisputable proof that the Romans never crossed the Atlantic."

"I don't think that was in doubt," Corrie said.

"Oh, it was," Lisa said. "I knew a manganese magnate who built a Roman villa on the banks of the Mississippi. Originally a Latter Day Saint, he couldn't stomach the abstemious lifestyle, and opted for a more bacchanalian belief system of his own devising. The central tenet was the notion that an entire Roman legion once crossed the Atlantic, sailed up the Miss, and came ashore exactly where he had built his house. I assumed there was something sinister going on, but aside from an over-fondness in speaking in Latin, he was a harmless eccentric who'd suffered a break from reality. Unlike most, he had the money to enjoy his fantasy without causing harm to others, except to his poor staff whom he insisted wear togas. I mention it because he also built a rather sturdy wall around his property. If we are delayed on our way to Savannah, it might be a suitable redoubt in the south."

"Let's worry about that *when* we're going south," Olivia said.

"Yes, but remind me to show you where on the map tonight," Lisa said.

Pete drummed his fingers on the wheel as, ahead, another obstruction loomed.

"Radiation's rising," Corrie said.

"How fast?" Pete asked.

"Can't say. I didn't write any of the readings down," Corrie said.

"Hang on, then," Pete said, bringing the car to a halt.

"Rising radiation would be a good reason to speed up," Lisa said.

"Yep," Pete said. "But we need a baseline, and the wind direction, so we don't drive into a hot-zone."

Corrie jumped out. Rufus clambered out over Lisa and Olivia.

"Careful," Olivia said.

"Shh," Corrie said.

"Zom?" Pete asked.

"Gunshot," Corrie said. She climbed up into the back of the truck, standing next to the tow cable.

Pete held his breath, straining his ears. The shot came a few seconds later, a dull, flat crack.

Corrie jumped back down, and jumped in. "Two shots, at least. Ahead and to the left. That's… yeah, west. Can't be more than a mile away."

"And the radiation?" Pete asked.

"The wind's coming from the north," Corrie said. "As for the level, I guess we should check again after we see where the gunfire's coming from."

It came from a church with an acre-sized parking lot occupied by a single, solitary van. The church was the largest of three one-storey buildings, and it was the tallest, though the spire was purely ornamental, a conical tower twelve feet in height. At the entrance to the car park, a weather-battered sign read: *Preserve the Faith. Conserve Christianity. Spread the Good News at the Nineteenth Annual End of Winter Jelly Jamboree. This Sunday. All welcome.*

The shooter was atop one of the single-storey cabins on the far end of the parking lot. The building and its neighbour were made of brick and wood, rather than being a metal-shelled static trailer. Even with a row of planters beside the door, shutters over the window, and a miniature fence to separate it from the parking lot, it was still too small to be the permanent home of a church leader. Four survivors, including the one shooter, stood atop the left-most cabin. Outside were the undead. Between twenty and thirty, with more drifting in across the open field behind.

Now that the tow-truck had appeared, the survivor had ceased fire, while four of the undead had broken off from the back of the pack, and lumbered towards the truck.

"That must be their van," Lisa said as Pete revved the engine, dancing the truck forward.

"Let me get on the back," Corrie said. "I'll shoot."

"Nope, we should save the bullets," Pete said. "Those guys clearly don't have any to spare."

"Nice idea, bro, but check the mirror," Corrie said. "We've got two more zoms approaching behind."

"New plan," Olivia said. "But it's basically Pete's plan. Him and me'll ride in the back. Lisa, you drive. Corrie, shoot if you have to. We'll try luring the zombies away. If that fails, then we'll stop to kill them all."

"I believe I'm the better shot," Lisa said.

"Right, but we have no idea if those survivors will try to rob us the moment we get clear," Olivia said. "Until we know they're friendly, we'll keep you as our secret weapon."

While Lisa reached forward to adjust the mirror, Pete opened the door, jumped down, and raised his axe as Olivia raised her gun. She fired at the zombie behind. From the other door, Corrie fired a handgun at the zombies ahead. Those twin sounds echoed louder than his footsteps as he ran to the rear of the truck.

One of the following undead had managed to clamber up to the truck bed and was halfway to its feet when Lisa jerked the truck forward a metre.

The zombie toppled sideways, thudding back to the asphalt. As it rolled, Pete swung. The axe slammed through the zombie's skull like an egg, cracking black brain over the drive.

"Gross," Olivia said, jumping up to the rear of the truck. "Quick, Pete."

He took her hand, clambering up. The moment he had, Lisa shunted the truck backwards. He almost copied the zombie in falling off, but grabbed hold of the tow-crane.

"One zom on the road," Olivia said, before turning around. "Sides look clear. Five coming from the parking lot cabin. Two down."

A gun cracked.

"Was that them?" Pete asked.

"Corrie," Olivia said. "The people on the roof are waiting. Well, three of them are. The fourth is doing a whole lot of pointing, mostly at the van. Yeah, if we can lure enough zoms away, I think they'll try for their vehicle. Five. No, six heading towards us now."

The truck shunted backwards a dozen yards, and again.

"Hold on," Olivia said. "I think Lisa's taking us back to the road."

"Do you reckon their van works?" Pete asked.

"Hope so," Olivia said.

The truck shunted backwards again.

"Zoms behind," Pete said. "On the highway. They must have followed us."

"Or the van," Olivia said, turning around. "Woah. That's a lot. Corrie!" She moved to the cab to warn Corrie while Pete looked at the road. He *had* wondered where all the zombies were, but hadn't dared ask lest he tempt capricious fate. Here was the answer.

Dozens drifted through the woodlands. Many more were now on the road, staggering along the highway behind the truck. He didn't look to see how many might be ahead. Lisa shunted them back onto the highway itself.

"There's a lot of them, aren't there?" Olivia said.

"Even after they were bitten, people ran away from the road," Pete said. "Of course they did. They were hoping to be immune. Hoping for safety. But they turned."

"We've got a minute. One minute, Corrie!" she added, raising her voice.

Corrie, now holding a carbine with the barrel braced through the door's open window, fired, but that wasn't the largest sound. An engine purred, grumbled, died.

"Here we go!" Corrie called.

"What's that mean?" Pete said, but grabbed on just as the truck lurched forward, and towards the undead approaching from the parking lot. He heard a gunshot. He heard an engine. He heard a victorious shout from Lisa. The tow-truck stopped, reversed again, and now they were speeding backwards towards the lurching pack of the undead. Pete gripped the tow-crane tight, and his axe tighter, getting ready for the crunch, but Lisa braked before she hit the nearest pair of zombies. As Pete staggered and nearly fell, Lisa changed gears, and drove forward.

"Better than a rollercoaster!" Olivia yelled.

"Can I get my money back?" Pete replied. Knees bent, he held on. Lisa wasn't driving fast, but the zombies behind were a quickly disappearing mass. When he turned his face forward, he was buffeted by wind, so couldn't see the van until the next time, marginally more gently, Lisa braked.

The van had stopped a few yards ahead. The back door opened, a man with a rifle jumped down, followed by another armed with a spear, while a woman stepped out of the passenger side of the van, apparently unarmed. She waved.

"They don't look completely hostile," Pete said.

"Let's go find out," Olivia said.

"G'day!" Corrie called.

"Howdy!' Pete said.

"Thanks for the assist," the man with the rifle said. The barrel was already aimed down, but he let go with his left hand, raising the gun to rest on his shoulder. "Where are y'all heading?"

"West," Pete said. "We're on a rescue mission."

"Seems like that mission was a success," the rifleman said. "Where did you come from?"

"From Indiana originally," Pete said. "But we've been travelling all over."

"Like where?" the spearman asked.

"Well, there are survivors up on Long Island," Pete said. "A couple of thousand or so, but they're about to leave, and are run by a quasi-dictator. There were supplies in Savannah, but lots of zoms, too. There *are* people down near Cape Canaveral, but they're basically pirates."

"What do you mean by *pirates*?" the spearman asked.

"With speedboats and guns," Olivia said. "We think they're scavenging fuel from the launch site. Norfolk was nuked. Annapolis has been abandoned, and the radiation's rising on the Delmarva Peninsula."

"That's… that's a lot to take in," the woman said, walking over. "Two days ago, we saw a zombie die."

"A lost soul returned to heaven," the spearman added with utter conviction.

The woman rolled her eyes, while the rifleman kept his face so expressionless it was impossible to tell on which side of the debate he'd land.

"We saw one die, and figured the rest were dying so it was safe to leave the fort for supplies," the woman said.

"You saw one die?" Olivia asked.

"Absolutely," the woman said.

"Two minutes, and they'll catch us!" Lisa called from behind the wheel.

"She's right," Corrie said. "We can't linger here. We're heading west. If you want to come with us, please do."

"Our families are back east," the spearman said. "Come rest, eat."

"We'd love to," Olivia said. "But we have to look for our friends. There's a junction up ahead. You take that eastward turn, we'll lure the zoms after us."

"Wait," the spearman said. He ran back to the van, dropped his spear inside, and pulled out a couple of jars. "Take this. It's small recompense, but I am reminded of Proverbs 24:14, wisdom is like honey, and this is as near as we have. The preserves were stored there for the competition scheduled for the Sunday after tribulation, so please, when we meet again, give us the score. Out of ten."

"The score? Sure," Olivia said. "Thanks. Where shall we bring it?"

"The church," the rifleman said before either of the other two could speak. "We'll leave a map. But we'll be hunkering down for another month or so. The zombies should all be dead by then." He turned around and walked back to the van. "They *are* dying, just not quick enough, that's all."

"Thanks for the preserves," Olivia said.

"Thanks for preserving our lives," the woman said.

Pete gave a nod, a wave, and returned to the truck.

"I take it we're not combining forces?" Lisa said.

"They're from a community nearby," Olivia said. "They wanted to get back. We could follow them, rest there, but they live somewhere to the east, and they were reluctant to give us an address."

"We have time for another hour's driving," Corrie said. "What we do today, we don't have to do tomorrow."

"But we can wait a few minutes to confirm whether the foe is following us," Lisa said.

"You didn't tell them our names, Pete," Olivia said.

"Nor did you," Pete said. "Nor did *they*. Or where they came from. But they're based nearby, and that was the guy's church, so it has to be pretty close by. Why didn't you mention Australia?"

"Because it would be false hope," she said. "Why didn't you?"

"I didn't think they'd believe me," Pete said. "But we found some more survivors. That's cool. And friendlies, too."

"Friendlier than that guy on Delmarva, and most of them on Long Island," Corrie said. "Not as friendly as Savannah or Cancun."

"Hey, I dunno, we got jelly," Pete said.

"A cherry conserve, and a pineapple and orange preserve," Olivia said.

"If it's orange, it's a marmalade, and should never be polluted with pineapple," Lisa said. "I have strong views on that. Ah, the tail has caught up with the comet." She adjusted the mirror. "Let us chase the stars."

They continued until the fuel gauge said the truck needed to drink, so took the first uphill exit. It led them to an ill-maintained home with echoes of past splendour.

Lisa killed the engine. "An ill-advised investment," she said.

"What was?" Olivia asked.

"This house," Lisa said. "I can't imagine why else someone would lavish so much on an architect to design a building and then fail to spend a cent on maintenance."

"I'll go watch for the zoms," Corrie said, wearily climbing out.

"I'll refuel," Olivia said. "C'mon, Rufus."

"I'll check the house," Pete said. "Early or not, I think we've stopped for the night."

There were mice, there were spiders, but there was only one corpse. From the photographs in the hall, the house had been built for a couple. He'd retired early, selling a business that had something to do with industrial packaging. She'd kept working long enough to be photographed at a ribbon cutting for an urban clinic. They had a daughter, who'd grown up, graduated, married, and had a daughter of her own. The graduation photograph had both mother and father standing proudly by their daughter. While there were photographs of the grandfather with his granddaughter, there were none of the grandmother. The daughter wasn't in the house, nor was the grandchild. Just the lonely old man, dead in his favourite chair, a pill bottle and glass close to his rodent-chewed remains.

"Looks clear," Pete called through the open front door. "There's even some food in the pantry."

"Cereal?" Olivia asked.

"Sadly, no," Pete said. "Not much of a view, either. I mean, there *is* by old-world standards. You can see hills and treetops, but you can't see the road at all."

"We are here, we have stopped, but should we continue?" Lisa asked.

"We could make another fifty, maybe a hundred miles, tonight," Corrie said.

"Depending on the roads," Pete said.

"It won't make much difference," Olivia said. "We'll still get to Sutton by mid-afternoon. We might not find anywhere better than this, so let's not risk damaging the truck."

"Then I shall see what feast can be mustered," Lisa said.

Pete dragged an armoire from the lounge out into the hall.

"Blocking the front door?" Olivia asked.

"No, the stairs," Pete said. "I figure there's too many ways in, too many windows, but only one staircase. We're up a hill, and this is pretty remote. I think were safe, but you're right, we shouldn't take any risks."

"Any more than we have to," Olivia said. "Those pills that old man took, they were for his heart. I don't think you can overdose on them. But he could have just stopped taking them. So was it suicide or not?"

"I don't want to think about it," Pete said.

"No, I suppose there's no point," Olivia said. "Do you think those church people really saw a zom die?"

"They seemed pretty certain," Pete said. "And I don't see why they'd lie. Doc Flo said the zoms *were* dying."

"But she didn't find proof," Olivia said.

"She was looking in New York, but here it is, in West Virginia," Pete said. "Wish I knew precisely where."

"Exactly," Olivia said. "I was wondering whether we should look for them, or take word to the ship to come look for them, but look where? All we know is, in a month or so, they might return to that church. The ship can't wait that long."

"We're on a rescue mission," Pete said. "We'll let Doc Flo worry about hunting for dead zoms."

Olivia crossed to the window, and looked outside. "We've got two choices, go find proof that the zoms are dead, or get revenge on the cartel. There's no guarantee either will be a success. Do you get that?"

"You mean you want to forget Sutton and look for that church group?" he asked.

"Not exactly," she said. "I *don't* want us getting to West Virginia to find the cartel long gone, the prisoners long dead, and then drive back to the ship empty-handed. It's not just us, Pete. It's Tess, too. Her mission was an utter failure. She found a handful of people, a lot of craters, and no proof the zoms are dying. The fact we branched off in pursuit of the cartel means she failed in that part of her mission. Except, now, here, maybe we do have proof the zoms are dying. So is that proof more important to the Pacific than us proving John Clayton is dead?"

"Is it?" Pete asked. "You tell me."

Olivia shook her head and walked off, but came back just as Pete had finished blocking the stairs. "The back door's locked. I've opened the curtains so it'll be easier to hear the glass break. I don't think the cloth would help keep the zoms out."

"We could put it to a vote," Pete said.

"Put what to a vote?" Lisa asked, coming out of the kitchen.

"Whether we go find the dead zom those people mentioned," Pete said.

Olivia raised a hand. "No votes. Because Lisa's going to go to West Virginia regardless, right?"

"I am," she said. "But I'd like to hear the alternative, if there is one."

"Doc Flo was looking for a dead zombie," Olivia said. "We've learned there is one nearby. Shouldn't we go tell her? Isn't that more important even than saving the life of a prisoner? And I know he would be just like us, imprisoned just like us, waiting for death, like us."

"Have you considered that it might be better *not* to tell Commissioner Qwong?" Corrie said. "If we turned south tomorrow, we might reach Savannah without needing to refuel. If we inform Tess of this news, she might feel duty-bound to send a team to investigate. A team including Dr Avalon. How long would that take? How dangerous would it be? What if, by then, that church community who were clearly desperate for food, have moved on or died? What if that delay is why the icebreaker runs out of food or fuel before it reaches safe waters?"

"This guy, John, the prisoner, who was he?" Olivia asked.

"My first employee," Lisa said. "He was older, and a man, and so a useful decoy. Because of that, he knew some of my secrets, but he kept them. After a few years, I put him in charge of my charitable foundation, but I'd promoted him beyond his competence. I had to find him a different position, but he was honest and loyal, and those are rare commodities."

"He's a friend?" Corrie asked.

"Not exactly," Lisa said. "Though that is a judgement on me, not him. Friendship requires trust, the one luxury I could not afford. Not then. He knew prison was a real possibility in any continued association with me. He accepted that, but did not expect this. I did not warn him. He is a good person. Even if he weren't, there are few who deserve such a cruel death as the sisters will provide."

"And that's why we won't put it to a vote," Olivia said.

20th April

Chapter 35 - Semi Wrecked
Lexington, Virginia

The last of the night's wind hurled the mist into a twinkling drizzle, which caught the first of the morning's light as it trickled down the windowpane. It had been a restless night with all five sharing the musty guest bedroom. That hadn't been the original sleeping arrangement, but a ghoulish soldier had crept out of the woodland at dusk, making it almost to the porch before Rufus gave a warning growl. Now, as the treeline slowly emerged from the shadows, all looked still, empty, and utterly lifeless.

"I think we're alone," Pete said. "Another ten minutes, and it'll be light enough to drive."

"Then we have time for tea," Lisa said, carefully coaxing the fire she'd set in an old frying pan. Above, she'd balanced a saucepan on an oven tray.

"It's just not the same as coffee, is it?" Pete said.

"I imagine our host's heart condition contraindicated a morning cup of Joe," Lisa said.

"How are we for water?" Olivia asked.

"We'll manage until we find a river," Lisa said. "Some run from the south, some from the north. We'll find a safe one soon."

Pete nodded, but kept his own counsel. "I'll check on the truck."

Rufus bounded off the bed, to join him.

"We ended up going a lot further south than north yesterday," Olivia said as they drove off, half an hour later. "We're— What was that?" Beneath their wheels, bone crunched.

"Crawling zom," Pete said, glancing in the mirror. He turned on the lights, but only one worked.

The sky darkened, the rain grew heavier, but there was no question of waiting out the storm.

"Where are we?" Corrie asked.

"In a straight line, only about fifty miles from Amelia Court House," Olivia said.

"Is that all?" Pete asked.

"We're down thirty-eight bullets since leaving the ship," Corrie said. "We topped up on food, but this truck is a real guzzler."

"We'll look for more fuel tomorrow," Lisa said. "And we can look for water after we cross the state line."

Between the rain and the gloom, Pete kept the speed at thirty, which was still sufficient to dodge the occasional undead pedestrian.

"There's a river!" Olivia said. "Just ahead. And there's a bridge."

The rain had dwindled to a drizzle, but the debate over whether the water would be safe to drink stalled when they saw the dead fish floating with the current.

Pete drove on. North then west, west then north, and increasingly uphill. Despite his brain telling him they had to be going down nearly as much as up, the curving terrain made his eyes think they were forever ascending.

"There's a road sign for Lexington," Olivia said.

Pete glanced to the roadside, but they were halfway up a hill with a steep slope on either side, and trees everywhere. Except ahead, where the undead emerged abruptly around a bend.

"Hold on!" he said.

"Veer left!" Lisa said.

But it was too late to stop, and the road was too narrow to swerve. He slammed into the loose pack, winging the first, driving over the second, and clipping a third with the bumper. The lights smashed. The wing mirror snapped. The windshield spider-webbed as a firefighter was thrown up the hood. The zombie kept rolling up and over the cab, thrashing as it fell into the truck-bed.

Before Corrie had time to shoot, before Pete had time to scream, and before even Rufus had barked a warning, the road ahead cleared, and they were through.

Pete kept the truck at a steady twenty miles an hour, not daring to go faster because of the arrhythmic clanking echoing around the cab.

"It's from the back. It's a zom," Corrie said. "We've picked up a passenger."

Pete braked. Olivia jumped out, drawing her sidearm before hesitating.

"Problem?" Lisa asked.

Pete followed her to the back. White bone jutted from the zombie's shoulder and thigh, the wounds oozing black pus each time it thrashed left and right.

"I don't think it's a good idea to fire bullets into our ride," Olivia said.

Lisa grabbed the zombie's twitching boot, dragging it across the truck bed until both its legs were over the lip, stepping back as gravity did the rest. She raised her boot, and stamped it down on the zombie's skull.

"Wipe that foot before you get in," Olivia said.

"We should take better care of the truck," Lisa said. "Our mission will be a lot more difficult to complete if we have to continue on foot."

Pete walked around to the front of the vehicle, to examine the damage. "Nah, we need new wheels."

"The Virginia Military Institute," Olivia said, pointing at a road sign, still a little way ahead. "That's why I remember Lexington. It was the setting for a book. You remember when Mrs Mathers had that book club, and she promised me it was a murder story, but it turned out to be a vampire romance."

"You were mad for a week," Pete said.

"It was false advertising," Olivia said. "But a military institute would be somewhere to look for a sturdier truck."

"A detour could delay our arrival," Lisa said.

"Like you said, if we end up walking, we'll arrive even later," Olivia said. "You want to come out for a minute, Rufus?"

The dog moved further back into the cab.

"Wise man," Corrie said.

There was an angry growl from the engine as they drove away, which rose to a persistent whine that climbed the octaves until it was beyond their hearing, though not beyond Rufus's who began whimpering in sympathy.

"New truck soon, pal," Pete said. "Promise."

"How about *that* truck?" Corrie said, reaching for her carbine.

Where the Lexington Turnpike met the Blue Ridge Parkway, a driver had misjudged how tight an angle a semi-truck-trailer could pivot. The rig and trailer had decoupled. The trailer now lay at a thirty-degree angle, propped against the trees of the woodland embankment.

Two people were in the back of the skewed trailer, passing small crates down to another two survivors below, while a fifth, armed with a rifle, stood guard in the road. All five wore near-matching bright red ski coats, probably recent loot. That all five wore the same colour suggested it was a uniform of sorts. The way the woman in the road carried the rifle suggested military. She was older, not old, but made to look her years by the comparative youth of the quartet by the truck. The barrel of her breech-loading rifle wasn't pointing at them, but the confidence with which she carried it suggested she didn't think she was outgunned.

"Don't suppose you need a tow?" Olivia asked, leaning out the window.

"Kinda do," the sniper said. "Kind of you to offer."

"We've got zoms not far behind us," Olivia said. "They might not make it up the hill, but you don't want to hope."

"If I can borrow your tow cable for ten minutes, we can right our trailer," she said. "Sergeant Jane Sayre, U.S. Marine Corps."

"We're the Guinns," Olivia said, opening the door and jumping out. "I'm Olivia. That's Pete, Corrie, Lisa, and Rufus."

"You're kin?" Sayre asked.

"We are now," Olivia said. "Me and Pete are on our honeymoon."

"You picked a fine spot for it," Sayre said.

"I'll go watch the road," Pete said. "Rufus, c'mon."

Sayre followed. "Jane Sayre," she said again.

"Pete Guinn."

"I was on embassy duty in the sandbox. Got back in January. You?"

"I sold carpets in South Bend," Pete said. "But I was conscripted up north."

"In Canada? That story was true?"

"You heard about it?"

"Heard someone was trying to set up a defence along the border," Sayre said. "Heard they were trying to do the same down south, too. What happened?"

"The nukes," Pete said. "A bomb came down on the army. The survivors scattered."

"So where are you heading?" she asked.

"West Virginia. We're looking for some friends. Odds are we won't find them, but we've got to look."

"You came from Canada, then? It's no better?"

"Not really," Pete said. "There's pirates in Cape Canaveral, and there's a couple of thousand people on Long Island, but they're thinking of leaving. Norfolk was nuked. Savannah's empty now. Atlanta, too. But we found some people yesterday, about halfway between here and Amelia Court House. They were based near a church with a sign out front for a preserve sale. If you were looking for more people, you could try looking there."

"We are, so we might," she said.

"They said they saw a zombie die," Pete said.

"Chuck, the guy with the hipster-hair, he thought he saw one die last week. Didn't see it myself."

Pete looked around, and guessed she meant the only one of the four youths who didn't have a buzzcut, though that young man's hair was barely long enough for a parting.

"What's in the truck?" Pete asked. "Food?"

"Ammo from the VMI," she said. "They set up a defence there, but a military college is not a fortress. They got overrun. Saw a lot of National Guard uniforms among the dead. We're up at Lake Moomaw, if you were looking for a place to rest up."

"That's the second offer in two days," Pete said. "You don't know how tempting it is. But we've got to go look for our friends."

"Inbound," she said, raising her rifle. It cracked loudly, and the staggering zombie fell, but she'd reloaded before it hit the ground.

"They're at Lake Moomaw," Pete said as they drove off, leaving the rig, now righted, still on the road. "I don't know where that is, but I bet we can find it. She said one of them saw a zom die last week."

"So maybe it really is happening," Olivia said.

"Maybe there's no need for Dr Avalon to come so far in search of a sample," Lisa said.

"Maybe not," Olivia said.

Chapter 36 - Babes in the Woods
Virginia

Two hours and a hundred curving, rising, falling, back-and-forth lost-in-the-hills miles later, Pete wished the trees had the decency to give each other a bit of space. There was rarely room for a view, and often no advance warning of curves and dips, or of the undead.

"Zoms!" Olivia said.

"Road's fine," Pete said, letting his eyes dart left and right at the low brush ringing the ever-present shield of trees.

"Loads of zoms!" Olivia said. "Two miles ahead. On the left."

"One mile, I think," Lisa said. "Large enough to kick up a dust cloud. I believe they're heading for the road."

"I can turn back," Pete said.

"Don't stop!" Lisa said. "We'll make it."

"Be ready to stop," Olivia said. "But maybe speed up."

He caught glimpses of them, or *it*, between the trees: a slow-moving dust cloud cutting along the bottom of a valley, churning abandoned fields to mud.

"We're through!" Olivia said as the road began to climb again. "Through, and beyond, with one field to spare."

"Are they following?" Pete asked.

"Not sure," Olivia said.

"Where was that?" Corrie asked.

"Not sure," Olivia said. "It kinda depends— deer!"

Pete braked, but the deer didn't even slow. It was sprinting uphill, along the brush, next to the road.

Pete set the animal as his marker, matching its speed. When he looked in the mirror, the horde was lost to view. Ahead, the deer darted across the road, disappearing along a track.

"We'll need a different way back," he said, easing his foot on the gas.

"We need to know where we are first," Olivia said.

The hills rose. The hills fell. The clouds grew denser, lower, buffeting in from the north. Occasional squalls pattered on the windscreen, there and then gone, hinting at a storm which never burst.

“Smoke, ten-o’clock, two kilometres,” Lisa said.

“Behind those hills,” Pete said. “Cooking fire?”

“I think it’s on the road or close to it,” Olivia said.

The blue hybrid lay on its roof, grey smoke billowing from the tip of the engine, and the front two wheel-wells. A trail of glass, paint-chips, blood, and gore marked where the impact had occurred. The collision had been with the undead, four of whom were still clustered around the car.

Corrie and Lisa walked towards the upturned car, and the undead who had turned towards them. Their guns rose as the undead approached. Four quick shots, and all four fell.

“Hang with me, pal,” Pete said, but Rufus paid him no heed, walking cautiously towards the wreck, before detouring to the roadside. He barked.

“Clear!” Lisa called.

“Dead,” Corrie said. “We were too late.”

Rufus barked again. He was at the top of the slope leading down into a wooded valley.

“Yeah, maybe not,” Pete said. “Rufus has found a trail. There’s blood here. Fresh blood.”

“There’s a child’s seat in that car,” Corrie said. “No sign of a kid. One adult dead, definitely. But maybe one missing, and one kid. A young kid.”

“Then we should hurry,” Lisa said.

“*I’ll* hurry,” Corrie said. “Woods might be different from desert, but I’ve spent years in the wilderness. Rufus, with me.”

“You both wait here,” Lisa said. “Come, Corrie.” She jogged into the woods before Corrie could object, with Rufus quickly overtaking them both. Corrie followed, leaving Pete and Olivia behind.

“Lisa really doesn’t like taking orders, does she?” Pete said.

“Or suggestions,” Olivia said. “We should check that car for clues as to where they came from.” She collected the fire extinguisher from the tow-truck. It fizzled rather than sprayed, but it dampened the smoke.

“Three go-bags in the back,” Pete said. “Maps… I don’t know what to look for. There isn’t much here.” He picked up a blanket with a Nemo print, another with a giraffe.

“We should clear the car from the road,” Olivia said as she unhooked the car seat. “Grab those go-bags.”

Bags, blankets, and child-seat were brought back to the truck. Pete used the tow cable to drag the car to the barrier, leaving enough space for a vehicle to pass.

"Do you think the car came from the same place as Sergeant Sayre?" Olivia asked.

"Lake Moomaw? There's nothing on the maps that would say one way or the other," Pete said.

With a rustle from the undergrowth, Rufus slunk back onto the road. Corrie followed, soaked nearly to the waist.

"We lost the trail in a river," Corrie said. "I think they headed downstream."

"One adult, carrying a child. They outran the undead," Lisa said, wiping her knife on an oily rag. "Do you wish to follow them?"

"The car was still burning," Olivia said. "We can't be more than an hour behind them."

"So why are we standing here?" Pete said.

"Because I *lost* the trail," Corrie said. "There's a bridge further down river. Looks old, maybe even derelict. But there must be an access track somewhere down the road. If I were wading through the river and saw a bridge ahead, I'd get out of the water. We can continue the search around there, but we might never find them."

"Let's go," Pete said.

It took ten minutes to find a turning, partially covered in bracken. A little way beyond was a locked gate with a warning that this was private land. Five minutes after that, the narrow dirt track became paved as it led to a forgotten bridge.

Pete stopped the truck short of the bridge, and climbed up to the roof.

"If I'm not back in an hour, honk the horn," Corrie said. "But stay here by the bridge."

"Wait—" Pete began, but Corrie had dashed off, and across the bridge, Rufus a few steps behind.

"I'll back-track up the riverbank," Lisa said. "If our survivor wished to return to the car for supplies, they would have come out this side. It's unlikely, but worth checking."

Olivia climbed up onto the truck bed, leaning against the cab. "That looks like a temporary bridge. For mining, do you think?"

"Or built while they explored for places to mine," Pete said. "Either way, it's been forgotten for decades."

They looked across the river.

"Do you think she'll catch up with them?" Olivia asked.

"Absolutely," Pete said. "If it were me, I'd look for shelter to rest and plan my next move. Maybe think about returning to the car for the gear."

"Maybe," Olivia said. "I think I'd keep moving. Head towards the nearest town."

"That has to be miles away," Pete said. "And I think, if you continue on in that direction, you'd run into that horde. Those zombies were on the other side of those hills. As long as we've got ammo and fuel, we're fine. Speaking of which." He jumped down, and grabbed a fuel can and the funnel.

They watched. They waited.

"We're not going to make it to Sutton today," Olivia said.

"Probably not," Pete said.

"I don't think we're even in West Virginia," Olivia said.

"We'll get there," Pete said.

"It'll be too late," she said.

"I know."

"And it'll be too late for us to get to Savannah."

"Maybe," he said.

"I'm not saying we should turn back," she said. "This just isn't what I expected."

"I think Tess did," Pete said. "And I think we should have."

They waited. They watched.

Lisa returned first. "Two zoms," she said. "No signs of living people that I could find."

They watched. They waited. They paced. They sat. Pete was about to say they should look for Corrie when three gunshots rang out from the far side of the river.

"Turn the truck," Lisa said. "We should be prepared for a quick escape."

As Pete got back in the cab, Lisa began crossing the river, but hadn't reached the far side before Rufus darted from the undergrowth. He sat, looking back towards the forest, from which, a few minutes later, Corrie appeared. She didn't stop when she reached Lisa, not until she reached the truck.

"They're dead," she said.
"The child?" Olivia asked.
"Infected," Corrie said. "Let's go."

The rain finally arrived before they reached the road. It became a torrent before they reached the upturned car. Rivulets ran down the hillside, growing into a river, washing the road clean.

When they saw a rooftop inching around a thinned grove, they pulled off the road.

"We should wait for the storm to pass," Pete said. "And we might as well wait inside."

No one said anything; there was nothing else to say.

21st April

Chapter 37 - Gridlock
Sutton, West Virginia

A storm is louder than an engine. The idea ran through Pete's head as he waited for dawn. It was better than thinking of the dead child. If they'd driven a few minutes faster, they'd have caught up with that car. But after a restless night thinking about maybes, it was better to think of the storm.

Two nights gone, and he wasn't even sure they had crossed into West Virginia. The ship would depart Savannah at dusk on the fifth day. Lisa wanted to attack at night. Assuming they arrived at Sutton today, attacked tonight, and were alive by dawn tomorrow, they'd have under thirty-six hours to get to Savannah. If they aimed straight for the lighthouse, rather than the pier in Thunderbolt, they could skip a lot of the suburbs. Assuming they could find the fuel, and enough vehicles for any survivors still being kept prisoner. Assuming the truck even survived as far as Sutton.

He watched the rain, thinking about the sergeant near Lexington, and the survivors at the church; that, too, was better than thinking about the infected child. He'd first thought the people in Virginia appeared friendlier than Long Island or Florida, but had overlooked what they had in common. Supplies were running out. From the stories Zach had told of South Africa and Mozambique, it was the same there. When supplies ran low, people fled. People fought. People died.

"Penny for them?" Olivia asked.

"I'd trade an oat bar," he said.

"All we've got is cans of beans," she said. "There was nothing at all here."

"We'll find some more food in Sutton," Pete said.

"Maybe some showers," she said. "I can't believe how much I miss our cabin on the ship. I dreamed about it last night."

"It was paradise, wasn't it?" Pete said. "Ah, come on. Let's get the others up and get moving."

The miles crept by faster than the road signs. The number of undead stumbling onto the road dropped with each new hill climbed. Each new crest brought a taller horizon ahead, but otherwise, the vista barely changed.

The houses near the road were increasingly barricaded with furniture and felled trees, but all were lifeless. Too often, the only movement came from the zombies trapped on the inside of those failed defences. Stalled vehicles had their fuel caps removed, though often still had moving corpses buckled inside.

"Tanks!" Corrie said, breaking the near silence which had consumed them all morning.

M1 Abrams main battle tanks filled the road, forming two columns, one on the northbound carriageway, another on the grass verge between it and the southern-bound road, stretching as far ahead as they could see.

Pete, driving again, slowed. "I'll take us onto the southbound."

"No, stop," Lisa said. "We should stop. We're not far from Sutton. Okay, yes, now I understand a little more."

"Understand what?" Olivia asked.

"Their plan," Lisa said.

"How far are we from Sutton?" Pete asked, bringing the truck to a halt.

"A little over five miles," Olivia said.

"I'll keep watch," Corrie said. "It's been twenty minutes since the last zom, but that's only counting what's behind." She climbed up onto the truck bed behind the cab.

"What do you understand, Lisa?" Olivia asked, following Kempton.

"Let me confirm my suspicions before I commit to any conclusion," Lisa said. "Rufus, stay on guard."

Pete drummed his hands on the wheel, then got out.

A crowing caw came from the trees on the down slope of the Appalachian forest. "No zoms," Pete said. "Lots of trees, but no zoms."

"Lots of tanks," Corrie said from the top of the cab where she turned a slow circle, scanning for movement. "Lots of birds, too."

"Birds are a good sign," Pete said. "Low radiation."

"Low here, but where did they fly from?" Corrie said.

Ahead, Lisa climbed up the first of the tanks while Olivia stood with carbine half-raised, looking ahead. After only a few seconds, Lisa climbed down, and motioned Olivia back.

"Trouble?" Pete called, as the two women returned.

"Experience tells us to rarely expect the opposite," Lisa said. "The tanks appear to be parked."

"There are plenty of bones," Olivia said. "Human *and* animal."

"So a battle was fought here?" Pete asked.

"I saw no casings," Lisa said. "The vehicles are fuelled. There are shells inside, and ammunition for the machine gun. At least forty M1 Abrams tanks, stopped in two rows, and at least as many support vehicles further back."

"They're still fuelled up?" Corrie asked.

"That one is," Lisa said.

"How far are we from Sutton?" Corrie asked.

"We're five miles from the Sutton Regional Jail according to that road sign," Olivia said.

"Yes, indeed I do understand," Lisa said. "The cartel employed a meteor to crack a walnut."

"And I'm still waiting on that explanation," Olivia said.

"One I shall provide as we drive," Lisa said. "Behind us, there was a side road leading up into the hills. I would suggest we park the truck there, and continue on foot."

"That zom should have caught up with us by now," Corrie said as Pete kept watch on the driveway leading up to the one-storey house nestled a hundred metres up the hillside.

"Found it," Lisa said, coming out of the house, a local map in her hand. "Now, can we find our destination? Yes. Yes, I think we can, though our difficulty will be these hills. However, I suggest we avoid the roads. In a straight line, our destination is two valleys over. The tanks are an obvious method of attack. Too obvious, perhaps. Or was that the point?"

"What point?" Pete asked. "We're still waiting on an explanation."

"When things work out well for an opponent, or poorly for oneself, it is often easy to ascribe to them prescient powers," Lisa said. "In reality, they've simply been fortunate. We'll need camouflage for our sniper's nest."

She went back into the house.

"I hate it when she talks like that," Corrie said.

"Glad it's not just me," Olivia said.

Ten minutes later, they were trekking through wild woodland, with Rufus as their early warning system for the undead, but though he was cautious, he was unconcerned.

"Still no sign of that zom," Corrie said, finally slinging her rifle. "Or *any* zoms."

"It's the perfect territory for surviving the outbreak," Olivia said.

"But the cartel weren't planning for zombies," Lisa said. "The jail is a clever idea, don't you think?"

"Depends what you mean," Olivia said.

"I knew the cartel were recruiting in prisons," Lisa said. "I simply put it down to a policy of eliminating the competition by controlling the labour supply. Yet here, the purpose becomes clear. For over a decade, they assumed a coming catastrophe which would devalue all currency. So why continue running a drug empire? Why continue recruiting in prisons?"

"They wanted an army, didn't they?" Corrie said. "How do you maintain an army in a specific location? Soldiers need to be fed and housed, and that's expensive. It's noticeable unless they have some other ostensible reason for gathering in such a large group."

"In Colombia, they had a coal mine and the miners," Pete said. "And this is coal country, isn't it?"

"It was," Lisa said. "Those pits still being worked were heavily unionised, heavily regulated, and often heavily protested. No, there would be too many questions asked by too many people, often in the national press. A jail offers an obvious recruiting ground. They wouldn't need to ensure universal support in advance. A few strategically placed staff, and a few more appropriately qualified prisoners, would suffice. Once the crisis began, and the inmates were locked in their cells, the remainder would be offered the choice of joining, or starving."

"Maybe," Olivia said. "But what was that you said about assigning prescience after the fact?"

"Ah, but there is the additional evidence of the tanks," Lisa said. "At the beginning of the crisis, the National Guard, and the police, were deployed away from the cities. Yes, partly this was to ensure the crisis truly was able to take hold. But I did wonder about the places to which the units were sent. Well, now we have an explanation for at least some of those destinations."

"Which is?" Pete said, irked from the rain dripping onto his neck, the sweat running down his back, and the damp creeping into his boots from the pine-needle-masked muddy puddles.

"Those tanks were deployed here for use by the cartel," Lisa said. "Unknowingly, of course. At the beginning of the outbreak, here in the United States, police, National Guard, and the army were deployed away from population centres. Was it to facilitate the spread of the virus? In some cases, yes. But the plan was conceived *before* the cartel, and their politicians, were aware of the plague they were about to unleash. The tanks are a store of ammunition and fuel. Each contains a thousand litres of diesel and is equipped with medical supplies and other personal equipment."

"Equipment the soldiers would have taken," Corrie said. "But they didn't, so why not?"

"Because of the plane," Lisa said. "Tanks. A jail. An airport. The plane dropped VX nerve agent, as the Australians saw in Colombia. At night, I would imagine, so the sentries didn't see the spray leaving the plane. Their vehicles would have been lit, as would their encampment, and we are only a few miles from the airport." She waved the map she'd picked up in the house.

"How do you know it was VX?" Olivia asked.

"The bones," Lisa said. "Some human, some bird. But all are now pecked clean. The birds in the trees had been feasting on the flesh, and the insects who'd beaten them to the meal. Some came to the feast early, and they died, too. The salient point is that the tanks, and their fuel, remain. Our enemy is not so numerous that they have salvaged that resource. And, of course, we now have a means of destroying them."

"You know how to drive a tank?" Olivia asked.

"I've flown a plane and driven a ship," she said. "I once operated a wrecking ball. A tank should be straightforward."

It was an interesting theory. A *terrifying* theory. Pete had no reason to doubt it. Not after hearing the stories, and seeing the video, of Colombia. But couldn't it also mean the cartel were so well provisioned they just didn't need those tanks?

Without the trees thinning, the hill crested, and they began to descend. A reflective flash of yellow caught an errant sunbeam, and had them detour a few hundred yards to a backpack, abandoned by a lightning-cracked stump.

"This might be a place locals could arrange to rendezvous," Lisa said, looking for prints while Rufus sniffed for a scent.

"No blood. No signs of a fight," Corrie said. "No reason for us to delay."

Pete looked at the bag again, but left it untouched, before continuing after the others, with Rufus leading the way, now downhill.

Rufus bounded back to Corrie, springing around, hackles raised, not growling, but clearly indicating something awaited them further down the slope.

A branch cracked. Cloth tore. Brush snapped as a body thrashed through the distant undergrowth somewhere below them.

"I see it," Pete said, angling forwards, but for every step he took down the hill, the zombie slid three, occasionally falling against a low branch or thick trunk where it would momentarily right itself before slipping again with the next unbalanced step. Pete slowed his pursuit, looking about, looking up. "Birds are gone," he said.

Below, the zombie had landed in a dip created by a partially uprooted tree. As it stood, its foot caught in a root, and it fell, face first. The zombie twisted so violently its thighbone snapped.

As Pete brought his axe down to shatter the zombie's skull, it was his turn to slip, landing shoulder-first on the moss and needle carpet.

"Not sure that was quieter than a gunshot," Corrie said, offering a hand to help him.

"But we must be silent from now on," Lisa whispered. "I see overhead cables. The road is ahead, and so our destination must be close."

"But left or right?" Olivia asked.

"Wait by the roadside," Lisa said. "I shall find out."

Chapter 38 - Springtime Traps
Sutton, West Virginia

Corrie and Lisa disappeared among the woodland running alongside the road. Pete leaned against a tree, while Olivia crouched next to Rufus.

"Whatever happens next, thank you," Olivia whispered.

"You already thanked me," Pete said.

"That was for coming back to Indiana for me. Now I'm thanking you for everything since. It's been fun, Pete. Terrifying. Depressing. Exhilarating."

"Exhausting," he added.

"But fun," she said.

"A whole lifetime in a couple of months," he said.

"Here's hoping for another few lifetimes to come. Do you have a map?"

"I left it in the truck."

"If we follow that road right-ish, we'll reach the tanks and the tow-truck."

"Do you think you could drive a tank?" he asked.

"We should try the tow truck first," Olivia said.

Pete nodded, watching for his sister. "Hope the cartel don't know how to drive a tank. Wouldn't want one of those chasing us down the road."

"Oh, don't," Olivia said. "There. Movement." She raised her carbine, but Rufus bounded forward, clearly unconcerned. Corrie came into view, and waved them over.

"There is a motel," Corrie whispered, when they reached her. "*The* motel mentioned in the note. It's barricaded like a fortress. The birds are hovering nearby."

"So there are people at the motel?" Olivia asked.

"I don't think so, but there *are* zoms," Corrie said.

They followed Corrie through the trees. Above the rustle of leaves, and the damp patter of another squall, metal clinked and knocked, growing in volume as they approached.

The two-storey hotel was a quarter the size of the parking lot, built in an L with most rooms having no better view than the vehicles in which the guests had arrived. Now, they had no view at all, as those windows were boarded from the outside. Ringing the motel was a recently installed chain link fence. Forming a defensive perimeter was a jumble of razor wire, but that wire was inside the fence, and in it were tangled the undead.

Lisa waited at the treeline, crouched low behind an ancient fern. "It is a prison," she whispered. "Similar in concept to that in which I was confined in Canada. However, I am certain that there are no still-human guards, only the undead."

"Found them," Corrie said, holding up a small pair of red-handled pliers. "I know these'll be slow, but it'll be quicker to use these than to go hunting for a better pair of wire cutters."

As they approached the wire, the undead saw, or sensed, them and became violently active, ripping their flesh as they tugged against the tangling barbs. But they all seemed to have become ensnared at the end of the compound furthest from this gap.

"They must have followed someone over there," Olivia said.

"Give it a few minutes longer, they'll tear themselves apart," Pete said.

"I'm not waiting," Corrie said.

Pete looked at the clothes. Not just those on the undead struggling to tear themselves free, but those rags on the ground. "That's a prison uniform," he said. "Two, at least."

"You mean they're prison guards?" Olivia asked.

"Inmates," Pete said. "Three, maybe four of them."

"We're in," Corrie said, holding the wire aside for Lisa.

"Rufus and I'll wait here," Olivia said. "Ten minutes and you're to be out of there. I'm counting."

"You don't want to come?" Pete said, as Corrie followed Lisa inside.

"Do *you* really want to go in?" she asked. "Just bring Lisa out. Ten minutes, no more."

The wire had been unrolled from that corner of the fence. The one-metre gap was where the two sets of coils hadn't quite met. The ground between was dotted with charred flesh, burned scraps of clothing, and pebbles which cracked underfoot. Except they weren't pebbles, but mud-smeared scraps of bone.

"It *is* a trap!" he yelled, even as he saw the wire, leading back into the roll of razor wire.

"But triggered long ago," Lisa said, calmly. "Hence the charred flesh."

"And why there's a gap in the razor wire," Corrie said. "But there's no shrapnel damage to the building. Must have been a firebomb. Lisa? Lisa!"

Kempton had jogged over to the motel, stopping by the boarded window to a downstairs room. She raised a cautioning hand while shaking her head before walking diagonally across to a road-facing room. The door had a key in the lock, still attached to a large and noticeable-from-a-distance keyring. She didn't turn the key, but drew her knife, and began levering at the wooden board.

"Let me," Pete said, using his axe as a pry-bar. From above came the muffled sound of glass breaking, followed by a fist smacking into the board covering the window.

"There are keys in the door," Corrie said. "This is the room you're supposed to enter, right?"

"Like their political brethren, the cartel always over-planned and under-thought," Lisa said, as the board fell away. "Step back, please."

"We've got zoms upstairs," Corrie said as fists began beating at a door. "And downstairs."

Lisa turned her head, shielded her eyes, and smashed the glass with her knife. "One more minute please, and we'll be leaving." After the glass fell, she leaned inside the room, but didn't attempt to clamber in. She sheathed the knife, and drew her sidearm as she walked over to the already broken window. "Yes," she said. "Glass inside, but one would expect that. Ah."

"What?" Pete asked, while Lisa walked to the still closed door.

"One minute, and we shall leave," Lisa said.

"You said that a minute ago," Corrie said. "We've got multiple zoms in multiple rooms."

"One minute," Lisa said, and fired three bullets into the door, near the lock. She tried the handle, but the door still didn't open. "Oh. That always works in movies."

"Let me," Pete said. He swung the axe at the door's already weakened frame. Two blows, and it opened.

Lisa went inside, took out a phone, and took a photograph.

"What is it?" Pete asked.

"A syringe," Lisa said. "The other room's door is rigged to explode with a gasoline-based firebomb. They used a grenade for the detonator with a wire attached to the door handle. When the door opened, the pin would have come out. But the wire was being kept taut by the curtain rail, which must have come loose when that trap by the fence exploded."

"Okay, fascinating," Pete said. "And now it definitely *is* time to leave."

"Of course," Lisa said. "After you."

Uncertain she would follow, but certain there was nothing he could do to make her, he jogged back over to Corrie.

"We're leaving," he said.

"Go on, then," she said.

He continued on to the gap in the fence. Only as he was making his way through did he look for Lisa. She was nowhere to be seen.

"Is it bad?" Olivia asked.

"Pretty much," Pete said. "It's a trap, but it reminds me of that place they were holding Lisa in Canada."

"Quick!" Lisa said, sprinting across the parking lot. "Leave the wire, there's no time," she added as Corrie made to bend it back after her.

"What did you do?" Olivia asked.

"Set a fire. We don't want some poor survivor to think there's any salvage inside. I would suggest we run before the gasoline explodes."

They sprinted back across the road, and didn't stop until they were ten metres up the slope. When Pete looked back, a thin plume of smoke rose from the hotel.

"If we follow the road, we'll reach the tow-truck," Lisa said. "But we should stay in the trees, at least until we're certain the fire has caught."

"Did you recognise any of the zombies?" Olivia asked.

"No," Lisa said. "There was a corpse, decayed, but tied to a chair. It is possible it was someone I knew, but I will take comfort in uncertainty."

"So what else did you find?" Olivia asked.

"Syringes," Lisa said. "From the clothing, the majority of the undead were former inmates at the jail."

"If they were wearing prison clothes, they were selected soon after the outbreak," Olivia said.

"Selected for labour, yes, but not for sacrifice until the sisters arrived," Lisa said. "The sisters set the trap. They must have arrived after the bombs fell, and after you had been flown to Corn Island. The prisoners would have been infected after the sisters decided to go elsewhere. I suspected as much when we saw the tanks. They were prepared but abandoned. There were too many convict-conscripts to accompany the sisters, one assumes aboard a plane with its limited number of seats. But the sisters didn't want to leave the convicts with such an impressive arsenal, so they were infected, and left behind as undead guards."

"With a fire bomb?" Pete asked, looking back towards the motel.

"With a series of traps, which acted against one another," Lisa said. "They left a bomb wired to an obvious access point which must have been triggered by a zombie. While it did little damage to the building, and none to the fence, the blast disarmed the trap inside the building. Altogether, it is a very amateur effort."

"But the sisters escaped," Pete said. "So where did they go?"

"That is the next mystery," Lisa said. "Ah, there we go."

The explosion wasn't loud, or fast, but it was relentless, a rising flood of black smoke with an orange heart, which grew wider and taller as more of the building burned.

"What now?" Corrie asked.

"It's time to go back," Olivia said. "If we hurry, we can make a hundred miles before dark."

"We'll need to grab some fuel from those tanks," Pete said. "I'm going to veto us trying to drive one, but maybe we could commandeer one of the army trucks. I don't think that tow truck will make it much further."

Rufus froze, turning to peer at the road, his ears pricked. Pete heard it a second later. An engine. No, *two* engines.

"Take cover," Lisa said, even as all four ducked down, hiding in the brush. Olivia grabbed Rufus's collar.

The engines belonged to two blue police motorbikes, which sped along the road, towards the smoking pyre of a motel.

"Cartel?" Pete whispered.

"Must be," Olivia said, hunkering down next to him. "Lisa, what do you think?"

"The next move is up to them," she said.

They didn't have to wait long before the bikes returned, speeding back the way they'd come.

Pete stood. "So?"

"It must be the cartel," Lisa said. "They are based nearby, and somewhere close enough to have seen the smoke. Anyone else living nearby, other than the cartel, would already have sprung the trap."

"They're at the airport," Olivia said. "They must be. We have to check. It's why we came here, after all."

Chapter 39 - Flying Underground
Sutton Airport, West Virginia

It was a long runway for such a rural town, while the encompassing wall was overly tall. What had begun as a low barrier to keep animals away from the tarmac now stood over three metres high, and was made of timber planks, repurposed furniture, part of a shed's corrugated wall, a car, plastic pipes, metal brackets, and even an upturned trailer. That trailer had most likely been towed by the tractor now parked in the partially deconstructed shed.

The other three buildings hadn't been dismantled. One was a hangar, one was a tower and service building, and the other looked like a double-height garage, outside of which the two blue motorbikes were parked. Almost as striking was the plane, a twin-engine jet, on-stand at the very end of the runway as if it were ready to take off.

"I see bones," Corrie said, as she peered through the scope. Again, they'd stopped within the shelter of the trees, about fifty metres from the fence and two hundred from the motorbikes. "Definitely bones. Outside the fence."

"Where?" Olivia asked

"Everywhere," Corrie said, handing her the scope. "They left the zoms where they killed them. And it looks like they killed them all."

"Sniper on the roof of the tall garage," Lisa said, scanning the terrain with a compact pair of binoculars. "One sniper, and one drinker. Four chairs. Maybe five. An awning. A grill, I think. Some other furniture. Maybe boxes. The details are difficult to distinguish."

"Five chairs could mean five sentries on duty at any time," Pete said, shielding his eyes with his hand.

"I think not," Lisa said. "Based on the size of the rooftop rainwater collection system, it's more likely there is one chair for each survivor here. Each *free* survivor. The twin-engine business jet parked on the runway will have an occupancy of ten plus two pilots, and fewer if they modified it for greater luxury or range."

"And the plane is *on* the runway," Olivia said. "They must have it ready for take-off."

Pete took the scope from Olivia and scanned the airport. "Why are they camped out on that roof when they could be in that tower? It's just as tall, and would be way more comfortable."

"But it's further from the jet," Corrie said. "Two bikes. One tractor. One jet. No other vehicles visible. There's a small patch of dug dirt near the partially dismantled shed. Could be graves."

"How do they kill the zoms?" Olivia asked.

"I'm reasonably certain the sentry has a rifle," Lisa said. "Darkness approaches. Either we act now or wait for dawn."

"Better we get this over with," Olivia said. "Anyone know precisely how?"

"We shall assume the jet has capacity for twelve," Lisa said. "There are no military vehicles parked inside the airport, and we know there are plenty on the road. It's safe to assume there are fewer than twelve people inside, and their escape plan involves a flight."

"We're still outnumbered," Corrie said.

"Surprise is a great equaliser," Lisa said. "I'll fetch the tow truck, drive it to the gate, and lure as many as I can there. You three remain here. Corrie, can you take out the sniper?"

"Not from here, but maybe if I get closer."

"Then do that," Lisa said. "Wait until I arrive, and begin with the sniper. Take out any others you can see. I'll drive onto the runway, and park in front of the jet. Mr and Mrs Guinn, I would impose on you to find a way through that fence. While they attack me, you can attack them from behind. If we've miscalculated the number present, you three should be able to slip away into the woods, liberate one of those military trucks before dawn, and escape to Savannah. Are we agreed?"

"Nope, but I can't think of a better idea," Olivia said, scanning the runway. "Pete?"

"I wish I hadn't skipped tank-driving class back in school," he said. "Let's do it."

"Then I shall return at dusk," Lisa said, and disappeared into the trees.

"I'm going to find a better perch," Corrie said, reaching into her bag. "Wire-cutters, if you need them. Rufus, come with me. If this goes wrong, you two watch for Rufus, and follow him to me."

The couple made their way down through the trees, to the edge of the woodland. "We can cut our way inside near that trailer," Pete said. "What do you think?"

"That there's no barbed wire," Olivia said. "Wait, look directly behind the tall garage, there's some pipework at an angle. Is that supposed to be a ladder?"

"I think we could use it as one," Pete said. "Oh, hang on. Look at the roof. They're disappearing. There must be a hatch in the roof, and stairs inside."

"So where are they going?" she asked.

The answer came a minute later when four people left the garage, to gather by the two bikes.

"Only four people. Maybe there are only four here," Olivia said.

"And only two bikes?" Pete asked.

"Maybe there are more inside," Olivia said. "Wait, they're leaving. They're all heading towards the gate. So who's on guard?" She turned back towards the distant tower. "Maybe there *is* someone in there."

"Zom," Pete said. "There's a zombie at the gate. Must have followed the motorbikes back. I think they're going to kill it."

"All four of them?" Olivia asked, even as the four stopped in their tracks.

"Truck," Pete said. "Can't see it, but I can hear it."

So, too, could the four people on the runway. None seemed to know what to do, so they waited halfway between the gate and the tall garage. Only the zombie moved, lurching towards the truck. Lisa sped up, braking only after she'd slammed into the lumbering monster, raising a rainbow of gore as the truck stopped and the zombie flew into the gate.

The four cartel survivors still just stood, clearly debating what to do next. Lisa opened the truck's door and climbed out, standing on the step, waving. One of the four raised a pair of binoculars to his eyes. He lowered them. Raised them. Lowered them again. All four began running, not towards the gate, but back to the garage.

"They recognised her!" Olivia hissed. "C'mon!" She ran for the wall. Pete followed, catching up just before she stopped near the upturned trailer.

Up close, he saw the pipework wasn't really a ladder, just a diagonal prop supporting the wall. A little further along, however, a table had been braced against the fence with its legs pushed through the links. While those legs had snapped, they still provided foot and handholds up which they could climb.

Olivia went first, and Pete was ten steps behind when he reached the other side of the fence. With the garage close, he couldn't see the gate, or the runway, but he heard an engine. It didn't sound like a plane, or a bike, but it was getting nearer.

Olivia had found a narrow door at the back of the garage, where she waited for him. She raised her carbine.

He drew his pistol. "Open," he mouthed.

She flung open the door. He ran inside, angling left, while she followed, going right. There wasn't much light inside, except from a narrow and open hatch in the roof, accessible via a set of scaffold platforms and ladders, at the base of which, in the floor, was a hatch that clanked closed.

Chapter 40 - To Kill, or Not to Kill, That is the Question
Sutton, West Virginia

"Clear," Olivia said.

"Gone," Pete said. "Down there. They went down there." He let his sidearm fall to his side. The hatch was secured with a wheel-lock mechanism. There was no obvious key or number-pad, and when he attempted to turn the handle, it wouldn't move an inch.

"It's a bunker!" Olivia said. "They've got a damned bunker."

"Check outside," Pete said. "See if there's more of them."

"More people or more bunkers?" Olivia said as she crossed to the door. "I can see Lisa." She stepped outside to wave.

Pete turned back to the hatch, uncertain if he should aim his gun at it or not. He looked around for a remote locking mechanism, and then for a camera. There were none, or none that were obvious. There *were* a pair of workbenches, a stack of tyres, three partially dismantled motorbikes, and two partially up-armoured cars. Both were county-sheriff sedans, with sheet metal panels affixed to the rear windows, and with more panels nearby, ready to be installed.

One corner of the shed was full of loose tools, and nearly as many toolboxes. Grabbed from nearby homes, presumably, and stored on and around heavier tools: a circular saw, a lathe, and an arc welder. Behind them was a generator, currently switched off. A cable ran from it up to the scaffolding platform, and then up the ladder to the roof.

As he heard running feet, he turned back to the door. It was Lisa and Olivia.

"What's up?" Pete asked.

"I was about to ask you that," Lisa said. "Olivia said there's a bunker?"

"There's a hatch in the floor," Pete said. "It closed as we came in. I can't get it open."

"They saw you and ran," Olivia said.

"Indeed," Lisa said. "However, we have an equally pressing problem approaching from the south. More zombies than I can count are on the road, about ten minutes behind me. Signal Ms Guinn. That forest will soon be no place to hide."

As Olivia went to wave Corrie inside, and to help Rufus over the wall, Pete climbed the platform ladder, leaving Lisa to puzzle over the hatch. By the time he reached the roof, Corrie was at the wall, and the undead were on the road. Lisa hadn't been kidding, there *were* a lot. Hundreds. Lisa had driven the tow truck into the airport, closing the gate behind her, but how strong was the gate?

He turned to look at the tower, before climbing back down into the shed. There, Olivia and Rufus were guarding the hatch.

"Where's Corrie?" he asked.

"With Lisa, gone to check the hangar and the tower," Olivia said. "Lisa thinks there must be another entrance to the bunker, and it's most likely to be in one of those buildings."

"I'm not sure," Pete said. "I mean, it's a long runway, isn't it? Too long for somewhere remote like this. I bet the cartel had it extended, and when they did, they put in the bunker. The tower and the hangar look older, like they were here before."

"Maybe," Olivia said. "Assuming it even *is* a bunker. Maybe it's just an escape tunnel. I can't see an air vent, or fans, or even a pipe. They had a huge tunnel down in Colombia, and this *is* mining country. That's if it belongs to the cartel at all."

"They ran when they recognised Lisa," Pete said.

"Maybe they ran when a scary old woman ploughed her truck into a zom," Olivia said.

"Yeah, sure, maybe," Pete said. "Except the cartel brought some prisoners here all the way from Delmarva."

"So it was owned by the cartel, but is that who they are?" she asked. "Look for cameras or a journal, a diary, or even a tablet with some recent video."

They'd found none before Lisa and Corrie returned.

"Have our hosts made contact?" Lisa asked.

"The hatch hasn't opened, if that's what you mean," Olivia said. "Did you find any more of them?"

"No, but we found another plane in the hangar," Corrie said. "It's a twin-prop with seats for four passengers, plus pilot and co-pilot. The jet has bullet holes in the cabin, the cockpit, and the engine. No blood inside, however."

"Considering the plane's position on the runway, it was shot to prevent it being used," Lisa said. "One can assume the damage *wasn't* done by the pilot, but that a pilot was here at the time."

"Right, because without a pilot, a plane's useless," Olivia said. "So why not shoot the pilot?"

"And why shoot the plane?" Lisa said. "It's all most puzzling. There was no sign of the tower being recently used, nor any beds or other comforts in the hangar. I imagine they must be sleeping down in their bunker."

"There's a few cans of gasoline over by the generator," Olivia said.

"And a proper fuel tank behind the hangar," Corrie said. She turned to the dismantled motorbikes, and the up-armoured cars. "Two cars, and two working motorbikes, so there can't be more than ten of them. You saw four?"

"Only four," Pete said. "And maybe that's all who are here."

"There aren't any kids," Olivia said. "There's a football, a few Frisbees, and some golf clubs in that corner, but no bicycles or soccer balls, no crayons, no real toys."

"So between four and ten adults," Lisa said, walking over to the two sheriff's cars. "The prop plane appears to be in working order, but perhaps their pilot is dead, or there are too many to fit into that smaller plane. It certainly appears they have plans to depart and to do so by road."

Pete walked over to the hatch. He gave the handle a kick. "So, what do we do?"

"Are they cartel?" Olivia asked.

"Those are two of the pressing questions, yes," Lisa said.

"It's getting dark," Corrie said. "We can't leave here tonight. And if we are staying here, we'll have to keep watch on that hatch in case they come back up. I'll bring the tow truck outside. We'll fill it up, and be ready to leave if the zoms get inside the fence."

"I'll take a look at those cars," Olivia said. "It might be they're a more reliable choice of transport."

"Why didn't they take one of the military vehicles in that convoy?" Pete asked.

"Another excellent question," Lisa said. "Perhaps those vehicles have been disabled."

The engine grumbled as Olivia turned the key. "Seems fine," she said, switching the engine back off. "They weren't in a hurry to finish preparing these cars. Add in the lack of beds upstairs and that tells me they have a lot of supplies down in their bunker. Lisa, what do you want to do?"

"I… I don't know," she said. "I truly don't."

"Looks like we've got a few hours to figure it out," Olivia said.

"I'm going to go watch the zoms," Pete said. He climbed the ladder, and returned to the roof.

More of the undead were approaching, but only in ones and twos, while the great mass which had followed the truck had spilled around the perimeter fence. Around twenty still lingered by the gate, and it was impossible to know how many more might arrive overnight. As the sun set, a chill arrived. A promise of a cold night he carried back down the ladder.

In the workshop-shed, Corrie had set a small fire in an old wheelbarrow.

"Have you figured out what to do?" Pete asked.

"We've determined the options," Lisa said. "But we've not settled on a final decision."

"We don't know who's down there," Olivia said. "Originally, here in Sutton, it must have been the cartel, but we don't know who these people are. Maybe they're former prisoners who escaped the cartel. Maybe they're survivors *of* the cartel. Maybe even employees of Lisa's who recognised her, but assume she's working *with* the cartel. We just don't know. So whatever we do, we've got to remember that."

"There's a lot of tools up here," Corrie said. "We could probably break the hatch open, but it'll open into a vertical tunnel in which we'd be sitting targets as we descend. We could drop down some burning gasoline. The fumes will probably kill them, depending on whether there's an airlock at the bottom, and whether they have another way out."

"But we don't know if they deserve execution," Olivia said. "We've got three days of food, but the ship will depart Savannah in under forty-eight hours. We'll have to do most of the driving tomorrow, in daylight. There's plenty of fuel, so I'd say we should take our truck and one of these cars. We'll stick the motorbikes atop the tow truck, and take them, too, in case we find a road too blocked for a bigger vehicle. Any delay could mean we'd miss the ship."

"We could block this hatch," Lisa said. "A few heavy weights should do it, or we could simply break some of the fence. The cartel do so enjoy using the undead as jailors, it would be poetic for them to share the experience."

"Only if we knew they were cartel," Olivia said. "Even if we did, didn't we stop an eye for an eye about a thousand years ago?"

"Plus, they might have a back door," Corrie said.

"Hang on," Pete said. "If they're cartel, we can kill them, or leave them to die, or let them be killed by zoms. But if they're not cartel, we can't do anything to harm them, yes?"

"Pretty much," Olivia said. "And since we don't know, since we can't know, we have to leave them be."

"Then we've got a bigger problem," Pete said. "Those zoms outside are spilling around the edge of the fence, but there's still a few dozen by the gate. There'll be more by morning. If we decide not to harm the people down there, we'll have to close the gate behind us when we leave, so the zoms don't end up killing them when they emerge from their bunker. There are no cameras here, right? So the people below will have no idea how safe, or not, it is up here."

"Unless they have another exit," Corrie said.

"Right, but we can't assume they do," Pete said, "not if we're debating what the moral course of action is. So, tomorrow, we'll have to shoot the zombies. It'll use up all our ammo, and at least an hour."

"We could fly," Lisa said. "And if we were to fly, we wouldn't have to leave here for another day. We'd have an extra twenty-four hours to puzzle this out."

"I thought the jet had been shot to scrap," Pete said.

"Yes, but I'm sure that twin-prop will fly," Lisa said.

"But can *you* fly it?" Olivia asked.

"Maybe the first thing to do is to go check," Corrie said. "Give it a proper once-over. If you can fly it, then maybe there's another option. If you can't, then we're back to square one."

Lisa nodded slowly. "Very well, yes. I'll check. Rufus?"

Pete walked over to the hatch. "Could we try tapping a message in Morse?" he asked.

"Corrie did," Olivia said, as she sorted through the packets and cans they'd brought with them. "There was no reply."

"We have to leave them be, then," Pete said.

"Morally, yes," Olivia said. "And I think Lisa knows it, but she's got to come to that conclusion for herself. There was a box of saucepans in the far corner. See if they're clean."

Among the pile of semi-organised loot were four boxes of factory-fresh cooking pots, though the frying pans had been removed from each. He brought over a large pan, then picked up a chair, moving it close to the wheelbarrow-fire. "It's not how I thought the mission would end," he said. "Nor is what we found at the hotel. I don't think the sisters ever got this far. If they had, they'd have gone on to Corn Island."

"I was thinking of Trowbridge," Olivia said. "When the sisters were supposed to be up in Canada levering him onto the presidential throne, they were actually heading down to the Delmarva Peninsula to look for Lisa."

"I was thinking of Australia," Pete said. "They organised that coup so they'd have a friendly government in the southern hemisphere. Maybe, after Delmarva, or after here, they flew to the Pacific."

"Well, that would be ironic," she said.

"Corrie and Rufus are checking the perimeter," Lisa said, when she returned. She dropped a bundle of straps on the floor. "The plane works."

"What are those?" Olivia asked.

"The harnesses for the two spare parachutes," Lisa said.

"And why have you got them?" Olivia asked.

"There were six parachutes. Rufus can't be expected to pull the cord himself, so we'll need to strap him to my harness."

"Back up a bit," Olivia said. "Actually, back up a lot. Why are you talking about parachutes?"

"Well, as I mentioned, I have *flown* before," Lisa said. "While I've never attempted a take-off, I can't foresee it presenting any insurmountable difficulties. If we knew there was an airport like this close to Savannah, then I would have few qualms about a landing. However, we don't know of any fenced runways. We will have little time to locate one, or even a clear section of road. However, we will be able to radio the ship from the air. Thus the most sensible option is to circle the icebreaker, radio them to deploy their boats, and then jump."

"What's wrong with driving?" Olivia asked. "We've found gas, and a couple of decent cars."

"We won't make it," Lisa said. "It took us three days to drive from Amelia Court House. There is no reason to assume a longer journey will be quicker. You're correct, we cannot harm the people down in the bunker, nor can we deliberately allow them to come to harm. We are *not* the cartel. That is the purpose behind everything I, you, and so many others have done, risked, and given up. No, we must be better than the cartel, and so we cannot allow these strangers to come to harm. Thus, yes, we must ensure the gate is closed behind us, unless we never open it in the first place."

"I'd still prefer driving," Olivia said.

"With no ammunition?" Lisa said. "There are at least thirty outside the gate now. Assume fifty by dawn, but the sound of each gunshot will bring more from along the perimeter. We will be without ammunition when we leave. Of course, it is important to remember that they followed the tow-truck here. Before then, they were following us, our truck. They will be most numerous along the road down which we travelled."

"We'll take a different route back," Olivia said.

"Indeed, with the unknown difficulties that presents," Lisa said. "Set that against the relatively low risk of jumping from an aircraft above a ship where the rescue will be effected by members of the Australian Special Forces. On balance, the plane is the only option if we are to catch that ship before it leaves Savannah."

"Let's talk after we've eaten," Olivia said. "We've got warm tea, spicy chilli, and canned cherries."

"What's Rufus having?" Pete asked as Olivia emptied a can onto one of the Frisbees.

"Hot dogs," Olivia said.

"Can I swap?" Pete asked.

"That's up to him," Olivia said.

Pete stood, and walked over to the door, spotting a torchlight. He raised a hand, waving before remembering there could be another exit to the bunker. But he recognised the bounding ball of fur that sprinted towards him, and straight over to the Frisbee.

"No swaps for you, Pete," Olivia said.

He took his bowl, and returned to his chair.

"The wall's holding," Corrie said as she came in. "Couldn't see any lights on the hillside."

"Do you know about the parachutes?" Olivia asked.

"Yep," Corrie said. "And if you want my opinion, I'd rather drive. I've never jumped from a plane, and I bet there's a lot of risk with your first jump, and I bet there's a lot more risk in jumping from that kind of plane. Yep, I'd prefer to drive, but I can't see us making it back to Thunderbolt in a day."

"We could have made it here in a day if we hadn't stopped," Olivia said.

"Sure," Corrie said. "But we stopped because we met people who needed help. Odds are we'll find similar people elsewhere. Both the sergeant near Lexington, and the people at the church, thought they'd seen zoms dying, so thought it was finally safe to collect much-needed supplies. I bet there are a lot of other groups like that. Maybe the sound of our engine will cause them to signal. And then there was that child. What if we came across another car like that? We'd have to stop. We'd just have to."

Pete ate a mouthful of the warm canned chilli. He'd had too many hungry days to be picky, but he enviously eyed Rufus's hot dogs as he took another small bite. Clearly noticing his covetous glance, Rufus began bolting his dinner.

"I'll have to jump with Rufus," Olivia said. "You can't, Lisa, because you'll need to be behind the controls until the four of us are out. Rufus will be calmest with me, but he still won't like it."

"I'll see if we've got something in the med kit we can tranquillise him with," Corrie said.

"Are we agreed, then?" Lisa asked.

"I'm not," Pete said, putting his bowl down. Rufus instantly bounded over. "Help yourself," he said, nudging the bowl a little closer to the dog. "If we parachute out over the sea, and if he's tranqed, Rufus won't float, let alone swim. If we don't tranq him, he'll struggle all the way down. Maybe Bruce or Nicko would be able to handle that, but not someone on their first jump."

"We're not leaving him behind," Olivia said.

"He'd stand a better chance of survival if we did," Pete said. "But I'm barely any happier jumping from a plane *without* Rufus. What if there's a storm over the coast? What if we get tangled in the chute? What if the chutes don't work? I think we'd be better off trying to land the plane."

"We don't know of a runway," Lisa said. "We'd have to pick a road or a field."

"Exactly," Pete said. "It'd probably be a crash, and could be miles away from the ship. Hopefully, the icebreaker would hear our radio message that we'd like to be picked up, and there is that army truck outside the marina. The zoms are going to be attracted to the crash, so we'll have to fight our way from the plane to cover. Hopefully, none of us break a leg during the landing. Hopefully no one dies during the rescue. But what if the ship isn't there? We'll have to fight our way to the marina to find out if it's been and gone, and if it *has* gone, we'll be stuck in Thunderbolt with the zoms, the gators, and the Floridian pirates not so far away."

"What are you saying, what do you want to do?" Olivia asked.

"I want to go to New Zealand," Pete said. "I'd settle for Australia, even the outback, but we've got to go where we'll do the most good. All those millions of people in the Pacific need Tess, and Leo, and Doc Flo. They need to know how bad it got here. They need to know there's no going back for our species. We can't do anything that'd imperil, or delay, that mission."

"A day or two won't matter," Olivia said. "Not when there's such a long voyage ahead of them."

"Except you're forgetting three things," Pete said. "Tess's original mission was to hunt down the cartel. Here they are." He stamped his foot. "Right beneath us. Does she have a duty to come flush them out?"

"No, because there's absolutely no way she can get from Thunderbolt to here," Olivia said.

"What are the other two things we've forgotten?" Corrie asked.

"Lake Moomaw," Pete said. "Would Tess feel obligated to make contact with them? And the third is the pirates off Cape Canaveral. The longer the ship spends in those waters, the greater the risk some of those boats find her."

"The pirates had weeks to go north. I don't see why they should change their plans now," Corrie said.

"I only spoke briefly with the commissioner," Lisa said. "But she is more than capable of making the hard choices. She did so with Long Island, after all. If she deems the risk is too great, she'll head south."

"Will she?" Pete asked. "What if she delays a day, and that day is the difference between having enough fuel and food to get to a safe harbour or running adrift in the open sea? What if the passengers have had enough, and mutiny?"

"That won't happen," Corrie said.

"Maybe not that specifically, but the longer the delay, the greater the chance something catastrophic happens."

"What do you want us to do, then?" Olivia asked.

"Forget Savannah," Pete said. "The one thing worse than delaying that ship is arriving after it's gone and ending up stuck in Thunderbolt. I guess we'd have to fuel up that truck, if we still can, stock up on food, if there's any left, and make for Lake Moomaw. Hopefully, they're as honest as they appeared, but would our arrival help them? We'd tell them about the Pacific, so wouldn't some among them want to head west? Is that the best thing for them to do? We didn't tell them about the Pacific the first time we met."

"Okay, but where would *we* go?" Olivia asked.

"Pine Dock on Lake Winnipeg," Pete said. "It's where we first met Doc Flo and Leo. It's a small town, a village, really, but it has a runway, and it has a waterdrome. When the Pacific sends out search teams, they'll want to use planes. Most runways won't be walled off like this, so where do the planes land? On the lakes. And when we left Pine Dock, there was a small garrison there. After the collapse, where would they go? Why would those soldiers go anywhere? Maybe that's where Judge Benton went, and it's the only place I can think of that Tess might send a team someday, other than New York."

"I don't want to go back to Long Island," Olivia said. "Okay, so we have a choice between Pine Dock or Thunderbolt? If I've got to pick a place to live for the next few months, it'd be Canada."

"It could be a lot longer than a few months," Lisa said. "Based on their projections for sending aid to New York, it could be a year."

"Maybe the zoms will be dead by then," Pete said. "Pine Dock doesn't have to be where we stay, just where we start planning how to get to the Pacific. If there's a garrison there, we can start bringing in other survivors. We can look for a route to the coast, a harbour for the ships to dock, even a long-range radio transmitter, or we could look for a boat of our own."

"Would we fly to Canada?" Olivia asked.

"I think so," Pete said. "It would be the quickest way across the Great Lakes."

"Then we've got the same risks whether we go to Savannah or we go north," Olivia said.

"I don't think so," Pete said. "In Georgia, we'd be hunting for a strip of land close to Thunderbolt. In Canada, we'd want the flattest bit of land we can find, and we can start looking as soon as we're over Lake Superior."

"If there are people in Pine Dock, there could be a radio beacon," Lisa said. "If not, I think I can find something as large as Lake Winnipeg, and a shallow beach on which to bring us down."

"You approve?" Olivia asked.

"When we came here, I didn't expect to find any of my people alive," Lisa said. "I did expect to find the sisters, and to gain some measure of revenge." It was her turn to stamp her foot. "This is what I get instead. My mission, my life's work, is done. I can do more good here in America than in a cell in the Pacific. There are people here who need help. Who need hope. I believe we can provide that. But it is for you three to decide."

"Corrie?" Olivia asked.

"I can't see us staying in Lake Moomaw," she said. "If we tell them about the radiation, and then about the Pacific, they'd want to leave. Pine Dock is about the only destination I can think of. So maybe we should go there, then go back for them. Maybe even go back to Long Island. We're basically continuing what General Yoon began. Pete's right. Where can we do the most good? It has to begin with Canada."

Part 4
Where We're Supposed to Be

Lake Superior

22nd April

Chapter 41 - An Unexpected Invitation
Sidnaw, Michigan

When he reached ten, Pete stopped counting craters and pulled the cabin-shade closed. "Where are we, do you think?" he asked, raising his voice over the engines' burr.

"It's been forty minutes," Olivia said. "Lisa said the plane flies at about five hundred kilometres an hour, so I guess around four hundred kilometres northwest-ish. So about as far as from Amelia Court House to Sutton."

"I never paid attention to geography, but wouldn't the next big city beneath us be Columbus?"

"Should be," she said. She pulled her own blind closed. "I guess it was."

At dawn, any further discussion on whether to drive south or fly north had been pre-empted by the undead. Over two hundred had gathered near the gate, with another hundred scattered around the perimeter. Even as they counted their bullets, more zombies appeared along the road, while a twenty-strong pack tumbled down the hillside beyond the fence. Without enough ammunition to shoot their foe, and facing so many that the fence was unlikely to hold, they had attempted one last, and fruitless, Morse message on the bunker hatch before boarding the plane. The take-off had been bumpy but over before fear had properly settled in. But now they were in the air, Pete couldn't help but think this was just the latest dumb idea in an increasingly long list. He could be on his way to Australia where there were clean sheets, stocked pantries, and hot showers, and where no day would begin with counting bullets.

"Thunder Bay isn't far from Lake Winnipeg, right?" Olivia asked.

"It's not close," Pete said. "Then again, nowhere is close in Canada."

"General Yoon was stockpiling supplies there," she said. "Supplies mean soldiers. And where would they go but north? People always go north in the horror movies. They do it in the books, too, so I know it's not just for the tax breaks. We'll find people. We'll help them."

"Are you telling me, or yourself?"

"Both," she said. "We made a deliberate choice not to help the people on Lake Moomaw. We've got to make what we do next count."

The plane buffeted and bounced.

"Last flight ever," Pete said.

"Except to Australia," she said.

"Okay, so it's the last flight without a proper pilot," Pete said.

"She managed the take-off and she's keeping us in the air, that's two-thirds of flying," Olivia said.

"Averaging a passing grade will be small consolation if we go crash-boom into the lake."

"There's always a parachute," Olivia said with a grin.

"Oh, don't," he said.

Rufus found it easy to sleep, but Pete didn't, so he re-opened the blind.

"Look at that," he whispered.

"What?"

"Zoms," he said. "Tens of thousands. More. Maybe millions."

"It's Indiana," Olivia said. "I think it has to be."

Despite its vast size, the horde was there and gone in minutes, though the trail of devastation gouged deep into the landscape kept them company for another dozen miles.

"Hey folks, you'll want to get up here," Corrie said over the plane's address system. "We've picked up a mayday."

Pete undid his seatbelt and followed Olivia up to the cockpit. "Can you turn the volume up?"

"We're already out of range," Corrie said.

"Where's the radio message coming from?" Olivia asked.

"That's Lake Superior just ahead of us, but they're in an IRS facility at a place called Sidnaw," Corrie said. "It was a woman on the radio. She said there are sixty children and a few adults in a fenced government facility surrounded by the undead. They have no ammunition. There's an airfield, but a jet crashed there during the nuclear war."

"I don't suppose you're familiar with the town?" Lisa asked. "It's not on our maps."

"Never heard of it, but we've got to help," Olivia said, grabbing hold of the doorframe, while Pete grabbed the seat.

"Indeed we must, if we can," Lisa said. "I'll turn us around and continue our hunt. But if we can't land, we will have to continue on, and hope we can return."

"She's back," Corrie said, tapping her headphones. She leaned forward. "I think it's there. That compound on the right."

"I'll turn the plane again," Lisa said. "I think we can land on the highway, though I'll need to fly low and confirm there are no overhanging wires. We will have quite a walk, so may I suggest you buckle up and brace, because it'll be an even longer walk with a broken leg."

Pete made his way back into the cabin, and checked the harness they'd rigged for a now-awake Rufus, who looked both expectant and irritated.

"You know that expression, out of the frying pan?" he asked, speaking low, and only to the dog. "This is what comes next in the dictionary."

"Sixty kids," Olivia said. "I hope we're in time. Have you heard of Sidnaw?"

"Not that I remember," Pete said.

"If we're not far south of Lake Superior, it's either Wisconsin or Michigan," Olivia said. "We can't be too far from the border."

"Except the lake's in the way," Pete said.

"You don't think we should land?"

"We have to," Pete said. "I just hoped, by air, we'd have gotten a lot further."

The plane lurched in mid-air.

"Hold on!" Lisa said over the cabin-address.

"That's not what you want to hear from your pilot," Olivia said.

With his sunshade still down, Pete couldn't see outside, but he was too busy trying to remember the brace-position to raise it.

The plane shook as the wheels bounced. They touched down again, harder, louder, squealing in protest. Now grounded, the plane veered left, then swerved right. The engines suddenly cut out.

"About a hundred zoms," Corrie said, pulling her way into the still-swaying cabin.

"Outside?" Pete asked, unbuckling his belt, before moving on to the now-growling Rufus.

"No. Outside the IRS facility," Corrie said. "Assuming the place encircled with zoms is where they're trapped. We're about two kilometres to the west, maybe three."

"Bring guns and ammo, and we can come back for the rest," Olivia said. "What kind of place is it?"

"The facility? It's a fenced compound, about a hundred metres on either side, containing a few warehouses," Corrie said. "It's off the road, though not by much, and just out of town, though not far away."

"What's the town like?"

"Like a village," Corrie said. "A few houses, a few barns, a few farms nearby."

"We have company," Lisa said. "Fifty metres ahead."

"Zoms?" Corrie asked.

"Absolutely," Lisa said.

Corrie pulled the door open and jumped down. Rufus barged his way after her. Two dull shots had sounded before Pete got outside. The air was cool. Fresh. Familiar.

"Smells like home," he said, looking around while, at a stop-start sprint, Corrie and Rufus circled the plane.

They'd come to a halt facing west on an east-west section of muddy two-lane highway. In the verge, on both sides, was an irregular jumble of partially crushed and completely wrecked cars and pickups, stretching as far as he could see, and now buried in the long grass. Beyond the cars, on either side, were trees.

"Someone cleared the road," Pete said.

"Indeed," Lisa said. "And as the runway is out of action, perhaps it was in anticipation of a plane. It is a question to ask our hosts over lunch." She raised her wrist to reflexively check a watch that wasn't there.

"We've got a zom behind," Corrie said.

"Let it catch up," Lisa said. "If there's to be a fight, we should do it far from the plane. What comes down can go up, but only after we've cleared the corpses from our new runway."

"You didn't dump the fuel?" Olivia asked.

"I wasn't sure how," Lisa said. "Still, not a bad landing for a first attempt."

"Wait," Olivia said. "Rufus needs his shoes. There's way too much junk on this road. Come here, boy."

A fluffy-winged cormorant landed on an overhead wire, not twenty yards back from where they'd come down. "Good job missing those wires," Pete said.

"I'm embarrassed to say I didn't spot them," Lisa said.

"Embarrassed? Wow. I'm just wondering what you'd have felt if we'd hit them."

"I can honestly say I would never have lived it down," she said.

By the time they reached the bus, nine zombies were dead, most having come from ahead.

"I need height," Corrie said, climbing up the battered vehicle. The tyres were shredded, the windows were smashed, the side had been caved in.

"A moment, and I'll join you," Lisa said, leaning against the bus's chassis.

"No worries," Corrie said even as she fired. "This is easier than dingoes. Just pass up a couple of mags."

Olivia plucked them from Pete's belt, and climbed up the side of the bus, using the shattered window as a step.

"Are you okay, Lisa?" Pete asked, giving his axe a practice swing.

"A few years ago, I hired a decathlon gold medallist to devise a fitness regime that would work every muscle in my body. I feel I should ask for at least a partial refund. The fuel caps have been removed from these wrecks, did you notice?"

"Yep. A lot of bones in the long grass," Pete said. "A few bullet casings, too."

"The passage of an overly heavy vehicle pushed these vehicles aside," Lisa said. "Probably after they took the fuel, but before they fired those bullets. Perhaps this is how the people at the compound expended all their ammunition."

"Olivia, how are we looking? Do we need to climb up there?" Pete asked.

"No, we're cool," Olivia said. "I haven't fired a shot yet. Ten to go."

"How far are we from Lake Superior?" Pete asked, raising his voice above his sister's methodical bang-bang-bang execution of the undead.

"About fifty kilometres due south," Lisa said.

"So we're not that far from Indiana," Pete said.

"We're a few hundred kilometres from Duluth, and the western edge of Lake Superior, where the Great Lakes end, and the western plains truly begin," Lisa said. "We must be at least five hundred kilometres to the nearest shore of Lake Michigan, and not much further to Chicago. I imagine that is far worse than New York."

"Clear!" Corrie called. "For now. That's forty-nine down. Anyone got more ammo?"

"For the carbine, no," Pete said.

"I have two magazines," Lisa said, "including that which is loaded."

"Then we're down to five mags and a bullet," Corrie said. "This could get close and personal."

"C'mon, Rufus," Pete said, "let's go scout the route."

Second guesses joined his misgivings but were forgotten when Rufus dodged wide around a door-less hybrid. From beneath, a foreshortened zombie crawled. The white bones jutting from its torn trouser legs scored deep gouges in the mud as it dragged itself towards them. Pete swung the axe down, the blade slicing through skull and face before clanging into the worn road.

"Fifty down," Olivia said as she caught up. She jumped up onto the hybrid's roof. "The road ahead looks clear. We've just got the zoms outside the compound itself to deal with."

She was wrong.

Chapter 42 - Burning Desire
Sidnaw Michigan

The southbound turning was signposted *The Edward J O'Hare Depository*, with a journal's worth of footnotes warning it belonged to the I.R.S. and was under federal jurisdiction. Identifying it as being the road leading to their destination were the corpses dumped in a field to the north of the highway. Zombies, obviously. Perhaps a thousand. Decaying slowly, but still giving off a stench thick enough to be visible if it weren't for the cloud of flies. They seemed to be hovering over the open graveyard, tasting rather than feasting.

Pete clamped his lips closed, swatting his hand through the air to clear it, but the flies didn't stray too far from their putrid swamp.

The south-leading side road was in better condition than the highway, and just as wide, but completely free of the undead. They found those zombies at the fence ringing the facility, and they were already dead.

The fallen infected lay in ones and twos around the outer-most of three high fences. Each fence was three metres from the next, three metres high, and supported by triangular steel fence posts, which were embedded in concrete and topped with razor wire. Where the fence met the road, there were three consecutive roller-gates, all closed.

Two figures were making their way through the long grass just inside the outermost fence. A man on crutches, his right trouser leg pinned just below the knee, with enough grey in his beard to put him past forty, but enough jet black to put him on the young side of fifty. His companion was a woman, about five-five to the man's hunched five-ten. She wore a broad-brimmed hat shielding her eyes and a flower-print scarf around her mouth and nose. Both survivors wore boiler-room-blue dungarees, with tool-belts at their waists, from which hung two half-metre-long sharpened metal spikes. The woman carried two long, and gore-flecked, spears.

"Hi there!" Olivia called.

"Were you folks on the plane?" the woman replied. She pulled down her scarf, revealing a twenty-something-year-old face that looked as tired as her voice sounded.

"Why'd you land?" the man asked. His voice was gruff, almost accusatory, and Texan to the woman's Minnesotan.

"We heard your mayday," Corrie said. "We came to help."

"Didn't need no help," the man said. "Didn't send no mayday."

"But we're grateful anyway," the woman said. "Hi. I'm Aqsa. Mr Grumpasaurus here is Abraham."

"We're the Guinns. I'm Olivia. This is Corrie, Pete, and Lisa. And this is Rufus."

Rufus yipped.

"Hey, Rufus! Where did you folks come from?" Aqsa asked.

"Corrie came from Australia," Olivia said. "But more recently, we took off from West Virginia."

"Ha! I told you, Abraham," Aqsa said. "Our prayers were answered."

"Yours maybe," Abraham said. "Pretty sure I was praying for the cavalry and I don't see no horses. Well, no point us talking out here where we're knee deep in guts, so y'all better come in." He limped towards the gate.

By the gatepost, the fencing took a ninety-degree turn, sealing the between-fence gap for the access road into the facility. A rectangle had been cut in that section of fencing, and re-secured with metal clips. There were no bodies on the road. No firearms at either Aqsa's or Abraham's belts.

"You lured the zoms to the fence so you could kill them with the spears, right?" Corrie asked.

"Hmm." Abraham grunted, pulling the outer gate open. "Noise brings trouble, and your engines made a racket fit enough to wake the dead. That's not a metaphor. More will come. If you want to leave, you better go now."

"Someone sent us a mayday," Lisa said. "If not you, who?"

The answer probably lay in the small crowd gathering behind the third, and innermost, gate. There were about twenty people, mostly bedraggled teens who were an even mix of anxious girls and nervous boys. Each carried a short metal spear. At the side, and a step behind, were four adults, leaning more heavily on their spears than the children.

"Anyone ask that plane to land?" Abraham asked.

"Me," one of the adults said. She wore jeans and a plaid shirt which didn't fit, and a green baseball cap beneath which were tufts of scissor-cut blonde hair. Mid-thirties, but maybe younger.

"Noise brings trouble, Yollie," Abraham said.

"A plane brings help, Abraham," Yollie replied.

"Does it?" Abraham asked.

"Oh, let them in," Aqsa said. "I want to hear about Australia."

Abraham swung himself aside so they could enter, then closed the gate before swinging to the internal gate, and opening that. "And who said you could abandon your posts?" he added, turning on the children. "Back you go until the all-clear's been sounded. Go on, now. You folks said you came from West Virginia?"

"And the other Virginia before that," Olivia said. "A ship was supposed to pick us up from Savannah, but we didn't think we'd make the rendezvous, so opted for Canada instead."

"Why?" Aqsa asked.

"It's a long story," Olivia said.

"Stories are for bedtime," Abraham said, turning to look back through the gates. He seemed almost disappointed that there were no more zombies.

"You guys have guns, and a dog to keep watch," Aqsa said. "So maybe we could start moving the bodies now. There *are* lots." The question was directed at Abraham.

"You got ammo for those guns?" Abraham asked.

"A few hundred rounds," Corrie said.

"Not enough, so grab a spear," Abraham said. "Walk clockwise inside the outer-most fence. I'll go the other way. Two of you do that. Two of you help Aqsa, and don't blame me if you get bit."

"Thanks, Abe," Aqsa said. "C'mon, the cart's over here. You'll want a scarf, too. I can offer you sea breeze or butterfly kisses."

"What kind of colour is a sea breeze?" Olivia asked.

"Oh, that's not the pattern," Aqsa said. "It's the perfume. Trust me, you'll need it."

Leaving Corrie and Lisa to patrol, Pete, Olivia, and Rufus followed Aqsa over to a row of large garages, each with a metal door, painted blue, except where a three-digit number had been painted in white in the centre. Waiting outside was a recently built cart. About the size of a car, and with a car's tyres, it had a metal frame, wooden sides, a ladder-

and-bracket crane, a hoist and winch with a ratchet handle, and a rubber sling. In the back were a pair of shovels, a box of gloves, and three bottles of bleach.

Aqsa walked over to a small table next to the cart, on which were a stack of folded scarves and an assortment of perfumes and deodorants, and against which leaned another five metal spears.

"I'd recommend butterfly kisses," Aqsa said, pointing to the scarves. "It's kinda citrusy, but very strong."

Olivia passed a scarf to Pete before spraying one for herself. "What are we doing with this cart?" she asked.

"Moving the bodies away from the fence," Aqsa said. "That's why we've got the winch. We move the bodies to that field across the road. We didn't think there'd be so many when we started. But we also thought we could power up the incinerator. Give it a shove, it's hard to get moving," she added, picking up the cart's handle. "You guys really came from Australia?"

"Me and Pete come from South Bend," Olivia said. "Just before the outbreak, he went down to Australia to find his sister, Corrie. They flew north, afterwards, to find me."

"And to make contact with the Canadians," Pete said.

"It's more romantic if you say it was just to find me," Olivia said. "We were married a few weeks ago."

"Congrats," Aqsa said, as they pushed the cart through the gate. "You flew *back* to America after the outbreak?"

"First time, yes," Olivia said.

"Hurry it up," Abraham said, impatiently waiting to close the gate behind them.

"He's a sweetie on the inside," Aqsa said as they wheeled the cart outside. "But on the outside, he's a cactus. So you went from Australia to Canada?"

"We fought with General Yoon and Judge Benton in Canada," Olivia said. "After the bombs fell, we tried to reach Vancouver so we could link up with the Pacific Alliance, but we got caught by the cartel."

"A cartel? You mean criminals?" Aqsa asked.

"Nasty people," Olivia said. "They were partly behind this mess."

"You mean the zombocalypse? How do you know?"

"That's part of the longer version of the story," Pete said. "But the cartel flew us down to the Caribbean, where we were rescued by some soldiers and cops from Australia. They were hunting the cartel, too."

"So you're cops, then?" Aqsa asked.

"Not really," Pete said. "I was deputised back in Broken Hill."

"We're *not* cops," Olivia said. "We're just people trying to make the world a little less worse."

"Cool," Aqsa said. "Next question, where's Broken Hill, and who are General Yoon and Judge Benton?"

"Let's start again," Olivia said, giving a slightly romanticised, and severely edited, version of the story while Pete hooked a chain around the legs of a corpse wearing a fluorescent vest.

With the chain attached, Aqsa turned the ratchet until the body was level with the cart. With a shove, the corpse was swung aboard, the chain was unhooked, and they moved on to the next.

It was slow, dirty, throat-gagging work. The scarves helped, but only a little. Finally, with eight bodies aboard, they dragged the cart down to the highway. After they'd slid and pushed the corpses into the ditch, Pete paused, taking in the wrecked vehicles along the roadside. There were fewer here than nearer the plane. His gaze settled on the birds feasting on the cloud of insects adventurous enough to taste the undead's diseased flesh.

"It's a lot of bodies," Pete said.

"I stopped counting ages ago," Aqsa said.

"How long have you been here?" Olivia asked.

"Since about two weeks after the outbreak," Aqsa said. "Back then, there were soldiers here, and more were supposed to come. It's because of the airfield. This was going to be a resupply base. But then the troop-plane crashed. We think because of the EMP."

"What happened to the soldiers?" Olivia asked as they shoved the now empty cart back towards the compound.

"Aboard the plane? They all died," Aqsa said.

"And the ones who were here?" Olivia asked.

"Captain Stahl led them away about a month ago. The captain put together a convoy with most of the adults, all those kids' parents, and the remaining soldiers, and led them south. There was supposed to be this big supply base with lots of tanks and guns in a town called Florence. He went to gather what he could. They never came back. I cycled down to look, and there was no sign of them, but that was about a week later. I'd have gone sooner, but there were too many undead. Since then, we've focused on staying alive."

"What kind of place is this?" Pete asked.

“It’s basically somewhere they burned documents,” Aqsa said. “There’s a big incinerator which should provide power, except it needs natural gas to get it started. We tried burning bodies with gasoline inside the furnace, but that was a complete disaster, so now we dump them on the other side of the road. We’ve got strong fences. *Really* strong. We’ve got a few solar panels for light and cooking. Water supplies can be a bit tight.”

“Talk later!” Abraham called from inside the gate. “Work now, or there won’t *be* any later. You’ve got another two to collect on the far side, so keep your eyes open!”

“He really is a sweetie,” Aqsa said. “Most of the time.”

Chapter 43 - Open Air Baths
Sidnaw, Michigan

They dumped the last cartload ten minutes before the clouds began dumping their rain.

"Perfect timing," Aqsa said. "We could all do with a shower. I'll fetch you guys some clothing."

"She was joking about the shower, wasn't she?" Olivia asked.

"I don't think so," Pete said, pointing to where a few of the older kids had run outside in t-shirt and shorts, and made a show of rinsing themselves beneath the rain.

"They're just showing off," Olivia said. "Oh, maybe not," she added, when one of the boys pulled out a bottle of shower gel.

"There's boiling water at the back of the office block," Aqsa said.

"That sounds way more sensible."

"Oh, don't mind them," Aqsa said. "It's all because of the pink hair crisis last week."

"The what?" Pete asked, but Aqsa had already jogged around the office. Pete hurried to catch up.

The inside of the compound was mostly concrete, dotted with a few warehouse-like buildings, separated with strips of worn grass, and dark streetlamps. The incinerator building was obvious from the chimney, while the two floors of windows made it clear this building had been an office. Of the others, a long low building, a short stubby one, a cluster of brown-clad three-storeys, it was pointless guessing what lay inside, but it was obvious what wasn't: housing.

"What's the plumbing like here?" Pete asked as they turned the corner.

"You're looking at it," Aqsa said, pointing at three steaming buckets, each behind their own, slightly ratty, privacy screen.

"Dare I ask what the toilets are like?" Olivia asked.

"Oh, those are fine," Aqsa said. "There's a septic tank, and the log book said it was emptied last November. Only twenty people worked here, and none of them actually *lived* here, but I don't think we'll fill it any time soon."

"What about showers?" Olivia asked.

"There's three over in the incinerator barn," she said. "But they don't work. When we still had gas for the generator, we powered up the pumps, but only got a trickle of water to dribble out the pipes. That's why the kids are washing in the rain."

"I left the Geiger counter in the plane," Olivia said.

"We'll get it tomorrow," Pete said.

"You think radiation might be a problem?" Aqsa asked.

"No, I'm sure it's fine," Olivia said. "But I've seen too many craters."

"Where?" Aqsa asked.

"We saw one near Columbus from the air, and another near Norfolk," Olivia said. "We know there were more, further east near Toronto. We heard about bombs in Brazil, South Africa, and Vancouver."

"It really was everywhere, wasn't it?" Aqsa said.

"You said there's not much water?" Pete asked.

"So far, there's been just enough," Aqsa said. "Sure, we all smell a bit, but it's not much different to what life around here was like a couple of centuries ago, that's what I tell the kids. That this is a valuable history lesson, which is probably why it's no one's favourite class. It's warm inside," she added. "And we've got plenty of clothes."

"Then that'll be five-star compared to last night," Olivia said. "So what's the story with the pink hair? A lot of the kids have dyed their hair, haven't they?"

"And did you see how a lot of the others have shaved their heads?" Aqsa said. "The kids got bored. Among some of the junk brought back here was a load of hair dye. They figured, why not? And whether by design or accident, everyone got their hair dyed pink instead of whatever colour they picked."

"That doesn't sound like an accident," Pete said.

"We've got sixty-three kids here," Aqsa said. "Princess is the youngest, and she's nine. Sally's the oldest, and she's fifteen. I swear, if it weren't for Abraham, we'd have gone all *Lord of the Flies* a month ago."

"So Abraham's in charge?" Pete asked.

"Him and Candice. She runs the kitchens. Dinner will be waiting just as soon as you wash. I want to go pace the perimeter." She left Pete and Olivia alone.

"Did you notice, when we came in, how the kids, and the other adults, were leaning on their spears?" Olivia asked as she pulled off her gore-flecked clothes.

"You mean that those spears would have to be clean," Pete said.

"Right, exactly. The kids, I get," she said. "The adults? I dunno, Pete, I don't think it bodes well."

The building had been an office, though most of the workrooms were upstairs. The downstairs was given over to store rooms, toilets, a small first-aid station, a few meeting rooms, and the staff break-area, which was now the cafeteria. It buzzed with chatter, most of which was coming from the children throwing questions at Corrie far faster than she could answer. As Pete's ears adjusted to the buzz, he realised most of the questions were about the Canadian singer Dan Blaze.

A pink-haired girl wearing a too-big hockey jersey and what, probably, were prescription swimming goggles, bounced over.

"Are you Princess?" Olivia asked.

"That's right, but you don't need to call me your highness. Not unless we're being formal," she said, without even a trace of irony. "Did you really meet Dan Blaze?"

"Sorry, no," Pete said.

"Oh. Never mind," she said, almost managing to hide her disappointment. "Find a seat, we'll bring you dinner."

"Thanks so much," Olivia said, and walked to the quieter, far corner of the cafeteria.

Six long tables nearly filled the space. Each table had five chairs on either side, and two at the end. From how the chairs were three-quarters the usual size, they must have come from a school. By the one wall with narrow, high-up windows were a pair of sofas, one of which was occupied by a grey-faced woman, covered in blankets. Pete nudged Olivia's foot with his own, and nodded towards the woman.

"Sleeping?" he whispered.

"Sick," Olivia whispered back. "Just enough tables. Just enough chairs. No space for many more. I think I get why the captain led a desperate mission for supplies. This place must have been heaving before everyone left."

The kitchen was in a glass-windowed office from which the panes had been removed, allowing a mix of steam and smoke to float into the cafeteria.

"They're cooking on open fires," Pete muttered.

"Some propane, too, I think," Olivia said. "But yes, that looks like a barbecue. And with how poorly their clothes fit, there can't be enough water for laundry."

"Or time, or electricity," Pete said.

"Sixty-three kids," Olivia said. "And I think Aqsa said there were seven adults."

Pete's gaze settled on the table where four of the grown-ups sat, just within earshot of Corrie, but still separate from the crowd of questioning children. Two men, two women, all in their late twenties to mid-thirties. They were better dressed than the children, in that their clothes fit. They didn't look at Corrie, though they were clearly listening while pretending not to be. Their manner was so overly nonchalant, it came across as furtive. They appeared healthy enough, but they'd not helped with the fighting, the clean-up, or, it seemed, with the cooking.

"And viola," Princess said, announcing her return.

"*Voilà*," the lanky girl carrying the two trays said. "Hey, I'm Sally. Sally Rutherford."

"That's Pete, I'm Olivia."

"From South Bend, right?" Sally asked. "You got married on the ship?"

"We did," Olivia said. "You heard that part of the story?"

"It's a sweet story," Sally said.

"Where's your dog?" Princess asked.

"He's with Lisa, patrolling the walls," Olivia said. "I don't think he liked being stuck in the plane. And before then, he was stuck in a car for a couple of days. Who's the woman on the sofa?"

"Candice. She runs the kitchens," Sally said.

"And those four?" Pete asked.

"Oh, that's just Brendon, Connie, John, and Yollie," Princess said dismissively.

"We'll let you guys eat," Sally said. "C'mon, your majesty. Someone has to take out the trash."

"Thanks," Olivia said.

Pete kept the smile on his face as he looked down at his tray. "Plain rice, pink meat, and candy."

"I think those are vitamin pills," Olivia said. "And I think everyone gets the same food."

"Reminds me of middle school," Pete said.

"Maybe that's where it came from," Olivia said. "So, what do you think?"

"Paper bowls," Pete said. "Saves on water for washing dishes. Food's plain, but I guess the vitamins make sure we get what we need. Plus, decent portions."

Olivia leaned forward. "Yeah, but how long have they got before this place collapses?"

Pete shrugged. "Dunno, but it's *we* now, isn't it?"

"Sun's setting," Abraham called from the door. "Ten minutes until lockdown. Anyone who wants fresh air, now's the time to get it. Sally, give Candice a hand."

Sally waved a few of the other teenagers over, and they helped the sick woman towards the door. When a pair of the children headed outside, paper airplanes in hand, Abraham limped his way after them. The other four adults made their way through a door at the far side of the room, while the other children begin meandering towards the stairs.

"So where do we go?" Pete asked.

"I guess we should check with Abraham," Olivia said.

But outside the doors, they found Lisa, Rufus, and Aqsa watching the two children throw paper planes across the rain-damp yard.

"Where's Abraham?" Olivia asked.

"Walking the perimeter," Aqsa said. "He'll come in when it's dark."

"Have you seen their vegetable garden?" Lisa asked. "It's quite something. Far more impressive than the effort we saw on Long Island. There should be quite a harvest in a few months."

"If we stay here that long," Aqsa said.

"You've been thinking of leaving?" Olivia asked.

"We stayed because this is where the kids' parents would come back to," Aqsa said. "Well, no. We stayed because we didn't know of anywhere better to go, and there's no way to get there if we did. It *is* safe here. There should be dinner inside for us. Would you mind keeping an eye on the kids? Five minutes, and they have to come in. When they say no, just tell them you can hear Abraham is on the way back."

"That's the nail," Olivia said, as the paper planes scudded across the wet concrete.

"The nail in the coffin?" Pete asked.

"No, on the head," Olivia said. "That they don't know of anywhere else to go. Yes, you're right, it's *us* now. We've got to help them, and we definitely can. You made the right call, Pete."

"I did?"

"Coming here rather than Lake Moomaw, or Savannah." She smiled. "Yes. This feels like where we're supposed to be."

After they ushered the children inside, they followed them upstairs. They found Candice leaning against the wall, and against Sally, in a corridor at the top of the stairwell. Some of the older children were carrying mattresses from a windowless door clearly marked as a utility closet. Princess, hands on hips, appeared to be supervising, or perhaps just judging.

"We thought you should have the store room," Candice said, her voice weak. "It's more private."

"Me and Aqsa sleep with the young ones," Sally said.

"The who?" Princess asked.

"I mean to say we sleep with her majesty's court," Sally said.

"And shouldn't her majesty be in bed?" Candice said. "Go on, or you won't be in a fit state to fight dragons tomorrow."

"Okay, night Candy. Night, guys." Princess dashed off.

Candice smiled. "Her family…" But she didn't finish the sentence. "The children are split into squads, roughly concomitant with their grades. The younger grades share the big office with Sally and Aqsa. I have this room. The older children share these offices, four to a room. Abraham sleeps downstairs."

"And the other adults?" Olivia asked.

"In the garage," Candice said. "Everyone here sleeps at the same time. Same bedtime, same breakfast. Yollie and her people prefer to stay up later, of course."

"Were you a teacher?" Olivia asked.

"In Green Bay," Candice said. "Vice principal of JFK High. Go Otters!" She coughed.

"You should get to bed," Sally said.

"We all should," Olivia said.

The utility closet barely qualified to be called a room, and really didn't have space for the three mattresses left on the floor, each partially leaning against the shelves stacked with linen.

Rufus took one look, then took two steps back out into the corridor.

"You and me both, buddy," Corrie said. "There's a sofa downstairs."

"Two sofas," Lisa said. "Sleep well."

Pete hung a flashlight from one of the metal shelves. "We've slept in worse places. Yep, this will do just fine."

23rd April

Chapter 44 - When the Levee Broke
Sidnaw, Michigan

Perhaps because of Candice, and perhaps because of exhaustion, there was no late-night chatter from the children. But there were other noises, all through the night, that kept Pete's sleep from being overly deep: children coughing, sighing, snoring; owls hooting, dry pipes pinging, the external cladding creaking; something scurrying above their heads, and even what almost sounded like a distant engine. Pete slept, woke, slept, woke, struggling against wakefulness in a battle for slumber he'd almost won when a yell came from along the corridor.

"Up! Up! Everyone up!" Abraham called as he stumped along the corridor, knocking on doors.

"What's wrong?" Olivia asked, the first to their door.

"The main gates are open," Abraham said. "There are zombies inside the facility. Saw it from the roof. Adults, meet at the stairs. We'll secure downstairs, then clear outside."

Lisa and Corrie were already in the stairwell, looking only marginally less confused than Pete.

"Is this normal?" Lisa asked, as Candice, then Aqsa and Sally, came to join them.

Some office doors opened, but when a few of the older children stepped outside, Abraham roared, "Back inside! Close those doors. Wait for the all-clear!"

"Normal, no," Candice said, now leaning on the bannister to stay upright.

"Sally, get Candice a chair," Abraham said, limping his way back to them. "Candice, you'll stay up here. We're going downstairs to check the building's still secure."

"What's happened?" Lisa asked.

"Good question. Yollie was supposed to be on guard, but she's not on the roof. I shone the spotlight on the entrance. All three gates are open. We're going to check downstairs is secure, then we'll close the gate, and *then* we'll clear the compound."

Sally brought a chair out of the nearest bedroom-office, placing it by the stairs and where it had a view of the corridor.

Lisa held out her carbine to Candice. "Are you familiar with firearms?"

"I think I can remember," she said with a smile.

"Then may I suggest Sally and Rufus stay on the landing below?" Lisa said. "Us six will split into pairs. If we hear Rufus bark, we know to retreat." She drew the pistol from her holster and held it out to Abraham. "And if anyone hears a gunshot, they know where to head."

"Aqsa and me'll take the front," Abraham said. "You four take the perimeter. Check the windows aren't broken, then close any doors."

Light in one hand, axe in the other, Pete and Olivia moved along the unfamiliar corridors, checking the equally unfamiliar doors. Most led to storage cupboards now crammed with loot. Toys were as common as clothes, and books were more common than either.

"Clear," he said, when they got back to the main doors where Abraham waited alone.

"Got the same report from your sister," Abraham said. "I sent her and Lisa to the roof. In about ten minutes, it'll be light enough to snipe. Aqsa's gone to brief Sally. She'll be back in a minute. Then we'll go close the gate. You two will cover my flanks."

"How many zoms are out there?" Pete asked.

"We'll count them after," Abraham said.

Footsteps preceded Aqsa as she ran to a halt in the lobby. "Good to go."

"Then you stay here," Abraham said. "When you hear *Rhapsody in Blue* knocked on those doors, you know to let us in."

"How does that song go?" Aqsa asked.

"Doesn't matter," Abraham said. "Zombies don't have rhythm. You hear any tune, you know it's us. You two, with me."

Olivia raised her handgun, suppressor attached, tactical light already on. Pete raised his axe.

Outside, a low mist hugged the ground, punctuated by the dim beams from above, and their own lights from below. One in Pete's hand, one attached to Olivia's pistol, and two taped to Abraham's crutches, with two more strapped to his wrists.

"Zom!" Olivia said, firing almost immediately.

A heavy thump shook the ground. Reflexively, Pete began to turn, but his light caught movement as a ghoulish shadow reared out of the misty darkness. He raised the axe one-handed, while keeping his other hand, and the light, aimed at the zombie's head as he swung, involuntarily yelling even before the sharp blade smashed through chin and neck. Partially decapitated, the zombie fell. Pete stepped sideways, sending his light searching for movement, and saw Abraham and Olivia, still moving towards the gate.

Pete jogged to catch up. Olivia paused to fire. Abraham didn't wait, but limped onwards toward the gate and the two undead staggering through. Abraham raised a crutch, swinging it low, toppling the zombie. Letting the other crutch dangle from its strap, he grabbed a short spear from his belt, thrusting it down, before limping in a half circle, out of arm's reach of the other monster. It fell as a rifle crack sounded from the rooftop.

"Close it up!" Abraham yelled, limping on to grab the innermost gate, tugging and shoving it across the entrance.

Pete joined him. Outside, on the access road, at least six shadowy figures roamed out of the early morning mist.

Another gunshot had him spinning around, but he couldn't see the zombie. He could barely see the lights coming from the office.

"Back inside!" Abraham said. "Stay close this time. Move!"

Visibility wasn't improving, but the mist was brightening as the sun began to rise. When a shadow stepped in front of him, Pete saw the cap first, the long hair, the almost human face. Almost. But he'd hesitated too long. The zombie lunged as he swung. Its hand caught around his axe, knocking it loose. Pete roared, charging forward, ducking beneath its flailing arms. His instinctive punch to the kidneys met only squidgy resistance, but his kick at the zombie's knee toppled it to the ground. Leaving it there, he ran on, drawing his sidearm as he sprinted towards the lights.

Olivia and Abraham waited in the doorway. As Pete reached them, he turned around. Once again, he could see nothing. They bolted the door at top and bottom before Pete slumped against the wall.

"Aqsa, tell Candice it's time for breakfast," Abraham said. "Whatever this day's going to bring, we might as well face it fed. The kids eat in squads. You two, with me. We'll seal the corridors, secure the mess and the stairs. When it's proper light, we'll clean up outside."

As soon as Abraham had shown them which room contained the partitions from the building's previous incarnation as an office, he limped off.

"Two partitions per corridor, do you think?" Pete asked.

"Make it three," Olivia said. "Do you think these zoms heard our plane?"

"Must have," Pete said. "There were at least six outside the gates."

"How'd the gates end up open?" she said.

"I've got a hunch," Pete said. "We seem to be four people short."

When the children came downstairs, the oldest split into two eight-person teams. Each team collected a wheeled mop-bucket containing ten short metal spears from a store cupboard. When the children reached the barricaded doors, each child picked up a spear, most of which trembled as they prepared to defend their home.

"Spears on the ground. Save your energy for when you need it," Abraham said, limping past. "Grub's up for you, Olivia. Pete, with me."

"The kids don't usually do guard duty, do they?" Pete asked, as he followed Abraham back to the main doors.

"Only in drills," Abraham said, detaching a flashlight from his wrist and hanging it on an empty fire-extinguisher bracket. "That's Team Awesome-Force and the Squid-Squad. They're the oldest."

"The kids picked their own names?"

"From TV shows, I think," Abraham said. "I wanted something more military. Candice overruled me. Said they ain't soldiers, so we shouldn't think of them as such. They may not be soldiers, but they'll have to learn. Sally's the only one who fights, and only inside the fence."

"You're a soldier, though?" Pete asked.

"I was," he said. "But that was years ago. Iraq. Two tours."

"Is that where you lost your leg?" Pete asked.

"Nope, that was in St Paul. Hit by a car while I was on leave."

"Oh. Wow. Sorry."

"What for? You weren't driving," Abraham said.

Pete hefted a spear. He'd have preferred to use his gun, but they had a finite amount of ammunition, and it was quickly being depleted. "Aqsa is from St Paul, isn't she? Did you guys know each other before the—"

"Shh!" Abraham hissed. He leaned one crutch against the wall, and unclipped a long-handled hammer from his belt. From outside came a concrete-scraping slither. Fingernails scratched against the door's metal kick-plate. A heavy thud came from further away; hopefully a zombie sniped by Corrie. From behind came a stilted clatter as the younger children began traipsing into the cafeteria.

Outside, a palm slapped wetly against the metal kick-plate, but a face slammed into the door's small glass window. Though reinforced, it cracked. The zombie slammed its head against the glass again. Below, on the ground, the crawler's fists rapped against the door. The hinges shook. The glass window cracked, becoming completely opaque.

Abraham limped sideways a step. "If the glass breaks, you spear them," he said. "If they slither inside, you deal with any on the ground. You leave the uprights to me. Stay clear of my swing. Save your bullets. Got it?"

"Sure. No worries," Pete said.

"You say that now," Abraham said.

The glass window dented in the middle, then popped inside.

"That's you," Abraham said.

Pete lunged forward, but as he thrust the spear through the broken window, the point dropped, skimming the wooden frame. He tried to correct the blow, but the spear point shaved the side of the zombie's face before ripping through the remains of its ear.

"Gotta aim high," Abraham said, utterly calm.

Pete tried again. The spear slammed into the temple, but cracked the bone, sending the zombie falling to the ground outside.

"Don't wait for the judges to give you a score," Abraham said. "Get ready for the next."

The hinges creaked. The wood-frame cracked. The lock snapped. The door swung inward.

Abraham launched himself forward, swinging the hammer up and into the zombie's face, crushing its chin, and sending it flying backward. As he swung his arm, he moved his crutch closer to the wall, while flipping the hammer so the backswing brought it down on the zombie's skull.

"We're going to need more partitions," Abraham said, taking a hopping step backwards. "But we'll draw them here. Kill them here. Keep 'em where we can see 'em. Squids, more partitions! Double-time, but keep back!" he yelled, dropping to a one-legged crouch, his right hand gripped around the now-vertical crutch as he punched the hammer straight into the skull of a zombie crawling through the broken door. "You were supposed to get the crawlers," Abraham said as he straightened.

"I'm used to fighting out in the open," Pete said, as he stepped into the doorway. Outside, the mist was lifting. He couldn't yet see the fence, but he could see the undead. Four of them, emerging from the fog: a soldier who'd lost her boots, a hunter in too-green camo, a hiker in an ice-white ski coat, and a biker in a shredded leather jacket from which the patches had been ripped.

Three zombies, as a carbine cracked, and the biker fell. Pete took another step forward, lunging at the hiker. Again, he misjudged the spear's weight, and tore a line through the zombie's scalp.

"Go for the legs!" Abraham called out as Pete jumped sideways. "Knock 'em down, *then* spear them."

"I miss my axe," Pete said, swinging the spear sideways, flinging the zombie from its feet. A carbine cracked again and again. Pete stabbed the spear down into the hiker's eye and stepped back. For as far as he could see, or for as little, there was no more movement, but above, the carbines still fired.

"An axe is a dumb weapon to fight zombies," Abraham said.

"I dare you to tell that to Clyde," Pete said.

"Who's that?"

"The Australian soldier who made them," Pete said.

"If I ever meet him, I will," Abraham said. "Axes are for vampires, maybe werewolves."

"You're into horror stories?" Pete asked.

"Not anymore," he said.

"Where do you want these?" Sally asked, having organised the teenagers, and collected more partitions from the offices.

"Behind us," Abraham said. "Block off the corridor. How's the rest of the building?"

"One window was broken," Sally said, "but Olivia got the zom before it got in."

"Fine. Make sure the kids all eat," Abraham said. "It'll be a long day for everyone once the fog clears."

The minutes stretched. The mist rose. The gunfire continued. Bodies thumped to the ground with increasing frequency until that, too, finally ceased.

Abraham limped his way up to the roof, leaving Pete alone by the door until Olivia and Rufus came to join him.

"That was less than fun," she said.

"How bad did it get?" he asked.

"Two zoms nearly got in around the back of the building, near the loading bay. They got stuck in the window. Looks like a lot more here."

"Most of them were shot by Corrie and Lisa," Pete said.

"How many?" Olivia asked. "Because I'm starting to worry about how many bullets we've got left."

Chapter 45 - Runaway
Sidnaw, Michigan

Abraham returned, with Aqsa, Sally, and Lisa, though not Corrie.

"Your sister's on over-watch," Abraham said. "Looks like fifty dead inside the fence. At least a couple of crawlers they didn't shoot."

"We didn't want to waste the ammunition," Lisa said.

"That's not our immediate problem," Abraham said. "Zombies don't hide, but we've got to check every inch of the compound before the kids can help us work. Before we can dump the corpses by the road, we've got to clear the fence, and that means closing the outer gates. And before we do that, I've got to check on the garage and see what happened to Yollie's gang."

"They ran," Aqsa said. "Princess said she heard an engine."

"Do you mean the plane?" Abraham asked.

"She just said an engine," Aqsa said.

"Well, it won't be a truck, will it?" Abraham said. "Sorry, looks like y'all won't be leaving by air."

"We're not leaving without the children," Olivia said.

"Hmm. Well, no one's going anywhere until we've dealt with this mess." Abraham limped off towards the garage.

"I'll assist," Lisa said. "Rufus, would you be so kind?"

"I guess we're on fence duty," Pete said.

"Gates first," Olivia said.

"First, I want to get my axe," Pete said.

"You'll want a spear for fence duty," Aqsa said. "Never thought they'd have gotten inside."

"Did Yollie know how to fly?" Olivia asked as they picked their way around the bodies.

"Brendon said he had his own jet," Sally said.

"Which one's Brendon?" Pete asked, spotting his axe beneath a dungaree-clad zombie with brain-matted braids. Seeing the lumps of bone and black pus coating the axe-handle, Pete left the weapon where it was.

"Brendon's the one with trimmed stubble and bad teeth," Aqsa said.

"And such bad breath you'd think a yak had died in there," Sally added. "Any place in the world you can name, he said he'd been there."

"And that it wasn't as good as people claimed," Aqsa said.

The inner gate had held, though there were now five zombies pushing against it. Far more milled about on the road, and along the outer fence where they pushed and shoved against the chain link.

"How do we do this?" Olivia asked.

"Easy," Aqsa said, raising her own spear to eye-height, balancing it on the chain link. "Here. C'mon over here. There!" She lunged, straight into a zombie's eye. "See?"

A minute later, all five were dead.

"Quick now, close the outer gate before more come," Aqsa said, pulling the inner gate open.

Pete dashed through, slamming the outer gate closed before any of the approaching undead could make their way inside.

"See, told you it'd be easy," Aqsa said.

"Has this happened before?" Olivia asked.

"That they got inside? No," Aqsa said. "Sally, go get an extra chain for the gate."

"I'll come with," Olivia said. "No one should go anywhere alone until we know this place is safe again."

"Cool. And come back with the cart, too," Aqsa said. She unlatched the internal barrier sealing the path between the outermost fence and the second. "Might as well start here. *This* we have done before. Most days, in fact, though I haven't seen this many in weeks."

"It must have been our plane," Pete said. "Sorry about that."

"What's there to apologise for?" Aqsa said. "If you hadn't landed, you wouldn't be here."

"And those four wouldn't have stolen the plane," Pete said.

"Hey, I'd pick you folks any time," she said. "And not just because you've got a dog."

"Those four were that bad?"

"No, I wouldn't say they were *bad*. It's just they weren't interested in staying," she said. "It's been obvious since they arrived. That was a few days after Captain Stahl left. They kept to themselves. They'd go scavenging, but they weren't interested in helping with the kids."

"They don't like children?" Pete asked.

"If I were being charitable, I'd say they didn't want to get attached." She braced her spear on the fence. "Hey! Here!" She lunged. "Easy."

Pete aimed his own spear, stabbing forward, before stepping back and lining up his next blow. "So why didn't they leave before?"

"No gas," Aqsa said. "That's what Captain Stahl was looking for. Enough gas to move everyone from here to somewhere more secure."

"Did he have somewhere in mind?"

"Nope, that was part two of the plan, but fuel came first. The captain took most of our gas, and the good trucks, to find more. What little we had left, we used in the generator to pump water up from the reservoir. Brendon said there's no more gas in town. All we've got left is an electric van, except we've got no way to recharge it."

"Ah. So Brendon was in charge of searching the town?"

"Him and Yollie and the other two, yeah," Aqsa said. "Those four did the looting. Abraham and me deal with the zombies. Sally and Candice take care of the kids. Well, now it's mostly Sally."

Pete stabbed the spear forward again. It was a lot to take in. "You lived in St Paul before?" he asked. "That's where you came from?"

"Before here, sure."

"It's a long way," he said.

"Three hundred miles, I guess," she said. "But it's not like I planned to come here. Abe and I started driving north, aiming for the border, but there were too many zoms, too many roads blocked by abandoned cars. We were lucky to find this place. I'd say it was an accident, but Abe had the idea we could continue east, and cross over the border, and the lakes, at the Sault Ste Marie crossing."

"That's gone," Pete said.

"It is?"

"General Yoon destroyed it to protect the refugees."

"Then we were seriously lucky," she said.

Pete stabbed the spear forward. "You knew Abraham well, then?"

"Not really. He was a customer, that's all. But recognisable, memorable, you know? I don't mean the leg, and back then, he still had his prosthetic, but he's the kind of guy it's hard to forget."

"What kind of business did you run?"

"A bakery," she said. "It wasn't mine, though. I started behind the counter just before it was about to go bankrupt. I said if the customers wouldn't come to us, we should go to them, so we bought a little cart, and camped out in a parking lot downtown. We didn't have the right permits, but before we were moved on, we'd made twice what we usually earned in a day. We had ten carts just before the outbreak. I thought things were really turning around."

"Tell me about it," Pete said. "Ah, but I got to marry the woman I love, so I guess I can't complain." He lanced the spear forward, and almost dropped it when there was a shout from behind the inner fence.

"They're gone!" Olivia called out.

"Who, Yollie?" Aqsa asked.

"And the other three, yeah," Sally said. "We bumped into Abraham and Missy Lisa. They're checking the perimeter, making sure this is the only place the zoms got in."

"*Missy* Lisa?" Pete asked.

"Isn't that her name?" Sally said. "Wait, it was Princess who told me. She does that, giving new names to people. Truthfully, it's easier to go along with it."

"I can't wait to hear what name she comes up with for you, Pete," Olivia said.

Except for a brief breakfast-and-bathroom break, they worked until noon. Once they were certain the undead hadn't broken through the fence, Abraham let the two oldest eight-child squads out of the office block. One squad joined him, the other went with Lisa as they patrolled the compound's interior, hunting for any stray undead lurking among the copiers and office equipment which had been dumped outside.

By two, they'd moved the undead who'd died inside the compound to the open graveyard by the highway, and began moving those who'd died outside the fence. Corrie and Lisa took their half-hour break to confirm the plane had gone, but returned with the oddest of news.

"It's still there," Corrie said. "They didn't take the plane."

"Did they leave the fuel?" Pete asked.

"And the ammo," Corrie said. "It's only two more mags, but it was in a pouch at the very front of a bag with the spare food. They can't have looked inside the plane."

"In fact, I don't believe they went in that direction at all," Lisa said.

"The engine Princess heard must have been a car," Aqsa said. "I guess they found one, and were waiting until they felt it was okay to leave us."

"They were waiting until they knew *where* they should drive to," Abraham said. "Long Island, I bet. Or that place you mentioned down in Virginia. But they'll die out there, I'm certain of it, so that's something."

Pete looked across at the children scrubbing at the concrete with water and brooms. The damp patches were already drying in a surprisingly warm afternoon. Ordinarily, the promise of summer's approach would have cheered him, but dry weather would mean no rain. What would they drink then?

24th April

Chapter 46 - Taking Stock
Sidnaw, Michigan

"Why so glum, Pete?" Corrie asked as she put her tray down next to Pete's.

"He's daydreaming about cereal again," Olivia said.

"Not just during the day," Pete said, pushing the pink cubes around his plate. "Even Rufus doesn't think much of this stuff."

Beneath the table, Rufus glumly munched his way through a portion of diced ham twice the size of what the humans were eating. The humans had rice, too, and a mug of herbal tea from Candice's secret stash. Pete would have been happy if the stash had remained a secret, but Candice had insisted. She now sat on her sofa. A boy sat next to her, reading aloud, but Candice was clearly asleep.

"Kellogg carved his first cornflake in 1894," Pete said. "That's well before electricity was widespread. Somewhere, there's a museum with a display of cereal-presses."

"You should probably learn what the machines are called before we start the hunt," Corrie said. "Maybe even what they look like."

"Wouldn't you need corn, as well?" Olivia asked.

"That's step two of my plan," Pete said. "Step three is getting the kids to plant and harvest it. Step four is making the cornflakes."

"And step five is eating them," Corrie said.

"Sure, but not just me," Pete said. "Four kids are working in the kitchen this morning. If we had a few boxes of cereal, the kids could get their own."

"You still need milk," Olivia said. "I can't remember the last time I even saw a cow. Not a live one."

"Oat milk," Pete said. "It doesn't need to be refrigerated. And no, I have no idea how to make it, but we'll figure it out. And we'll figure out how to box up the cereal so we can sell it to the Australians when we next see them."

"You've really given this some thought," Corrie said.

"Is it any wonder?" he said, before reluctantly spearing another pink cube. "Ah, it's not just the food. I tried giving Rufus a wash out in the rain this morning. He's no cleaner, and neither of us is happier. We need cereal, and we need showers. They're two of the pillars of civilisation."

"There I can help," Corrie said.

"You can fix the showers?" Olivia asked.

"Theoretically, yes, but don't get your hopes too high," Corrie said. "I took a look at the solar panels and the electric van. I can definitely rig the solar panels to charge up the van's battery. It shouldn't take more than a few hours."

"To fully charge the van?" Olivia asked.

"No, to build the charging station," Corrie said. "To charge the van, theoretically, should take six hours on a clear day, assuming I can dismantle a transformer from the data centre."

"There's a data centre here?" Pete asked.

"A small one," Corrie said. "There's a mini server farm in the building right at the back of the compound. It's too small to be for general use, so it must be a back-up for something really important. If we ever get a bit of surplus power, it'd be fun to have a nose-around."

"Get the van working first," Olivia said. "That was really handy back when we were escaping Michigan."

"The battery would be even more useful than wheels," Corrie said. "We can use it to run the pump, and drag some water up here from the reservoir."

"How far away is that?" Olivia asked.

"A couple of miles," Corrie said. "According to the schematics, they dammed a chunk out of a lake to use as a water treatment plant for the town, and expanded it a bit when they built this place."

"So if we fix the solar panels, we'll get water?" Olivia asked.

"And as much water as we want," Corrie said. "There's about ten thousand litres in that natural gas tank they converted to store rainwater. Realistically, it'll be gone in a month. Sooner if the weather warms up a bit."

"The food will last about as long," Olivia said. "The ham and rice all came from a semi-rig delivering bulk stocks to prisons."

"Talk about cruel and unusual," Pete said. "So in one month we'll either starve or stink ourselves to death?"

"I don't know about food," Corrie said, "but once we've got a bit of power, we can pump up enough water for everyone to have a cold shower every other day."

"Can we heat the water?" Olivia asked.

"Probably not," Corrie said. "I'm assuming we'll want some electricity for charging lights, running a stove, and maybe showing a movie at night."

"What are we cooking on at the moment?" Pete asked.

"Propane and charcoal," Olivia said. "The coal will be gone in three days. The propane might last a week longer."

"So we need more power," Pete said. "Would normal car batteries do?"

"Sure, in a pinch," Corrie said. "But we'll need more solar panels, too. Maybe a wind turbine."

"Those are huge," Pete said. "No way we could move one."

"Think smaller," Corrie said. "Like a weather station at a school."

"Is there a school in town?" Olivia asked. "We should ask Aqsa." She turned around. "I can't see her. Or Abraham. *Or* Lisa."

"They were walking the perimeter," Pete said.

"Ah, cool. So we need some solar panels or wind turbines," Olivia said. "Can we use the kerosene from the plane?"

"Sure, but when it's gone, it really is gone," Corrie said. "Are we sure we want it for this?"

"Maybe not. Either way, we'll run out of food in a month," Pete said. "What about the crops they've planted?"

"They'll need another two months," Olivia said. "If we're really lucky, we might each get a lettuce, bean, and strawberry salad twice a week for four or five weeks. That's *one* bean and *one* strawberry."

"So we'll have to hunt," Pete said.

"Not with the carbines," Corrie said.

"Has anyone seen a bow?" Pete asked.

"Nope," Corrie said. "Since the birds around here will be eating corpses, or eating the insects which eat the corpses, I'd say we want to avoid hunting. Fishing might be an option, up at the lake."

"Could we drive the kids up there in the van, and have them fish while we stand guard?" Pete asked.

"Sure, maybe," Corrie said. "But you'd use up a day's worth of electricity. We can only charge the battery during daylight, but we can pump water, or recharge devices, at night."

Lisa leaned on the table, sighing as she sat down.

"How is Missy Lisa this morning?" Olivia asked.

"How did that name begin?" Lisa replied.

"You can blame Princess, but I think it's stuck," Pete said. "How's the perimeter?"

"Only one zom during the night," Lisa said. "What did you make of that van?"

"I was just saying I think I can power up the battery," Corrie said.

"Good. The moment you can, I'll use it to turn the plane."

"Why?" Olivia asked. "You can't be planning to fly out of here?"

"We're not leaving the kids," Pete said.

"Of course not," Lisa said. "However, a plane is a useful asset, but only if we can get it into the air. Once airborne, we could fly a maximum of eight hundred kilometres, conditional upon the weather. If our goal is still to drive north to Canada, we will have to first travel west, to the western edge of Lake Superior. We will have to go through, or around, the city of Duluth, and over the St Louis River. Knowing where the bridges still stand will reduce the amount of backtracking we have to do, thus reducing both the amount of fuel and time the journey will take."

"You think we should leave?" Pete asked.

"Of course," Lisa said. "Not immediately. Not today. But it is inevitable. This Captain Stahl was aware of the compound's weaknesses, which is why he took such a desperate gamble in taking nearly every able body away in search of fuel. We have a strong fence, so departure does not have to be rushed. However, we cannot delay preparations. I intend to fly over Duluth, then follow Lake Superior across the border to Thunder Bay before returning. After radioing down my findings, I'll parachute out, overhead, and you can drive out to collect me."

"Seriously?" Pete said.

"I have never jumped from a plane, Mr Guinn," Lisa said. "I wouldn't call it a regret, but life, even after the end of the world, should be filled with new experiences. Besides, our last landing was blessed with good fortune, but only because the nearby undead were clustered outside this facility. Jumping would be the safer of the two options."

"Why fly over Thunder Bay?" Corrie asked.

"Because General Yoon was creating a supply base there," Lisa said. "It might provide us with a temporary refuge, or an alternative to Lake Winnipeg, or a place to loot in the months ahead. If it was atomised, better we know now. I'm sure there are many other places worthy of an aerial survey, but with such limited fuel, and with the bridges across the St Louis being the priority, there will be time for Thunder Bay, but no further. I would aim to fly the reconnaissance mission within the week, but we must first plan how we'll transport the children north."

"Did you discuss this with Abraham?" Olivia asked.

"I did," Lisa said. "And with Aqsa. They're agreed with the general idea, but want further discussion of the specifics."

"Right. And I guess there aren't any buses hidden here?" Pete asked.

"It isn't that type of facility," Lisa said. "This is a place for the disposal of documents. The long building contains industrial shredders. They could strip a tree to chips in seconds. Imagine what they could do to the undead. However, we would require Rube Goldberg to design a mechanism to get the zombies to walk into the mouths of those machines."

"And a lot of electricity to run them," Corrie said. "What kind of documents?"

"You didn't notice when you went to the bathroom?" Olivia asked.

"Tax records," Lisa said. "Rather mundane ones. But this does provide us with a surfeit of paper. Sadly, there's nothing so useful as an armoury. This place, I'm afraid, was nothing more than a pork farm."

"I'm pretty sure there were never any animals here," Pete said.

"The other kind of pork," Lisa said. "The White House needed a vote, so gave a congressional representative a federal facility, with its federal salaries. Afterwards, they looked for ways to make it break even, or at least not make such a loss."

Rufus gave a forlorn yip.

"I think he needs to walk off his breakfast," Pete said.

"Me, too," Olivia said. "How about we take a look at the town, see if there are some buses, or some solar panels. Or, even, some cereal."

"One of us should stay here so as not to cause concern to the children," Lisa said.

"That's me, then," Corrie said, pushing her tray aside. "Hey, kids, who here wants to play around with electricity?"

Well over thirty children copied her by standing up.

"Good luck with that," Pete said.

Chapter 47 - The Trash House
Sidnaw, Michigan

"This reminds me of how people attempted to deal with the plague," Lisa said as she sprayed a vanilla-scented body-spray onto a bandana.

"Surely you're not *that* old," Aqsa said.

Olivia laughed, while Pete ran his finger along the collection of body-sprays and perfumes. Forest fresh sounded more like a toilet cleaner than a deodorant, so he picked frosted ocean, mostly out of curiosity. Spritzing a bandana, he tied it to his face.

"We must get you another of these," Olivia said as she checked Rufus's increasingly tattered police coat.

The dog yipped his agreement.

"You don't use a lead and collar?" Aqsa asked.

"More often than not, he is the one leading us," Lisa said.

With Rufus setting the pace, they hurried past the stinking roadside graveyard. Beyond, Pete was glad to pull down the bandana. After five minutes with frosted ocean in his nostrils, he knew why some scents didn't exist in nature.

Rufus sprinted from one infrequent wreck to another as they followed the main road into the town. There were fewer cars abandoned on the road than on the stretch near where they'd landed the plane, but more vehicles had been parked, or pushed, into the driveways outside the increasingly frequent homes.

"Can't see any tyre tracks," Olivia said. "If those four drove this way, there'd be tyre marks in the mud."

"Maybe we were wrong about them," Pete said.

"I was wrong when we first met them," Lisa said. "I can claim exhaustion, but I'm usually far better at judging people's intent."

"Hey, I was wrong, too," Aqsa said. "It happens."

"Not to me," Lisa said. "The fuel caps here are all open," she added as Rufus returned from another fruitless foray.

"And that front door's ajar," Pete said. "I'm guessing that was opened by Yollie and her people."

"How long since you last came down here, Aqsa?" Olivia asked.

"Weeks," Aqsa said. "There's just been so much to do inside."

Rufus had darted ahead again, before dashing to the right. He gave them a found-something glance, before turning his attention to a cluster of close-to-road ranch-style homes with barely a property marker between them.

"Nope, we weren't wrong," Olivia whispered, pausing at the curving trail torn through the lawn and onto the road. "That was done by tyres, and they're recent."

"Very recent," Lisa said. "One car, I believe. Heavily loaded."

Pete raised his axe. Aqsa levelled her spear. Lisa whistled. "They aren't here," she said. "And nor are the undead. But one car with four passengers leaves little space for supplies. Shall we see whether they left any behind?"

As Rufus prowled the long grass, Pete walked to the nearest home. He knocked the blade against the door, listened, looked again at Rufus, and then tried the handle. It wasn't locked.

It was a small house, filled with trash. The living room was crammed with furniture. One small sofa matched an equally trim armchair, but two other chairs had been brought in and positioned on either side of a low coffee table. On the table, and beneath, were scores of crushed beer cans, and nearly as many empty glasses.

"Smells like an ashtray," Olivia said. "Are you coming in, Rufus?"

The dog took one sniff and backed off, settling into an alert crouch on the porch, watching the main road.

"Beer cans and snack wrappers," Lisa said. "I believe we have half an answer to a question we'd not thought to ask. I'll check the other cabins. Rufus, with me."

"How often does Abraham leave the compound?" Olivia asked, as she picked her way across the stained rug.

"No more often than me," Aqsa said. "He and I deal with the undead, and that can sometimes take all day."

"And Candice?" Olivia asked.

"She's sometimes too weak to make it downstairs," Aqsa said, using her spear to push through the litter. "There's a mirror here."

"Pill bottles in the bin here," Pete said. "They look to be all they bothered throwing away."

"What kind of pills?" Aqsa asked.

"Oxy," Pete said, picking up a jar. "And it's empty. I think all the bottles are."

"You do *not* want to look in the bathroom," Olivia said. "The bedrooms aren't much better. I think we should leave before we catch something."

"Why not just sweep the trash outside?" Pete said.

"In case me or Abraham went for a walk," Aqsa said. "When we sent them out for supplies, they came here instead to get drunk and high."

"Looks it," Olivia said. "But they'd still need to find their beer and pills. They did actually search the houses. Did they ever bring things back to the compound?"

"Sure," Aqsa said. "Clothes. Sometimes toys. Occasionally food. They always said there were zombies. Always said there'd been a fight."

"I can't see any dead zoms," Pete said, stepping back outside.

Lisa stepped out of a cabin opposite. "They wrecked one house, and moved onto the next," she said. "More pertinently, the small cabin is their stash house."

"That sounds promising," Aqsa said.

"It's not," Lisa said.

It wasn't.

"There's food!" Aqsa said, deeply affronted as she picked a label-less can from the neat stack on the countertop. "There's more in the cupboards. This is… It's disgusting."

"It's a lot for four, but not for seventy," Lisa said. "Most of the remaining food requires cooking. A fire would produce smoke which might be seen or smelled from your compound. There are children's clothes, in bags, in the bedroom. Other bags contain soap and similar."

Pete picked up an empty cardboard box from the floor. "Shotgun shells."

"They found ammo?" Aqsa said. She shook her head and walked back outside.

Pete and Olivia followed.

"I don't get it," Aqsa said. "I get that they might drink and get high, but why not bring the canned food back?"

"Us and them," Lisa said. "It is a story as old as civilisation. I suspect this one began with the discovery of fuel, or the lack thereof. There are ten empty gasoline containers, only four of which have been used recently. Your captain, who went in search of more, must have stripped the town first. While little gasoline remained, there was enough for one car, and a car only has room for four. But which four? How do you pick among the children? How did they each ensure the car didn't leave without them? It had to be those four who would leave, and only those four, and so they kept a car ready with whatever ammo they found, and with food. When the day to flee never came, they began eating the food."

"But why not bring it back?" Aqsa asked.

"After the first few days, the first week, it would have seemed suspicious," Lisa said. "Abraham believes in order, in rules. It is essential to keep so many teenagers in line. Them, and us. If Abraham, or you, were to search the town, you would learn there were supplies to be found. The fuel would have gone into the generator, they would have been trapped, and so they couldn't allow themselves to become attached. I imagine they would have left whether we arrived or not, but our arrival gave them the excuse to flee. Four of us replacing four of them. I imagine, aloud, they said they were doing the right thing, ensuring that there were fewer mouths to feed. Yet, truly, they knew that with our arrival, their lie would be discovered. They had no choice but to go. I imagine they have gone due east, to Sault Ste Marie. Did you tell them that the crossing was destroyed?"

"Me? No," Pete said.

"Nor me," Olivia said.

"Since there are no tracks leading west past the compound, they went east," Lisa said. "Where else could they go? That tall young man who styles himself Little John said he came from the southeast, from Green Bay, barely escaping the refugees, and zombies, who fled Chicago. Aqsa, you came from St Paul, and that's to the southwest. I know we said we came from the south, and we said there were survivors on Long Island, but we were hoping to go north. For those reasons, crossing the border to Canada makes sense. With their limited information, going east is sensible, and so that is what they have done, and why they will die within the week."

"You got all that from a few bags?" Aqsa asked. "You should have been a detective."

"People are simple," Lisa said. "No matter our wealth, language, or religion, we share the same base desires and simple goals, and this is the simplest explanation. I could be wrong. They could have driven to Fort Knox because they believe the government stored a time machine there with which they can undo this catastrophe."

"Okay, yep, driving to Canada is more likely," Aqsa said.

"Indeed," Lisa said. "I would suggest our mission has crystallised. Our two priorities are to confirm there truly is no more fuel to be found in this town, but also to learn what other supplies remain in people's homes. Uncooked canned food in particular. While doing that, we should make a note of the largest vehicles which are still roadworthy. I would suggest we divide forces. Two should begin taking back what is here, two more should check the town. A gunshot will be the signal for danger."

"Pete and I'll start on the town," Olivia said. "Keep an eye on them, Rufus."

"Time for a mental reset," Pete said, stretching as they walked back to the road. "There are no zoms in town, no gas, some loot."

"Some zoms do turn up at the compound every day," Olivia said.

"True, but I was thinking maybe things aren't as bleak as they first seemed," Pete said.

"Lisa's still right, we've got to leave," Olivia said. "Ah, no. Ahead."

Beyond a set of railway tracks, which cut diagonally across the road, shambled a ragged figure in a lime green overcoat whose sleeves overhung its hands.

"I'll get it," Pete said. But the zombie didn't hurry, so nor did he.

"There's no rust on the train tracks," Olivia said.

"Is there a station in this town?" Pete asked, while keeping his eyes on the shambling creature.

"I don't think so," Olivia said. "Abraham said there's a bar, a post office, a few agri-businesses, and the airfield, all of which were stripped before the captain went south. But trains run on diesel. It's getting close."

Pete raised the axe level with his waist, ducking as he swung low and wide. The zombie's flailing arms created an air current which brushed Pete's face, but the axe sank deep, slicing through the necrotic tissue just below the creature's knee. It fell, thrashing, even while Pete straightened, bringing the axe down in a two-handed sweep.

"Okay, yeah, I'm starting to agree with Aqsa about spears," Pete said. "Axes are great for ships, but out here, I'd want… what's that weapon that's as long as a spear but with an axe head?"

"Do you mean a pike?"

"One of them," Pete said. "I can't see any more zoms. Can't see a locomotive, either."

"No, but we made good time following the train tracks up in Canada," Olivia said.

"I wouldn't want to drive along them in a bus," Pete said.

"Two buses," Olivia said. "I'd prefer three, in case one breaks, but that's if we can find enough fuel. Diesel, I guess. Which, now I say it aloud, is exactly what that captain was looking for."

They kept walking, scanning the buildings, the cars, occasionally crouching to see beneath.

"If we found a loco with fuel in the tank, we could drive the kids away by train," Pete said.

"Do the trains here link up with Canada?" Olivia asked.

"Eventually. Somewhere. Probably," Pete said.

"We'll need to find a railway map," she said. "And if there wasn't a station in this town, what are the odds we'd find that map here? The sign says that's St Claire Street. Oh. Look at those houses, they've all got external tanks. Oil, maybe? No, it's propane," she added as she walked near enough to read the battered warning sign. "Nearly empty, but not completely."

"Do you think we could transfer that back to the compound?" Pete said.

"Not safely. Not easily. Not without a truck," Olivia said. "Maybe we could bring the kids down here and heat up some water for a wash, or cook some food. Is it worth the effort if our goal's getting out of here? No, we need a bus. Yep, that house there, with the grey garage doors."

"No way could you fit a bus in there," Pete said.

"No, but we won't find one in this town," she said. "Maybe Lisa can spot one from the plane, but we'll still have to drive the fuel to the bus once we find it. I'm wondering if those guys were so lazy they only checked the cars that were parked outside."

The garage doors were still locked. So was the wider than usual front door, which was placed at the top of a shallow ramp, separated from the sidewalk by a neat row of rose bushes.

With one swing from the axe, Pete splintered the wooden front door, revealing a wide hallway with coats hanging on low hooks, no tables, and one wheelchair with very thick tyres.

"That explains the ramp," Olivia said. "Pete, it's an electric wheelchair!"

"I don't think Abraham would want it," Pete said.

"No, I was thinking of the battery," she said. "And maybe we can use the motor, too. We'll ask Corrie."

"Smells like zom," Pete said, as he stepped inside. "And rat, edged with a hint of damp. Those four drunks didn't make it this far, though, so maybe we'll strike gold."

Olivia drew her sidearm, then slapped a palm against the wall. "No, can't hear anything."

The internal doors were half a metre wider than standard, and slid rather than swung, with the closest opening into a living room whose windows faced the main road. The guest sofa and matching small chair were almost unused compared to the cracked leather recliner immediately in front of the TV. The left arm was folded down, while on the right arm were more buttons than on the TV remote.

"He had good taste," Pete said, flopping into the chair. "Oh, this is perfect. Talk about a dream chair."

"She," Olivia said. "I'm stereotyping, but there are a lot of western romances on these shelves. No photos."

"There's one here of a sunset over a lake," Pete said, pointing to the wall between the TV and the window.

"I mean no photos with people in them," Olivia said. "You search the kitchen, I'll take the bedroom."

"Just one more second," Pete said, before reluctantly pushing himself back to his feet.

The kitchen cupboards were built off the ground, with a foot-high gap between floor and base, under which the mop-drone and robotic vacuum cleaner could both easily traverse. There was one of each, parked in a charger next to the fridge.

"This is *so* my dream house," he whispered.

None of the cupboards were above his chest height. Above them, on the wall, were more photographs: a lake, a forest, three different mountains. Inside the cupboards, he found genuine treasure and real disappointment. Enough of the shredded packaging remained that he could recognise his favourite brand of sugar-cinnamon cornflakes, but the mice had beaten him to the contents. The same was true of the pasta, rice, and even the cheat-bake spice packs. But the tins were intact, even if their labels had been chewed. It was the same with the glass jars which, from their colour, must contain some variety of tomato sauce.

"Pete, come see!" Olivia called.

He placed the jar on the counter and followed his wife's voice into the bedroom.

It had been sky blue, with a custom-built bed, lower to the ground than normal. Next to the bed was another chair. This was entirely mechanical, though with narrow wheels, and a narrow frame: a getting-about-the-house chair.

"She's on the floor," Olivia said, holding up a revolver. "I think she sat on the edge of the bed, so she could look out the window as she died, but she fell forward, not back, and ended up on the floor. She left a letter."

"You mean a suicide note?"

"Not really. It's for her sister, Gilda. She was Glenda. Gilda was the photographer. The letter's a thank-you that she didn't think would ever be read." Olivia placed the letter on the bed, next to the revolver. "I'd like to bury her, if that's okay?"

"Sure, but why?"

"In case Gilda ever comes here," Olivia said. "It's... I was thinking about Nicole. How I had to leave her in our apartment. You can see the sisters loved each other so maybe, one day, Gilda will come here. We can't bury everyone, but that doesn't mean we should ignore all the bodies."

"Yeah, I get it," Pete said. "We could check a few more houses, then one of us could dig while the other packs. I found some food in the kitchen. Mice got the packets, but there are plenty of jars and cans. And there's a battery vacuum cleaner. Want to bet whether there's an electric car in the garage?"

There wasn't. While there was space for a car, it was missing, but the low shelves against the north wall contained enough bleach to scrub the entire compound.

They found a pull-along trolley in the garage of the next house they checked, and they found a shovel in the third. They didn't find any more food. It looked to have been taken long ago, probably soon after the outbreak. They wheeled the cart back to Glenda's house, where Olivia began digging while Pete packed the kitchen. The food didn't amount to nearly as much as he'd thought, only filling one and a half suitcases. He filled the rest of the space with an armful of paperbacks before loading the bleach from the garage.

He swapped with Olivia while she took a turn emptying the kitchen in the next house along. It didn't take long to dig the grave, nor to fill the cart, but they hadn't quite finished before Lisa and Aqsa, with Corrie and Sally, hiked along the highway towards them.

"You guys okay?" Corrie asked.

"Sure," Pete said, leaning on his shovel. "We're burying the owner of this house. It's representative of all the people we can't lay to rest."

"I'll take a turn," Aqsa said.

Pete climbed out of the hole so she could jump down.

"How well stocked is the town?" Lisa asked.

"Hit and miss," Pete said. "The mice did a more thorough job than Yollie. I guess we've found enough food for one meal for everyone. If the rest of the town's like this, maybe we'll find ten meals, maybe twelve. No fuel, yet. There's a robot mop in there, and a wheelchair and vacuum cleaner. Can we use the batteries?"

"Maybe to run a few lights," Corrie said. "But we have a shortage of power, not storage."

"Let us see whether that can be found," Lisa said.

"It's not much food," Abraham said. "But it *is* variety. That'll be appreciated."

He and Pete stood in the doorway to the stockroom pantry where Candice, sitting on a folding chair, supervised four teenagers who were unpacking the haul. One cleaned the cans with a bleach-coated rag. One dried. One added a new label, which was often a guess, while the last put the cans onto the shelves.

"Never scoff *at* a free meal, Abe," Candice said. "John, put the jars of tomato sauce aside, we'll have those tonight."

"Can we have pasta?" the tower-block-tall young man asked.

"Oh, I do so wish," Candice said. "I went to Naples once, to visit the ruins of Pompeii. I'd never tasted *paccheri* like it. I spent years trying to recreate the texture, but I think there was something in the water."

"Like ash?" John asked.

"We'll leave you to it," Abraham said, and limped back along the corridor, gesturing Pete should follow. "How many houses did you search?" he asked, when they were out of earshot.

"About half," Pete said. "I guess we'd need another day to search the rest, and a third day to go through the businesses and any nearby farms."

"Half, you say?" Abraham said. "And how many of those had already been searched?"

"By Yollie? Only the ones near their stash-house," Pete said. "But the locals didn't leave much behind. It was mostly a jar or two here and there. I'd say we've got enough for three meals each, so maybe we'll find that much again. Plus we found clothes, and those alkaline batteries. That'll keep some reading lights on at night for at least a month."

"Right, but no gasoline," Abraham said, but grudgingly added, "Still, it's a good day's work. I best patrol the perimeter before dinner."

"I'll give you a hand," Pete said.

"No, you've earned your rest," Abraham said, and limped off.

News that there was going to be something different for dinner had brought most people down to the cafeteria early. One of the older squads were sorting the recently found clothes, dividing them into individual piles to be collected after dinner. Even the western romances he'd thrown into the bag had found a few takers. From the copy of *Lost Among the Sage* lying on the floor, there'd already been a few giver-uppers, too. He picked up the book, skimming a few pages as he took what was becoming his usual seat.

25th April

Chapter 48 - Mind Your Head
Sidnaw, Michigan

Pete lanced the spear into the zombie's eye. Red-brown pus arced from the wound. Reflexively, he stepped back, and lost his grip on the spear. It fell, with the corpse, on the far side of the fence.

"Again?" he muttered, and began the long trudge back to the main gate, which was the sole entrance to the between-the-fence walkway and where they'd stashed the spare spears.

Abraham, who'd been performing the same unwelcome chore on the other half of the fence, was there when he arrived. "You done?" he asked.

"There's a couple more left, but I lost my spear," Pete said.

"Told you to take a spare," Abraham said.

"That *was* the spare," Pete said. "I just need more practice."

"You'll get that, sure enough," he said. "I'll finish up. Y'all make sure you've got everything you need today. Everything," he added.

"It'll be fine," Pete said.

"Says the man who just lost his weapon," Abraham said.

"I'll triple-check my gear," Pete said, and made his way back to the cafeteria, and almost bumped into Lisa and Aqsa as they opened the door. They had weapons in hand, empty bags on their backs.

"Where's Corrie?" Pete asked.

"Sitting with Candice," Lisa said.

"She took a turn for the worse last night," Aqsa said. "We're going on a hunt for pills."

"But it is not so grim as that makes it sound," Lisa said. "I believe we know what's wrong with her. The symptoms do seem very similar to those experienced by the chief engineer on Tamika's ship. Tiredness, leaden limbs, and a numbness in the extremities except where there's a tingling. With him, it was a blood flow problem ultimately corrected by an operation on the valves in his heart. But first they tried a pill regimen. It almost proved sufficient in itself. While I don't recall which specific pharmaceuticals he was prescribed, I'm sure we can find something in town to match the symptoms."

"Do you want me to come with?" Pete asked.

"I doubt Abraham would be happy with any change to today's plans," Lisa said. "We must remain focused on our longer-term goal, Mr Guinn. Fuel is critical, more so now than ever."

There was an edge to Lisa's tone, a nervousness not usually there, an inevitability in the outcome of this last desperate bid to save a dying woman. He watched the two women walk towards the gate, already wondering who might get sick next.

Rufus bounded outside, running a short sprint the length of the cafeteria-office building before stopping expectantly by Pete.

"Just waiting on the wife, bud," Pete said.

Olivia came out with Sally at her side, and Little John causing an eclipse behind. John, the second oldest, and by far the tallest, of the children, had finally been given Abraham's dispensation to join an expedition.

"A few more of you, Rufus, and we'd have a team to pull this cart," Pete said as they dragged it towards the gate. Most of their supplies were aboard: empty fuel cans, hoses, a few chains, and four spare spears each.

"What do you think, Rufus, would you like to be a sled dog?" Olivia asked.

Rufus's silence matched that of the two teenagers.

Abraham gave them a nod as they wheeled the cart through the gate. He said nothing, either, but his anxiety was obvious.

"You're from Green Bay, aren't you, John?" Pete asked.

"Sure. Mostly."

"So is Candice, isn't she?"

"Think so," John said. "I didn't know her. Not before I got here."

"And you're a fan of Robin Hood?" Olivia asked.

"Who?"

"How come the nickname?" she asked.

"Oh. My dad was Big John," he said. "There were four Johns when he played."

"Football?" Pete guessed, finding dragging the cart far easier than dragging conversation from the young man.

"Yeah. Until his knee gave. He did some commentary, and we had a bookstore."

"Sports books?" Pete asked.

"Sure. Some," John said, finally opening up a little. "Signed stuff, you know? Sold some memorabilia, too."

"How did you end up here?" Olivia asked.

"We were trying to reach my aunt's farm," John said. "But it'd been overrun. Same thing happened with Chicago, then Green Bay. We sort of fell in with a load of other people on the road and ended up here."

"Sounds like what happened to everyone," Pete said. "We all end up in weird places."

Beyond the reeking roadside graveyard, Pete pulled down the bandana. Rufus took that as a sign to scout ahead. They crossed the junction with Lake Street, then walked over the railway line, and past the brackish and fly-filled Trout Creek. Past Milltown Road, past St Claire Street, and almost straight past Aqsa who ran out of a house, utterly confusing poor Rufus.

"Hey! Found it," she said.

"The pills?" Pete asked.

"We think so," Aqsa said.

"They should assist," Lisa said, following her out. "How many zombies were at the gate today?"

"Six," Pete said.

"We've seen none so far this morning," Lisa said. "But we found a canned feast lurking in a locker in that house's garage. I suspect the owner had just discovered the joys of couponing."

"We'll fill up on our way back," Pete said, dragging the cart onward.

"Yollie and Brendon did the bare minimum, didn't they?" Sally said.

"They didn't even do that," John said. "They quit even before they left."

"They were just plain dumb," Olivia said. "Now they'll be dead. The only way we'll survive is if we help each other. Me and Pete, we're the proof of that, right, hon?"

"One hundred percent," Pete said. "We all chip in, we all do our bit, and we'll all be just fine."

"In Canada, that's where we're going, isn't it?" John asked.

"Yep, Lake Winnipeg," Pete said. To the north, birds circled and swooped. He counted eight with blue-tipped wings and a blue crown, but otherwise they were mostly white, at least underneath. Large birds, too, with a half-metre wingspan. But beyond that they weren't crows, and weren't usually seen in downtown South Bend, he'd no idea what they were. "Got to find me a bird book," he said.

"And in Canada, we'll meet your people from the Pacific?" John asked.

"I hope so," Pete said.

"But not soon," Olivia said, quicker to grasp the inference. "The commissioner's ship has to sail down the length of South America, then up to New Zealand. They should be able to fly from there to Canberra, where the new U.N. government is based. They'll have to discuss what Commissioner Qwong, Captain Adams, and Colonel Hawker found before putting together a search mission. I think that mission will be approved, but it could be months before they reach the coast. It could be fall before they land on the lake."

"Fall? Oh," John said. "So not until Thanksgiving?"

"Cheer up, Thanksgiving comes earlier in Canada," Sally said.

"Let's not worry about it too much until after we get to Pine Dock," Olivia said.

"We can leave the cart here," Pete said when they reached the post office at the junction with Erie Street. "We'll check out the airport, confirm there's nothing there, then come back and continue east for two miles, then work our way back, picking things up as we go."

Rufus let out a growl, dropping into a ready-to-spring crouch. Pete grabbed a spear from the back of the cart, watching the long grass move as the unseen zombie crawled towards them.

"Just one, I think," he said.

"John, watch the south," Olivia said. "Sally, the north."

Pete stepped out into the road, to meet the creature. Small. Young. And again, he wondered what had happened to the younger children from nearby. There'd been a few mentions of an earlier convoy which had fled the town, but like the mission on which their parents had disappeared, discussion of it was taboo.

He took another step forward, and stabbed the spear down, trying to finish the crawling child while it was still partially concealed by the long grass, but it rolled out of the way and onto the muddy asphalt, reaching for him. He braced his boot on its thin chest, and plunged the spear down, into those forever-young eyes.

"Let's move on," he said. "Quick now."

"It's a kid," John said.

"Some are," Sally said.

At the end of the road, they came to the runway. It wasn't an airport. Even air*field* would be a generous description for the grass landing strip into which a C-17 had crashed. There were no hangars, no tower, just a few battered sheds, a lot of debris, and nearly as many sun-bleached bones.

"The captain came to collect the guns," Sally said. "They couldn't find any."

"It must have been a civilian rescue flight," Olivia said.

"So why are we here?" John asked.

"For the tractor that turned the planes around, and pulled the roller to keep the field flat," Pete said. "There has to be one, but no one would use it for an escape vehicle. Plus, maybe the wreckage, and bodies, stopped people from searching too hard for fuel. There's a shed in the north, another over in the west. Let's split into two, check quick, and be gone in half an hour."

"You can have the north," Olivia said. "Sally, me, and Rufus will take the west, and I bet you the first box of cereal we find that we finish first."

Despite the high stakes, Pete took his time as he picked a path through the battlefield of twisted seats, spars, skulls and other debris from gravity's victory over the plane. Built at the edge of what had been the grass runway, the shed was the size of a double garage, though with only a single door, constructed on a cement base with a wood frame and sloping wooden roof. The walls were now singed from the post-crash fire, while the roof sagged inwards under the weight of the starboard wing tip.

Pete launched his boot at the jammed door, shoving it ajar, but raising a loud creak from the roof, and a soft groan from the precariously balanced section of wing.

"Perhaps that wasn't the best idea," Pete said. "You stay here, John, watch the grass for movement. I'll take a quick look around, and be back in a minute." He took a theatrically deep breath before squeezing inside. "There *is* a tractor," he said, speaking loudly to reassure the teenager. "Big beast, too. Tyres nearly as large as a person, unless that person is you, John. But it's buried beneath half the roof."

"Zom!" John yelled. "Ha! Got it!"

Pete squeezed back through the door. John's spear was buried a foot deep into the soil, pinning the zombie by the neck.

"Good job," Pete said.

"We fought them in Green Bay," John said. "They came to the store. Abraham should let us fight. Most of us know how. There's no point pretending they're just going to die."

"Maybe not," Pete said. He handed the young man his spear. "Take this. I'll check the tractor for diesel and be back in a minute."

He squeezed back inside, and picked his way over and around the jumble of fallen shelves, overturned tool lockers, fallen roof-spars, light-fitments, and shingles.

"You done?" John called.

"Almost there!" Pete replied. "There are keys in the ignition. Fuel cap's closed. We might have struck gold. How's it looking out there?"

"Empty," John said.

"Stay alert," Pete said. He eased under a pair of shelves, dropping to his knees to crawl beneath a tool locker, now leaning against the tractor. The jungle of debris creaked as he reached the seat.

"I'm going to try the engine," he called, stretching for the keys.

"Say what?" John called back.

"The engine," Pete yelled. Above him, the roof shifted. He ducked his head lower so it was at least below the seat. But it was increasingly obvious the only way this tractor was getting out of here was if it ploughed through the debris. He turned the key. The engine coughed. The debris shook. The needle in the fuel gauge danced before settling in the red. He turned the key. While the rumbling ceased, the creaking didn't.

"There's fuel," he called. "But not very much."

"You okay?" John called.

"Coming out!" Pete yelled back, uncertain John could hear him.

Something heavy fell from the roof in the far corner. Something heavier hit the mat of shingles above his head. Dust and grit fell like rain as he dropped to his knees. He closed his eyes, holding his breath as the grit-shower continued. The creaking continued, too, growing louder, deeper.

He hunkered down, close to the tractor's tall rear wheels, deeply regretting having made his way inside. A metallic screech was cut short as the artificial roof above dropped.

Pete ducked lower, reflexively breathing in, and getting a lung-full of dust. As his coughing finally subsided, so did the sounds around him. Most of them. There was a drip of water, a screech of metal, and a pattering swish he couldn't place.

"Not good," he murmured, as he opened his eyes and saw very little. He reached for his belt, looking for his flashlight. His hand still worked. That was something. Despite a general, and growing, whole-body-ache, he wasn't in any great pain.

He found his flashlight, and turned it on. The debris had fallen around the tractor in an almost square cocoon. While there were plenty of gaps and crevices, there was only one large enough for him to crawl through, and a hand was already stretching through that.

"Zom!" he said aloud, ducking back against the tractor. He reached for his holster and was joyfully surprised to find the gun still there, but he didn't draw the weapon because he couldn't see the zombie's head, just its grasping hand.

Should he try a shot, and risk the sound causing another avalanche? Or wait for the zombie to force its way forward, perhaps bringing down even more of the roof? Neither would get him out of this self-building tomb, so he opted for option three.

Keeping his eyes on that questing hand, he eased himself up and onto the tractor, dragging his legs in, and his knees up, so he was sitting in the footwell with his head well below the steering wheel. He turned the key. The juddering engine shook the new walls on either side of him. The zombie's hand thrust forward, and he could now see the head, but he didn't reach for his gun. Instead, he reached for the pedals.

The tractor jerked forward, surprisingly quickly, surprisingly far, easily ploughing a route through the shed's fallen roof and thinner walls. Everything went white as he drove into daylight, and then a different kind of white as the tractor slammed into the remains of the plane's wing, which now lay on the overlong grass. Pete was flung sideways, ripping his coat, and his arm, on the debris as he clambered to his feet. He drew his gun, looking for the zombie, but it was still hidden in the wreckage. He spun around, looking for more, and only saw three figures, running towards him: Olivia, Sally, and John. He waved even as he backed away from the wreck.

"Are you okay?" Olivia asked, as she reached him.

"A few scratches, that's all," Pete said.

"Let me see," Olivia said. "That cut will need glue, and maybe stitches, and definitely needs a clean. The med-kit's by the cart."

"There's a zom in there," Pete said.

"We found a few behind the other shed," Olivia said. "But we also found diesel, so let's go get the cart."

"What happened to you?" Corrie asked when she opened the compound's gate for them.

"The sky fell on my head," Pete said. "A shed did, anyway."

"Good thing his head's full of rocks," Olivia said. "How's Candice?"

"Sleeping. And genuinely a little better," Corrie said. "Is that fuel?"

"Diesel, maybe," Olivia said. "We're not sure."

"Guess how much," John said.

"Sixty gallons!" Sally said, before Corrie could answer.

"It's enough, isn't it?" John asked.

"It's a start," Corrie said. "A really, *really* good start. Take it to the garage, I'll come test it."

"And take the food to the kitchens," Olivia said. "And remember to wash up," she added as Sally and John wheeled the cart inside.

"Abraham went to kill some zoms on the far side of the compound," Corrie said. "Three of them."

"Oh. There were a few crawlers up at the airfield," Olivia said. "But we didn't fire a shot, and we found fuel, and a bit more food. Candice is really okay?"

"She seems to be," Corrie said. "We'll know for sure in a few days. You brought back a bicycle."

"We found it around the back of the post office," Olivia said. "There were a couple more in the yard of a house just this side of the junction. I was going to take Sally and John out again to pick them up after they've eaten. Then, tomorrow, I think we need to cycle out to search some farms. This town's been picked over too often. We got lucky with that fuel, but only because it was hidden beneath some corpses after the plane crashed. We gave the containers a bit of a clean, but they need another scrub."

"Then you take over the watch here. I'll take care of those," Corrie said.

26th April

Chapter 49 - Passing Sorrows
Sidnaw, Michigan

They were woken with tragic news.

"It's Candice," Abraham said, his voice a half-whisper from the doorway to their office-bedroom. "She's passed."

Pete pulled himself out of bed, quickly dressing.

"How and when?" Olivia asked.

"She stopped breathing," Abraham said. "It was peaceful. I didn't notice. Not at first. That was about two hours ago. I didn't want to wake anyone early, but the kids should know before breakfast." He paused. "I don't know what to do with her body. I don't want to throw her out with the zoms, but I don't want her grave to be a reminder to the kids. It's only a few weeks since they all lost their parents."

"What do you usually do?" Olivia asked.

"She's the first to have died under my watch," he said.

"We could bury her next to Glenda," Olivia said.

"You mean the house in town belonging to the woman in the wheelchair?" Abraham asked.

"It's a nice spot," Olivia said. "Tranquil. Peaceful. Pete and me can dig the grave after breakfast. We'll bury her this afternoon. If the kids want to say goodbye, we can take them down there in groups. If they don't, there's no pressure."

"That might do," Abraham said, he began pulling the door closed, but paused. "Thank you," he added, before limping down the corridor.

"I guess it was inevitable," Olivia said.

"And we still don't know what was wrong with her," Pete said.

"That's something we're going to have to get used to," Olivia said. "Let me see your arm. Hmm. It needs a new dressing, so we better look for more of those. And more antiseptic. More glue, too. And then we should look for some proper sutures."

"You think it needs stitches?"

"I don't know if that glue will hold, so yep. No anaesthetic, either, so it'll sting. And that's something else we'll have to get used to. C'mon, brave face for the kids."

Two hours later, Pete stood over the dug grave. "That's something else we'll have to get used to."

"Hopefully not too often," Olivia said. "No zoms?"

"Not yet," Pete said, glancing at Rufus who had his eyes on an occasionally rustling juniper bush. Though the plant was taking full advantage of sun, rain and a lack of pruning to sprout in every direction, it was far too small to conceal even a child, undead or not. "Sun's high. I think we've left it too late to go to any farms today."

"It'll wait until tomorrow," Olivia said. "And we found sixty gallons yesterday. That's a lot. Time's not so pressing we can't spare a few hours for this. Memorialising our friends is important. Did you see John this morning? He might be as tall as a giant, but he's only fourteen. I don't think he slept a wink last night."

"You mean I should remember they're just kids?" Pete said.

"And remember what they've lost," Olivia said.

"You mean their parents?"

"And the younger kids. You must have noticed they're missing."

"Sure. Do you know what happened to them?"

"They were evacuated to St Paul," she said.

"Where Aqsa and Abraham came from?"

"Exactly. Everyone knows what happened to St Paul, and so what happened to the younger children. They know what happened to their own parents. Then we came along, speaking of craters and cartels. Yollie and her people left. Now Candice has died. That's a lot to deal with, even without the zoms."

"You think the kids will break?" he asked.

"They're already broken," she said. "We all are. But what's stopping them from cracking is the belief that we've got a plan. That and Abraham."

John and Sally helped bring the body to the grave. Aqsa and Abraham didn't. They both wanted to be there, but their absence gave the rest of the children an excuse not to attend.

Olivia said a few words, and a brief prayer Abraham had handwritten. "Thank you, Candice," she finished. "You kept the children safe. We'll remember that, and continue the work."

"Thank you, Candice," Pete said, uncertain what else to say. John echoed him. Sally simply shook her head.

"Let's get back," Olivia said. "C'mon, Rufus. Home."

Pete gestured towards the houses. Olivia shook her head. He nodded, but reluctantly. Time really was running out. When they got back to the compound, they found it was running out a lot faster than they'd realised.

Abraham was overseeing the children as they carried containers from inside the rarely used buildings further from the entrance. As they pulled the gate closed, he limped his way over.

"Sally, John, help straighten those lines," Abraham said. "We're setting out anything which can hold water. It's going to rain later."

"What's happened?" Olivia asked.

"Corrie used that diesel you found to power up the pump," Abraham said. "We got a surge, then a trickle, then nothing. She's gone up to the reservoir to find out why. Took Aqsa and Lisa with her."

"Are we short of water?" Pete asked.

"Always," Abraham said. "That storage tank is holding, but I thought this would keep the kids busy."

When the rain came, it was more a trickle than a shower. With Corrie not back, and with the children increasingly subdued, Olivia declared it bath time. It was a lacklustre effort that ended up with everyone soapy rather than scrubbed, and damp rather than clean, but it filled the time until Corrie and Lisa returned. They didn't bring good news.

"We've got nineteen days of water," Corrie said.

"What about the reservoir?" Abraham asked.

"Is there a zom in the pipe?" Princess asked, having come over with half of the semi-clean children.

"Don't say things like that," Little John said.

"It's dinner time," Abraham said. "John, get everyone inside. We'll come tell you everything in a minute. Go on. Don't make me say it twice." The children drifted off. Abraham turned back to Corrie. "You were saying?"

"The reservoir, and filtration system, was carved out of a small lake," Corrie said. "Sometime before the power failed, someone opened the valves so the pipes leading here became an enclosed stream. But, between the reservoir and the lake proper, there's a dam. The sluices are closed. To open them, we'd need power. The trickle we got earlier was the rain and surface run-off which had filled the reservoir. When I turned on the pump, we sucked it dry. This storm will have refilled it a bit, but not enough. Nineteen days, and that storage tank you built will be empty."

"Unless it rains," Abraham said.

"Yep," Corrie said. "And when it rains, the reservoir fills, but we can't use solar panels to charge the electric van on a cloudy day. We can ration water, and we could build some more rainwater collection tanks in the town linked to roofs and guttering. Or we could just drive the van up to the lake, and fill up some barrels. Water is a problem, but not an insurmountable one."

"Food will be," Abraham said. "We can't make more of that. Not here. How long do we have before it's gone?"

"Thirty-five days," Lisa said. "We can fish in that lake, but we can't live there. We can cycle to nearby towns, or drive that van. However, food is no more a problem than water. Our shortage isn't in water, or food, or labour, but in time. Our plane set down a week ago. I still haven't taken it up again to scout Duluth and the land between. The flight should take place soon before we leave, but the longer we wait, the greater the chance a heavy storm could wreck the aircraft. But why do we want to scout Duluth?"

"To get to Canada," Abraham said.

"Indeed," Lisa said. "Though I was speaking rhetorically. Ultimately, we want to get to Pine Dock because it is a possible contact-point with the Pacific. Otherwise, we want a lake for fresh water, and for fishing. There is one such place a lot closer than the border. Lake Superior is only twenty miles north."

"What about the radiation?" Abraham asked. "Didn't you say the lakes had been bombed?"

"We can check the readings as we search for a suitable redoubt," Lisa said. "The van's log book says the vehicle has a theoretical range of a hundred and twenty miles. That would be in a wind tunnel at the factory. On good roads, in good conditions, I would expect one hundred. We should hope for eighty, which gives us a forty-mile driving radius. Duluth is a hundred and eighty miles away, but L'Anse is twenty. We could easily ferry everyone there. Say ten per trip, and we'd have it done in ten days. We can then return for the crops in those planters. We'll have lost nothing, but gained a lot."

"You want to give up on Canada?" Abraham asked.

"No," Lisa said. "Canada should be plan-A, but we don't need to travel there in one go. We need a fresh water source, and a food source. So let us relocate to Lake Superior, and then continue our search. However, before we drive north, let us confirm there is no fuel in the one obvious place nearby. Florence."

"Where the kids' parents didn't return from?" Abraham asked.

"But I went and came back," Aqsa said. "There were lots of vehicles, but they were all driven into a sort of wall, like a fortress. There were lots of zombies, too."

"But after those vehicles were driven into position to form that wall, were the fuel tanks drained?" Lisa asked. "Perhaps they were, and that is why Captain Stahl continued his search. Perhaps they weren't, but there just wasn't enough for the captain's needs. Perhaps he didn't look."

"That's a long shot," Abraham said.

"Yet a necessary one," Lisa said. "Once we go north, it will be harder to search anywhere to the south. Around here, the fuel was seized in the early days of the outbreak. The same must be true near Florence. Thus, if we find nothing in that redoubt, we'll find nothing anywhere near it. Now is the time to look. We are still relatively close, and we still have bullets."

"How much fuel do we need?" Pete asked.

"Six hundred gallons," Abraham said. "Assume one thousand miles to get us to the northern end of Lake Winnipeg with a detour or two. A bus can make five miles to the gallon. We'll need three buses, so six hundred gallons is the bare minimum."

"In the week since we landed, we've only found sixty gallons which someone else had syphoned, stored, and forgotten," Lisa said. "We'll find no more within walking range."

"Florence isn't within driving range," Abraham said. "Not of that van."

"So we'll cycle," Olivia said. "Just me and Pete. If there's no diesel there, we'll know by nightfall tomorrow. But Aqsa, you went there, you tell us if we're wasting our time."

"I didn't look for fuel," she said. "I was just looking for our people. For anyone. There was no one, but there could be fuel. It's possible."

"Sixty miles, we can manage that in a day," Pete said.

"May I remind you, if you wish to return, it will be twice that distance," Lisa said.

"We can still manage it in a day," Olivia said. "You guys can finish clearing out the town. We might as well get all the supplies up here. Sorting and packing will keep the kids busy."

"But we'll tell them you're going to look at some farms," Abraham said. "Florence is the place no one comes back from. I don't want them worrying about you two as well."

27th April

Chapter 50 - Twisted Weather
Michigan and Wisconsin

The sun was reluctant to rise, hiding behind yellow-tinged skies as rain drizzled against the office-bedroom window. But by the time Pete and Olivia got downstairs, the rain had ceased, though storm clouds still hovered overhead.

"Do you have everything you need?" Corrie asked, as Pete checked the improvised saddlebags slung behind the bike.

"Handgun and suppressor, and three mags," Pete said. "Spear and crowbar, and a knife."

"And a carbine, water, a map, lunch, and a med-kit," Olivia said, tapping the bags slung on her bike. "We're set, Corrie."

"And the Geiger counter?" Corrie asked.

"No worries, sis," Pete said. "We'll be back before dark."

"But if we're not, don't start worrying until around midday tomorrow," Olivia said. "We'll take it slow and steady, and we'll hide from the rain."

"Are you sure you don't want me to come?" Corrie said.

"There's just not enough adults here," Olivia said. "We'll be fine."

"You're clear," Abraham called, limping back from the gate. "If you're going, get going. But come back safe, you hear?"

Once they were away from the highway, and heading south, Pete began to enjoy the ride, mostly because the air was fresher. The ever-increasing pile of zombies outside the compound had created a miasma over the entire neighbourhood. Which wasn't to say that the countryside beyond was pristine. The fields were overgrown, except where the bare earth had yet to, and would never again, be planted. The fields were dotted with stagnant puddles, which often spilled onto the roads. While the water was never more than a few inches deep, it slowed them to near walking pace. Infrequently, the fields were dotted with sun-bleached ribcages from the cattle which hadn't survived long enough to be slaughtered. They'd died in clusters, never alone.

Pete puzzled over that for a few miles. Had the farmers released the cows into the fields before they'd fled? Or had they died while grazing before the utter irreversibility of the apocalypse had become apparent?

"No zoms on the road," Olivia said, slowing to pull alongside him.

"Yeah, I hadn't noticed," Pete said. "Should have, but I was too busy looking at the cows. No zoms. Maybe they're dead."

"Well, I'm not going to bank on it," Olivia said. "It might seem like a year, but it's only a week since we flew over that massive horde. I wonder if the lack of zoms is linked to the lack of cars. You realise we haven't seen one for at least a mile?"

As he turned to look over his shoulder, a brake cable detached from his handlebar, rattling as the loose end caught against the spinning front wheel. Reflexively, he clenched the brakes, and nearly went flying as only the front wheel ceased turning.

"You okay, hon?" Olivia asked.

"It's just the brake cable," Pete said, reaching into his bag for some tape. "I guess we go slower from now on."

"We're in no rush," Olivia said. "There's a squirrel over there. Just gone up that tree. I think you scared it. Ah, no, I take it back. It wasn't you. There's a zom in that field. Oh. There's one behind us on the road now. Well, so much for our tranquil bicycle ride."

Just before a sign saying that Iron River was only five miles further on, they came to a car with an open fuel cap.

"First car since... since when?" Pete asked, taking out the map.

"Maybe five miles, if you mean actually on the road and without a zom trapped inside," Olivia said, leaning her bike against the car. "I bet someone stayed behind in Iron River, then came north looking for fuel like we are now. How big is Iron River?"

"Big enough we'll go around," he said. "We can keep an eye out for smoke, but we're not searching for more people until after we've finished with Florence. What are you doing?"

"Checking the car's trunk," she said. "Yep. Thought so. There's some loot in here. Nothing worth taking. Clothes and tools, mostly. A little stove. It's camping gear. Maybe people our age. People who spent an occasional weekend out in the woods. They took what they could carry, but if they didn't run the car dry, someone else thought to grab the last bit of fuel." She closed the trunk, and picked up her bike. "Don't say it. Don't think it. Just look at that sky."

It had turned a familiar and ominous shade of green.

"It is that time of year," he said.

"We should get that plane in the air as soon as we can," she said.

"*While* we still can," he said.

Before the storm arrived, they found shelter in a trackside barn, near a shallow hilltop. It was from there they watched the tornado arrive, and where they desperately hoped it wouldn't turn their way.

"I wonder who they were," Olivia said, as Pete watched the twister rip across the open farmland on the other side of the shallow valley.

"Who?" he asked.

"The people who first sheltered here," she said. "They stayed long enough to light a fire and empty their bags. They left toothbrushes, half a paperback, a blood-soaked shirt and a mud-streaked t-shirt. Cutlery, string, candles, and a block of soap."

"Is that surprising?" he asked.

"Not really, just that it's all neatly lined up on this table. They figured someone else might have need of it, except you could pick up those things in pretty much any house."

"Maybe this was where they were supposed to meet someone," Pete said. "They got separated out on the road."

"They'll regret not keeping their toothbrush," Olivia said. "It's a good thing sugar's going to be scarce for a while. I do not even want to think about what we'll do if we need to pull a tooth."

"We should grab some tools from a dentist's," Pete said. "Not today, but on our way to Pine Dock."

"From Thunder Bay, maybe?"

"Or Duluth," he said. "The twister's turning east."

"Look at the destruction it's left behind."

"Not just destruction," he said. "Those are zombies. The zoms are following the twister!"

"Please turn around," Olivia said. "Please turn. Not you, Pete. The tornado. It'd rip the zoms to shreds as easily as a person."

"And spray the infected pulp wherever it goes," Pete said. "Infected rain. Hang on."

"What?"

"It's not just infected blood and brains it'll spread," he said as he took the Geiger counter out of the bag. "Doc Flo said infected material only remains contagious for a few minutes while out in the open, and never more than an hour. But radiation… yep. The reading's higher than it was back at the compound."

"How high?" Olivia asked. "Actually, no, don't say. We can't do anything about it."

"We'll take another reading on the other side of that valley," Pete said. "We can change our clothes, our boots."

"And the bikes," Olivia said. "We'll have to ditch the bikes. But not until we can find spares. Oh, Canada, we can't reach you soon enough."

In silence they watched the slow-moving maelstrom churn eastwards.

"If a tornado hits the plane it'll be gone for good," Olivia said. "I don't think Lisa wants to fly it, not really. She comes across as self-assured and devil-may-care, but it's an act, like everything else about her. She'll do it, if she has to, but if this storm hits the compound, she won't be able to."

"If it hits the compound, it's over," Pete said. "How far are we from Florence?"

"Ten, fifteen miles," Olivia said.

"We could be there in an hour," Pete said. "Rain's dropping. The tornado's moved on."

"It could come back," Olivia said.

"Yep, but we're not really safe here," he said.

"What about the radiation?"

"Like I said, we really should get out of here."

Chapter 51 - The Place From Which No One Returns
Florence, Wisconsin

Halfway between Iron River in the northwest, and Iron Mountain in the southeast, they found the town of Florence. Aqsa had described a wall made of vehicles, but Pete had still pictured a ramshackle fort. This was a fortress encasing nearly half of the small town. Tanks were parked between the houses, and in the roads. Their cannons were aimed out and down, ready to obliterate any approaching army of the undead. The larger gaps between tanks and houses were filled with cars, bricks, and scaffolding, the smaller gaps with furniture and other salvage. Beyond lay an outer wall of bone, evidence of the battle fought here.

"Now I understand why Aqsa didn't know whether there was any fuel left," Pete said. "It'll take a week just to untangle a single tank."

"There were defenders, but they fled," Olivia said. "So guess what that means?"

"They took the gas with them," Pete said.

"Yep. But they'd have had a central fuel store. It'll be around there we'll find any spare vehicles. Captain Stahl wouldn't have needed them because he drove here, so maybe we'll get lucky. What's the radiation like?"

"It's dropped."

"Cool," she said. "We'll find some new clothes in there somewhere. Maybe some more bikes, but we'll hide ours for now over by that stack of bookcases."

"Why hide?" Pete asked as they wheeled their bicycles across the yard.

"Because it's a fortress, Pete," she said. "If we didn't have to get back to Sidnaw, we'd surely think about staying. Other people might be here."

"Maybe for a night or two," he said. "I wouldn't linger."

Four bookcases had been set in a U on the house's front yard. Cinder blocks had been placed on the lower shelves to add stability. Inside the bookcase-U were the pecked-clean bones of five people. The skulls appeared intact, but it would be a coincidence to find five immune people dead in one place. Unless, perhaps, everyone in this fortress had been the immune survivors of a much larger, previous conflict. Even that didn't seem plausible as, on their way to the house, they came across more bones, more brass, and more slowly decaying corpses of the undead.

The house's back door was blocked from the inside. So were the windows, but not on the next house along. There, the glass had been cleared from the frame, with a helpful set of steps placed beneath, and with a footstool inside.

"Guess we aren't the first to come here looting," Olivia said, as she climbed inside. "Iron River's not that far. It's— Woah!"

A uniformed figure staggered out of the kitchen, arms banging into the walls. Olivia ducked sideways, reaching for her belt. Pete, still halfway outside, jumped in, charging with the spear raised, lancing it through the zombie's side, and then into the wall beyond. Even pinned, the zombie still thrashed with painless vigour.

Olivia swung the crowbar heavily through the air, and into its temple. The zombie sagged forward, finally still.

"Not exactly the welcome I was hoping for," Olivia said, wiping the crowbar on an already musty couch.

Pete eyed the spear, then shook his head, and drew his sidearm, to which he affixed the suppressor. Olivia did the same.

"She was wearing a uniform," Pete said, stepping into the doorway, looking up and down the hall.

"Hopefully from a clothing stash next to where they kept the fuel," Olivia said.

"Hopefully, that's not where she got bitten," Pete said. "Think we're clear."

The front door was closed, but not barricaded. When he opened the door, he saw the keys were in the lock. It was a disturbing detail, as was the vista beyond. The road and the front yards were filled with cars, and bones, from a failed attempt to build a secondary line of defence.

"Fuel caps are closed," Pete said.

"Step ladders by the sides of those houses," Olivia said. "They look like they're pinned to the walls. A major effort went into fortifying this place." She took out a phone. "I borrowed this from John. He wanted me to bring back footage of what we saw." She snapped a few photographs, then a short panoramic video.

Wary of crawlers, they gave the abandoned cars a wide berth, walking slowly as they scanned the boarded windows and once-occupied rooftops for signs of more recent life. A lot of effort had gone into this fortress. More effort than Pete had seen anywhere since they'd travelled with General Yoon's army. Even more effort than on Long Island.

"Forts are defensive," Pete said. "So what were they defending?"

"I'll tell you what they *weren't* defending," Olivia said. "Their families. The tanks had a crew of four, yes? But their families didn't live in this town. Once the tanks were in position, the rest of the fortification could be built in a day, with the help of the locals. Then they all waited, but after the bombs fell, if not before, at least some of the soldiers would have gone looking for their families. Inevitably, the rest left, too."

"Then to whom do these bones belong?" Pete asked.

The decaying corpses were still a constant presence, inhibiting the weeds, littering the driveways, lining the roads.

"I guess they belong to the people who chose to stay," Olivia said.

Not all of them, because before she'd taken another step, a gunshot echoed across the rooftops. The second shot confirmed from which direction the gunfire came. Two turns, and two roads less clogged with vehicles and corpses, later, they reached an inner line of defence. The fence had belonged to a school, and it had been reinforced, doubled in height, turning that school into a keep. Here, where it backed onto playing fields, four of the undead pushed against the fence, clearly enlivened by the shooting. Olivia motioned they should back away, and they quickly detoured into a backyard.

"Sniper must be on the school's roof," Olivia whispered.

"Can't be much of a shot," Pete said. "I didn't see any recently dead zoms."

They backtracked through back yards, until they reached Olive Avenue and the road-entrance to the school-keep. A new roller gate ran across the road. To support it, and the fence on either side, holes had been drilled in the road into which metal poles had been planted and held in place with mounds of quick-drying cement. On Pete and Olivia's side of the gate were two zombies, recently killed. On the other side were two people, two motorbikes, one military truck, and one Abrams M1 tank. This tank wasn't part of any defences, however, and its cannon was elevated and aimed eastward.

Pete and Olivia took shelter between the corner of a church and a sprawling witch-hazel, watching the two people. Both were men, and both wore military fatigues, but the clothing was clean, so it must have been recently found. Both carried rifles, too. The man sitting on the tank's cupola, who was reading a paperback, had his weapon lying next to him. The other held his weapon in one hand, with most of the weight taken by the gun's sling, while the other hand held a cigarette. The gun might be a carbine. Maybe an M16. Possibly an AR-15, but probably a fully automatic military rifle. Neither man was clean-shaven, though both had trimmed beards, which made it hard to gauge their ages.

He turned his gaze upwards, scanning the school's roof for a sentry until Olivia tugged on his arm. She'd unslung her carbine, and had leaned it against the church's wall, placing her empty holster next to it. Her bag dangled from one shoulder while she had the crowbar in her hand. She motioned he should unbuckle his holster, so he did, slipping the pistol into his belt at the small of his back.

"What's wrong?" he mouthed.

"Can't tell," she mouthed back. She pointed towards the main entrance, and mimed knocking.

He nodded.

On either side of the gate, and its supporting section of fence, more cars had been used to build a wall, but Pete was more interested in the other gate, further along the road, and beyond the tank: a gate which seemed to run eastward, and without any further obstruction. The school *wasn't* a keep; the fortress had simply been partitioned in two.

"Hey," Olivia called out as they approached the roller-gate.

The man on the cupola dropped his book, reaching for his rifle, though he relaxed as his eyes settled on Pete and Olivia. Though he picked up his gun as he stood, he didn't raise it. The smoker, meanwhile, simply gave a half-hearted wave before taking another drag on his cigarette.

"Are you guys with the army?" Olivia called out.

"Pretty much," the smoker said. "Where you from?"

"North Michigan," Olivia said, even as Pete was cycling through the various possible answers. He fixed a smile on his face, trying to spot the trouble his wife had seen. "We're looking for food. We'll work. We'll fight."

"Always looking for workers," the smoker said.

"Cool," Olivia said, and tugged the gate open a few feet. Leaves and dirt were gathered beneath, suggesting it didn't get opened very often. "I don't suppose a woman called Eliza came through here a few days ago," Olivia added. "I've got a photo." She reached for her bag, drew her gun, and fired two shots into the smoker, and half a magazine into the man on the top of the tank before Pete had his own sidearm raised.

"Watch the school," Olivia said, as she ran over to the tank.

"Why fire?" Pete asked, training his gun on the entrance, as he followed.

"Because I know that smoking guy," Olivia said. "He was at Notre Dame with the nephew."

"They're cartel?"

"Three cop badges on his belt kinda proves it," she said. "And... yep. He's even got that damned tattoo on his arm. A three-branched rose bush."

She picked up the rifle still lying atop the tank. "I think I know why the captain never returned from here," she said. "And why there are so many uninfected corpses outside."

"So we should run," Pete said.

"No, we should attack," Olivia said. "This is a prison camp, and we've got people to free."

Their footsteps echoed, as they ran inside the school. Their pace slowed from a sprint to a tiptoe sidle from one classroom to the next, but each was empty. If the cartel were keeping prisoners nearby, it wasn't in the school.

The first two classrooms contained neat rows of folding cots. All empty, except for a few blankets dropped during a hasty retreat. The third contained tank shells. Shell crates were neatly stacked against the far wall, with an empty hand cart in the middle of the room.

"I guess that's why he was smoking outside," Pete said.

"There are bullets in here, Pete," Olivia said from the door on the opposite side of the corridor. "Says it's .50 calibre. That's for a machine gun, right?"

"And there's more in this classroom," Pete said, quickly jogging to the next room along. He looked down, at the scratches on the floor left by the frequent passage of heavy carts. "And there are a lot more classrooms in this school. If there were people here, friendly or not, we'd have heard them by now."

"Yep, we should leave," Olivia said. She took out the phone, snatching some footage before doing the same with room containing the shells. "Shells and bullets. Okay, let's go."

"After we hide those bodies," Pete said, opening the door to the shell-room. He grabbed the empty trolley and hauled it out into the corridor.

"Why hide?"

"Because if we move them, and open the gates, then maybe anyone who comes looking for them will think they became zoms."

"There's blood on the tank," she said.

"Maybe they'll think it was left when the guards got infected," Pete said. "It'll just take a minute, and it's the best we can do."

They hauled the cart outside, and dragged the bodies onto it.

"Casings," Olivia said, picking them up. "Although I guess there are so many here, it doesn't matter." She threw them wide, while Pete dragged the cart towards the gate leading into the rest of the town.

"Wait, what about the motorbikes?" Olivia asked. "Look at the leaves piled around the truck. They must have come here by bike."

"So two bikers, here alone," Pete said. "They were probably checking the shells were still here."

"No, I mean shouldn't we hide the bikes?" Olivia said, before adding, "No. They were killed by zoms, and zombies don't drive. Hang on." She drew the handgun from one man's holster, walked back to the tank, firing three shots into the air before letting the gun fall. She returned to the bodies, drew the knife from the other man's belt, stabbed it deep into his side, before dropping it next to the bike. She put the rifle back on the tank. "Yeah, it's not the best fake crime scene."

"In a day or two, it'll be perfect," Pete said.

They pushed the gate leading into the town wide open, and wheeled the cart into the first garage they came to.

"I say that's enough," Olivia said, pulling the garage doors down. "There are zoms inside this part of town. Hmm. That's quite a trail we left in the mud, and we forgot about the gate leading out of town and to the east. Yep, I think we should stop pretending we're master criminals, and get out of here."

"Wait, your carbine," Pete said. "You left it behind the church."

"We grab that, then we go," Olivia said. "Oh, this is just like West Virginia."

Pete stepped over a skull. "Do you think the defenders were killed with VX?"

"Maybe," Olivia said. "It would explain the bones. It doesn't explain why the cartel is here of all places. Oh. Perhaps it does."

"What do you mean?"

"Give me a minute to think it through," she said.

They made their way to the rear of the church. Olivia picked up the carbine, then turned to look back at the tank.

"What is it?" he asked.

"I wonder if we should look for clues as to where their base is," she said. "It has to be close. Pruitt was the governor of Michigan. The nephew was a cop in South Bend. Here we are, not far from Lake Michigan, and not that much further from Indiana. And when we bumped into the nephew again, that second time, it was on the Canadian side of the Great Lakes. I think this is the region they always planned to claim. If it was bombed, they'd have gone down to Colombia. If it wasn't, it makes for a far better kingdom."

"Mikael was exiled to Florida," Pete said.

"Right, not to Colombia," Olivia said.

"Okay, so does it matter now?" he asked.

"Only in that I'd like to know where they are so we can avoid them," she said. "Wait, do you hear that? Oh, Pete, we got it wrong. The bikers were waiting, weren't they? They were just outriders, and the rest of the convoy is just about to arrive."

"In here," Pete said, pulling open the church door, and nearly gagging on the stench.

The door led into a boot-room with rows of pegs for snow-coats. More recently, it had become the last resting place for some of the townsfolk. From the bullet holes in the skulls, they'd been shot. From the lack of flesh on the bones, they'd been uninfected. The trail of bodies continued into the vestry and then into the church itself. They had clearly been executed, and he thought he could guess who they'd been, when they'd arrived, and where they had come from. Pete returned to the vestry where Olivia was half-crouched by a cracked and dusty window, which overlooked the school.

"Think we found out what happened to Captain Stahl and the kids' parents," Pete whispered.

"Car," Olivia said. "Car and two bikes. Big car. It's stopped by the outer gate."

A trio of shots rang out. Then came a rattle as the gate was pulled back. The engine noise continued, briefly, as the vehicles drove in and up to the school: two blue police motorbikes and one black SUV with tinted windows over which a grill had been fitted. At the front of the car was a wide wedge of steel for us as a plough, but from how the front passenger climbed out first and then held open the rear door, this vehicle was primarily used as a limo. The VIP didn't get out of the SUV, though.

The two bikers had dismounted, and crossed to the tank. One picked up the rifle. The other picked up the bloody knife, before pointing towards the open, inner gate. He said something, but Pete couldn't hear what. Nor could he hear the reply, but the knife, and rifle, were dropped, and the two bikers ran into the school.

Finally, the passenger got out of the car. Pete was expecting a muscled giant, a two-ton movie villain, not an older woman dressed all in black, leaning on a silver cane. Then he realised.

"The sisters," he whispered, and raised his gun.

Olivia, one hand now holding the phone close to the window, grabbed his wrist with the other. "Wait until we can see them all."

Herrera took a step away from the SUV, looking up at the treetops to the east where a quartet of crows had begun cawing. She turned to speak to someone still in the car, presumably her sister, but turned as the two bikers returned from inside the school.

"Attack?" Pete whispered.

"Not until the driver gets out of the SUV," Olivia whispered. "We can't let them get away."

Again, it was impossible to hear the conversation. Herrera got back into the SUV. One of the bikers jogged to the inner gate and pulled it closed while the SUV turned around and began driving back the way it had come. The bikers followed, only pausing to pull the outer gate closed before continuing on, eastwards.

Olivia lowered the phone, and checked the video she'd just taken, pausing on a still of the woman in black.

"That's the woman from the video at Lisa's mansion, isn't it?" she said.

"I think so," he said.

"Time we went back, then," Olivia said.

"We should have shot them," Pete said, stepping over a corpse, and towards the door.

"The driver never got out of the car, nor did the other sister," Olivia said. "We might have got one, but not the other. If we'd been caught, they'd have made us tell them about Sidnaw. No, we know the most important thing: they came from the east. I'd say that's absolute confirmation we should head west."

"Yeah, but will Lisa want to?" Pete asked.

Chapter 52 - Change of Plans
Sidnaw, Michigan

They arrived back in Sidnaw drenched in sweat, dripping with rain, and with the sun nudging the horizon. Outside the gates, Abraham and Lisa were loading zombies onto a cart.

"Started to think you'd found a hotel for the night," Abraham said.

"The cartel were in Florence," Olivia said. "Leave the zoms, let's get inside, and we'll tell you what happened. We've got to change our clothes, then we'll join you."

"Radiation," Pete added, throwing the contaminated bike onto the pile of the undead.

Fifteen minutes later, the adults had gathered in the hallway outside the cafeteria, except for Corrie who was once again on guard, but this time on the roof.

"What's going on?" Sally asked, opening the door to the cafeteria.

"We'll tell everyone in a moment," Abraham said. "Just make sure everyone eats. Give us ten minutes." He pulled the door closed.

"It was the cartel," Olivia said. "The army used the school as a supply dump for tank shells and bullets. I guess they got shipped there with the tanks. The cartel left two people on guard. I recognised one from South Bend. We took them out, checked inside, and hid the bodies. We were going to let the zoms in, to cover our tracks, when we heard engines. Two bikes, one black SUV. We took video, and I kept the phone, but there's a contamination risk. We saw that woman who was on the video from your house on the Delmarva Peninsula."

"Margalotta Herrera," Lisa said. "Born Masha Sidorova on the outskirts of Yakutsk sixty-five years ago. She and her sister, and their brother, were exiled after the demise of the USSR. She is the chemist. Where she is, her sister is never far behind. Did you see her sister?"

"I think she stayed in the car," Olivia said. "Someone was definitely inside."

"These sisters run this cartel?" Abraham asked.

"They do," Lisa said. "Margalotta was responsible for the murders in my house on the Delmarva Peninsula, among other horrors. What happened next, Olivia?"

"They drove off. We came back," Olivia said. "We never had a clear shot, not really."

"Bringing this news back was more important," Lisa said.

"There's more," Pete said. "We saw a tornado on our way to Florence. That was near Iron River. That's when we checked the radiation figures."

"Not much we can do about radiation," Abraham said. "Not much we can do about twisters, neither."

"And we found a lot of bodies in a church," Pete said. "Shot, mostly. I think it was Captain Stahl and the other people from here. They must have arrived when a lot of the cartel were there, and were executed because they were such a large group, they'd have been a threat."

"I didn't see anyone," Aqsa said.

"Did you get to the school?" Pete asked.

"Behind some gates with a tank outside?" Aqsa said. "Yes, I saw that. I didn't go in. I was… I was looking for living people, or for their abandoned trucks."

"The cartel must have taken the vehicles away," Olivia said.

"Did you take any photographs of the bodies?" Aqsa asked. "Maybe we'd recognise someone."

"They've been dead a long while," Olivia said. "None were identifiable."

"Wouldn't do us any good if we could put a name to the bones," Abraham said. "And it won't do the kids any good to hear that part, so we'll keep it to ourselves. Let's leave them with hope."

"They didn't leave anyone on guard?" Lisa asked.

"No," Olivia said. "They didn't look for their two scouts, either. They just left."

"Good," Lisa said. "Their army is too small to sustain a permanent garrison, or to take significant numbers of prisoners. Aqsa, you were fortunate they had no one there when you arrived. If they executed Captain Stahl and the parents there, then they won't have been subjected to prolonged questioning. It is a small comfort, but comfort nonetheless."

"Doesn't help us much, does it?" Abraham said. "Any idea where they came from?"

"Somewhere to the east," Pete said. "Quite a way to the east, or they'd have stumbled across this compound by now."

"Somewhere close to the shores of Lake Michigan," Olivia said. "With Pruitt being the governor of Michigan, and the nephew working as a cop in Indiana, it makes sense. If Colombia was supposed to be a base for seizing control of the Panama Canal, wouldn't they look for something similar up here?"

"Like the crossing at Sault Ste Marie?" Lisa asked. "A crossing destroyed by General Yoon to prevent the spread of the infection. That is something the sisters could not have foreseen. Yes, it is an interesting theory."

"Can you add to it?" Abraham asked. "Maybe take a guess at where they are?"

"If we learned anything from West Virginia, there will be an airport and a prison," Lisa said. "But where they were isn't necessarily where they are now."

There was a rumble of feet, then a shushing from inside the cafeteria.

"We'll save the theorising for later," Abraham said. "How much danger are we in?"

"No more than yesterday," Lisa said. "We are simply aware that we are in far more danger than we first realised. We should avoid going south, or east. Sadly, we can't use the plane; it would be too easily spotted from a distance."

"Doubt it would fly after that storm," Abraham said.

"How far would those sixty gallons of diesel get us?" Pete asked.

"We've got six drivers," Abraham said. "So, say six pickups filled with the kids and not much more. Maybe three hundred miles. Depends on the roads. Could be a bit more. Could be a lot less."

"So we'd get to Duluth, and maybe a little bit beyond," Pete said. "That should be safely far away from the sisters. We're more likely to find a few buses in a city."

"Are you suggesting we should look for pickups tomorrow, and leave the day after?" Aqsa asked.

"Yeah, maybe," Pete said. "Or maybe the day after that. We shouldn't rush our departure, but we certainly shouldn't linger. We've still got the electric van. We could drive north, tomorrow, up to the lake. We can look for a redoubt, or some bigger vehicles, up there. We can ferry the kids up in cars, and we'd still have the van to bring up some of the food. Then we could follow the lake west. We don't need to sprint to Duluth, but I'd still aim to be north of there within a week. On the way we'd have the lake for fresh water, maybe some fish. We can look for fuel and better vehicles abandoned by people who took to their boats."

"I don't like the delay," Abraham said.

"It isn't much of one," Pete said. "Tomorrow, while we go up to the lake, you can find the pickups. We'll need to charge the cars' batteries, change the tyres, and fill up the tanks. The kids will have to repack. We wouldn't be ready to leave until noon, anyway, and by then, we could be back with the news that we've found somewhere, or that we've got no choice but to take our chance with a sprint westwards."

"Agreed," Abraham said. "If not tomorrow, then the day after, at dawn, we'll leave. We better tell the kids. No mention of their parents, okay?"

"I'll go swap with Corrie," Pete said.

Half an hour later, Olivia came to join him on the roof.

"I liked how you took charge back there," she said.

"I just wanted to end the debate," he said. "I do want to get away from here, but I don't want us to die somewhere worse. I get Abraham's point, and I really don't want to linger, but I don't want to die three days from now stuck on some rooftop in Duluth."

"Or trapped in a pickup, surrounded by zoms," she said. "Making the journey in stages is a good idea. That's got to be the lesson from our own attempt at getting to Pine Dock. We had to tell the kids about their parents," she added. "Princess asked. What could we say?"

"Better not to lie, I guess. How did they take it?"

"They're upset, but I think they all knew," she said. "No, it is better this way. When we leave here, we can leave a lot of the past behind."

28th April

Chapter 53 - A Busy Harbour
L'Anse, Lake Superior

"I feel like a farmer always worrying about the rain," Pete said as he peered through the office window. "Rain will keep the cartel at home, but I think it's stopping."

"We're hunter-gatherers, not farmers," Olivia said, coming over to join him at the window. "Speaking of which, we should look for some books on them."

"Farmers?"

"Well, yes," she said, "Though I was thinking of hunter-gatherers. But we should look for some books on meteorology, too. There's no excuse for us just guessing at the weather."

"We'll need to find a library," he said. "You're right, the knowledge is out there. We'd be foolish to ignore it."

"We need a library *and* a hydroelectric dam," she said. "Give it a couple of weeks and we'll have found them both. I can hear the kids, so I'll see who wants to take Rufus for a walk. Meet you at breakfast."

He'd never seen such a long queue outside the cafeteria, though the delay wasn't for the food, but for the baggage check-in. Princess had a clipboard, a set of scales, and a wobbly rectangular plyboard frame. Before a child could enter the cafeteria, they had to check their bag was underweight, and not too large to fit in the frame.

With a queue outside, there was none inside, so a minute later, he was sitting in his usual seat, a bowl in front of him.

"What's the story with the bags?" Pete asked his sister, who'd beaten him to breakfast.

"The kids were up all night packing for the trip," Corrie said.

"All of them?" he asked.

"Princess insisted. You know what she's like; it's easier when she gets her own way. I bet it won't be long before she renames herself queen."

"That's where I draw the line," Pete said. "The baggage check was her idea, too?"

"Yep, and the weight and size limit. Do you want to guess how she came up with the specs?"

"By measuring her own bag?" Pete asked.

"Pretty much," Corrie said. She pushed her bowl aside. "Where's Rufus? I was hoping he'd finish this for me."

"Taking a walk," Pete said. "Aren't you hungry?"

"That's my third portion," Corrie said. "We won't be able to take all the food with us. Better we don't leave so much here we're ever tempted to come back. But even though I vividly remember too many hungry days and hungrier nights, there is a limit to how much of that ham anyone can eat. Did you want Rufus today, or can I borrow him? We'll have to take some of the kids with us, and if I'm watching them, I could do with someone else to watch for the undead."

"No worries," Pete said. "There's a good chance we'll never get out of the van, and if we do, it'll only be to stick a hose in some car's gas tank."

"Cool. On your ride today, keep your eyes open for a firehouse."

"You think we'll find fuel there?"

"Nope. Look for some local directory, or map, listing industrial facilities at risk of a major fire. Chemical factories, that kind of thing. They'd be built away from towns, and might have a few vehicles we can borrow, but they'd also have sturdy fences. I'm thinking somewhere like that could be a good place to spend the night. Maybe even two nights, while we go ahead to check out a route through Duluth."

"Sure," Pete said. "Experience tells me we're likely to stop at the first likely spot we find, though."

"No, we can't travel like that," she said. "We'll need a specific rendezvous in case some of our convoy gets separated."

"I'll see what I can find," Pete said. "Where's Lisa?"

"With the van," she said. "She was up even before Princess."

The van was packed, and ready to go. So was Lisa.

"If I were wearing a watch, I'd pointedly glare at it," she said.

"It's barely dawn," Pete said.

"Which means we're now wasting daylight," she said. "And we still have to wait for your wife to have breakfast."

"What's that saying? More haste, less speed," Pete said. "Never really understood it before now."

"To a well-ordered mind, the two are not mutually exclusive," she said. "We have twenty-three empty containers which won't be dissolved by diesel or gasoline. We will require more."

"And some way of marking which is which," Pete said, checking the van's cargo-cabin.

"Coloured cloth tied to the handle," Lisa said.

"That'd do," Pete said. "Hoses, funnels, a few tools. Yep, looks like we've got everything."

"I packed us a lunch, too," she said. "I considered adding a few bicycles, but I think it would be better if we plan not to misplace the van."

"It'd be hard to plan for that," Pete said. "But speaking of plans, what are yours?"

"In what regard?"

"The sisters," Pete said. "Now you know where they are, what are you going to do about it?"

"Nothing until the children's safety is assured," she said.

"And after?"

"I shall return to Florence with a high-powered rifle," she said. "I shall ascertain the sisters' location, and end their existence from afar."

"I figured it was something like that," Pete said.

"They represent no greater threat to the future than any other ill-led gang, so I don't do this for the future, but for myself," she said. "It is revenge, cold and simple, and that is why I will undertake it alone."

"How will you find them?" Pete asked.

"Hopefully through questioning one of their foot-soldiers," she said. "Failing that, I will follow their vehicle tracks, though I have a suspicion where I might find them. They planned for a nuclear apocalypse, where the northern hemisphere would be a ruin, and their future power would come through control of the Caribbean and the Panama Canal. Their preparations in the United States, with Pruitt, with Indiana, and with the jails, was for if the devastation was not so severe as assumed. After the outbreak, they decided to turn the plan on its head and claim the far richer prize of America. On the shores of Lake Michigan, just north of the border with Wisconsin, and north of Green Bay, Pruitt set up a scientific preserve. Some of that land was given over to a forensic body farm, some to agricultural, aqua-cultural, or arboreal pursuits. It seemed an odd thing for her to do, though now I believe we know why. I imagine that is where the sisters went after the outbreak. They may have moved, of course, but it will have been to somewhere between Lake Michigan and Florence."

Pete closed the van's door. "You don't have to go searching for them," he said. "I won't try to talk you out of it, but you really don't have to."

"I do, in the same way you had to board my plane the moment I told you the location of your sister."

He let it go, raising a hand to wave at Abraham who was finishing his morning patrol of the wire.

"You're clear," Abraham called. "Two zoms at the far side. I'll deal with them when you've gone."

"Which I think means we should leave," Lisa said.

"I'll grab Olivia."

Lisa drove. Olivia tried the radio. Pete watched the passenger mirror as the compound, then Sidnaw, disappeared behind them. The road ahead was monotonous, and little different to what he and Olivia had seen while cycling south the previous day. Abandoned cars, looted homes, stray zombies staggering out onto the road ahead, and behind them. Flooded roads and swampy yards through which the van skidded to avoid large groups of the undead.

At Covington, they turned north, and it was then Pete noted something he'd been looking at without seeing. Like with the stretch of road near the plane, the vehicles here had mostly been pushed to the roadside by some very heavy machine. Not always, but often enough to suggest that at least one large vehicle had driven these roads after the exodus of the local population.

As they approached L'Anse, the abandoned cars grew more numerous, but here, too, they'd been shunted off the road by something far heavier than the electric van. The vehicles grew more numerous still, with two artificially narrow lanes becoming one, then none when they reached a professional roadblock.

Cars had been upturned, then stacked on their sides in a long line that ran across a junction from one corner house to another. In front was a line of cars, parked so as to act as a support for the metal wall. Behind, indicating how this work had been completed, was a crane, its hooked cable swinging gently in the rising wind.

"Can anyone see any people?" Olivia asked, leaning forward in her seat.

"Not in the houses, not on the roofs," Pete said. "Where are we?"

"Just outside L'Anse," Lisa said. "The lake is directly ahead, though still a mile or so distant."

"Too far to hear the waves," Pete said. "Pretty sure I can hear something, though. I'll go check."

As he opened the door, the sound became more distinct. A soft roar, not like waves, and not like anything else he'd ever heard. Instinct told him not to stray too far from his best means of escape, so he pulled himself up to the van's roof. He couldn't see immediately behind the wall, but he could see the road fifty metres beyond. Rather, he couldn't see the road at all.

"Zoms," he whispered, dropping back to the cab. "Hundreds of them, just the other side of the barrier." As quietly as he could, he pulled the door closed. The car-barricade shuddered and shook. Lisa put the van into reverse.

"Take us west," Olivia said. "At the next junction, go west. We don't want to lead them back to Sidnaw."

One detour led to another, and then to a halt when they came to five cars abandoned in the middle of a nowhere-junction. Two of the vehicles had crashed, while the others were almost parked.

"Why are we stopping?" Olivia asked.

"Because of the zombie in the driver's seat of that red SUV," Lisa said. "I doubt the undead remembered how to drive. In which case, the driver fled while infected, stopped to die, and we'll find fuel in the tank."

"Wait," Pete said, checking the mirror. But the road behind appeared empty. "Okay, I guess."

"How many do you think you saw behind that barricade in L'Anse?" Olivia asked, following him out of the van.

"I could see hundreds, so it must have been thousands," Pete said. "Maybe the Canadians set up L'Anse as a refuge from which they were running an evacuation of the U.S. After the bombs, they used the town to run an evacuation of Canada."

"Or those refugees were trapped there while waiting for an evacuation ship which never came," Lisa said. "Regardless, we still need fuel."

Pete followed Olivia towards the wrecked car, tapping the spear on the ground, watching for peripheral movement that would betray the presence of more of the undead. "Think it's just one," he said, raising the spear. The zombie extended its neck, snapping its mouth through the window towards him as he braced the spear point on its cheek, before lancing the point forward, into the zombie's brain.

"Yep, just one," Olivia said.

Lisa brought over a rag, hosepipe, and wooden peg. A minute later, gasoline was dribbling into the can. A lot less than a minute after that, the trickle had ceased.

"That's it?" Pete asked, holding up the rag. "I haven't finished cleaning the spear."

"About an inch," Olivia said. "Yep, that's it."

At the next cluster of stopped cars, it took less than a minute to confirm all eight had their fuel caps open.

"Did you see all the bags in the back?" Pete asked. "There must be some food in there."

"I wouldn't bet on it," Olivia said. "And I wouldn't touch it."

"No, but someone took the fuel, but not the food," Pete said.

"It speaks poorly for our hopes of finding sufficient supplies around here," Lisa said. "This raises the question of our next destination, and at what point we return to Sidnaw."

"Let's try going north again," Olivia said. "If we find more zoms and more barricades, we know we've got to head straight for Duluth, and I'm inclined to say we should leave Sidnaw before dusk."

They began angling northwards, occasionally spying a car with a resident zombie, but they didn't stop until they came to another car-barricade, except this one had already been torn apart.

Lisa stopped. "The road sign said this was Baraga."

"Found it," Olivia said, tapping the map. "We're north of L'Anse. It's on the other side of Keweenaw Bay."

"How far?" Pete asked.

"About five miles in a straight line, but only if you can swim."

"Then we are unlikely to find anything here," Lisa said. "However, we *are* here, and it is less than an hour since we left the compound. If we return now, we will leave today, and make camp tonight somewhere on the outskirts of Duluth."

"We'll have to do that anyway," Olivia said. "But that wall was broken by something big driving out. Maybe they came from Canada, and maybe they left a map behind telling us not to go to Thunder Bay. I think we should check."

"And give Corrie a bit longer to fuel up some cars," Pete said.

They drove slowly into the town, past solitary homes with boarded windows. Where houses and stores were clustered close together, they were ringed with felled-tree walls, surrounded by a brush-and-branch moat. Each had become a fortress unto itself, though all were now abandoned.

"Reminds me of Canada," Pete said.

"So do the flags," Olivia said. "There. See. Oh, it's hidden by the trees, but I saw a maple leaf and a stars and stripes. The Canadians *did* come here. But was it before the bombs, or afterwards?"

"I see a zombie," Pete said. "Behind us now. Side road. Only one."

"How far do you want me to drive?" Lisa asked.

"Until we see water," Olivia said. "Then we'll turn around. Then... yeah, we'll leave today. We'll decant the fuel from the plane, and see if we can get to the outskirts of Duluth. At least we'll be far away from the cartel."

When they reached the lake, in a moment as profound as in Florence, their plans changed again. At the marina, moored to the seawall, was a forty-five-metre-long ferry with an ice-blue hull and snow-white superstructure.

Chapter 54 - The Voyage of the Voyager
Baraga, Michigan

Lisa stopped the van on the slipway. "We have company," she said. "Two undead, twenty metres away, behind those shipping containers."

"Turn the van," Pete said, opening the door. "We need to be ready to leave."

Olivia followed him outside, spear tip low to the ground.

The two zombies staggered around the edge of the shipping container. Their clothing had been reduced to tattered rags, while their skin was a patchwork of charred flesh and mud. One was tall, the other was short, and neither had been recently turned. Otherwise, it was difficult to discern anything about the people they'd been.

"Bet someone tried a gasoline bomb on them," Olivia murmured, drawing her arm back.

"I was just thinking that," Pete said, taking a step sideways so his backswing didn't accidentally hit his wife.

"On two," Olivia said. "One."

"Two," Pete said. He stepped forward, swinging the spear low like a scythe into the tall zombie's legs. It staggered forward, but didn't fall. Its charred hands swung in an arc that missed Pete's head as he ducked under, turned, and stabbed the spear forward and up, into the back of the zombie's head. He stepped back as Olivia threw. Her spear soared through the air, quickly crossing the few metres distance, and slamming into, and through, the smaller zombie's neck. The weight of the spear caused it to fall.

"I didn't think of that," Pete said, stabbing his own spear down into the twitching zombie's eye.

"Well, it *is* a spear," she said. "But I need a bit more practice."

"We need pikes," Pete said.

"What are those weighted balls connected by a bit of rope called?" Olivia asked, pulling her spear free. "We need those. Or trip wires. Or just a whole lot more bullets."

Lisa, having turned the truck, had climbed up onto the cab's roof. "I believe we are alone," she said, jumping back down. "Or sufficiently so we can safely inspect this ship. Shall we?"

Scraps of sail floated on the water's surface, and a few severed ropes were tied to the quay, but there were no other boats in the harbour, except for the large ship tied to the seawall.

"The waters closer to shore must be too shallow for such a large ship to dock at the quay," Lisa said. "Thus, the captain knew this harbour well, and this ship can't have been here long."

"She's called the *Voyager IV*," Olivia said. "Nice to see this boat was continuing the family tradition its great-grandma began. Ships live a long time, don't they, so maybe the *Voyager I* was just a hollowed-out canoe."

"Looks like a decently thick hull," Pete said. "Lots of portholes. Some seats on deck. I think it's a passenger ferry."

They stopped at the end of the seawall, and opposite the on-deck gate in the ship's rail. The gate was closed, and there was no ramp bridging the gap, but there were two loose ropes, either side of the gate, running to the seawall's rail. Four sturdier ropes secured the ship at aft and stern.

"Looks like we've got to jump," Pete said.

"Then jump we shall," Lisa said, holstering her sidearm.

"No, me first," Olivia said. "Move back." She leaped as the ship rose, and slammed heavily into the closed gate. Time stretched while she caught her breath, but she hauled herself over the gate, and onto the deck. "Clear," she said, swinging the gate open.

It was an easier jump for Lisa, and easy enough for Pete.

"Now what?" he asked. "Start with the cockpit?"

"Start by looking for bloodstains, bullet holes, and bones," Lisa said.

"It's a National Parks ferry," Olivia said, tapping a sign affixed to the deck. "I guess that means it didn't usually cross the border."

"I'm sure it will be capable of doing so," Lisa said. "Though that will depend upon the state of the engines."

"You want to sail to Canada?" Pete asked.

"Don't you?" Lisa asked. "This ship can't have been here long. We need to ascertain who its last passengers were, where they went, and when. More important still is whether there's fuel aboard. Can we sail this ship, and, morally, can we steal her?"

"Morally? Absolutely," Pete said, though doubt crept in when he saw inside.

A year ago, the *Voyager IV* had been a cross-lake passenger ferry. More recently, it had been a school. The interior was decorated with children's drawings, mostly in crayon, and mostly of ships, sunsets, and seas. If any of the kids had drawn a more accurate representation of their new world, it hadn't been pinned to the walls. More recently still, the main passenger cabin, with its long rows of seats, had become a dumping ground for supplies left behind by those who'd brought the ship to this remote lakeshore.

"Shoes. Books. Screwdrivers," Olivia said, sifting through the debris, until she found a bag. "Underwear, still sealed in plastic. That's all that's in here." She put the bag on a seat.

"I've got a bag of soap here," Pete said. "Bars, all identical, at least fifty."

"They had too much to carry," Lisa said. "I shall look for a logbook in the cockpit. May I suggest you continue your search of this deck?"

"It's never wise to split up," Olivia said.

"We don't have time for caution," Lisa said. "Not when we might be aboard our salvation."

Pete drew his pistol. "Gunshot means trouble," he said.

"When has that ever not been the case?" Lisa said.

"How old do you think these kids were?" Olivia asked Pete as the couple moved down a broad corridor signposted as bathrooms.

"About the same age as ours," Pete said. "But if they thought they were going to come back here, they'd have left someone to guard the ship."

"No, I'm not thinking about that," she said. "Well, I kinda am. We better check these bathrooms."

He nudged the door with his boot. Inside was dark, so he turned on his flashlight, knocked it against the wall, then listened for an undead reply. "Clear," he said, ducking low to shine the light beneath the stalls. "Not clean, but it's clear. What was that about the kids' ages?"

"They triaged their supplies, offloading for weight," she said. "I think that means they won't come back. But does it mean we should come here?"

"It's further from Florence," Pete said.

"But closer to L'Anse, and not really any nearer to Duluth," Olivia said.

At the rear of the ship was another large passenger cabin, though this had a small galley-bar, against which a pirate leaned.

"Where did you find that hat?" Olivia asked.

"On the bridge," Lisa said, taking off the black felt bicorn with the white skull and crossbones motif. "I believe I would have liked the teacher who ran this school. That's what it was, according to the log on the bridge. Before the outbreak, it was a ferry used as an occasional icebreaker during the winter months to bring provisions to the more remote island settlements. After Manhattan, and after the ferry brought refugees to Thunder Bay, it was seized by General Yoon, and converted into a floating school. More recently, it was seized by some Americans who wished to cross the lake and head home."

"How recently?" Olivia asked.

"Between one and four weeks ago," Lisa said. "I've yet to find a date, so I've had to infer, but considering the precarious mooring, I would say closer to one week than later."

"Which brings us to the all-important question," Pete said. "Are they coming back?"

"Is that really the *most* important question?" Lisa asked. "But no, I don't think they will return. The teacher's original cohort of children were transferred to Vancouver just before the bombs fell. She was from Texas, and had got to know a few soldier-refugees from the most southerly states. In turn, they had met a few others, and so on. Together, they claimed the ship. Those who didn't wish to travel with them were offloaded. There is then talk of an island, of gathering supplies, of listening on the radio for messages, and so on. Ultimately, they found themselves running low on diesel. They had gasoline, however, and so decided to use it to drive south, thinking that would be safer."

"They went home?" Pete asked.

"I would say they drove *towards* Texas," Lisa said. "Which does bring us to the most important question, the answer to which is no, there is almost no fuel aboard."

"Pity," Pete said.

"Not especially," Lisa said. "We have the kerosene in the plane, and the sixty gallons you found yesterday. We can look for more here, or we can use the van to search nearby."

"If today is anything to go by, we won't find much," Pete said.

"I saw a fish outside," Lisa said. "In the *fresh water* lake. The toilet cisterns can be filled by hand. There's a small shower down in the engine room, again with a water tank which can be fed by hand. We will have a queue all day long, but it *is* a shower."

"Wouldn't the outflow be immediately outside the ship, from which we'd be drawing water and catching fish?" Olivia asked.

"This is not a problem if we move," Lisa said. "And we don't need to move far, not if we can find a sailing boat. We can anchor this ship in a remote bay which doesn't have road access, then use a sailing boat to scout for fuel and fish. We can sail a little further to look for vehicles on the northern shore. General Yoon was evacuating people by ship from the east *to* Thunder Bay. Where they boarded the ships, we will find their vehicles. I'm uncertain as to Thunder Bay's fate, though my initial reading of that log was that it was no better than anywhere else, but perhaps we can find vehicles there. Aboard, while we search, we will have food, water, and some basic comforts, and we will have security."

"As long as we have fuel and some working engines," Pete said.

"Let's do it," Olivia said. "We can get away from the cartel, and when we're on the other side of the lake, the two of us can drive off to Pine Dock. We can see if there's anyone still there before we bring the kids. We can even leave a message there for Tess and Doc Flo, and go back later in the summer to see if there's been a reply. Oh, Pete, we have to. It might not be permanent, but nowhere is."

"What if the engines don't work?" Pete asked.

"We can't test them now, due to the noise," Lisa said. "But they must have worked a week ago. There is no reason they wouldn't work still. If they don't, though, we are still further away from Sidnaw."

"We'll put it to a vote," Pete said. "Not here," he added. "I mean we'll see what Abraham and Aqsa say, though I can guess what that'll be. It's still early. Should we check the rest of the ship for zoms?"

"I can't imagine how a zombie could have found its way aboard," Lisa said.

"This upper deck seems safe," Olivia said. "Let's bring the kids here and do a proper search of below decks afterwards. It's still early. We could probably get the kids up here today, but I'd like to spend a bit of time checking some other vehicles on the way back. We'll have to return by a different route, so maybe we'll get lucky, and find enough diesel to get us all the way to Canada tonight."

"How much trouble are we in?" Abraham asked, as Pete jumped out of the van.

"None," Pete said. "Oh," he added as he saw the front of the van. "That was zoms. We stopped to check out twenty or so cars parked by a house. A pack of about a hundred lurched onto the road. Didn't realise the damage was so bad, but the engine sounds fine."

"Did you get much fuel?" Abraham asked.

"Better. We found a ship," Lisa said. "And we think we should relocate there this afternoon."

"Not until Corrie returns with the cars," Abraham said. "Tell me about this ship."

"You do that, we'll go help Corrie," Pete said.

"Let's put the van on to charge, first," Olivia said. "Wow, we're really going to need to give it a clean."

With a new spear in hand, he and Olivia went to find Corrie, though Rufus found them first. The dog darted out to meet them, before leading them back to an open garage where Aqsa and Sally stood guard, while John and Corrie changed a tyre.

"You're back early," Corrie said.

"How close are you to being finished?" Pete asked.

"Why, is there trouble?" Corrie asked.

"We found a ship," Olivia said, and quickly explained.

"We could sail to Canada?" John asked.

"Yes, once we find more fuel," Olivia said.

"We've got six vehicles," Corrie said.

"That's good," Olivia said. "We'll only need five if we're taking the van."

"You haven't seen them yet," Corrie said. "Two SUVs and four pickups, and this is the largest of them."

Pete took in the rusted blue beast. The cab had space for two people sitting behind the driver, but not if one of them was John.

"We'll have to ride in the back," Olivia said.

"Not you," Corrie said. "You'll be driving. So it'll be the kids in the back."

"Me and Sally, we can drive," John said.

"Even then, most of the kids are going to ride in the open," Corrie said.

"Can we rig some walls to the rear of the pickups?" Pete asked.

"Maybe," Corrie said. "Plus, we've still got all our gear to carry."

"We found some gasoline," Olivia said. "Are there any gas-powered vehicles which are larger?"

"Not that I've seen," Corrie said. "How much more time should we spend looking?"

"None," Pete said. "Let's get these back to the compound and figure it out."

Pete stood alone in the gathering dark, watching the undead approach the fence. Fifteen, so far. They'd appeared as they'd driven the second trio of cars back to the compound, but had surely been following the sound of the first three. Above, the sky had grown artificially black, though the storm had yet to break. Was the impeding tempest the omen, or was it the undead? Either way, the weather would be worse for that ship on the lake. There was nothing he could do about that, so he just lined up the spear, and waited for the zombie to lurch close enough to strike.

As he killed his eighteenth, the rain began to fall. Heavy droplets, large and cold. He stood a moment longer, while visibility dropped further, and the rain fell heavier, pattering on the new corpses lying outside.

"You're wet," Princess said, when he entered the garage where Corrie and Abraham were working.

"Rain can have that effect," Pete said. "Need a hand?"

"Nope," Abraham said. "Go dry off. Get some food. Get yourself packed."

"Have we reached a decision?" Pete asked.

"We're leaving tomorrow," Abraham said. "We're all travelling together. So we've got to finish adding some walls to the trucks."

"You're distracting them," Princess said. She had her bag with her, so wasn't there just for the company, but out of anxiety.

That same anxiety was worn on Olivia's face when Pete ran into her at the doors to the office building.

"Is there trouble?" Pete asked.

"Absolutely," Olivia said. "But no, not really. Lisa's telling her life story, though she's framing it as a fairy tale. Aqsa's packing up the store room."

"I didn't think we'd have room for much."

"No, but we might risk a second trip back here for supplies," Olivia said. "We decided, or Abraham did, that we'll make one trip, all of us together. People take priority. We'll fill all the extra space with food. But depending on how the journey goes, maybe we'll come back with the van to pick up the rest of the pantry." She looked behind her, down the dim corridor lit by a sole hanging flashlight. "I don't think we *will* come back. I think we *should*. It'll use up fuel, of course, and be dangerous driving down roads full of woken zoms, but we won't find much food in some remote house up on the peninsula."

"We won't catch much fish until we find a rod," he said.

"Exactly. I was thinking about the trouble we had in Thunderbolt, and there we had Tess and Clyde, and the sailors nearby. Here, we've got kids. It'll be twice as dangerous for them, twice as terrifying for us."

"But even if we brought all the food, it won't last us long," Pete said. "Fish has to be the answer. We'll find some rods in Baraga before we leave."

"And we'll have to empty the trucks' fuel tanks," she said. "That's how we'll be transporting a lot of the diesel. Assuming the ship hasn't been sunk by this storm."

"I was worrying about that," Pete said. The world went briefly bright as lightning speared through the sky. "That was close."

"We never collected the kerosene from the plane," she said, "so watch for the bang."

"Can we use that in a ship, do you think?"

"Corrie said there wasn't enough left in the plane for it to be worth the risk. We'll take four pickups, one SUV, and the van."

"We're taking the electric van?"

"It's got enough charge," Olivia said. "And we'll take the charging point, and the solar panels. Because if the ship has been sunk by this storm, or if the engines don't work, we can use the van to drive around looking for fuel. It'll be quieter than a truck."

"I had to kill eighteen zoms by the fence," Pete said. "They were summoned by the combustion engines, but that van wasn't as quiet as a whisper."

"I know," Olivia said. "If the ship is there, it won't be better than this. There'll be nowhere to run around, and a lot of seasickness if the weather's like this. We'll have flushing toilets, but no paper. We'll have a shower, but no way to launder towels. It gets us away from the cartel, but they don't have a monopoly on violence. We don't know who we'll meet in Canada, assuming we ever get that far."

"We'll make it work," Pete said.

"I know. But this is only the beginning of the journey," she said. "I just so wish we could have begun it this afternoon."

29th April

Chapter 55 - Waiting on the Weather
Sidnaw, Michigan

Pete wasn't woken by the storm, but only because he'd barely slept. He could blame the thunder crash and lightning flash, but they were just a proxy for his fears of what the next few hours could bring. At three, and hearing footsteps outside, he went down to the cafeteria. There he found a small pack of younger children, and Sally, checking their previously packed bags.

"Where's Abraham?" Pete asked, as the tap-thud-tap of his crutches usually came soon after the patter of feet in the corridor.

"Still working on the trucks," Sally said. "Missy Lisa's helping."

Pete nodded. "I guess if they needed our assistance, they'd ask for it."

"You think *those* two would ever ask for help?" Sally asked.

"Good point. Fetch some of those blue cleaning cloths from the storeroom," Pete said. "Clean ones," he added. "Bring a box. I'll check the bags. If everything's there, I'll tie a cloth to the top, and we'll take it over to the corner. When we've done all of them, we'll cook up all the food we can."

He picked the most anxious child to begin with; a ten-year-old called Kyle who'd lost his parents in Chicago. The neighbours who'd rescued him had died on the journey west. Captain Stahl had found him some fifty miles to the east. His story was far from unique among the children, and far from the most horrific.

"One change of clothes," Pete said, moving the disordered items into a neat pile. "Soap, toothbrush, toothpaste, and two bandages. One book. *Truckers*? Good choice. One can of fruit. One can of stew. *No* cans of pink ham." That got a nervous chuckle. "One water bottle. One blanket. One hammer. A can opener, flashlight, and a waterproof coat. Pencil. Paper. Spare batteries. And a giraffe. Cool. How are your shoes?"

"Fine."

"Let's see. Great. So let's get this all back in the bag," Pete said, carefully repacking the bag. It all fit. Just. "Now put it on. Let's check it's not too heavy. Great. So we'll tie a cloth to that, and call it done. Who's next?"

It didn't amount to a great wealth of worldly possessions. There had been a lot of supplies left aboard that ship, so the clothes and soap could be replaced with a few more cans of food. But food alone wouldn't save this child, nor the many others like him. Better they maintain this thinnest veneer of normality for as long as they could.

It didn't take long to check the other children's bags. Leaving Sally to supervise breakfast with half the children, and setting the others to tidy the cafeteria as busy-work, he went outside. The thunder and lightning had ceased, but the rain still fell. Though it was less heavy than last night, it was pooling into a swamp to the left of the gates. Checking those were still closed, he followed the lights to the garage where Abraham and Lisa were inspecting the pickups.

"Great job," Pete said.

"It's not," Abraham said. "We've got four walls, but no roof. Walls ain't that high, neither."

"They are higher than a zombie can reach," Lisa said.

Rusty corrugated steel sheets had been bolted to the inside of each truck's bed, with a metal support pole for extra rigidity running diagonally to the opposite side.

"Where did you find the corrugated sheets?" Pete asked.

"Behind that server building," Abraham said. "Still raining out there?"

"It's easing," Pete said.

"Good," Abraham said. "We'll carry most of the fuel in the tanks, and will syphon it when we arrive. The older kids will ride in the front, so they can get out to fight if they have to. Younger ones, they'll be stuck in the back. I'll promote one older kid to NCO in charge of the others, but it's not going to be a fun drive for anyone."

"It will be a short one," Lisa said.

"About a third of the kids are already up," Pete said.

"Figured they might be," Abraham said. "What about the zoms?"

"Two outside that I could see," Pete said. "I was going to wait until light before dealing with them. You two should get some rest."

"Plenty of time for that when we're on the ship," Abraham said. "I want to load up the spears and tools, and other bulk supplies. It won't take long. We can't bring many."

"Then I'll go keep the kids quiet," Pete said.

Breakfast came, breakfast went, and still the rain fell. By nine, they'd taken the bags to the garage, allocating each, and so each child, to a vehicle. And still the rain fell.

He and Olivia trekked out to the fence to kill the zombies that had arrived during the night, though there were only three around the entire perimeter. This time, they didn't bother moving the bodies to the graveyard. When they returned to the office building, they found Abraham waiting by the doors.

"We'll wait until two," he declared. "If the rain hasn't stopped, we'll leave anyway."

"You should get some sleep," Olivia said.

"Never could sleep during the day," Abraham said. "Reminds me too much of the hospital. You'd sleep during the day because there was nothing much to do, but then you'd be awake at night, and be alone with your thoughts. No, better to keep active. What about the plane?"

"No way it can fly in this weather," Pete said.

"I was talking about the fuel," Abraham said.

"It's too dangerous," Olivia said. "I slipped in the mud when killing those zombies earlier, but I had the fence between me and them. There'll be enough fighting out in the open when we get to Baraga. If you won't sleep, at least sit down for a bit. If you do that, maybe the kids will, too."

Abraham grunted, but limped away.

"He's worried," Pete said. "But so am I."

"For us, it's the waiting," she said. "For him, it's that the waiting is finally over, but the destination is as fraught with danger as here. I think the sky might be brightening a bit, there in the south."

They watched the clouds for a minute. Another.

"Maybe," Pete said.

"Great. Time for one last meal," Olivia said.

The deluge dropped to a drizzle, and Pete began a patrol of the fence, but quickly gave up and returned to the gates. The zombies along the perimeter were unlikely to be a problem. On the track leading to the highway, though, were three. He made his way inside the fence, squelching through the sodden, well-trodden mud, dreaming of dry boots.

"Over here, then," he called, tapping the spear against the wire.

He didn't like talking to the undead. It seemed wrong, in so many ways, and always left him wondering what he'd do if one ever replied. This one didn't. It pawed at the fence, nearly tugging its fingers off as they caught in the chain link. The rain had rinsed streaks into the mud on its face, giving it a near camouflaged look, offset by the bright blue waterproof, shredded front and back during the attack which surely must have caused infection. Pete aimed, and thrust, twisting the spear up as the zombie fell, letting gravity free the body from the weapon.

"C'mon," he called to the other two. "Let's get this over with."

And it was over, in only a few minutes, and so was the storm. The sky truly was brightening now as the sun barged through the clouds. There was even a little warmth in the rays, a harbinger of the summer about to begin.

It was an omen, he decided. A portent of better things to come. He made his way back to the gates, and then back into the compound, just as Sally came running out. Rufus quickly overtook her, splashing to a halt in one of the deeper puddles.

"You're worse than the kids," Pete said, before turning to Sally. "Is there trouble?"

"I was going to ask you that," she said. "And if you wanted any lunch."

"I think I'm done with pink ham," he said.

"Missy Lisa wanted to know whether we're still leaving at two."

"I'd say so," Pete said. "What did Abraham say?"

"He's asleep," Sally said.

"Good. He needs it. In a few hours, the roads will be a bit dryer. Let's get the trucks out front, and we can get the kids aboard."

Rufus darted towards the gate.

"What is it?" Pete asked, following the hound. He heard it a moment later. "Engines!" he called. "Sally, warn the others. Keep the kids inside."

As the sound grew nearer, it became easier to identify. Two engines. Two cars. His first thought was Yollie and her people, finally returning from their jaunt east. Would he allow them to join the exodus, or leave them with the compound and its last supplies? As much as their betrayal infuriated him, it was no real choice. They needed drivers. They needed adults.

The vehicles drove into view, travelling slower than the weather demanded. The first was a sheriff's car from Elkhart County. The second was a black Humvee with a mud-covered crest on the side. Not a military vehicle, but perhaps used by a different government agency. The sheriff's car drove up to the gate. The Humvee stopped a length behind.

"Howdy!" the driver said, as he climbed out. "Captain John Abernathy. Looks like we're in the right place. Mind opening the gate?"

"What do you mean, the right place?" Pete asked.

"I hear there's some kids inside. We're the rescue party," Abernathy said.

Pete nodded, and pulled the outer gate open, before walking to the middle gate. They weren't ever actually locked, just pulled closed and latched, so there was no point pretending they would actually keep these people out. Three in the cop car, including Abernathy, probably the same again in the Humvee. From what he could see of the passengers in the sheriff's car, they were dressed in civilian gear, though with police-issue vests. He could see a couple of long-arms, too, in addition to the handgun on Abernathy's hip.

"Who told you about this place?" Pete asked.

"Word got passed from one person to another," Abernathy said. "You know how it goes?"

Pete tugged the last gate open. "We've just finished lunch," he said. "But I'm sure there was some left over."

Abernathy got back into the car, and drove it on, and into the compound. The Humvee followed. Noting the zombie which followed that loud engine, Pete tugged the gate closed. He had his spear, but not a gun since that was with his dry travelling clothes up in their room.

He followed the vehicles inside, now wondering what it was about them that had made him think of his gun. The sheriff's car from Indiana? No, not that. Or not *just* that. If this was a rescue party, where was the bus to carry the kids?

"Are you with the police, or the army?" Pete asked Abernathy as he climbed out of his car. Two passengers got out of his car, another two climbed out of the Humvee.

"These days, is there any difference?" Abernathy asked. "But I was a captain in the South Bend P.D."

"I didn't think South Bend had survived," Pete said, his instincts confirmed.

"In the end, it didn't," Abernathy said. "We turned the University of Notre Dame into a fortress, but had to relocate last month. We'd have come here sooner, but we were still settling into our new base. How are the kids?"

"Who's this?" Abraham called out as he, Aqsa, Rufus, and Lisa came out of the cafeteria.

"They say they're from South Bend," Pete said, hoping the others would understand the inference. "They say they built a fortress out of *Notre Dame*."

"But we had to leave a month ago," Abernathy said. "We've moved to Lake Michigan. Things aren't too bad up there. You guys have an airport here in town?"

"A landing field," Lisa said. "Eliza Keynes," she added. "And it's wonderful to see the police again. Or are you military?"

"A little of both," Abernathy said. "This landing field, where is it?"

"Oh, to the north, but a C-17 crashed months ago. It's unusable," Lisa said. "Let's talk over some tea. Or we have coffee, if you prefer." She raised a hand, pointing towards the garage.

That seemed to be a signal. A shot rang out, a second. Fired from the rooftop. Uncertain what the plan was, Pete tackled Abernathy, pulling the man to the ground. Above and around him, bullets flew, but immediately in front was a fist, which slammed into his face. As they rolled in the mud, Pete punched back, but Abernathy kicked, butted, and jabbed. Whoever he really was, he was a brawler. Pete gave up hitting back and rolled away, across the mud. He jumped to his feet, and realised the shooting was over.

Lisa stood over Abernathy, her gun aimed at his head.

"Clear," Abraham said, from the Humvee. "There's no one in there."

"Rufus was shot!" Aqsa said, kneeling next to him.

"Is he okay?" Pete asked.

"I don't know. He's bleeding," Aqsa said.

"Take him inside," Abraham said.

Pete walked over to the nearest corpse, a woman with a leather holster at her belt, which was worth far more than the cheap revolver she'd not had time to draw. Pete tugged it free, but there was no one to shoot. Slowly, his brain cleared.

"Corrie and Olivia were on the roof?" he asked.

"With the carbines, yes," Lisa said. "Are you okay?"

"Fine," Pete said, taking a step towards Rufus, but Aqsa had picked him up and was carrying him back to the office from where John was already running to meet her. "Yeah, I'm okay."

"Then please relieve him of his gun and knife," Lisa said.

"Why did you shoot? I'm here to help," Abernathy said, as Pete pressed his looted revolver into the man's back while he plucked the knife and sidearm from Abernathy's belt.

"South Bend fell a few days after New York," Pete said as he stepped back. "Notre Dame was burned down by the cartel. How many of these bodies do I need to check before I find a tattoo of a three-leafed branch?"

"My name is Lisa Kempton, I'm sure you're familiar with it."

"No," Abernathy said.

"Bull," Abraham said. "Everyone's heard of her, but you know her for a special reason. You work for the Rosewood Cartel."

Abernathy shook his head.

Lisa shot him in the leg.

Abernathy screamed, rolling over to clutch the wound.

"We don't have time for torture," Lisa said. "Instead, I will make you an offer. That injury will prevent you from outrunning the undead. This defeat will prevent you from returning to the sisters unless you seek a more absolute death. Instead, you may take your car, antibiotics, bandages, and food, and drive wherever you wish. We'll give you sufficient supplies to last until your leg has healed, and the sisters have forgotten about you. This is the best offer you will get, because it's an escape from your old life, and a chance to be reborn."

Abernathy rolled into a sitting position, still clutching his leg. He looked from Lisa to Abraham, then to Pete. "Okay," he said.

"Capital," Lisa said. "Before we begin, understand that I know some of the answers to the questions I'll ask, and so if I believe you are lying, and so your information is worthless, I will shoot you. Where did you really come from?"

"Near Lake Michigan," he said. "Michigan State. Just north of the border with Wisconsin. There's a tract of land the state owns, and where they operated some scientific research places. Nothing to do with the undead," he added.

"A location arranged by Governor Pruitt," Lisa said. "I think I might now know why she fled her state at the beginning of the outbreak."

"I don't know anything about that," Abernathy said.

"Were you really a cop in South Bend?" Pete asked.

"I was," he said. "I was just a cop."

"So how did you end up working for the cartel?" Pete asked.

Abernathy shook his head. "Gambling," he said. "I could never pick a winner."

"And?" Lisa prompted. "Do please remember there is a limit to how much blood anyone can lose."

"You know who runs the cartel?" Abernathy asked.

"The Herrera sisters, yes," Lisa said.

"They have a nephew," Abernathy said. "They wanted him to learn a trade. They sent him to be a cop, and told him to work his way up. I just had to keep an eye on him, keep him out of trouble, but then the world blew up. There was a rendezvous in Michigan. The nephew never arrived. His aunt did."

"The sisters?" Lisa asked.

"Just one," Abernathy said. "Margalotta. She said her sister was dead."

"That's wonderful news," Lisa said. "And why are you here?"

"For the airfield. We heard there was a C-17 here."

"It's in pieces," Lisa said. "Both the plane, and the landing field. Why do you want a plane?"

"There's a redoubt in Colombia, an underground storehouse with enough supplies to last a century. That's where we're heading."

Pete laughed. "Sorry. Sorry," he said. "I almost wish there was a plane to take Herrera there, just so someone could get a photo of her face when she lands."

"The mine in Colombia was blown up," Lisa said. "Her people have been eradicated."

Abernathy nodded. "Figured as much. I *am* a cop. *Just* a cop. I don't like these people, but sometimes you have to do bad things to stop something worse."

"Oh, I wholeheartedly agree," Lisa said. "You are looking for a plane. You heard of Sidnaw from prisoners, yes?"

"Yes," he said.

"They told you that there was a compound containing their children, and an airfield nearby?" Lisa asked.

"Not *their* children," Abernathy said. "We heard about this place from two guys, two women, in a car. About five days ago."

"Yollie," Abraham said. "What happened to those four?"

"What do you think?" Abernathy said.

"If you found no plane here, what were you instructed to do next?" Lisa asked.

"We were to drive on to Duluth," he said. "Look for a plane and runway there."

"And then what?" Lisa asked.

"Pick up a tank from a place called Florence," Abernathy said. "We figured that'd give us a fighting chance against the undead."

"Then I believe I have the answers to all my questions," Lisa said. She fired, shooting Abernathy in the head.

"Lisa!" Pete said.

"Oh, I do apologise, did you want to ask him something more?"

"I… I guess not," Pete said, looking down at the corpse. "I better go check on Rufus."

"Not until we figure out what we're doing next," Abraham said.

Corrie jogged out of the office, Sally at her side.

"More trouble?" Pete asked.

"I don't think so," Corrie said. "Couldn't see any from the roof."

"How's Rufus?"

"The bullet gouged his side," Corrie said. "John's holding him, Aqsa's shaving him, and Olivia's trying to keep him calm so the cut can be cleaned and glued. I don't know if it's damaged any muscles or tendons, but we're going to have to sedate and stitch him, and then keep him docile until it's healed."

"We've got to get to the ship," Abraham said.

"Agreed," Corrie said. "I saw you talking to him. Did he tell you anything?"

"He connected a few dots," Lisa said.

"She can fill you in when we're on the ship," Abraham said. "The Humvee's diesel, and it's got a nearly full tank, which is bigger than that SUV's. I think we should take that with us as our lead vehicle. Any objections? Sally, grab a squad, and get the SUV unloaded, and the fuel out of the tank. Go on, now. Quick."

"Yollie told them about us, about this place," Pete said after Sally had run off. "That's how they knew."

"Another point of discussion when we're aboard the ship," Lisa said. "Gather up the guns and ammo, and then empty that car of anything we can use. You should leave immediately. But I am going to Florence."

"Want to share why?" Abraham asked.

"Because the tank at that school is Margalotta's backup plan," Lisa said. "In many ways, it would have been better if they'd had a working plane here. If she flew to Colombia, we would know her fate was sealed. But with a tank, she is unlikely to reach the southern border. Oh, I can hope the zombies will get her, or she will succumb to radiation or starvation, or even to mutiny. Until then, she will continue to rain misery upon our bleak world."

"But why go to Florence?" Abraham asked.

"I'll blow up the school," Lisa said. "There are shells there, yes? Those are easily turned into a mine. No shells, no tank, no bullets. No escape for this most vile creature."

"Sounds good," Abraham said. "Except you've forgotten we need six drivers."

Lisa walked over to the sheriff's car, and plucked a carbine from the back. "An M4. With a full magazine. There are three more on the seat. And… ah." She opened a bag. "Another four magazines in here, along with some magazines for a nine-millimetre pistol. John or Sally can take my place as driver. Should you get into difficulty during that drive, you now have the ammunition to swiftly, and safely, deal with the undead from a distance. You don't need me, but Margalotta must be stopped for the sake of any survivors south of here."

"She's right," Pete said. "Yollie and her friends might not have been the best people, but there's no way that Abernathy or Herrera spent the time to learn that for themselves. If we blow up the school, we'll hasten the end of Herrera. It's the least we can do, and all we can do. So I'll go with Lisa to make sure it's done."

"What did I just say about drivers?" Abraham said.

"That you need six, and you've got John and Sally," Pete said.

"No, this is my fight, Pete," Corrie said. "I'll go with Lisa."

"It's everyone's fight," Pete said. "Besides, we need you to get that ship working. The kids need Abraham and Aqsa, and I can't let Olivia go without me."

"I'm pretty certain she'd say the same thing about you," Corrie said.

"Well, I won't give her the chance," Pete said.

"Enough arguing," Abraham said. "Pete and Lisa can go. That's it. No one else. And you better go now, before anyone gets there before you. And don't go into battle without saying goodbye to your wife.

Made that mistake myself, once. Never got the chance to make the mistake a second time."

He limped away.

"He was married?" Pete asked.

"Take his advice," Lisa said. "Say goodbye to your wife."

"Why does that sound so final?" Pete said, and jogged back inside.

Chapter 56 - Chicken-Wire for the Soul
Florence

It was a hasty departure, for which Pete was glad; there wasn't time for second thoughts. They took the electric van for the journey south, but bicycles for the return journey north. The quieter electric engine should allow them to hear other vehicles as they neared Florence, while the bicycles certainly would during their escape. At dusk, the ship would pull anchor and move into deeper waters. If, as was most likely, he and Lisa didn't reach Baraga in time, they would, tomorrow, head up to the tip of the Keweenaw Peninsula, and signal with Morse. There was no plan for if they got no reply, nor for if the ship's engines didn't work.

"Another one-way mission," Pete said, speeding up so as to outrace a zombie by the woodland's edge.

"Oh, I think not," Lisa said. "Except in that we will never return to Sidnaw. I was never much of a cyclist. I look forward to correcting that oversight."

"You do know how, don't you?" Pete asked.

"Oh, certainly," she said. "The principle, at least. I did ride a motorbike, as much as I never truly enjoyed it."

"The two guards we killed at the school had motorbikes," Pete said. "Maybe those bikes are still in Florence."

"Wonderful," Lisa said. "Though I can't imagine a worse form of transport in our broken world. Mr Guinn, I don't believe I've said it before, but I am very glad to have employed you."

"You didn't really hire me, did you?" Pete said. "It was all a con."

"Then let me say I'm glad to have met you," she said. "I will apologise, too. There was an opportunity some years ago to execute the sisters. I didn't do so because I was persuaded there was a chance to bring them to justice."

"No worries," Pete said, not really listening. He let his hand drop to the newly looted M17 pistol at his hip. In his pocket was another. Next to him was a pump-action shotgun, taken from the back of the sheriff's car. He was better armed than he'd been since Canada, but then he'd been travelling with an army.

"I do worry," Lisa said. "Rather, I can't help but be consumed by regrets. I am concerned that I will gain another in this mission."

"Like I said to Corrie, it's everyone's fight," he said. "If you want to take a lesson from how things turned out, then maybe it's to let other people help. If you'd told the world everything, right from the beginning, maybe that would have stopped all of this."

"I am sad to admit that you might well be correct," she said. "Certainly, nothing I tried worked."

"Let's put a pin in that debate until we're both safe on that ship," Pete said. "But I was serious when I said the kids need you if they're to survive the next few weeks."

"They will need us both," she said.

"Great, so what's the plan?" he asked.

"Park outside. Approach on foot. Start a fire in the school. If the enemy are present in the town, we will cut a way through an unwatched section of fence. Hence the wire cutters and gasoline. Considering the hour, I can't imagine any circumstance in which they will depart today, not when Abernathy might drive on to Duluth."

"So attack at night?" Pete asked. "We better leave the bikes outside of town. I don't want to waste time looking for more tomorrow." He checked the range-gauge, but his experience of driving the van told him it was an optimistic guess. "Might have to cycle the last few miles anyway."

"No matter," Lisa said. "I'm sorry for Rufus."

"He'll be fine," Pete said, leaning forward so as to better concentrate on the road. Ahead, it glistened from where the storm had created a swamp out of two neighbouring fields.

"I should have asked Abernathy why he was so intent on leaving North America," Lisa said.

"Keep your regrets for later," Pete said.

"Oh, they keep me company most nights," she said. "I was wondering whether it might be radiation."

"Let's not worry about that until later, either," Pete said, though he then tried to remember when he'd last looked at the Geiger counter.

To take his mind from that, from what was soon to come, and his own oh-too-many regrets, he focused on the road.

Minimising collisions with the undead kept him occupied for another twenty miles, while the range-guide's sudden descent to zero kept him occupied for another ten. But when a man's voice grumbled a few feet from his ear, he nearly swerved into a tree.

"Work 'em harder," the voice said. "We've got an hour to finish."

"What the heck was that?" Pete said, bringing them back onto the road.

"Apologies," Lisa said, taking a radio from her pocket. "I took this from the sheriff's car. Only one handset, and with quite a short range."

"That was them, you mean?"

"Abernathy's colleagues, the cartel, yes," Lisa said. "We are nearing Florence. It is safe to assume they have reached it before us."

"Keep listening," he said. "But turn the volume down. I'll look for somewhere to park."

He pulled the van off the road while they were still in the outer, unwalled suburbs, parking opposite a fire-damaged elementary school. They'd picked up nothing more on the radio, which he hoped was an indication they'd remained undetected.

The presence of the undead seemed to confirm it. He counted three among the smoke-blackened ruins. As they made their way through the backyards to the south, he nearly tripped over a fourth, crawling out from beneath a raised, and broken, porch. He stamped his heel down on its hand, then its head, pushing the decaying face deep into the mud. He had to slam his boot down again to crack bone, and make the zombie go limp.

"Should have brought a spear," he whispered.

"There's a shovel," Lisa said, pointing to a tool lying next to a tooth-marked ribcage. There were no other bones, suggesting some animal had dragged them away.

"Or a bayonet for the shotgun," he said.

But the backyards soon gave way to a new fence. Beyond, he could make out a running track. Beyond that was the high school.

"That's the school," Pete said, ducking back behind the fence. "Me and Olivia approached from the other side."

Lisa took out the radio, checking the volume was on low before she stood, looked, and lingered too long for Pete's comfort. He tugged on her arm. She ducked low, and held up the radio.

"It seemed a sensible way to see if there was a sniper on the roof," she said.

"Foolhardy," Pete said.

"Yet it appears to have worked," she said.

A window shattered somewhere between them and the elementary school.

"Zoms," Pete said. "We'd be too exposed if we cut the fence here. Let's use the houses as cover, and get closer. See how many we're up against."

They detoured west, and soon found the city's tank wall. The undead were awake behind them, roaming rather than following. Though he could hear them, he couldn't see any yet, nor after he'd sprinted across the road and to a house where the wooden boards hung loose from a broken window. Regretting not having picked up that shovel, he used the shotgun as a lever to pry enough boards free that he could look inside.

"Looks clear," he whispered. "Go on."

"Such a gentleman," she said. She cleared the glass, and climbed inside.

He remained outside a moment longer, listening for the undead. By the time he was inside, she had the radio raised to her ear.

"There's something odd going on," she whispered.

"They've spotted us?" he asked, looking back outside. He saw a zombie, staggering across the road, though not yet heading to the house.

"I think not," she said. "But they don't sound afraid. I don't believe Herrera is here."

"Pity," Pete said.

As he reached the house's front door, he heard a gunshot. Muffled, but clear. He looked to Lisa. She took out the radio, listening for a second before shrugging. "Nothing. But it is hard to hold a rifle and a radio."

"Someone's shooting zoms," Pete said, opening the door a crack, and looking outside. "We'll make for the church. It's not far, and there are so many bodies inside, no one would visit. But there's a fence between there and the school, a fence and a gate."

"Hence the wire-cutters," she said, patting the bag. "I fear we will have to leave our attack until nightfall, though it is possible we have missed our opportunity all together."

On leaving the house, they dashed from one piece of cover to the next, each time pausing to listen and watch. But there were no undead inside the fortress. There were no patrols. From house to tree to fence to house, they ran, undetected. During the stop-start dash, they heard another three shots, but none of the bullets were aimed at them. When the school once again came into sight, it was clear that the sniper wasn't on the roof. When they had a clearer view of the school from behind the church, it was obvious why.

Three army trucks were now parked next to the tank outside the school's main entrance. On the roof of the tank stood the sniper. Pacing behind the trucks was an overseer, gun in one hand, baton in the other with which he swiped at the prisoners, though only after they deposited their heavy crates into the trucks.

Pete counted eighteen prisoners before the emaciated faces began to repeat. Three trucks, so three drivers, meaning there was at least one more slave-driver inside. With eighteen prisoners, he'd bank on there being a lot more than that. But he couldn't see any other vehicles, or Margalotta's up-armoured SUV. This work gang were collecting the shells, and presumably the tank, and it was a job that must surely be close to complete.

"Inbound!" the sniper called out, his words muffled but still clear. "We got a big one coming in!"

"Bet it's hungry," the overseer jeered. "What, don't you care?"

The prisoners began moving more quickly. None were able to run because each had a length of rope or chain around their ankles.

Lisa nudged Pete, then pointed down the road. The outer gate, leading east, was open. About twenty metres further down the road, and on the verge, a prisoner had been tied to a stake, which had then been encased in chicken-wire. The wire had been bound too tight for the prisoner to move, and tight enough a zombie could reach, if not bite, the skin beneath.

The sniper languidly raised his rifle, and turned away before firing. "Missed," he called out.

"Don't you want her to live?" the overseer called. "Or is it you want to be next?" He swiped the baton low, tripping a prisoner who sprawled forward, landing heavily on the school's concrete steps. The overseer swiped the baton again. "Who said you could stop! Who said you could rest!" Each word was followed with a blow until another prisoner reached down, and hauled the injured man to his feet.

The sniper slowly loaded another round, then fired. The zombie fell. "Five yards. Next time, I won't bother."

"Who wants to be next, then?" the overseer barked as the prisoners ran outside, staggering beneath the weight of the crates. "Who's next?"

"Go to the gate," Lisa said, letting her pack fall. "Be the distraction."

Pete nodded. He leaned the shotgun against the wall, unclipped his holster, and repositioned it at the small of his back. He took the other M17 out of his jacket pocket, and slipped off the safety before returning it to his coat. Finally, he walked back around the church, giving it a wide berth as he approached the gate.

Seeking inspiration from the church, as he approached the gate, Pete bellowed, "Have y'all heard the good word?"

That got the attention of both the sniper and the overseer, and a few of the prisoners, though two then hurried back through the doors, and into the school. Pete ignored them, clasping his hands in front as he approached the gate, keeping his eyes on the overseer.

"Just kill 'im," the overseer said.

It was an instruction Lisa followed. He heard a crack, and saw the sniper drop. Pete did the same, falling to a knee as he reached for the gun in his pocket. As he did, one of the prisoners leaped on the overseer, who had made the mistake of turning his back on the detainees. Another prisoner joined the first, and Pete left the gun where it was, and sprinted to the gate. By the time he'd hauled it open, the overseer was down, dying, his own knife embedded deep in his guts. The man who'd stabbed him gave the blade a twist, before pulling it out.

"Thank you," the prisoner said. "There are two more inside."

Pete handed his pocketed pistol to the nearest prisoner before drawing his holstered M17, and running to the door.

As he pushed it open, he heard feet behind him, but didn't look. Instead, he ran inside, and along the hall, raising his gun when he saw a figure running towards him. Pete saw clean clothes, not rags, so he fired. Two shots into the vest, one into the shoulder. The slave-driver staggered sideways, into the wall, then collapsed with a bullet in his brain, fired by the freed prisoner now at Pete's side.

"Two to go," the freed prisoner said.

From deeper inside the school came the sound of gunfire. A burst, cut short. A figure staggered out of a classroom's open door. Pete almost fired, but this woman was covered in blood and mud. He recognised her as being one of the pair who'd rushed inside the moment they'd seen him.

"Johnny?" she asked.

"The cavalry's here," Johnny said. "Did you get them?"

"They're down," she said. "The others?"

"Dead," Johnny said.

"Then we haven't got much time," she said.

"True enough," Pete said. "Let's get out of here."

"No, we've got to disarm the bombs, first," Johnny said.

"What bombs?"

"Son, you don't realise it," Johnny said, "but these people are part of a cartel who had a hand in causing the chaos we're living through. No way were we letting them take these shells or that tank. We set a bomb in the truck, another in the gym."

"Why the gym?" Pete asked.

"That's where most of the supplies are," Johnny said.

There had been eighteen prisoners. Four had died when the last guards had been swarmed, torn apart by a fully automatic burst. But through their sacrifice, the remaining prisoners had got close enough to exact their revenge.

"We knew they were going to kill us," Johnny said to Pete when they all gathered outside. "They've killed everyone else. Worked some to death. Murdered the others. There were hundreds of us. Hundreds of prisoners. Until it was just us. We knew our time had come. They thought staking one of us out to be torn apart would guarantee compliance, but that speaks to their own fears, not ours. No, we were going to jump them, but wanted to set the bombs first. In case."

"Capital," Lisa said. "So perhaps we can reset some of the explosives as we leave. One for the tank, one for that truck, one for the school. There should be enough space in the rear of these two trucks for everyone."

"We didn't think we'd survive," Johnny said.

"No, but you have," Lisa said. "Though that poor woman who was trapped in the chicken-wire cage won't live long unless we can get her some treatment."

"Hang on," Johnny said. "When I said we didn't think we'd survive, I mean we didn't talk about what we'd do if we did. There's the kids to think of."

"The cartel have them prisoner?" Pete asked.

"No, we had to leave them, weeks ago," Johnny said.

The penny dropped, and hard enough to cause concussion. "From Sidnaw?" Pete asked.

"How did you know?" Johnny asked.

"That's where we came from," Pete said, "but the kids are somewhere else, somewhere safe, so let's blow this place up, and we'll take you to them."

Chapter 57 - Storm Cloud
Baraga, Michigan

"Mom!" Sally called, running to the emaciated woman who'd been held captive in the chicken-wire cage.

"Dad? Dad?" John asked, frantically moving from one unwashed freed prisoner to the next.

"John, help Sally!" Abraham said. "Get everyone aboard the ship. Quick, now. Pete, are we in trouble? Were you followed?"

"Only by zoms," Pete said, walking away from the pair of army trucks. He'd parked his next to Lisa's, and she'd parked hers next to the pickups which had been driven from Sidnaw. They'd stopped right at the harbour's edge, but it was still a long hike along the seawall to the ship.

Olivia jumped down from her truck-roof sentry post and jogged over. "Oh, Pete, you don't know how glad I am to see you're okay. You are okay, aren't you?"

"No worries," he said.

"There won't be as long as you promise not to do anything like that again. Who are these people?"

"Prisoners of the cartel," Pete said. "The last of them. They were loading shells and ammo into these trucks down in Florence."

"Did I hear Sally call that woman Mom?" Olivia asked.

"Yep. I think her name's Jenny, or Jennifer. The cartel had caged her inside chicken-wire, and left her out in the open. As long as the others worked, the gangsters shot the approaching zoms."

"I… I don't know what to say to that," she said.

"Yep. Do you see the guy with the beard?" he asked.

She turned around. "That doesn't narrow it down much."

"The guy at the back, talking with Abraham. That's Captain Johnny Stahl."

"As in the soldier who led the parents away in search of fuel?"

"Exactly."

"So these are the kids' parents?"

"Some might be, I'm not sure," Pete said. "There wasn't time to talk before the drive. During it, I was filling Captain Stahl in on the Pacific, and he was filling me in on General Yoon."

"Does he think she's alive?" she asked.

"Sorry, no. He only met her once, a few days after the outbreak. He was running a supply train network to Thunder Bay, moving people west and supplies east. He has a couple of guesses where we might find supplies on the northern shores. He was transferred to running part of the U.S. evacuation just before the bombs fell, and ended up in L'Anse, which is how he ended up in Sidnaw, though I didn't have time to ask how the zoms took over that harbour town."

"How did they get caught?"

"In Florence," Pete said. "Though I didn't get the details of that, either."

"Oh, there'll be time," Olivia said. "Are the cartel following?"

"Nope, but the zoms are," Pete said. "We blew up the school on our way out. Or these survivors did. They'd already set the bombs by the time we arrived. The cartel thought the prisoners were broken, but they weren't. They'd rigged some bombs and were about to attack when we jumped in. Me and Lisa were basically the distraction that ensured victory. Lost a few of them, though."

"But you brought a lot home," Olivia said. "How are they?"

"Emaciated. Exhausted. Traumatised."

"No, sorry, I mean will they be a help, or do they need it?" she asked.

"They all need a meal, and a sleep, a wash, and probably another three meals after that," Pete said. "Give them some time to recover, and they'll be a lot of help. It's exactly who we needed."

Olivia looked around at the ship. "There's a lot of kids on deck," she said. "All looking towards the shore. Looking for their parents, I suppose, since you certainly didn't bring back all of them."

"The other prisoners are all dead," Pete said, turning back to the road. "There were hundreds. There should never have been any. Ah, but we did what we could. How was the drive?"

"Here? Fine," she said. "Slow. We took a short cut down some back roads, and had to backtrack a few times when the roads were blocked. One track was basically washed away. We could probably have forded it, but didn't want to take the risk. We haven't been here very long. We've still got to syphon the trucks, but I'm waiting to hear whether the ship works."

"We still don't know? Right. How's Rufus?"

"Not happy," Olivia said. "We can't stitch his cut without anaesthetic. Whether it would be ethical to use anaesthetic on him, rather than keep it for a person, is a debate I'll keep until we find some, but we do need to search. I've set a squad to read to him, and that seems to be keeping him calm."

"Really, what's the book?" Pete said.

"No, the book is to give the kids something to do while they sit with him. If they keep calm, so will he. That's the theory, and it seems to be working so far. Zom."

"Seen it," Pete said. "Do you have a spare spear?"

Olivia raised her gun. "After the ruckus from all of these engines, there's not much point trying to be quiet." She fired, but the sound of the shot was lost beneath the grumble of an engine.

"That's a good sign," Pete said. The ship went quiet. "I hope it was a good sign."

"Two more inbound," Olivia said. "If the ship's engines work, let's get the diesel out of these trucks, and then get out of here."

"I'll go grab some help," Pete said. He turned towards the ship where Aqsa and Corrie, fuel cans in hand, seemed to be having an argument with Lisa. As he began walking towards them, they began walking towards him, so he waited.

"Is there a problem with the ship?" Pete asked, as his sister approached.

"The hull's as dry as Tibooburra on a Monday morning," Corrie said. "The engines work. I'm ready to take her out into deeper waters. Plus, one of the newcomers, Hannah Stone, used to work a tourist-tour boat on the Mississippi. She worked maintenance above the waterline, but she knew her way around the engine room. She says this ship isn't too dissimilar. We're ready to go."

"Except Lisa wants to leave," Aqsa added.

"What, why?" Pete asked.

"Our shortages are universal," Lisa said. "Most pressing are medicine and food. Either we spend the next two hours searching this harbour town, possibly with no result, or we spend one hour driving back to Sidnaw. We know we can find food, and some very limited medical supplies, in Sidnaw. Limited is better than none."

"We can't go back," Aqsa said.

"Why not?" Lisa said.

"Um, the cartel?" Aqsa said.

"I'm with her," Corrie said.

"The newcomers have not eaten properly in a month," Lisa said. "We will have no food left by midnight. It is all well and good saying we can catch fish in the lake, but without line or net, and at night, I don't hold high hopes for salmon at breakfast. I will take one truck, fill it with food, and return before dark, but only if I leave now."

"Not travelling down the roads we just took," Aqsa said. "I was at the back, and I had nothing but zombies in the rear mirror."

Olivia fired. "Inbound. Three more coming!"

"You won't be able to load up the truck on your own," Corrie said. "I'll go with you."

"No you won't," Pete said. "We need you to prepare the ship. I'll go with Lisa."

"*We'll* go," Olivia said.

Pete didn't give Corrie time to express her unhappiness at being left behind, though it was written across her face as the three of them jumped into one of the army trucks. The shell and ammunition crates rattled across the back as Lisa drove them south.

"Are you trying to hit them?" Pete said, as Lisa winged one, then a second zombie.

"I'm just anxious to get back to the ship," Lisa said. "There was a time I liked driving, but that ended long before the outbreak."

"We've got time, though," Olivia said. "About two days, right? Margalotta's going to wonder where Abernathy is tonight, but won't start looking until tomorrow."

"A point in favour of not letting this task wait," Lisa said, slowing before swerving to avoid one of the undead. "I should confess that I do have an ulterior motive."

"When do you not?" Olivia said. "As long as you understand we're getting the food, and then returning to the ship."

"Absolutely," Lisa said. "During the drive from Florence, I had Ms Stone for a companion in the cab. She told me a most interesting story about why Margalotta is suddenly so desperate to leave Michigan."

"Why?" Pete asked.

"Did Captain Stahl not mention it?" Lisa asked. "Do you recall, as we overflew Indiana, we saw a great mass of the undead?"

"A horde," Olivia said. "Millions of them, big enough to wipe a town from the map."

"There is more than one," Lisa said. "A second formed from among the refugees who flocked to Sault Ste Marie, and found the crossing destroyed. A third emerged from the ruins of Chicago. Margalotta is thus trapped between an anvil and a furnace. She has no choice but to flee."

"How does that tie into this trip back to Sidnaw?" Olivia asked.

"We shall collect the food and bring it back before nightfall," Lisa said. "But I would like to destroy the plane first. Abernathy came looking for a plane, after all. The highway on which the compound is built would be one of the potential routes for Margalotta to take if she were driving east."

"There's no way that plane could possibly take off," Pete said. "Not after that storm."

"I didn't inspect it," Lisa said. "But since she seeks a plane, she must have a pilot, and probably a mechanic. It would be unfortunate if, with her demise so near, we were to leave a means of escape in her path."

"Where could she go?" Olivia asked. "All her redoubts were destroyed."

"Except one," Lisa said. "The airfield at Sutton. I don't know if the wall around that runway will hold, and we don't know if the people in the bunker will welcome her, or hide as they did from us. However, there was a storage tank of aviation fuel behind the hangar. And, of course, she would have gone through Sutton before coming to Michigan. Presumably by air, and flown by the same pilot she is now hoping will take her to safety."

"Which is why she's looking for a plane," Pete said. He slapped his hand against the dash. "We should have let the zoms onto the runway in Sutton."

"No, we did the right thing," Olivia said. "The *just* thing. No one should sit in judgement on strangers. Except for the Herrera family. Them, I'm very happy to judge."

After the first five miles, the number of undead on the road began to thin. By the time they reached the highway, and the plane, it had been five minutes since they'd seen one.

"There's no way that plane is going to fly anywhere," Pete said.

The wind had tugged the aircraft from the road. The port wing was bent, while the cockpit window was cracked.

"For my own peace of mind, I'd like to make certain," Lisa said. "One minute, please." She opened the cab door, and stepped out.

"You know we haven't seen a zombie in ages?" Olivia said.

"It's all the driving we've been doing," Pete said.

"You mean in a circle back and forth to Baraga?" Olivia said. "If the zombies are not on these roads, they were certainly on the back roads north of here. If we do make it back to the ship, this absolutely will be the last time we drive through these parts."

"We'll make it back," Pete said. "Here's Lisa."

"That was far easier, and far less satisfying, than I anticipated," Lisa said, climbing back behind the driver's seat.

When Pete looked in the mirror, he saw a thin wisp of smoke drifting from the cockpit's cracked windows. "Did you set a fire?" he asked.

"After cutting a few wires," Lisa said.

As they continued on to the facility, Pete kept one eye on the cracked mirror, watching the growing plume of oily smoke rising from the plane, so didn't see the zombie until it lurched from behind the partially crushed bus. Lisa braked. The zombie tripped, falling face first onto the road, right in front of the slowing tyre. The skull popped, but the sound was lost in the far louder explosion behind them.

The truck rocked as the blast wave overtook them, while shrapnel pattered along the roadway behind.

"Ah, apologies," Lisa said. "I forgot the plane's fuel tank was far from empty."

Pete looked at the smoke cloud rising behind, and the many smaller plumes rising from the scattered and burning debris. "You'd need more than a mechanic to get that in the air," he said.

The truck bounced across the slowly rotting undead shot by Corrie when they'd first arrived, then through a new swamp created by the recent storms. Though it was shallow in depth, five metres of road already lay beneath an opal-black mire.

"It's the bodies," Olivia whispered as the tyres splashed through the noxious ford. "All those bodies dumped in that field created a dam for all that rainwater. If we hadn't already left, I can't imagine we'd want to stay. There's the turning. Looks clear. No zoms. That's good."

"I've got the gate," Pete said, jumping out as Lisa stopped. He pulled the outer gate open, then the inner. The middle hadn't been closed. As the truck pulled inside, he left the outer gate open, closing only the inner gate before taking a moment to scan the road outside. There were a lot more corpses than he'd remembered.

He walked over to the cab.

"I think it best if we find a ramp down which we can empty the last of those shells," Lisa said.

"And I think you should leave this to the professionals," Olivia said. "What do you think, Pete, the loading dock at the back of the office?"

"Should be about the right height," Pete said. "You park there, I'll go grab the handcarts. We left them in the garage, right?"

"Get two," Olivia said. "And I think there was a stack of empty plastic crates in there. Grab those for anything the kids didn't pack."

Pete slapped the cab, and made his way across the cracked asphalt, around Abernathy's abandoned sheriff's car, and towards the garage.

It hadn't been a bad refuge, in that it had kept them alive. But looking around now, it had been a close-run thing. They'd been lucky finding the ship in Baraga, the fuel at the airport, and arriving in Florence in time to help the prisoners escape. Yes, they'd been lucky, but luck always turned.

He opened the pedestrian door at the side of the garage. The cavernous room was dark, but not as empty as he'd expected. As his eyes adjusted to the gloom, he saw the up-armoured SUV. Then he saw the barrel of a gun. Slowly, his eyes focused on the hand with the chemical burn on the thumb, the black-sleeved arm, and the malevolent face with a crowing smile.

"Trap! It's a—" he managed to yell before something heavy slammed into the small of his back. He fell forward. Something cold pressed into his neck.

"Move, and I'll shoot," a woman said. Not Margalotta Herrera, but one of her guards.

He felt hands at his sides, plucking the gun from his holster, the knife from his belt. Hands roughly checked beneath his coat, before the gun's barrel was drawn back from his neck.

"On your feet," Herrera said.

"Got 'em," came a shout from outside, and that voice didn't belong to Olivia or Lisa.

With a gun in his back, and with Herrera behind that, he was marched outside, to the open parking lot in front of the office. There, Lisa and Olivia knelt, hands on their heads, with two men holding handguns behind. Another woman stood to one side, holding a shotgun.

"My dear Lisa, how glad I am to find you here," Margalotta said. "It has been so long, hasn't it, old friend. Nikita, how many?"

"Only three got out of the truck, ma'am," the woman with the shotgun said. "There were none inside."

It was his shotgun, Pete realised, incensed. He recognised the red clips on the strap. Okay, so he'd taken it from Abernathy's police car, but even so. His internal rage slowly shifted to understanding. The Elkhart sheriff's car was parked in full view of the gates. Abernathy had been *sent* here. Of course, there was one way to clear things up.

"Did you go to Florence yet?" he asked.

Margalotta waved a hand. The woman behind him kicked at his ankles, sweeping him from his feet, then kicked again, at his spine. Pete managed to roll with the blow, though it still hurt, but made a play of the pain, staying curled on the ground while he tried to formulate a plan.

In the distance, he heard an engine. Margalotta had reinforcements inbound, so if he were to act, it would have to be soon.

Margalotta turned back to Lisa. "I did so hope we would meet again."

"I'm certain you've prepared a tedious speech," Lisa said. "I have no time for it."

"You are correct," Margalotta said. "There is no time. I had such plans, Lisa. I wanted weeks. I hoped for months. I had an operative who believed he could keep you alive for years."

"He's dead," Lisa said. "All your people are dead. Your nephew is dead. Your brother is dead. Your mine in Colombia is a crater. Oh, and do you recall Mr Clemens? Of course you do. He returned to England to dismantle your organisation in Europe. This is what your schemes have been reduced to, Margalotta, a concrete prison surrounded by a putrescent swamp. Fitting, don't you think?"

"Not quite all," Herrera said. "You think you're so clever, you think you know our plans. You don't. You never did."

"If they include the bunker in Sutton, then yes," Lisa said. "Or your brother's ship, the *Archangel*? That was sunk. Trowbridge is dead. But do you know the most amusing part of this calamity?"

Pete coughed as an alternative to swearing. His plan had been to claim there was a map to Trowbridge's location in an office upstairs as a bid to split the group up, and so even the odds. But that wouldn't work now.

Margalotta drew a long, thin knife and stabbed it into Lisa's shoulder.

"No, Lisa. Make me laugh. What is the most amusing part?" Margalotta said, as she slowly pulled the blade out.

"Love you, Olivia," Pete said, and rolled backwards and sideways. A gun cracked, but he kept moving, curling and turning, tackling the woman who'd been stationed behind him. He knew his attempt had failed because she was already bringing her gun to bear. Better to die trying, so he tried to topple her over, until her head exploded in a shower of blood and bone. As she collapsed, he scrabbled for her gun. Another shot sounded, then a burst, before he had the pistol in his hand and had spun around. Olivia and Lisa had both tackled Margalotta. Three gangsters were down. The last, the woman with the shotgun, had taken cover behind the police car, clearly better aware of the sniper's location. Pete's finger curled around the trigger. He didn't let go until the gun clicked empty.

"Clear," he said.

"Reload, re-arm," Lisa said as Olivia rolled the old gangster onto her back. Lisa, clutching her arm, grabbed one of the fallen handguns and aimed it at Margalotta.

Pete retrieved his shotgun, and aimed it at the gate, but lowered it when he saw who was running towards them: Corrie. He ran to meet her. "Where'd you come from?" he called as she opened the gate.

"The ship," Corrie said. "You should have stayed a little longer to hear what the prisoners said."

"One moment," Lisa said, picking up a gun. Margalotta was slowly getting to her feet.

"You won this hand, I see," Herrera said. "And what now, Ms Kempton? Do you really think an Australian prison cell will hold me?"

Lisa fired. Once was enough.

"Is that all of them?" Corrie asked.

"I think so," Pete said. "How did she know about Australia?"

"Yollie," Corrie said. "That's why I followed. You know how Abernathy said Yollie and her friends were the reason he knew to come to Sidnaw? You should have asked Captain Stahl exactly what Yollie told them, and why that didn't lead to a mutiny."

"Perhaps you could tell us," Lisa said, leaning against the sheriff's car.

"Let me see your arm," Olivia said. "Okay, no, this is bad. Very bad. I'm going to find some bandages."

"And while we wait, perhaps you could enlighten us as to what brought about this fortuitously timed rescue," Lisa said.

"It's not fun having secrets kept from you, is it?" Corrie said. "Remember the night we arrived, the kids weren't much interested in any part of our story except the second-hand tales of Dan Blaze. Because I was recounting what Zach told me, and because I was telling the tale to kids, I skipped a lot of the stuff about the cartel being involved in the coup during that first telling. I said there'd been a change of government. That's about all Yollie and her people knew. So when she told Margalotta, that was all Yollie had to say. They were tortured, all four of them, to make sure that the story was accurate. And it was, as far as they knew. But Margalotta took that to mean her coup in Canberra had worked."

"She wanted to get to Australia because she thought the government was loyal to her?" Pete asked.

"It gets better, or worse, depending on your point of view," Corrie said. "They've been camped near Florence for the last few days. They knew we were here, but they were hoping the hordes would travel north to south, or perhaps wipe each other out as they bumped into each other. Then, they were going to make contact, find out how we were going to get back to Oz, and ingratiate their way onto our plane."

"So why did they want the tank shells?"

"In case we had to drive some of the way," Corrie said. "That was their plan-B. Plan-A was that they could kill us and fly south, but that depended on Abernathy finding a plane."

"We'd already won?" Lisa asked.

"Depends on what you think victory looks like," Corrie said. "If she'd lived long enough to reach Oz, it would only be to hang, but she'd have caused a lot more misery en route."

"How'd you get here, sis?" Pete asked.

"The Humvee," Corrie said. "I always fancied driving one."

"There's three zoms at the gate," Pete said. "I don't think we'll be able to collect that car."

"Start by packing the food," Lisa whispered. "The ship needs the supplies."

It might have been the labour, but by the time they'd loaded the truck, and Margalotta's SUV, Pete was sweating a river.

"I think that's it," he said, walking around to the cab where Lisa was resting.

"She's asleep," Corrie said, before leaning forward to check. "Yes. Just sleeping. Blood loss, I guess."

"Then better we get her to the ship," Pete said.

"Want me to take care of it?" Corrie asked.

"I need the practice," Pete said. He drew the pistol from his recovered holster, and walked over to the fence. Stopping two metres away, he raised the gun, and fired.

Ten zombies. Fifteen bullets. He was improving, but he'd still keep his eyes out for a pike. As he'd begun shooting, Olivia and Corrie had switched on their engines. As the SUV contained fewer supplies, and didn't contain Lisa, it would take the lead and so act as a battering ram. As the last zombie fell, and before any more could lurch around the perimeter, Pete threw the gate open, and jumped into the SUV's passenger seat. This time, since the cartel knew where this redoubt was, they wouldn't close the gates behind them.

Olivia drove over the just-fallen undead. Pete checked the mirror to see that Corrie was following, and again when they reached the highway.

"East then north," Olivia said.

"East then north," Pete echoed, again checking that Corrie was behind as they turned onto the road.

"We'll head all the way to Covington this time," Olivia said. "No way am I risking any more back roads. We'll go to Covington, then north, almost up to L'Anse before turning for Baraga."

"Good plan," Pete said, turning in his seat as an alternative to compulsively checking that Corrie was following. "Nice car. A bit showy."

"Looks better than it is," Olivia said. "I never trusted a car with seat warmers."

"Was there any interesting loot in the back?" he asked.

"Some wine that might once have been very expensive," she said. "A few knives and revolvers, and a box of what I think were Margalotta's keepsakes. Nothing I'd call treasure."

"No copy of the Constitution?" he asked. "Or maybe a set of Washington's false teeth, or Franklin's original stove?"

"No, why?"

"I dunno. I was just hoping that she'd done something more since the outbreak than go to Delmarva, then Sutton, then Michigan," he said.

"I don't think so."

"So she really did just care about murder and revenge?"

"And murdering for power," Olivia said. "I guess it was like she said right at the end, that this was all a game to her."

"Then she lost," Pete said. "But I don't feel like a winner."

"It is over," Olivia said. "Finally, properly over. Zom," she added, swerving around the legless soldier crawling across the road.

"It's not," Pete said. "It's just beginning. We'll have to put to sea tonight, hunt for diesel tomorrow, and make getting to the northern shores of Lake Superior a priority."

"Because of the zoms?"

"Because we don't know how many more of her people are lurking in these parts," Pete said. "I'm not going to trust any strangers we meet this side of the border, not for a long while."

"Pine Dock," Olivia said. "That's still the goal. Maybe not to live, but just to leave a message for Tess. Still, we've got time, now. We've got— Woah!"

She braked as a deer sprinted across the road ahead of them.

"That was close," he said.

"Yeah, but there are deer, Pete! Oh, that is something. Something wonderful. If there are deer, there could be— squirrel!"

And not just one. A pack scampered across the road. Followed, then overtaken, by a herd of deer mixed in with a pack of dogs. Olivia slowed again, and slammed her hand on the horn.

"There must be a fire," Pete said, looking up at the sky. "Yep, there's a smoke cloud ahead."

"The herd's thinning," she said. "Okay. Cool, there's a sign for Covington." She eased onto the accelerator. "That doesn't look like smoke. And how *could* it be smoke? There's been more rain than dry these last few weeks."

"There! Turn! Turn now!" Pete said.

Instead Olivia stopped, because she had seen it too. The road had reached the crest of an incline too shallow to really be called a hill. But beyond, to the east, the woodland thinned as the land fell, curling into a valley. In that valley, and on the distant hill slopes, were the undead. More than Pete had ever seen in one place. More than thousands. Millions. A wave. An ocean. Felling trees, churning mud, sending up a dirt cloud as they marched inexorably westwards.

"Go north, now," Pete said.

"Tell me twice," Olivia said as she turned onto the track.

He checked the mirror for Corrie's truck. And checked it again for the cloud, but while he could see his sister following, it was impossible to tell if the horde was. Ahead, there was nothing. No zombies. No wildlife. Not even any birds. Even they had taken wing, escaping the inevitable death obliterating the land behind them.

"It's not just a beginning," he said. "It's an ending, too. A real end to all we knew."

Epilogue - An Absolute Good

Pete leaned against the deck rail, almost too tired to think, but still too tired to sleep. Above, the stars were out, and nearly as bright as the light spilling from the ship. Below, the waves languidly splashed around the hull, as the ship gently moved with the current, away from the shore.

"I hoped I'd find you asleep, but I thought I'd find you here," Olivia said.

"It's hard to sleep," Pete said. "I keep thinking how close we are to home. It's the horde," he added. "All those people. How's Lisa?"

"She's asleep," Olivia said. "Hannah and Aqsa are keeping an eye on her. Jenny, Sally's mom, is a nurse. When she's recovered, she'll be able to give a more accurate diagnosis. They say that's why Jenny was picked as the human sacrifice at Florence, because she'd been helping keep everyone else alive."

"And how is she?"

"Don't know. Corrie's opinion is that if we can avoid infection, everyone will live. Everyone will have long-term issues, but they're the survivors. Psychologically, they never gave up, so they shouldn't give up now."

"I guess we need to look for more medicines," Pete said. "What about Rufus?"

"Him, I'm more worried about," she said. "The glue's already working its way loose. I guess we'll just see how it goes, same as with everyone."

"And the kids?" he asked.

"Depressed. Shocked. Upset. They'd mostly accepted their parents were dead, but not knowing let them have just a sliver of hope."

"Jenny's the only parent?"

"She is. And she and Captain Stahl are the only survivors of the group that were once at Sidnaw. The kids will be okay. The worst has happened. The last few days has been a shock, but they got through it. There'll be some rough days ahead, but I think they'll get through that, too. Princess has appointed Lisa pirate captain."

"She didn't want the rank for herself?"

"Oh, no, she's pirate admiral, which at least means she's not a pirate queen. But she made it clear Captain Lisa answers to her. The subtext being, Lisa's not in charge. John implied… I don't think the kids had a meeting, but they've got a better idea of who Lisa was, what she did, and why. I don't think they want her making the decisions. Not anymore."

"Agreed," Pete said. "Abraham's a better leader.'

"Ah, no. John only came to me because Abraham had told him to ask you."

"To ask me what?"

"What the plan was," Olivia said.

"How should I know?"

"Because you went all the way to Australia, and then came all the way back," she said. "Congratulations, Pete, you've got yourself a new job."

"As leader? I don't think I want it."

"Don't worry, you'll have lots of people to tell you when you're doing things wrong. So what's first?"

"I don't know about first, but we've got to reach Pine Dock," he said. "Maybe not all of us, but we should leave a message there for Tess. More immediately, we need a hydro-electric power station. Fresh water, electricity, and fish."

"And we'll need a washing machine and a dishwasher," Olivia said. "Two things they didn't think to put on this ship. Until then, we'll need to find silverware, dishes, and a ton of clothes."

"Or some dish soap," Pete said.

"At least we have fresh water," she said.

"We'll start tomorrow by looking for a rowboat," Pete said. "Considering where we found this ship, I don't think it can cope with shallow waters, so one of us is going to have a swim."

"Think of it as a bath," she said. "Maybe we can find some remote houses with propane tanks, and use that to cook some food, and maybe even do some laundry."

"What about the horde?"

"We'll just keep an eye on the sky," she said. "We'll know when the horde is coming."

"And what if they come all the way to the lake?" he said.

"Yep. And there's the radiation, and the run-off from all the towns and cities along the lake," she said. "But that helps. This ship is safety, but it's not a sanctuary. We don't want to get too comfortable. Captain Stahl has the addresses of General Yoon's supply dumps. I told him to tell you about them in the morning. By then, Corrie will have a better idea of how much fuel the engines use, and we'll collectively have an idea of what supplies we're most in need of. We did an absolute good, Pete. You, me, and Corrie. Especially you, though I'm taking just as much credit. We didn't save the entire world, but we did save one small part of it."

"For now," Pete said.

"Which is enough," she said. "We didn't give up. We didn't turn back. We did something to be proud of, you and I." She leaned in close, until a scream from inside had them both take a step towards the door.

"Nightmare," Pete said.

"Kid or adult, do you think?" Olivia asked. "We're awake, so let's go check."

"Yep, we might have scored a victory, but life goes on," Pete said.

"It does," she said. "I am so thankful it does."

The End.

Printed in Great Britain
by Amazon

28287295R00228